The Curlew's Cry

TIA JONES

Gomer

The author wishes to acknowledge
the support of Literature Wales's
Writer's Bursary.

Published in 2016 by
Gomer Press, Llandysul, Ceredigion, SA44 4JL

ISBN 978 1 78562 152 9
ISBN 978 1 78562 153 6 (ePUB)
ISBN 978 1 78562 154 3 (Kindle)

A CIP record for this title is available from the British Library.

This book is published with the financial support of the
Welsh Books Council.

Printed and bound in Wales at
Gomer Press, Llandysul, Ceredigion

I f'annwyl blantos,
Owain, Angharad, Rhiannon a Gwilym

Acknowledgements

A big 'thank you' to all the people who have helped me with this novel, especially John Rowlands, Nick Fenwick, David Jones and Vera Andrew, whose specialized knowledge of the foot-and-mouth outbreak of 2001 proved invaluable. I am similarly indebted to the Williams veterinary surgeons for responding so patiently to my questions and for explaining so many different procedures so expertly, just as Sion Thomas did when he showed me around wind farm sites and loaned me a quantity of statistical information. Not least, I owe a huge debt of gratitude to my long suffering family, who have constantly come to my aid with comments and useful pointers. Finally, thanks to Ceri Wyn Jones and Gomer for making this happen once again, and to my editor, John Barnie, for such sterling work.

Tra bo dynoliaeth fe fydd amaethu
A chyw hen linach yn ei holynu,
A thra bo gaeaf bydd cynaeafu
A byw greadur tra bo gwerydu,
Bydd ffrwythlonder tra pery – haul a gwlith,
Yn wyn o wenith rhag ein newynu.

Dic Jones
(from 'Cynhaeaf',
Cerddi Dic yr Hendre, Gomer)

1

Bethan looked repeatedly back over the stretch of white sand to the dark shape on the edge of the tide mark, aware that the distance between them was considerable. She was already mentally and physically spent, but at least she was on dry land. Standing into the wind made her tired eyes run, forcing her to blink repeatedly as she stared hard to be absolutely sure that what she saw was real – that the blob standing near the dinghy was indeed a child, her little girl, and not some trick of light. It was difficult to distinguish distinct shapes against the grey mass of shale that had been heaped up by the force of water to the top of the beach. In her exhaustion, her eyes danced out of focus as she scanned the top of the beach to reassure herself that the small human shape by the inflatable was still there. Impossibly torn by the need to be in two places at once, Beth couldn't afford to go back the several hundred yards to check that Clare was all right. She hesitated, dazed like an animal in headlights, wanting to run both ways, knowing it was pointless to call out in the high wind, with no hope that the little girl could understand why her mother had left her there, seemingly abandoned. Thankfully she could not hear the child crying miserably as it stood close, yet unable to place her small hand onto the dinghy where a man's body lay. All Beth could hear was the continuous roar of retreating surf. She raised her arm briefly in a wave of reassurance, knowing her gesture to be futile. Clare was too young to comprehend any of it. Why her mother had chosen such a drastic course of action that had put their lives in such peril. The girl had been frightened in the storm but Bethan had been there for that part of their atrocious journey. Hopelessly compromised, Bethan silently begged her to stay where she'd told her to, safe by the boat next to her unconscious uncle. Soon, surely, there must be someone who would be out? An early morning coastguard, warden or surfer, when they'd be spotted. Bethan had spent what little reserves she had pulling the dead weight of Tegwyn out from the surf's edge, but without the buoyancy of the waves to help, she was unable to pull him any further up the beach that would bring her closer to Clare.

She knelt down again and continued mouth-to-mouth resuscitation, counting and pushing down just above the heart. She knew instinctively what she was doing, staying professional as she had countless times in a hospital ward. Only this was different. Never before had resuscitation meant saving the life of the person she loved. Pumping and counting on the point just above where his ribs joined, she willed him to breathe. 'Come on Tego, breathe. Just one breath. Please, please breathe. One, two, three, four.' There was nothing in his face or waterlogged flaccid skin to give her hope. She stopped herself from screaming but would not give up, pumping him furiously.

'You can't leave me, Tego. Not now, not after everything. You promised,' she thought, feeling a sense of hopelessness, looking for a sign.

She glanced again up the beach, to see what she'd dreaded. The child was moving off, away from the safety of the boat. She'd started to walk in the opposite direction from where her mother was. She hadn't seen her, bent down attending to Tegwyn, and didn't now look in her direction as she stood up, waving her arms, shouting for her to stop. Clare continued to wander across and down the beach, back towards the wind-whipped sea. Bethan knew she was searching for her and hadn't seen her. Whatever she did, she mustn't go back to the dangerous, surging wall of water where the boat had capsized. Against the noise of the wind and expanse of sand she had no hope of getting Clare to stop or turn round and look, to see her, so that she would know she wasn't alone on the beach and hadn't been forgotten and that no one was left in the water. If only she had stayed by the boat until someone came to her. But what was the sense of time to a small child? Even Bethan could not say how long she'd been on her knees pumping Tegwyn's chest. How could she expect her daughter to wait, traumatized as she was by what she'd been through. Who could expect her to stay next to a stranger's body? He might have been her mother's brother but to Clare he was a stranger having only met him for the first time on the boat hours before. It was also very likely he was already dead and she was waiting beside a corpse. Bethan had taken the impossible decision, leaving her daughter in order to try and save Tegwyn, but once the little girl had decided to leave the safety of the dinghy, that choice now put her own daughter's life in jeopardy. She couldn't leave Tegwyn, nor could she let her daughter wander back to the sea's edge. With a last thrust on Tegwyn's chest, she got up, forcing her aching legs to run, calling out after Clare.

Home on leave, Martin Price had been jogging his usual route, his dog Meg running on ahead as he rounded the point to see the expanse of Porthmawr beach that lay in front of him. Immediately his gaze was drawn to the surf smashing over the pockets of rock that stood in deep water fringing the cliff, white wild sprays sent impressively into the air as each wave hit the granite. It was only when he brought his gaze back towards the beach that he saw something unusual. Firstly, there was an unfamiliar boat, an inflatable, perched on the high-water mark and as he followed the retreat of the tide he saw the scene unfolding below him on the sand. He slowed down as he scanned the beach for some evidence of a catastrophe, looking back at the boat where he was sure now it was not a bit of clothing as he'd first assumed, but a body lying lengthways on the inflatable's floor.

As he moved nearer he continued to scan the beach making out another object, a waterlogged piece of driftwood at the edge of the retreating tide and was there a hull of a boat floundering in the surf at the water's edge? He was about to turn away and up towards the empty car park to see if there was anybody about, or any RNLI crew members, when he saw the woman. She was at the far end of the sand. She seemed to be running and waving her arms and as he watched from his vantage point he suddenly saw another figure, smaller and more distant. It was going in the direction of the sea and he realized that the woman was running after it, only she was never going to reach it in time at that pace. He knew the beach, the deep submerged pools and the race that could easily suck an unsuspecting foot from under it. The pull of the outgoing tide would do the rest sucking it under, only releasing the body far out at sea.

'Emergency, lifeguard, ambulance,' adding, 'police'.

He put his mobile back in his pocket, zipping it securely and calling his dog ran down the crumbling cliff path onto the beach, chasing after the woman, only realizing as he got nearer that the other person, still intent in going toward the surf, was a child. He quickly caught up with the woman as he put out a hand and pulled on her sleeve. She gasped with fright until she realized that the man was a stranger. She pointed in the direction of Clare.

'Stay here, I'll get him.' Without waiting for any kind of explanation Martin dashed forward, his dog in pursuit, running on to the sea's edge where he plucked up the child before it reached the water's edge. It wasn't the boy he'd supposed, but a little girl whose eyes stared at him as he swooped her into his arms, cradling her shivering wet body into his own, smiling down at her face feeling a sudden surge of pleasure at having saved her from the sea.

'I've got you. Everything will be all right. Look,' he said as he tried to point against the wind. Not knowing their relationship he didn't know how to refer to the woman coming towards them.

'See, she's there.' Pointing again and slowing down so that the child could see the woman.

Bethan hugged her quietly, her child, sobbing suddenly in relief, Martin standing by them. 'Oh Clare, *cariad*. Thank God you're safe. I'm here. Mam's here, it's all right.' Caught up in the trauma she didn't remember to thank him as he stood over them poised, waiting to help her. Then she remembered the others. 'My brother and Tegwyn, they're over there,' she pointed to the dinghy and beach. 'They're in a bad way. We've nearly all drowned.'

'I've already rung for help,' Martin said, touching his breast pocket where he kept his mobile. 'I called the emergency services when I saw the dinghy.' His dog wagged her tail at his voice, and he stroked her muzzle pushing up into his hand, ready to run again.

He desperately hoped the emergency services wouldn't be long and there weren't more bodies in the sea, or pinned under the upturned hull being tossed in the waves. He was no hero let alone a strong swimmer and knew he was no match for the churned up wild surf.

'Where are they?' Martin asked again, his relief palpable as Bethan swung her arm up the beach pointing to the brown mass that was Tegwyn. He started to run toward what he'd originally thought had been a bit of driftwood.

Not long after the noise of its engine, they caught sight of the welcome yellow of a Sea King helicopter, its lights beaming out of the drab sky as it came into view, flying low across the beach. It circled twice before landing on firm sand. With the precision of a hive of bees, the emergency crew emerged from the helicopter door, ducking under the rotating blades racing straight into action to save life. The sight and sound suddenly reminded

15

Martin of his time in Kosovo, his six-month assignments an engineer in the British Army with only a fortnight off in between. He thought of the face of his close friend Garry, Gareth Morgan, smiling inanely at him in bright Balkan sunshine on the side of that hill; the broad cocky smile of his mate standing by some broken bridge in a war of brutal repression and widespread displacement as the former Yugoslavia was blown apart. Garry had stopped and shared out some sweets, and then a cigarette, with two men who pointed the alternative route avoiding the blasted bridge. Theirs was a remote village that could have been Llanfeni, nestling in the mountains among other close-knit communities, Serbo-Croat instead of Welsh, Dalmatian and Dinaric rather than Cambrian; the homes of peasants and men of the land now being forced to flee in a diabolical act of ethnic cleansing. Half a mile on Garry had been blown to bits by a mine.

Coming home to Wales, Martin had insisted that he should be the one to take what was retrieved of Garry's possessions back to his family in Pembroke; the quiet grief of another South Wales tragedy, deep-veined, black as coal. Whenever he was reminded of the Balkan crisis, he couldn't help but see the happy-go-lucky face of Garry followed by the sanctimonious features of Tony Blair, unable to conceal his own delusion of grandeur as he stood next to Bill Clinton on TV, seeing himself as some kind of modern-day saviour. It didn't help the soldier to be reminded, bringing back worry and anxiety about his next tour, so he tried to concentrate his attention on the emergency crew who'd taken over, strapping Tegwyn and Richard onto stretchers, both with breathing masks over their grey faces. Carefully but quickly they were lifted aboard the helicopter, and once the blades had accelerated, it took them to hospital. Wrapped in blankets, Bethan and Clare were led away by ambulance staff into a waiting ambulance at the top of the sand, leaving Martin to talk to the police.

2

During those long bleak days Penny wasn't sure Richard would pull through, but she was determined not to let his farm slide, so that if he returned to anything like normal – and as the hospital professionals kept telling her, he was lucky to be alive – she wanted him to see she'd worked for the both of them and given him something to aim for as he improved. With Mervyn's guidance she became adept at milking, with the twice daily routine, and handling cows every day she began to know them, not just as part of a herd but as individuals. So it wasn't the life-changing field trip to the Arctic to study whales that they'd promised themselves, or the African wildlife safari. Penny was faced instead with the more down to earth study of animal husbandry. Dairy cows may be more docile, but she soon learnt they were still intriguing, and once she got to know them better, she found they had quirky individual habits with a bucolic charm all of their own.

Milking them twice daily, they became more than mere cows and unlike her beef suckler cattle who did not require such close attention, Penny found the Friesians gave her a solace from her gnawing fear that Richard's injuries would leave him in a vegetative state – either that, or he'd die. She couldn't afford to dwell on either, however, as she raced to and fro to the hospital, hoping each time that there would be a change for the better, and glad to be able to leave with a ready excuse to get back to the milking. The cows became a vital distraction, their presence a comfort, keeping her busy so she didn't have to think about the future. She knew they'd think her soft, the hardened hill farmers, but as she got to know her herd and their place in the hierarchy, she'd pick up on a particular gait, a torn ear or tail carriage that said a lot about them and their individual personality much more telling than any obligatory tag number.

She gave them names, Blackie, Daisy and Sunny, all especially unique, nice cows.

Then there was Mavis, a bit cheeky and prone to throw a side kick if she was in a mood. Lastly her favourite, Maud, the leader of them all. First to food, she would stand by the large rollers that acted as brushes and having enjoyed a rub along their length was unwilling to allow the other cows the same luxury as she stood guard over her private masseur. If a cow came too close, the alpha female would stiffen and arch her neck, giving a fierce stare, and if that wasn't enough, she would hit the poor cow in her abdomen pushing her against the wall as she did so. Not a gentle trait to be so domineering but it was necessary all the same for the herd to have a leader. Getting the best position and the most food, she produced the strongest calves and had plenty of milk, so that Maud's offspring excelled in their elevated position, and several of her daughters vied for leadership when the time came. She may have been matronly and dominant, with her white patch over one eye that gave her a threatening look, but once Penny got to know her she soon realised that Maud was as soft as butter with humans, lowering her head for Penny to rub it as her rough tongue licked Penny's coat in mutual appreciation. The sweet, warm breath of cows in milk. Penny would sit talking to them, telling them how Richard was. Sometimes, alone in the parlour, she'd let her guard down and cry as they watched her, and she was sure they felt sorry for her as she released her pent up anxiety, their knowing body language a 'there, there' as they chewed the cud in patient understanding. Useless with the tractor, she left all that work to Richard's uncle Mervyn without whom she'd never have managed. At the weekends Tegwyn would lend a hand, too, allowing the old man a rest.

Unsentimentally, but nonetheless saddened, the old farrier made a decision that had been niggling him for months. On that Saturday morning, he covered the seat with his old slope, and lifted up his sheepdog Taff, his light frame hidden by his thick coat, and put him on the passenger seat of his van where he lay, his eyes looking at his master, his tail un-wagging, knowing. Mervyn drove the short journey to the vet, carried him in and onto the table where a nurse shaved a patch of his hair from his front leg. Mervyn kept a hand on his head as the vet administered the dose, a hand on his arm in recognition of a painful but right decision that sent the dog to sleep. Later that day, he set about digging a hole and buried him near the cottage, under a hedgerow with a high bank that would shelter him from the Atlantic winds, where, in summer, dog roses flowered appropriately. He stood there quietly, thinking of his constant companionship of sixteen years and the understanding that had existed between them as they worked the flocks of sheep – all the 'aways' and 'come-bys', the '*saf yma*' and '*tyrd ymlaen*' until the working day ended with a 'that'll do'. A habit of a lifetime, whenever he stopped, pausing by a gate or door to put his hand down automatically for that warm muzzle that had shadowed him through his working day. Somehow the death of his dog was a sign for him to let go, to be content to potter about after a laborious life he'd enjoyed with the stoicism of the old school of farming – men who worked marginal land where nature and natural disaster ruled. Easier to let go now with the farm flourishing under Richard, knowing he had a stepson to follow on who also now had a son. At least, that had been the plan until the accident after Richard's mad dash across the sea to save his sister Bethan which had proved so ill-timed, nearly drowning them all.

Once again it had been up to the old uncle-cum-stepfather to step into the breach. Too old for the rigours of hill farming, all he wanted to do was sit down in his kitchen with Elin, listening to the radio in gentle companionship. He knew she would never recover from her stroke, loving her still for all she'd been to him. It pained him as he watched her trying to talk in front of Penny, whom she had never known. Incapacitated as she was, she'd just looked across at her son's partner, her head at an angle unable to convey what she was thinking, while Penny was unable to pick up any nuance that would signal an understanding which someone might have done who'd known the old lady in better days.

Nor did it help that Bethan, Elin's daughter, had come home changed. No longer her easy warm self, but an agitated nervous woman who put the room on edge, so that instead of settling the old couple, her presence made her mother uneasy, causing Mervyn to fuss. Penny tried to make conversation to gain her sister-in-laws's trust, taking an immediate liking to her broad face and wide mouth, but Bethan's blue eyes held her off and Penny knew that she needed more time to readjust to home life after what she had been through. So didn't push herself onto the family, and as soon as she could she made her escape back to the animals and farm.

She couldn't understand anyone allowing herself to be treated in the way Richard said that Bethan had been, but what did she know of other people's marriages? Ralph may have been a cheat but he'd never have held her a prisoner in their home, or beaten her up. And, as for Richard, well he was incapable of violence. Perhaps she'd just been lucky with the men who'd been attracted to her and Beth's situation was more common than she'd imagined.

3

The past year had been a momentous one for the Davies family, and as the New Year changed to herald another century, Richard knew he was lucky to be alive to see it in. Against the odds he'd come back from the brink and all he could remember of their torturous journey that nearly ended his life was getting into the boat, and the dolphins, before the increasing swell of the sea and the rising wind brought on the ensuing storm. Then, thankfully, nothing – knocked out before he could witness the rashness of his decision or the hopelessness of his sister's plight. Nothing until he woke in a hospital bed, with his head bandaged, a tube sticking out of his arm, and another uncomfortably up his nose. A machine monitored his breathing. He'd surprised them, as the nurses told him later, pulling through against the odds. He put it down to stubbornness, deep rooted farming resilience that refused to let go.

That was six months ago and apart from a scar where they'd drained a build-up of fluid from his head, and a slight propensity to forget which was a common enough complaint, he had made a complete recovery. He was still not allowed to drive, though he'd take the tractor and quad bike out on the farm, leaving Penny do any driving on the road. The biggest miracle was that she was there, she'd stayed with him, helped him convalesce, and under his direction and with Mervyn on hand, Penny did more and more jobs on the farm, becoming proficient with his herd of cows and a dab hand at milking. She thrived on the responsibility of managing the herd, the small successes of pulling a difficult calf alive, of spotting the symptom of a potential illness before it became a problem. In the evening she insisted on making supper for the four of them, enough for Mervyn and Elin in Y Bwthyn using her organic meat range, or fresh fish with lots of salads and roasted vegetables – nothing but the best for Richard, tempting him back to health with her home food. Although it had come as a surprise that Penny proved to be a natural on the farm as if she'd spent all her life in the countryside rather than the city, it was the fact that she loved him that was the more astonishing to Richard. Middle aged, balding with a poor sense of dress, boring, predictable and at times prosaic, Penny made him feel wanted and he still couldn't believe his luck that this sophisticated woman of means seemed genuinely to love him for what he was, expecting that he'd wake up one day to realise it had all been a glorious dream. Only she was still there in his house after a difficult year, eating meals with him and sharing his bed, warm and inviting, hugging him to her. For the first time in what had been a hard life, Richard Davies, a mild mannered and quiet farmer, was truly happy.

It came out of the blue when she told him, so that after having avoided hospitals for most of his life, Richard found himself there for the second time in the space of a year. This time he was waiting in the pale green corridor outside the antenatal clinic where his partner had been taken. A nurse popped her head around the door and called him in. Penny was lying on a bed and next to her a small monitor showing a vague moving shape in grey. The nurse rolled the ball around her stomach trying to locate the baby's heartbeat. The sudden unmistakable sound of a swish-swish beat made them both smile, confirming that he was going to be a father again after all this time. It wasn't so much being a father at his age but Penny as the mother that was so astounding to him.

Caught up in the aftermath of their tortuous journey, Penny hadn't considered a missed period as anything other than the beginning of an early menopause and never thought about going to see a doctor, not until it was too late even to consider a termination. So now she was having regular trips to the antenatal clinic, under a high-risk category as a mature mother, and every month Richard found himself sitting in the cafe run by the WVS sipping a strong cup of tea, waiting for Penny to come back from the obstetric consultant. He couldn't get over the fact he was going to be a father again, that Tŷ Coch would have the sounds of a baby after a gap of nearly twenty years and was determined he'd make a better effort this time round. Thinking of his daughter Rhian gave him a pang of guilt, knowing that he'd not been a good father and had let her down. Not quite estranged, she rarely got in touch, and even less came for a visit. This time he'd make sure he'd be more hands on, the new man, there helping with nappies, and reading bedtime stories. It seemed absurd, ridiculous really, that she was there at all. Used to wealth and the city with all its sophistication, she'd opted for the middle of nowhere, a small isolated Welsh village, sharing her life with him on his dairy farm overlooking Cardigan Bay with nothing other than the farm, its puny income, it's thin soil, and beautiful views to sustain them. She was not like the majority of incomers who moved in briefly to set up a business on good rates, only to leave when the grants or dreams ran dry, heading back across Offa's Dyke. To top it all, she was carrying his baby – beautiful Penny who despite the odds had stayed, continuing to live and work from rural Wales and determined to make a success of her business. She owed it to herself, she explained to him; it was her way of sticking two fingers at her ex and luckily for Richard she had grown to love living in the country.

The opposite could be said of Bethan, who having loved her farm home as a child, now seemed out of kilter with her rural roots. Her ordeal only came back to her like bits of flotsam in random fragments, so the family was still unsure of everything that had happened. Nor had she been knocked mercifully unconscious, but was the only adult in the boat's cabin having to go through the hours of terror at the height of the storm. Even her daughter Clare had succumbed to a fitful state of sleep as the boat was tossed in huge waves. She also blamed herself for the journey in the first place and had at the time been convinced that Tegwyn, like Pete, had been lost overboard, leaving her not only responsible for their deaths but also with the task of bringing the boat to safety, solely in charge for the life of her brother and child. It was only as dawn broke that she saw Tegwyn's silhouette still clinging to the tiller as they approached land and he tried to steer the boat to safety. Then heroically he'd managed to get them up on deck and into the inflatable that he pushed off into the rolling surf as he stayed behind trying to keep the boat upright for as long as possible. Later she'd found him rolling like a waterlogged log in the surf and had managed to pull him up onto the beach.

At the time of the accident Bethan had also gone to hospital and received treatment for shock and exhaustion but was discharged after twenty-four hours. Perhaps if they'd known what she'd really been through, she'd have been kept under observation for longer. She'd been persuasive and was eager to 'go home', as she'd put it, to look after Clare and be with her family. The medics in the hospital didn't know her history.

On the face of it she seemed happy, jubilant to be back at Tŷ Coch, to be close to her Mam, and stepfather. The news that her brother Richard and Tegwyn were making progress and the likelihood that her brother would make a full recovery, convinced her that she was also fine. She tried to dismiss the tell-tale signs to the contrary, refusing to listen to the tremors that had resurfaced in her head. Rather than acknowledge that anything was wrong she over-compensated, keeping herself busy, unable to sit still, up and down like a yo-yo pretending to be in high spirits at being home again. Once he'd been given the all-clear by the doctors, Tegwyn who'd waited most of his life for this moment, didn't waste another minute to take Bethan and Clare home to his smallholding of Tan y Bryn divided by a few fields from Tŷ Coch farm.

She was closer to him, and he felt she'd be safer there while still near the family farm that had been her childhood home. If anyone came looking for her, Tŷ Coch would be the obvious place and this way Richard would have the time to raise the alarm. Let him dare, Tegwyn thought. No one was going to damage his lovely Beth ever again; he'd see to that. In his way he tried to do everything to accommodate her and Clare, happy to redecorate the house if she had wanted, only she insisted she liked it the way it was, it was all the more homely for being shabby. He'd made an effort planting a climbing rose over the front porch and had raked over a patch in the yard, adding topsoil for her to have a garden, keeping his wood business away from the house so that Beth wouldn't be bothered by anyone driving up. He didn't want anything to alarm her and he made sure she was never alone, either staying home himself or accompanying the two of them over the couple of fields to Tŷ Coch to be with Richard and Elin, so that he could sort some of his backlog of work. The moss operations were going well, and the newly designed iodine plasters were becoming available in chemist shops. They'd had a very busy two years and the owner of the business, Dr. Trelawny, could afford to give Tegwyn some time off. If he was intrigued by their obvious history, he kept his questions to himself and Tegwyn was content just to have Beth with him at last. What he wanted was to be happy and to hear her laugh again as he had when she was a little girl. Only it had been different then and easier to get a child to come out of her shell as he made a fool of himself around the yard to make her forget for a moment her dad's sudden death. That was back then, but Tegwyn was determined that whatever had happened between her and Malcolm, he'd regain the Beth he knew and loved.

He'd been forewarned by the brothers, Richard and Simon, that Beth was still suffering from what had happened in Ireland and from the loss of her baby, and he expected her to be edgy at first. But it was only after she moved in with him that he realized just how altered she had become and he felt way out of his depth in knowing how to help her. He hadn't bargained on her sudden swings from joy to anxiety which were intense, extreme, and exhausting. With it came a persistent wariness and although it had been many months since it had all happened, Bethan's behaviour hadn't really improved. On the surface she may have looked better as she'd regained some weight, but she still reacted in fright to mundane and innocuous sounds and sights. The ideal he'd imagined them sharing had not become the reality – it was more like a campsite for a fleeing refugee than a home. No matter how he tried to reassure her, she remained unsettled and restless with a sense of being hunted, looking over her shoulder and ready to grab her child and run. But holding a candle for her for so long, Tegwyn was not going to give up on her, and he would do what it took to regain her trust as if she was a frightened, snared animal. It was unfortunate that her daughter was the image of her father with mousey features, freckled skin, and quick brown eyes – a smaller feminine version of Malcolm. Tegwyn had met him only once, at the time of their wedding when Llanfeni had been temporarily filled with merry Irish, and like a rugby international there'd been a lot of drinking and shenanigans. Tegwyn had succeeded in getting savagely drunk before turning morose. Sick in the small hours he spewed up his loathing for the man who had stolen his girl, but not before he'd scarred his car, running a knife along the sides and bonnet. It had been some sort of recompense that she'd had the scales taken from her eyes and been desperate to come home, and to him.

It never bothered Tegwyn that her family had been against him – and Elin still was, sitting in her chair with her fixed stroke-sloped face slanted in persistent disapproval. So what! She'd never liked him, sloping around up to no good, old enough to be her father. Even when she'd needed him most in their days of crisis, she couldn't conceal her dislike as he stared at her swollen stomach – her lifting of a shoulder as she pulled her coat over her pregnancy, remarks made to belittle him in front of her children. Only she had no choice with her husband dead and the farm literally bellowing for attention and herself unfit for manual labour. Beggars couldn't be choosers and Tegwyn had stepped in, taking on the daily milking and the slog of another's toil to keep the farm from going under – animals milked and fed, fields tended, knowing there was no reward, no inheritance, as Tŷ Coch was not his birthright but Richard's when he was old enough to take the reins.

Only Elin had sussed that he was sweet on Beth, and unable to cope without his help, she watched him like a hawk and was relieved when the inquest into her husband Ianto's death was over and Mervyn her other neighbour and, more importantly her ally, moved in with them.

With a middle-aged farrier there was no longer any need of a wild teenager, and Elin and her son Richard were glad to see the back of Tegwyn. Only Beth cried at his going, but it hadn't turned out the way Elin had wanted. Sending Beth off down to Cardiff had been a mistake in the first place in Tego's eyes, as it was there she'd met Malcolm which led to what her stupid mother called 'a good marriage' that had turned nasty and been her downfall. Now that she was home again Tego wouldn't let her go, and although he'd been hailed as a hero after getting them into the dinghy and off the boat before it sank, he knew that behind his back, tittle-tattle slipped like sludge through the community, sure that there was something sinister to be unearthed and finding it odd that he, a non-swimmer, had survived while others hadn't. His only priority now was Bethan's welfare, and this time he was in a better position to provide for her. The rest of them could go and piss in the wind for all he cared.

It wasn't only Bethan O'Connor, née Davies, who had run away and returned home, for the man who'd saved them on the beach had also come back to see his family, his running a tool to help him control his demons. Luckily for the Davies family he chose the coastal path south to Llanfeni.

A soldier's leave always seemed so short, and already Martin was aware that his days in the UK were drawing to an end. It had been a wet spell, all along the western coast but unlike the residents, serving Brits didn't complain, relishing the unpredictable weather, enjoying the fat drops of rain that fell on his face as he and Katie walked up onto the fell. It was invigorating after the dry death-heat of his last tour of duty and no wind or rain would spoil his few days with his sweetheart, laughing at her girly grumblings, teasing her until she chased after him, stopping to embrace and hold her close, kissing the raindrops on her face that ran down onto her lips, the ground beneath them soft and giving. It wasn't so different up north, from the Welsh hills, and Martin could see himself settling down with her and helping in the family business. Katie's father was a self-made man who spoke his mind and appreciated a grafter, and Martin had enjoyed getting his hands dirty – he was used to taking orders and prided himself on his physical fitness. Fighting overseas had made him prouder of his roots and the fact that he was British. Surrounded by sea, he felt the island people shared a common ground, town and country alike, very different to what he'd been subjected to in the former Yugoslavia where communities were in the process of being ripped apart.

What had seemed like a good idea at the time had turned out to be a wrong decision and since his mate's death, Martin wanted nothing more to do with the army. As a teenager the offer of a career there had seemed more exciting than working at the oil refinery on Wales' west coast or a job with the county council and in the early days the army had broadened Martin's horizons, teaching him new skills. He enjoyed the camaraderie, all soldiers together, especially the company of Gareth Morgan who he trained with and who became a close friend. He was a little older than Martin and like the brother he never had, the raw recruit was able to open up in his company. They were Welsh, had a similar physique and were both highly competitive in everything they did. In their cups they boasted of their glory days – lads aspiring to wear the red jersey and play for Wales and just missing out – watching instead on the plasma screen at their local club, pint in hand, and vocal in their supporting role. They prided themselves on keeping fit and if Martin had the edge in speed, it was Gareth who'd win the sapping stamina runs up on the Beacons, Cader Idris or Snowdonia. Yes, at the beginning, with Gareth for company, he'd enjoyed being in the army, travelling overseas and seeing something of the world, stationed in Germany, and later in Cyprus where he'd learnt deep sea diving. It was a world away from what was facing him now and he dreaded returning. On his last day, he asked Katie to marry him.

'Mrs Katie Price,' she thought to herself, liking the sound of the name, better at any rate than Dobson that made her think of carthorses.

'Do you have to go back tomorrow?' she pleaded with him, twiddling her bit of sparkle on her finger. 'We could go into Leeds, catch a show or film. Celebrate our engagement.'

'I promised them I'd call and I've got to be back at barracks on Sunday. You know I'd love to stay here with you, and as soon as I can, I'm quitting the army.' He shrugged, giving her one of his grins, leaving the sentence unfinished, not wanting to guarantee something he couldn't control, his wish dangling in the air.

'I know Martin. I'll just have to wait, won't I! Just you make sure you look after yourself and don't do anything daft like getting yourself killed.'

'Try not to,' he replied light-heartedly, feeling anything but, with Gareth's death still haunting him. He changed the subject abruptly. 'I don't know what to give them from Yorkshire. I don't like going home empty-handed. I suppose I can get my Nan some of those soft mints. What do you call them?'

'You'll have to take some rhubarb or we'll never hear the end of it!' Dark sheds full of long pinkish shoots with curled yellow leaf that had become popular once more. As a crop the sheds full of forced rhubarb paid them better than fell lambs.

'Of course I'd love some rhubarb, perhaps I could buy some for the Davies family.'

'Probably be able to run to that, and if you play your cards right you can come up to the sheds and help me pick it in candlelight.'

'Very romantic. You must think me daft.'

'Yeh, but that's why I love you.'

'Ever since the beach, you know when it happened. Well, it's become a bit of a ritual and when I'm home on leave I try to go and see them make sure they're OK.'

'You're a good man, Martin Price!'

He allowed himself to smile as he shook his head. 'No, I'm not, but they've sort of become an extension of my own family I suppose, and at any rate they seem pleased to see me.' He didn't tell her it was a place he had to return to, a place where he'd spent time racing with Gareth along the coastal trails, the memory all he had left, and needing to be there before returning to a conflict zone.

'Hardly surprising seeing as you're their hero. And mine,' she said, kissing him.

'As long as I'm yours that's all that matters. I'm a bit superstitious, silly I know.' It would niggle if he didn't call at Tŷ Coch, especially if things went badly.

'How old is the little girl, what was her name again?'

30

'Clare, must be about six or thereabouts, I suppose. Why?'

'Then she'll be old enough to look after a lamb. And, before you say no, I've just the thing. I've got a cade lamb here.' He looked nonplussed, needing her to explain. 'The ewe must have jumped a fence early, and the lamb's the result. Apart from being puny, he'll never grow into anything worth much, and he's not even a pedigree. But, it would give her something to look after, that would be her responsibility. Kids love being in charge.'

'Do they now! And I get the message you don't want it?'

'Just a time-consuming nuisance. See, I'm not such a softy! It managed to kill his pure-bred mum being born and she was worth the hundreds, not this miserable mongrel, and I'm left with a dead ewe and this little runt nobody wants.'

'Can't you give him to another mother?'

'Perhaps in six weeks when the flock's due to lamb but I'll have enough pure-bred lambs then, rather than waste my time with this thing, and by then it'll too late to adopt.'

He was about to protest but Katie stopped him. 'Look, it's no skin off my nose, but I can't do what Dad says and knock him on the head and it's not worth a trip to market, just for him. He's a nuisance in the shed getting under everyone's feet. So you'd be doing me a favour and get Dad off my back.'

'How can I take a lamb back to Wales?'

'More sheep than people in Wales, Martin! They're hill farmers aren't they? Put him in the front, like a dog and he'll be fine. They don't get car sick!'

'What loose in my car? What if it jumps about?'

'We'll feed it first and it'll go to sleep, heater on and radio to listen to, you'll be fine. I'll give you a bottle made up and some powdered milk and we can put him in a cardboard box if it makes you happier so he can't jump out.'

Unable to think of another reason not to accept Katie's offer,

Martin shrugged a reluctant OK wondering how he'd been talked into accepting a pet lamb.

Although he didn't want the animal bleating and peeing in his car on his journey back to Wales, he was pretty sure it would please Clare and it would be worth it just to see her face light up when he turned up with a live lamb for her. And, if it didn't work out he knew Tegwyn would be capable of dispatching it.

'You sure you want to get rid of it?'

'Yep.'

'At least let me give you something?'

'You already have!' she said waving her ring at him. 'Honest, Mart, you're doing me a favour. I'll get a couple of empty feed bags to put on the floor in case of accidents. All she has to do is call it, and show the bottle and he'll come running to her. Like a puppy.'

He knew he fancied her, and enjoyed the time he spent with her in Yorkshire, but if it hadn't been the fact that his best friend had been blown up and that he was having to face going back abroad, Martin wondered if he'd be quite so keen to get hitched. He left reluctantly for home, driving through a blanket of fog and coming out suddenly onto a pocket of hill that had broken through the dense cloud into the early sunshine, giving the landscape a fairytale feel – a small copse of leafless trees circled by the grey, concealing all root or attachment so that it seemed to float on air. Prehistoric ridges trailed away into the mist. The road conditions deteriorated as he dropped lower and by the time he'd reached the motorway, driving was treacherous, with freezing fog and virtually no visibility. Martin became more tense, struggling to see the way ahead. He gripped the steering wheel tighter – those silent shapes, shrouded in cloth, expecting a machine gun pointing at his face or, silent in the denseness, a knife to slit his throat. Clammy and with a quickening heart and shortness of breath, he knew he was experiencing a panic attack, sensing the unseen enemy as dimmed light peered through the dense moist cloud. He forced himself to drive on and concentrate only on getting through the fog. The sudden bleating of the lamb made him jump, then he welcomed it's reality. It stood, briefly complaining, then turned round and lay down, resettled in the car's heat.

With all his footings taken from under him, the soldier craved security, the need to belong to something solid. What he'd seen, and the death of his friend, had changed him and although he had never been attached to the soil, he sought the appeal of something fixed. Perhaps he'd always been that way and the war highlighted his need. As a boy he'd been in the minority, not being part of the young farmers' club, his teasing of the 'joskins', a smokescreen for his envy, and in part it had been why he'd joined up, to belong, to be one of the lads in a different uniform. He was a natural mechanic. Now, years later, on his last two leaves, he saw local sons becoming their fathers, married with children and running the family farm; the older generation moving out to a purpose-built bungalow. He resented their easy, ready-made choices. They hadn't seen or done anything of the kind he had – the stark choice of kill or be killed. They were content to tend their cows and sheep, the tractor and the plough, and his Katie was the same. He realized it was part of her appeal, belonging, hefted to the land. Happy in her environment, she was a capable modern girl, a shepherd in her own right on her quad bike, with mobile phone and sheepdogs, tending the upland flocks; Herdwick, Swaledale, Scottish Blackface, all tough hill sheep and Martin wanted to be part of the same solid structure, hoping that by being in that environment it would give him a new stability, an anchor to make him safe, happy to grow rhubarb no longer from shoddy but still forced in dark sheds using candle power for harvest – another Victorian food that was back in vogue with the London chefs. The soldier needed that sense of ancestry, of lives formed by wool, water and cold granite rock; not an illusion of heat-induced haze in a sea of shifting sand, but a dependable, pure landscape.

His guilt would never leave him, as he'd witnessed his mate blown up in front of him by a roadside bomb he should have seen. It had put paid to any appetite for adventure and now all he wanted to do was get out, before he became another statistic. As he drove he thought of how he could set up his own business and mend tractors or other machinery. He knew he was a coward wanting to flee as he listened to the news of an impending war in the Middle East, but he needed to watch out for his own skin, as anyone would. The soldier didn't sleep well, reliving what had been, and what was likely to be before him, his agitation and fear getting worse as the end of his leave approached and another tour of duty loomed in Macedonia.

Richard stayed with Penny through her labour, and after the long slog, witnessed the natural birth of his son. With both of them parents to grown up daughters, Dafydd Sion Davies, named after the two grandfathers, was their first son, and both Mum and Dad were hugely proud. He rang his daughter, euphoric with his news.

'Congrats, Dad! I can't imagine you a dad.' She laughed, thinking the news had come seventeen years too late.

'It's hardly sunk in, Rhi, but you'll come and see us won't you and meet your little brother?'

'Sure, Dad. I'm glad you rang because I've got some news too. I'm moving to London. I've got a job and I'm off from here.'

'Oh. You're leaving Wales? What sort of job, Rhi?'

'Fashion. Designing. Hats, Dad, they're the next big thing!'

It sounded better, bigger than it really was; a tentative offer on someone else's market stall.

'Well, that's brilliant. Have you got somewhere to live?'

'Yea, Ryan's found me a place.'

He wanted to ask who Ryan was but let the question hang unasked.

'It's OK, Dad, Ryan's my boyfriend, he's in a band, The Lites. You wouldn't have heard of them, but he's cool.'

'As long as you're happy.'

'I am.'

'You'll keep in touch.'

'Course. And, you've got my mobile number.'

She didn't tell him that she had to run, to get out of the house and away from Les, Nesta's man. He'd only moved in with them so he could bother her. Only her stupid mother couldn't see it. Thinking her daughter was stirring it, making it awkward. A dirty lech, using Nesta to get at her daughter, deliberately getting in the way to brush against her as she tried to pass. Irritating enough, but he raised the bar by trying to catch her on her own, spying on her and making lurid suggestions. Once he'd nearly managed to force himself on her and she'd only just managed to get him off by biting him and running out of the house half-dressed. When she told her mother, instead of chucking the shit out, she'd tried to laugh it off as a silly bit of flirting.

'You must be blind, Mam, if you can't see him for what he is.'

Only her mother wouldn't be told. 'She must be desperate,' thought Rhian as she slammed the door shut and headed off to the railway station, glad to leave the valley behind and head up to the anonymity of a big city, and London was where Ryan was.

Penny's two daughters were less generous when they heard the news of a new 'brother' and before even speaking to Sophie, Charlotte had grabbed the phone and told her mother just what she thought before cutting her off.

'You little bitch,' muttered Penny, tempted to redial and give her a piece of her mind; a young spoilt, prejudiced snob.

'How did she take it?' Richard asked, seeing her disappointed face.

'Not brilliant, and the little vixen put the phone down on me before I could even tell Soph.'

'Teenagers! They'll come round.' He didn't add the awkward stepchildren bit, selfishly intent on addling any other union, for nothing could dent Richard's happiness.

Apart from sleep, that is, which did dent even the milk farmer's joy, well versed though he was in rising in the small hours. Sion's arrival put this in a whole new context for he hadn't been prepared for the sleepless nights and crying. Both he and Penny had forgotten how much new babies cried and how the whole process was utterly exhausting. At least the younger mother had energy on her side, but for the farmer and his partner the first months of baby Sion's life were totally draining. Naturally Penny had insisted on breast feeding and no to dummies, so the result was hours of complaint, constant walking around the kitchen, all part of being the new man with his son strapped to him in a baby sling as he tried in vain to placate the baby's protests, leaving Penny to catch up on lost sleep.

It wasn't how he'd remembered the first time round. Then he'd left the day-to-day rearing of his daughter Rhian to Nesta. Now fully immersed in all things baby, he felt he'd been hit by a sledgehammer, for he was not an occasional helping hand but was on call twenty-four hours. What with the needs of the baby, the cows' twice-daily milking, as well as all the other jobs needing to be done on a farm, Richard looked in a perpetual daze. Although his sister Beth offered to help, he didn't trust her, nor did he think it fair for her to help with their baby after her own miscarriage when she had lost a son. It was all too soon and although she was getting better, Richard didn't think her fully recovered mentally. In his eyes, his son was too precious to risk leaving with his disturbed sister, even if she was a qualified nurse and mother. As it was, he reasoned with her, justifying his stance by the fact that as Penny was feeding the baby herself, it wasn't very practical for anyone else to help out – because the baby would soon need another feed and there was little point in upsetting its routine.

He knew his rejection had offended her and hoped his sister would come to see it for the best, but since their conversation she'd stopped calling in, going directly to Y Bwthyn to her mother and stepfather. In a few months it would become easier for everyone, but for the moment there wasn't any routine and every waking minute was taken up with feeding, winding and changing and little else, so that even if he wouldn't admit it to his sister, he regretted his hasty decision, longing to be able to hand his baby over and leave him get on with the farm. Pulling on his overalls and going out was a welcome relief, getting away from the confines of the house which Penny insisted in keeping artificially warm for the baby, glad to get into fresh air and walk his fields to collect the cows.

The bracing sea air cleared him of his mugginess, as he called them through the gate in a long established ritual. They filed quickly down the lane, passing his mother's cottage and into the milking parlour, heads down to their feed, as in rotation he washed their udders put the claws on as they ate their cake to the steady rhythmic beat he'd known all his life. Sometimes Mervyn would help him finish, but as often as not Richard was left to do them on his own.

Working methodically, content now as a proud father, this shy, undemonstrative man brimmed with a joy that was infectious as he took Sion around the farm with a renewed sense of purpose, his years of labouring now rewarded, as he would able to pass the farm on to the next generation. It was a need as ingrained in him as the soil he worked. Fixed firmly in a baby sling, Richard sang to Sion as he walked, his sonorous voice ringing out in the yard. His mother with her window open could hear him, a smile trying to form and escape from her mouth as she remembered the songs of his youth; *hwiangerddi* and *alaw werin*, that he'd sung at the local *eistedfoddau* and if she could, she would have told him how glad he'd made her, hearing him sing again, '*Nawr lanciau rhoddwn glod mae'r Gwanwyn wedi dod a'r gaeaf a'r oerni a aeth heibio. Daw y coed i wisgo'u dail a mwyniant mwyn yr haul*', by Bob Tai'r Felin, a new season full of the hope of spring.

Waiting for his tea in the kitchen, he'd pick Sion up and sit him on his knee with another such rhyme, making him giggle with delight as his big hands bounced him in the air while Penny looked on smiling indulgently at them, her one wish being that her daughters would eventually, in their own time, choose to come back to her.

For Richard, Sion was the reason to push all the harder in order to keep the farm running successfully so that when the time came he had a thriving business to pass on. He knew his mother liked Penny who was somehow more on her wavelength than Nesta had ever been, taking her fresh flowers and homemade cakes with nutmeg, ginger and other spices. Then she produced a grandson and although Elin couldn't say so, Richard knew she was delighted and content at last, knowing there was another generation at Tŷ Coch.

Across the fields at Tan y Bryn, Tegwyn was also struggling with a home filled with his new family, and on a rare morning when he'd left Beth, he relished the freedom of the hill, as he walked over the rough, uncultivated land. On his way to the moor his eye caught a pair of black-coloured birds perched above the face of a disused lead mine, the shale their nesting place hidden within gorse and heather. Not rooks or crows with their red bill and legs, but a pair of choughs seeking sanctuary. He was quietly pleased at his spotting them, careful not to disturb their nest as he pulled up onto the silent moor, knowing theirs was a special secret, wild and unpeopled place where he'd spent hours moss gathering and dreaming of Beth, quite different from several hundred feet below where the land was heavily stocked with grazing animals in fenced fields, and 'yard' was too grand a word for what served as one on his smallholding and plain house that hadn't had much spent on it over the years. It had met his simple needs, though, and the house had the spartan carelessness of a solitary male. Not that he was slummy, far from it, but having lived alone since the death of his parents, Tegwyn was just not used to sharing. Apart from a brief period when he had been married, and quickly divorced, he'd since run his business and his life on his own, out most of the time and only home to sleep. He kept his machinery and wood equipment in two outbuildings and his two saw benches were housed under a zinc-roofed open area at the top end of the small yard. There were no animals but piles of various wooden planks that were stacked tidily. Along one side, neat tied bundles of fencing stakes were ready for sale, their softwood tips treated with creosote to help prevent rot. Long since empty pigsties had been converted for storage and were stacked full of seasoned hardwood, ready for the open-fire and wood-burner customers who'd become increasingly important to his business's profitability.

Ironically relying on electricity to heat his kitchen, Tegwyn often didn't bother to put a match to the open fire in the small living room which he rarely used. Out working during daylight hours when he came home in the evenings, if he hadn't bought a burger or fish and chips in Llanfeni on the way home, he'd call in at the pub for a game of dominoes and a pint, though less often now with his old mates, the original moss gatherers, Frank and Dic, as their health deteriorated, so that most of the *hwyl* had gone, living on embellished stories of their glory days. Now he tended to live off micro ready-made meals for one, sitting down in the kitchen to watch the telly.

That was until the arrival of Bethan and her little girl. Whereas before his home had been a place to eat and sleep and not much else, it had been transformed in a day into a shared home for the three of them. Anyone – but especially her presence – exposed the sparseness of his house, something he'd been hitherto unaware of. Now, looking at it through her eyes, he saw it for what it was, shabby, unwelcoming, and cold. Not unclean so much as faded, with bare walls in tired, dull paint, and no adornments. There were only the most basic utensils in the kitchen, and elsewhere he'd managed with the old lino and the odd rug. Upstairs there were two bedrooms and a box room, served by a single toilet, sink and white bath, with a small mirror on the window shelf, toothbrush and toothpaste in a plastic cup, and packet of disposable razors, as his only toiletries. At the time, he thought he'd improved things, but looking at it with them there it looked bare. He set off to buy new – two chairs for the kitchen table, a rug by the fire in the living room, and sofa to brighten the place up, but the bright colour merely emphasized the lack in the rest of the house.

It wasn't just that, though. He'd told Bethan to go and buy whatever she wanted. It was a newness for him that had nothing to do with furniture or other household fittings – the space within the house, that personal vacuum in each room which he'd got so used to, which he hadn't even considered, until it was filled by Bethan and Clare. Now the reality of sharing his home with someone else, however wished for, caused Tegwyn to constantly readjust his own space within the four walls of the cottage. Not that he didn't want them – hadn't he spent his nights dreaming of just such a resolution. It was just that he hadn't realized the impact their physical presence would have on him. Like them, he also needed time to adjust and learn to become familiar with their ways and needs. There were family nuances between mother and child which they took for granted, but which he needed time to become part of, something that wouldn't happen overnight. Having Bethan with him had been a fantasy he never really believed would become reality, and now she was here Tegwyn found himself clumsy around them, his middle-aged, inbuilt routine difficult to break in order to accommodate theirs, with the kitchen, bathroom and bedroom all shared. Even though he had wanted this, he nonetheless felt it as an intrusion.

Still recovering, Bethan hardly noticed the plainness of Tan y Bryn. She was just grateful to be safe and to have Tegwyn, a person she'd known all her life, there to look out for her. There was Clare as well who changed her priorities. These were of a primal nature, a mother's instinct to protect her young, and for the first time in a long time, she felt secure knowing he'd already risked everything for her, and would again to protect her. This was now her home and these the back lanes where she grew up with no bogeyman to jump out at her, and she was determined to be as she had been before she ever went to Ireland, and put Malcolm out of her mind so she didn't live in the fear he'd created. She had to force herself not to look over her shoulder as she walked over Tan y Bryn fields to the lane that joined them with Tŷ Coch, Tegwyn insisting on accompanying her until she had enough confidence to go alone, knowing he watched her from the gate, making sure she came to no harm, playing along with her insecurities, sure that the Irishman wouldn't step on his turf. To begin with she skirted round, keeping close to the edge like a mouse hiding from beady eyes that would swoop if it was spotted, but as the days drew into weeks and nothing happened, Beth gradually became more confident, backtracking the lanes and the land she knew so well.

One morning she crossed the field's middle and swinging her leg over the gate she waved back at Tegwyn who'd waited, watching to reassure her that she was safe, before she vanished behind the high hedge and down to Tŷ Coch. Richard also kept an eye out, timing her movements to coincide with the end of his milking so that he'd be sure she'd passed safely to see their mum in the cottage. At least there she was more helpful, keeping Elin company and tidying up, releasing Mervyn to a bit of space so he could potter outside. Her mum wanted to know why she hadn't sought help and come home earlier, but she couldn't talk very easily and it took time for Beth to understand her. Some days it was awkward between them, with a lack of communication, and Beth thought she had more in common with the mother-in-law she'd left behind than with her own mother sitting in an easy chair by the kitchen window, the opposite now of everything she used to be. She remembered her mother as always active, never sitting down until the end of a long day, busy on the farm, always with jobs to do. It was work that she'd loved and had pride in, and to see her reduced to sitting in a chair by the window to watch was sad. Not for the first time, she wished she could put back the clock; that she'd never left, nor met Malcolm, so that none of it would have happened. It was a silly thought, really, the idea of living life so as not to upset a previous pattern. Deep down it was a fear of not succeeding.

'I'm sorry, Mam,' she said, tucking in her blanket. 'I know I should have stayed. If I'd been here you would never have had your accident.' She looked down at her with a conciliatory smile, 'But he'd already got me by then, you see, and I couldn't tell you, could I? It was all too late and all the family had their own problems. I had planned to, Mam, but there was never a good time, what with you in hospital and Uncle Merv and Rich so upset.' They both knew it was water under the bridge but it bothered Bethan that she'd let her mother down. 'Originally

I'd bought an open ticket for me and Clare so I didn't need to rush back, but he'd seen to that, and I was gullible enough to swallow his story. I should have seen what he was up to but I didn't. I'm sorry mam, for everything. I know I've let you down.'

Elin tried to put her hand out, to pat her daughter's in reassurance, her attempt at a smile causing her to dribble which Beth gently wiped away before kissing her on her head. 'I hope you can forgive me, and this time I'm home for good, and I'll look after you I promise.' Enough for one morning, Beth didn't want to burden her mother with it all and kept off the subject of any mental problem, or what had happened to her following her trip home and the subsequent avalanche of a collapsing marriage, losing her baby, and his involvement in her kidnap. Her union with Malcolm had been an unmitigated disaster, a prison sentence where she had been the captive. She wasn't even sure if the family had told her the truth or what she knew or understood, but she could see that her mother was alert and lucid in her head even if she couldn't speak or articulate easily. Her mum understood, she always had.

Moira knew he watched her but didn't care what was reported or seen. He could hang for all she minded and buttoning up her coat against the west wind, she raised the sealed envelope in a gesture of defiance towards the window of the Georgian house, got into her car and drove off down the road from her bungalow and away from the village, to post her letter somewhere he couldn't get it. Not that it mattered as he knew darn well who it was for and where it was going, and as for the contents he could guess accurately what it contained:

I'm so glad you are both safe and home with your family. Thank God for that, as the weather was atrocious! As you know, I am not a sentimental person, but your flight has left me bereft and I find it difficult coming to terms with the hole your absence causes me. I feel a desolation, almost insurmountable, without you and Clare, and I never thought I would grieve again as I do now. To lose a son and daughter-in-law and a precious granddaughter by the hand of another, now despised, son. As you can imagine, he wishes me dead and I for my part reciprocate the sentiment emphatically. Without him and what he has done I would still have Kieran, you and Clare. Hell is too good for him, but at least he has not got you or Clare.

You must not worry about me. I have always been resilient and I entertain myself with my racing, whiskey, and my cronies at the bridge table, and still do the daily crossword to keep myself sharp. The idea of the internet seems good although I don't understand modern technology, but I have started to make inquiries – please thank Penny – I would love to talk to you both and see a picture – what an idea! A big hug to Clare from her Granny and your guardian angel watch over you both.

Your loving mother-in-law, Moira

Her letter, or rather the tone of it, came as a shock to her daughter-in-law who knew that Moira was neither religious nor melodramatic. She felt bad about the way she'd compromised her and guilty at abandoning her, and the morning's post worried Beth as she studied the postmark to see to what lengths Moira had gone to post it away from the O'Connor home. It had been six months since they'd left, and whereas Beth had Tegwyn and the family close at hand to look after them, she'd left Moira stranded and alone with Malcolm. She had in the process taken her daughter, Moira's beloved granddaughter, with her, as well as getting Moira to help them escape, and it was this sense of betrayal, mixed with regular nightmares of Malcolm trying to catch her, that caused her panic attacks.

The dreams were nothing so simple as snuffing her out, there was no humane gun to the head, stunning her like a cow, no proficient slit to the throat, but vivid dreams of him enjoying himself. What he wanted was to watch her suffer and beg at his orchestration; a freak conductor to a torturous melody that would involve Clare, her Achilles heel. That chorus that would always wake Beth, calling out 'No!' as she involuntarily grabbed Tegwyn in fright. It played over and over, not just in the small hours, catching her out when she least expected it in a sinister refrain, even in the middle of the day. But if Bethan still had trouble with her waking nightmares, Tegwyn was getting used to her behaviour, believing that she only needed time and her panic attacks and bad dreams would diminish. Half asleep, he'd wrap his arms around her, soothing her as he held her close until she relaxed.

Between the demands of Dafydd Sion and his cows, Richard had already lost most of his night's sleep. The young bitch Fly's constant barking in the small hours was the last straw. Getting up from their bed and leaving Penny curled half asleep, he crept downstairs and slipping on his coat and wellingtons walked across the yard to the shed where Fly was, to give her a row. The little bitch was so pleased to see him, she leapt up, tail wagging excitedly only to be chastised by the tired farmer. 'Fly! Shut up you bloody dog,' Richard said, threatening to smack her, his voice a growl in reprimand. The young dog slunk back to the corner of the shed not understanding what she'd done wrong as he slammed the door shut.

As he walked back across the yard he was determined to have a word with his sister about her. Officially the puppy had been bought for Mervyn, as a replacement for Taff, who he'd put down. But the old man hadn't bonded with the young bitch and tended to leave it in its shed unused, so that, bored, it had got into the habit of barking. He would raise the issue when he told her about the old mare. It seemed that she'd managed to hold in foal to one of Madoc's bloodlines, one of the last of the line from her late father's horses and it would be a good present for his sister and give her something to look forward to, come April. She had always been with horses which had been part of the attraction to Malcolm, but soured by being made a fool of in the hunting field, followed by another public humiliation in front of his racing cronies, she had become incapable of handling any thoroughbred. Richard and Tego would change all that and it was about time Beth was re-introduced to her old love of the Welsh cob. It would butter her up into taking the dog off his hands and would give her something constructive to work on. She'd always been good with the farm dogs and it was worth asking to see if she'd be willing to take on the young dog before lambing got under way. Kill two birds with one stone, thought Richard, pleased with his idea – stop the dog yapping at night and help take Beth out of herself and get involved in the farm.

4

A visit from Martin always lifted their spirits, and he made a special fuss of the little girl he'd lifted from the surf's edge, giving her a wink that was only for her, like her dad used to, to make her feel special. When he went back and opened the front door of his car, bent down and lifted out a noisy lamb, Clare's face lit up. He carried it up to her. 'This little miss is for you,' he said holding the lamb as it tried to wriggle out of his grasp. 'It hasn't got anyone to look after it and I thought I know just the person who would be able to. Do you think you can?' She nodded uncertainly, looking across to her mam for permission, as she stroked the lamb's face. Responding to a small finger, the lamb immediately suckled, making Clare laugh.

'See, it loves you already! Here put your hands out, like mine,' shifting the bundle across to Clare's outstretched arms. 'It's quite heavy, don't let it go.' She closed her arms around it, holding the lamb tightly, her mother close by in case it escaped. 'There, it's happy with you. It's yours now, so do you think you can look after it and feed it for me when I go away?'

Clare nodded enthusiastically. 'I can keep it, Mam?'

She wasn't going to be able to say no, even though she'd end up looking after it as the novelty wore off.

'Go on then, we'll find some straw and put it in the shed, but you'll have to feed it.' As they walked towards the shed, she turned back to Martin. 'I didn't know you were going away again so soon?'

He nodded, his mood changing suddenly, his jaw tightening, and though he spoke lightly enough, Beth could see he'd become ill at ease. A sufferer of acute anxiety herself, she could spot the tell-tale signs, the strain on the soldier's face, his grey eyes not really engaged but fixed and distant, looking out to sea remembering another time or place. She saw his shaking hands as he tried to conceal them by wrapping them across his chest to stop the tremor. Behind his forced smile, she sensed his unhappiness, and although it was cold standing in the yard, there was a latent sweat on his skin. She wanted to put her hand out and hold him, to let him know she understood, and he saw her look of concern and didn't want her pity. How could she possibly know what he had been through. What experience had she ever had of war, watching buddies destroyed by roadside bombs, limbs blown up like bits of rubbish falling to the side of the road. She could have no idea what he'd been through or what atrocities he'd seen, and her pathetic pity suddenly angered him. What right had she to recover or be optimistic about life when he had saved them but failed to save his real friend Gareth. And now he was being forced to return, to be on guard, to be a go-between in a wasted bitter war. The Balkans was not his problem.

On an impulse she wanted to give him something to hold onto.

'That's brilliant, Martin, I've got something.' She ran upstairs before he could object, and opening a small drawer in her bedroom, pulled out the silver Byzantine cross from the back, hidden underneath her underwear and came back down. 'I want you to have this. It came from the Ottoman Empire and has protected soldiers in the past.' She held it out to him in her open palm, willing him to take it from her. 'Please don't say no, just take it. Put in your pocket if you won't wear it round your neck.' No longer a stolen, sullied love token, but a talisman returning eastward. Easier to take than reject, he took it without studying it, putting into his coat pocket to chuck later, as he smiled quickly, his lips becoming tight, glad to leave them, the memory no longer good or important to him.

'By the way,' he said. 'I've got myself engaged.'

'That's brilliant Martin. Congratulations!' He turned on the engine, knowing he had to drive on to his barracks.

At the time of the near drowning on the beach, Llanfeni primary school teachers had been alerted to the Davies's trauma and when the time came they had been fully prepared, ready for any telltale signs of the little girl's stress, and to make allowances for it. Huddled in the staff room, they had listened, at third-hand, to Bethan's story, including the flight from Ireland, savouring the details, sucking them in like strands of richly sauced spaghetti, and gasping at the audacity of it, their eyes sparkling at the malice of it all, wanting more.

They made sympathetic noises of disbelief before pronouncing judgement, nudging closer to each other over the kettle and sink, reinforcing the bonds of community. Initially the teachers and school staff took particular care, monitoring Clare closely, making sure she was always at the front of the class, but as the weeks slipped by, she became a little less prominent. When out in the playground, she was always accompanied by an older child acting as guardian, but in time, seeing no threat, the headteacher relaxed this scrutiny and allowed the little girl to integrate and make her own friends as she adjusted to being another normal schoolchild.

The present Martin Price left them delighted Clare, who after a few days of help had mastered the mixing of the milk powder with warm water, and the feeding of the ever-greedy black-faced lamb. She was so proud of being in charge of the woolly thing that she managed, by persistent nagging, to get her mum to drive them down to school so she could show it off to the class and her teacher, Mrs Williams, who duly made the appropriate noises. Many of the children, brought up on farms were less impressed and they soon got bored of the bleating animal until it peed on the floor, making them giggle. Enough! The teacher quickly ushered parent and lamb out while trying to prevent the children from treading in the puddle.

5

Bethan had not expected to like Richard's partner and it had come as a nice surprise to have her preconceptions proved so wrong. Penny was the opposite to what Bethan had imagined her to be, down to earth and hands on, she was not in the least stand-offish and she just got on with whatever needed doing, getting her hands dirty and working tirelessly on the farm. She seemed to thrive on the physical involvement, in stark contrast to Richard's ex, Nesta. Although the whole family knew of some of Beth's problems, Penny, unlike Richard, had no qualms about leaving her son with her. She was only too grateful to get a breather out in the yard or fields for a short time without Sion. Savvy, she was also up to speed with all the new technology and although the remoteness of where they lived limited access, Penny had already got the farm onto a computer network, as well as mobile phones, and she showed Bethan how to use email, so she could communicate with her mother-in-law in Ireland, without Malcolm knowing.

Yet for all the new advances in communication, Mervyn was the first to hear the breaking news on his radio. Sitting in the kitchen with his first cup of the day, he'd switched on the radio as he did every morning to catch the end of *Prayer for the Day* and then at five forty-five, just after he'd taken a cup to Elin and seen what sort of a night she'd had, he'd come back to the peace and quiet of the kitchen, with the ticking clock, to listen to *Farming Today*. There was no preliminary chit-chat this morning, the programme went straight to the news of an outbreak. He knew it could become serious if not stopped. Foot-and-mouth had been identified in swine in Essex. He looked across to the calendar hanging on the wall making a mental note of the day. Most animals were in at this time of year which he thought was a bonus, but to be on the safe side he knew he'd let Richard know, and without finishing his tea, he got dressed and crossed the yard to the milking parlour, quietly thankful that Essex was a long way off, and glad they no longer kept any pigs.

'Oh hello Mervyn, is everything OK?' Richard asked as he saw his stepfather walk along the aisle towards him. 'It's not Mam is it?'

'No, no she's all right, still in bed with her cup of tea.'

'Well, I've nearly finished here, if I'd known you were coming I'd have left the cows, but you could make yourself useful and hose down for me. I want to get to market prompt.'

'I've just heard on the radio there's been an outbreak of foot-and-mouth reported and I thought I'd better let you know straight away.'

'Foot-and-mouth? Where? What animals have been infected?'

'Pigs in Essex.' Mervyn saw Richard let out his breath, relaxing slightly as the outbreak was nowhere close. Mervyn's news was still a worry, but not an immediate threat and he couldn't remember the last outbreak or what had been the consequences, having never experienced the disease at first hand, only the descriptions of older farmers.

'Did you tell Penny?'

'I haven't been to the house yet, I came out here to you first.'

'Damn,' he thought to himself, wondering about the implications and how it would affect the running of the farm.

'Did they say anything else?'

'No, just restrictions in place around the outbreak while they carry out tests.'

'Foot-and-mouth. That's all we need! We've only just started to recover from the BSE crisis. When was the last outbreak? I can't remember.'

'In the 1960s, it started in a farm in Shropshire. You must have been quite young.'

Richard tried to recall. 'I only vaguely remember. I think I read something, but that's about it. No one round here had it did they?'

'No, it didn't affect us here, and it was different in those days. Farmers used their local market so there was much less movement of stock and less risk of the disease spreading.'

'How long did it last, Merv?'

He wanted to know the implications and what they could do to avoid it.

'Several months, I seem to remember, mostly over the border. Shropshire and Cheshire had it bad. You were only a youngster and had enough on your plate, what with what happened to your dad, so it's not surprising you don't remember it.'

'What caused it?'

'Contaminated pigswill with infected Argentine lamb. Cledwyn Hughes was the minister of agriculture then, I remember that.'

'Is that what's happened in Essex? Infected feed?'

'I doubt it's pigswill today with all the rigmarole and rules, but it's too early to say and you know Defra, they never give more information out than the industry knows already.'

'Except for more rules and regulations.'

'And a lot of help they are.'

'You don't have to tell me. But could be serious for us Merv?'

'Potentially. But, we're a long way away from the outbreak and they should be able to get it under control with all the new technologies in identifying infectious diseases.'

'Well, let's hope so. We're lambing next month. We need to tell Beth, as she'll be handling the early ewes and help you with the year's lambing.'

Obviously bothered by Mervyn's unwelcome news, Richard wanted to know the extent of the last outbreak and he continued to quiz Mervyn.

'Were a lot of animals lost?'

'Thousands probably. I know the Duke of Westminster's pedigree Dairy Shorthorn herd was one of many. Based near Chester, so it was on the Welsh news a lot. Three hundred valuable cows slaughtered, and their genetic lines all lost.'

'I'd hate to see my cows go like that. God, just as everything was getting better and we were finding our feet. Mad cow disease and now this.'

'We haven't got it, Rich, and being fairly isolated, it's unlikely the disease will travel this far west.'

'I hope you're right. But, it wouldn't do any harm to take some precautions. I'll put some disinfectant mats out by the gate to the road.'

Back in the house the normality of the domestic scene was so tranquil that he wondered if Mervyn had got his facts right and was almost loath to bring up the subject with Penny sitting feeding Sion, the kettle singing on the hob and the smell of toast and homemade marmalade, inviting after coming in from the cold.

'And how's my lovely girl and son this morning?' He bent over giving her a kiss.

'Ooh, your face is cold, Rich,' she said, feeling his cheek against their little nest of warmth in dressing gown, baby, and milk. 'You could do with some breakfast. The kettle's on, toast? And coffee?'

'Thanks, *cariad*. Did you have the news on?'

'You must be joking! It's been Terry Wogan for us, hasn't it Sion. Why? Should I have?'

'Mervyn's heard there's been an outbreak of foot-and-mouth. Do you mind if I put the TV on. I need to hear the news.'

Penny immediately leaned across to switch the radio off, not sure of the implications, but she could see that her husband was sufficiently worried to realize the potential seriousness of the situation. It always seemed to happen whenever anything looked too good, or was going overly well, a nasty twist of fate would bring you back on your uppers. Only yesterday she'd left Beth in the house with Sion and joined her husband outside. In the sunshine the farm looked vibrant, expectant of spring on the cusp of another season of lambing and calving. Leaning over the gate watching the cows contentedly grazing off the last of the winter kale, Penny had listened as Richard had talked over his plans for the field rotation; man and woman warming their backs in the brief February sunshine, imagining their fields full of summer growth – valuable nutrients from red and white clover in the hay meadows, and oats and peas that would go into the year's silage, like a rich filling in a grass sandwich; their aim to make Tŷ Coch farm operate as near to self-sufficiency as possible, negating the need to buy-in concentrate, with the exception of essential trace elements for the health of their stock. Hopefully, if all went to plan they'd be able to reduce their costs by needing less bought-in animal cake as well as making their meat even more accountable and additive-free, a win-win situation she had optimistically thought. This vision of the future pleased her as she'd slipped her arm through Richard's, seeing their shared path, working the land for their family's future. She loved the sudden understanding of what it was to be tied to the land and governed by nature as she looked out across his fields and even the sun obliged her sense of well-being, illuminating the winter hillside. Where a month earlier heavy cloud had given way to a covering of snow, the hillside now shone in a fresh brightness and the dead bracken was a stark chestnut brown below dark patches of gorse. White blobs of sheep spread across the sloping sides of the common, interrupted by hawthorn in a perpetual slant against Atlantic winds, their stubborn roots offering a windbreak to sheep in severe weather and giving a bearing for the shepherd in poor visibility. In that brief period of morning sunshine, the hill stood magnificent in an almost florescent light against the dark purple heather. That was less than twenty-four hours ago and the overview had soured with quickening cloud, heavy rain and driving winds.

'Mervyn thinks I ought to take those young calves to market as soon as possible. So I'm going to take them today.'

'Why? They're barely two weeks old, Rich.'

'Because if this disease spreads, Mervyn thinks they may close down the markets and we'll be lumbered with them. They will still need feeding and there will be nowhere to sell them, and we've got the lambing about to start. Anyhow, fifty quid is better than nothing, and the Friesians will never fatten. If I go now I should be back by dinner and it'll give me a chance to see what's happening. Have a word with the union, and find out what's being done to stop the outbreak spreading. Will you go over and tell Beth? Just so she knows.'

'Why? Can it affect sheep?'

'Yes, all cloven hoofed animals are at risk.'

In the market the mood was full of the breaking story, the effect on prices being immediate as animals were either being sold for a pittance or returning home unsold. For all the talk, no one seemed to know what was happening – how many actual cases had been confirmed and where? The union was still waiting for Carwyn Jones, the National Assembly rural affairs minister and Westminster agriculture minister Nick Brown to call a meeting with them. Richard saw Alun and Elwyn who farmed Bryn Coed, a few miles over the hill from Tŷ Coch. Big sheep farmers, the men were in a pen of broken-mouthed ewes, sorting them into suitable groups for sale as Richard joined them.

'*Bore da,*' he said to them. 'How's trade?'

'Pah!' said Alun, raising his eyes to the heavens.

'Everything's down,' Elwyn grumbled.

'And it'll drop again if they don't sort it out pretty bloody quick, how did you get on?'

'Gave them away. No one wants Friesian bull calves. Twenty-five each and that took a lot of persuasion. Better than taking them home. No profit, only lessening the loss.'

'And there won't be any profit if they have their way. The politicians don't want farmers in this country.'

The older of the two brothers, Alun, raised his head in the direction of a white-coated official.

'I suppose you remember the last outbreak?' Richard asked.

'So do you, Richard Tŷ Coch! Cheeky bugger! It was only twenty years ago! The Isle of Wight.'

'No, I didn't mean that one. The one before then, you know that spread across the whole country.'

'Oh, then. That was terrible, back in the Sixties. You don't remember it?'

'Fair play,' Elwyn said, winking at him, 'you were only a boy, but your dad Ianto would have.'

'Were there many animals killed?'

'I'd say half a million or more. Spread round the country, thousands of outbreaks all over.'

'No cure?'

'Nope.'

The news sobered them, as other farmers leaned closer, listening in on the old brothers' conversation, only to be broken up by the sound of the microphone and the banging of a wooden stick on metal as the auctioneer stood above them on a plank, calling reluctant buyers in to the aged and brokers' section, selling for slaughter.

'Good ewes, with plenty of meat on these,' he announced, seeing a few dealers eyeing up the lots, none willing to show any keenness to buy, waiting for the lowest price and knowing they had the farmers over a barrel. There was little demand for mutton.

'What do you think, Mr Ali?' as a slim olive hand felt along a sheep's back weighing up their worth.

'Who'll start me off? Forty, forty, come on they must be worth that. Thirty I'm bid, thirty-two ...'

Alun slipped a fiver into the brown hand as the hammer went down.

'Thank you, Mr Ali, they'll kill out all right.'

Having seen enough, Richard left the market. As he drove home, the realization that his calves had sold for ten pounds less than an old ewe bound for the Halal market was an unpalatable truth.

There was an air of anxious expectancy, as Richard listened eagerly to news bulletins. Like farmers up and down the country, he hoped for a containment of the outbreak, worrying about cross-contamination, as he re-doused disinfectant onto the mats across his lane that evening after the milk lorry had gone, in the hope of keeping the disease out of Tŷ Coch.

6

It didn't take long for the novelty to wear off, and like many pets, it ended up with a parent doing the daily chores of feeding and cleaning. The pet lamb had thrived initially and Beth didn't think much of the fact that it had been slow to finish off its milk. It was only at dinner-time that she realised there was something wrong. The lamb lay listlessly, grinding its teeth, wet with saliva around its mouth. She left the bottle in the straw, planning to come back in a couple of hours after going round the in-lamb ewes with Fly. It would be no great loss if the pet lamb died, knowing all too well that cade lambs often didn't flourish on the bottle, and she didn't think Clare would be unduly upset. It was time-consuming and she had plenty of more profitable jobs to get on with.

When Richard returned form market full of the foot-and-mouth outbreak, he insisted they all walk round the farm to double check the stock. The farmer wished he could make his land secure and prevent the wild animals from moving freely over it. Ever since bovine TB, he mistrusted the scientists and still secretly blamed the badger population for spreading the virus. There was nothing he could do other than try to block up any holes in his fencing, even though he'd been told only cloven-hoofed animals were susceptible, and when Tegwyn came home from work, Richard insisted he wipe all his forestry equipment with disinfectant. Tired after a hard physical day, Tegwyn nearly fell out with his brother-in-law over his knee-jerk reaction to the outbreak.

'You don't think you're over reacting? I haven't been near Essex, or anywhere near any pigs, Richard!'

'Better to be on the safe side.'

'*Duw*, they'll sort it in no time. That's what Dr Trelawny thinks.'

'Since when was he an authority on foot-and-mouth? Even the vets don't know, and they're meant to be the experts.'

'I suppose it was all the talk in the market?'

'Prices dropped like a stone and no one had any useful information. It was all speculation but no guidelines for us to go on. So I'm just taking all the precautions we can.'

More surprising was the government's swift action in closing the meat export market the same day as the outbreak was confirmed. The effect pleased the European farmer, while causing the home market to collapse.

'I can't understand it,' Richard said, coming in from the following morning's milking. 'Why haven't they put a stop to animal movement here?' He increased the volume on the TV, as if the news was going to be any clearer by being unnecessarily loud. 'You'd have thought it would have been the first thing they'd have done instead of penalizing us by closing our export trade.' He had been doing his homework, trying to read up on the disease. 'Typical French, first BSE and now this. We all know the outbreak originated outside the UK but we get penalized. Contaminated meat coming in from abroad. Like rabies, foot-and-mouth is not an endemic disease in this country, so it has to be brought in.'

'They are slaughtering all the infected animals aren't they?' Penny asked, "and killing animals on adjoining land. Won't that halt it?'

'I hope so. But they've been so slow, fussing about the EU implications instead of sorting it out at base. Getting information is impossible. Phone lines are permanently on hold, and how long can you wait? Nearly forty minutes and still no answer to your question. Can we take our fat bullocks to market and bring them home if the price isn't good enough? Or do they have to go straight to slaughter regardless of any price offered?'

'The girl in the office wasn't sure. They couldn't give an update because they hadn't received any from the ministry. They advised us to wait.'

'They don't know what they're doing. Half of them haven't a clue about farming, and all the red tape and form filling we have to do. It means nothing but work. In many ways we're worse off now than before. At least in those days some of the Ministry men knew what a cow and sheep were. They had some experience of agriculture. But today! Well, it's a bloody shambles. Look what happened with my calves. Even with the outbreak confirmed, many of the farmers drove their animals back home. So who knows where the disease is spread. No good closing the door after the horse has bolted!'

'You can't blame the farmers. You'd do the same in their position.'

'Of course. But what if any were infected? Or, got infected in the market? Heaven knows where they all are now. Half way round the country. I'm glad to have got rid of the calves even if the price was lousy. It's one less thing to worry about.'

'Yes, quite.'

'And what about all the hefted sheep? The flocks roaming on the hill where there are no fences, barriers or anything?'

It seemed impossible to contain Britain's sheep flocks and cattle herds effectively.

'How long is the incubation period?'

'I don't know, and I can't even get a definitive answer on that, but it could take weeks to show, Pen. And the ground could still be infected. I just don't know, and I can't get to speak to anyone who does.'

Several more days passed without any decision before it dawned on Whitehall to belatedly announce a suspension on all animal movements within Britain. Livestock markets and work at all abattoirs were also suspended for seven days to allow the grey-suited men, wearing unsuitable shoes for muddy fields, to get up to speed, chasing the outbreaks in a desperate catch-up.

Richard and Penny continued their daily routine, looking at their animals more carefully with each milking, and hoping rather, than believing, that they could remain isolated from the disease as they watched the evening news reports of the rapid spread across the country.

Without a second thought, Tegwyn took the dead lamb and threw it down into the dingle so that Clare would not see it, knowing that by morning carrion would have done the job of disposing of it and that within a few weeks, there'd be plenty of new lambs to take its place.

It was only when Bethan mentioned it in passing to her brother, that the lamb's death took on a new dimension. Immediately Richard convinced himself that it had died of foot-and-mouth and in a panic scrambled down the bank at the back of Tan y Bryn in search of the carcass. Finding nothing other than a scrap of bloodied wool, after a sleepless night of worrying, he lost his temper as he yelled at his sister, accusing her of bringing the disease to his farm.

'Richard, it just died, like lambs often do. It's got nothing to do with foot-and-mouth.' She tried to reason with him, his face livid as his father's used to be when he was angry.

'Where the hell did you get it from?'

'What? Oh, the lamb. Martin brought it. It was a present for Clare.' She could see it didn't make sense. 'He had it from Yorkshire, from his fiancee Katie's farm.'

'Why? What happened to the ewe?'

'Apparently it had died.'

'It died! What of?' He sounded almost pleased at his deduction, nodding grimly at Bethan.

'Died in labour, Richard. Do you think he would have given you an infected lamb! They don't have foot-and-mouth there, for heaven's sake Rich. The lamb just died from the powdered milk, as they do. Martin thought he was doing us a favour. He saved your life in case you had forgotten, so I don't think he'd bring a sick animal to ruin your farm. Come on bro, you're overtired that's all, and it's just an awful coincidence. Nothing more.'

After he'd been placated and gone back down the lane to Tŷ Coch, Teg was glad to sit down. It had been a physically tiring week. He wasn't young anymore and found the labour of moss gathering cold, wet and tiring. Nor was it the same without Dic, and although he and Frank tried, they couldn't recreate the camaraderie of bygone days when life didn't seem so pressured. Even the pub had lost its allure. Locals who once played darts and dominoes were dying out, replaced by Sky and widescreen televisions for entertainment – a world of visual communication that negated any need for conversation, leaving communities void of communal spirit. Only the catastrophic led to a resurgence of that spirit. However, the foot-and-mouth catastrophe was different to other natural disasters, as the countryside shut down and the public were kept away, watching the burning pyres on television, removed from the harrowing reality – the revolting image of dead cattle, heads lolling among stiff legs with sticking-out hooves. Piled high onto lorries, their bodily fluids dripped out as they were driven off to be burned in hastily prepared pits in their thousands.

On the news, Nick Brown, the minister for agriculture who had announced that it was not a national crisis, now insisted on the closure of footpaths to minimize public footfall, while many sports fixtures, including horse racing, still went ahead.

Malcolm scanned the news, hoping to hear of the out-of-control spread of the disease that would cause the British farmer devastation, and more specifically spell ruin for Tŷ Coch farm so that he would have to delay his plans to travel overseas. He could postpone his trip until the foot-and-mouth had cleared up, and although it did not infect horses, like dog muck on his shoe, he didn't want to step into anything foul that could come back to taint Irish soil.

In the early light, Richard saw the soreness. It was more than just a touch of lameness, as two of his cows hobbled slowly down the lane after the others for the first of the day's milking, saliva dribbling from their mouths in obvious discomfort. In that moment Richard knew all his precautionary work had been for nothing. He left them unmilked in the collecting yard to go inside and ring the vet, knowing the consequence.

Dai Lewis, white-clad in protective clothing, with wellingtons to match, looked more like a scientist than a Defra marksman as he got out of his truck with an array of armoury in the back. There was none of the normal banter but, sombre-faced, he greeted Richard, offering brief condolence. Over the last few weeks he'd learnt not to dwell, not to show too much sympathy as farmers and their families broke down while they watched their animals being killed. Accompanied by two younger men, he followed Richard to his herd of dairy cows still standing patiently in the collecting ring unaware of their fate. It was very different from his day-to-day work as a licensed slaughterman where he'd be called on to put an animal out of its distress, or some old cow down after a long life. What he had to do in the last two weeks, and today, was destroy a lifetime's work – to shoot indiscriminately every cloven-hoofed animal on a farm, whether it was young or old, already ill, or showing no outward signs of the disease whatsoever, and to do this as proficiently as he could.

Squeezing his lips together, Richard cleared his throat in an attempt to remain stoic as he led the way. He didn't want to be there but equally felt obliged, honour-bound to his loyal cows to make sure they were at least shot quickly. He knew it would be hard, but after witnessing the first few shot at close range, their kind faces splattered with blood and brain as they fell, he could not stomach it, begging Dai to stop as the noise of the guns boomed, drowning out the desperate bellowing of his beloved cows. The marksmen were as quick as they could be with their shotguns, sometimes shooting twice into a staggering animal. A deathly silence followed as the dead cows continued to bleed and tears ran down Richard's face numb with the shock of it all. As gently as he could Dai told him to go inside. Better not to witness the killing of the young cattle, the calves, the sheep and lambs. It would be less clinical in the fields, not point blank and less easy to have a clean shot as animals ran, but Richard shook his head; he was their dairyman, herdsman and shepherd and he had no choice but to be there. Horrific and harrowing as it was, he watched his animals being gunned down. The young cattle, spooked by the noise and the white-suited men, galloped to the furthest end of their respective fields, fidgeting restlessly, panicking afresh each time a rifle was fired. Because of the range and movement, not all of them died quickly, and Penny's terrified Welsh Black store cattle, bellowed and ran, trying to jump the stone walls to escape.

In the farmhouse Penny tried to entertain Sion, offering her a distraction from what was happening outside. It hurt to know that her Welsh Blacks were being slaughtered but it was worse for Richard who had a lifetime's work destroyed, never to be replaced. Knowing the farm was all that he had ever worked for, Penny knew that witnessing the slaughter of his stock would upset him terribly and there was nothing she could do. Each shot was a powerful reminder of the carnage taking place. The constant gunfire caused Sion to cry, and only when the men had left the yard to go to the outlying land would he quieten.

On the sloping fields, sheep were shot with their lambs that were still so young they were barely able to run as they stumbled after their mothers, until nothing was left – no life, no bleating or movement other than a sea breeze whispering its salt sorrow over such killing fields.

Because of the fear of contagion, no one was allowed to leave the farm, which meant that Clare was forced to stay away from school. From her bedroom window she had also witnessed the destruction of the animals. She watched the men in their white clothes with guns shooting all the ewes and lambs in the fields which her mam had had to pen, to await the marksmen. Beth tried to pull her away from the window, but mesmerized she also stood there, horrified, an arm around her daughter, watching the slaughter of their sheep. She recognised some of the specially marked ewes that she'd helped lamb, appalled now, at the bodies being obliterated by bullets. When it was over the family was left in shock; each member stunned by the calamity. Mervyn had pulled Elin's chair away from the window to save her the sight and they sat quietly in the kitchen, saying nothing. At Tan y Bryn, Tegwyn was the only member of the family who'd been up to his neck in work trying to keep the burning pyres supplied with enough wood. Issued a special licence, he left in the early hours with his forestry equipment in order to source timber, debark it so as to increase the burning temperature and get it to the sites as quickly as he could. In and out, he had to show his card, get himself and his machinery and vehicle sprayed, and come home, often very late, absolutely shattered. To try and cover up the smell of smoke and where'd he'd been, he'd talk to them about the horses, one of the few animals, thanks only by the structure of their feet, that were not contagious and so were safe. The cobs, hens, and Fly the sheepdog, were the only animals left on the farm that a week earlier had supported over a thousand animals. Tŷ Coch farm and the surrounding land were left in total isolation, rotting like lepers. Mats, with military demarcation points across the farm's entrance, were manned by a sentry who would brook no crossing.

7

Richard leaned over the gate, the smell of burnt flesh still acrid in the still air, that no sea breeze was able to clear. He might have been able to bear a natural calamity, but this was the result of human laxity, a sloppiness compounded by bungling incompetence that left him with nothing. The foul smell remained, permeating the farm's soul, lingering on the growing spring grass, devoid of grazing. He'd been through the mill in the last few months and all to no avail as he'd fought to keep his farm clear, while Penny whose stock was on a different holding, suffered the same fate, leaving the land barren. The hideous day when they'd come to shoot his animals was etched in his mind – cows and sheep mown down, literally, days after Beth had worked so hard to help bring lambs safely into the world.

He couldn't bear to think of his beloved cows, and yet he couldn't stop thinking of them either, as they'd stood, quiet and trusting, before they staggered as they were shot in the head, one by one. Some went down like lead, but for the unlucky ones their 'sweet spot' for oblivion had been fractionally missed, causing acute pain as blood poured from their heads covering their lovely black and white hides in thickening streaks of red and he felt so guilty. By his hand they'd died, and for all the advancers in modern agriculture it was him, not his father or grandfather, who'd failed in his duty as custodian and lost the Tŷ Coch dairy herd.

Even now it wasn't over, for in another bureaucratic cock-up the dead animals that had been lifted by JCBs and piled high were not collected immediately. Instead they hummed in the heat with the sick smell of death, as they putrefied further, lying bloated and exposed in the spring sun. With farms all over the country in the same state, only the army could cope with the sheer numbers. Called upon by Westminster in catch-up, their expertise and manpower was needed to sort out the bureaucratic shambles. When Martin turned up in his uniform at Tŷ Coch, Richard, who'd wrongly blamed him for the outbreak at there, was grateful it was him and not a stranger. He knew them, he was one of them, a rural boy who'd grown up on marginal land squeezed between sea and mountain.

Martin knew that Richard Davies had already been through enough as he sat down and with the help of the auctioneer, forced to negotiate the cost of it all with a hard-nosed Ministry official to make sure there was no shenanigans. How much were his cows worth? The cows with unborn calves, the years of milk production, the gentle stroking to and from parlour to the fields in buttermilk yellow? What price? The pure-breds, that had taken him most of his working life to build up? How could he replace them or their bloodlines, let alone place a value on them? They didn't understand that it was like shooting your dog or cat; that his animals were part of the family albeit living out and grazing his extended garden of fields and hill.

He watched them, still recognizable, until they were finally carted off in large containers open to the sky so that stiff legs could be seen sticking out, and through it all he remained white and impassive, trying to deal with it by working, walking animal-less, avoiding the places where the swelling heaps had scorched the grass dead. Only after the carcasses had gone and the place was silent did he break – no great grieving sobs of outrage, but the barely perceptible crumbling of hope, of any belief that they'd want to farm again after what they'd been through. Their son Sion was the only one who remained untainted, gurgling in innocent contentment. Penny had never seen her husband cry, never witnessed a collapse so profound – her generous, quiet farmer who always took what nature threw at him in stoic resignation, with a philosophy of acceptance which was something that had made him so appealing to her. It was the opposite to how her ex viewed the world, and now this disease, made worse by man's incompetence and greed, threatened to overwhelm him.

Although he might have felt totally alone because of the nature of his work, there were hundreds of farmers up and down the country also staring out onto empty fields recently culled of all livestock, their situation made worse by the fact that they were unable to come together to share in their collective loss, making it all the more acute in their enforced isolation.

There was little else to talk about, and with all the livestock markets closed, there were more than usual in Y Fenni pub with opinions on how the outbreak was being handled. Talk revolved around new outbreaks, who'd been affected and how the politicians were handling the crisis. Not surprisingly any local unaffected by the outbreak offered opinion on the shambles. Glyn Williams, who worked for the council, leaning over the bar to have his pint refilled, told them what had happened to Dai Lewis a few days previously.

'Typical of the Ministry,' he said, with a gripe of his own. 'How was Dai expected to carry on his work when he hadn't been paid? He'd no money for diesel or ammunition for him or his staff. And do you know what they suggested he do. You wouldn't believe it.'

'Well, tell us Glyn,' said Frank, keen to hear.

'Why don't you use public transport, to save on costs!'

'What public transport? *Duw, Duw*, stupid fools!'

'Yeh. But can you see it? Hmm! All in their white suits, splattered with blood and muck with guns and rifles and boxes of ammunition getting onto a fucking bus in town to go off to another farm and do a bit of shooting!'

'Clear the bus pretty quick!'

There was a chuckle of appreciative laughter.

'*The Good, the Bad and the Ugly*, or *Straw Dogs – The Guns of Llanfeni*!'

'I've always said we're being run by morons and there's the proof. So what did Dai tell them?'

'He didn't mince his words.'

'No, I bet, and …?'

'Oh, I think when they had it spelled out for them and they saw the implications, a cheque was sent.'

'Dai was pretty furious. It delayed the whole process, and fair play he was doing his best to get the infected farm animals slaughtered as quick as he could to stop the disease spreading through the whole of the county. And then having to deal with the bright sparks in the smoke dilly-dallying with their daft ideas. Well, it made his blood boil. All right for them sitting in their offices but he was the one on the ground, having to deal with all the farmers.'

'It's the kids I feel sorry for. How do you explain it to them?'

'I remember when we had to have Don put down. Mair was so upset. And, fair play the dog was on its last legs. He'd had a good life but you try explaining that to a child.'

'They don't understand.'

'Did you see that family on the TV trying to stop them coming onto the land, standing there with their children as a barricade by the gate to block the truck?'

'Llwyn y Gog?'

'Yeh.'

'Awful.'

'Dai said the farms with children or just a few animals, like pets, were the worst. He's got a daughter. He could imagine what shooting her pony would do to her.'

'The whole business is a bloody waste, so unnecessary. If our government cared, like the French, for their agriculture, we'd never be in this mess, foot-and-mouth would never have got into this country.'

Glyn looked round and lowered his voice to his small group.

'Some farmers couldn't care less, in fact they're glad to get it. I know two farms not a million miles away from this spot who will make a lot more money from the compensation being paid them.'

'I even heard they tried to get the disease onto their land, to deliberately infect their sheep,' added Frank, unconcerned as to who heard him.

'I'd be careful what you say, there's many who wouldn't agree with you.'

Elwyn Evans walked over to them, tapping Glyn on the shoulder. 'For the record, Glyn Williams, those farmers ought to be shot along with their animals. So don't you go around smearing us with the same shitty brush. You've always got a few who are dishonest, even in the council.'

The inference was plain. 'Cheat if they could get away with it – steal – anything to fiddle the system to a make a bob. Doctors, lawyers, bankers, yes and farmers, you've always got your rotten ones. So I'd mind what you say.'

He went back to the group of farmers who all gave Glyn a black look. Muttering into his mild, Glyn couldn't resist adding, 'Not pennies. Compensation running into the millions.'

At first Richard Davies sat numbed in the house, unable to go out, staring at the wall in their kitchen. He wouldn't answer the phone, even when Rhian rang from London. He wouldn't pick up the kettle or even smile at his son, just sitting in a blank space, looking at the clock unaware of the its ticking; not slumped but upright on a hard chair at the table as if expecting something to be placed before him, only he didn't eat, hardly slept and would barely talk to his wife or baby. Penny knew there would be problems after what he'd been through and at first she tried to engage him in conversation, keeping the subject-matter trivial, her attempts at being light-hearted betrayed by the tension in her voice. When Richard didn't respond, she tried plonking Sion on his knee in the hope that the baby would snap him out of his darkness. Like a weight of flour, Richard put him down on the floor, ignoring any protest. He had no interest in her or them, sitting there at the table, not lifting his knife or fork. For several days she tried to get him to engage with family life, but he put up an impenetrable barrier. Neither Mervyn nor Tegwyn could distract him, and in desperation when Penny suggested Beth talk to him, Tego wasn't so sure.

'I'm not sure that's a good idea. Beth's not in a fit state, she's taken it pretty badly herself. She's been a whole month lambing, only to see them all slaughtered just as they should be flourishing. Bad enough after all her hard work but, well, she's not strong emotionally. You know.'

'But she's OK isn't she?' asked Penny.

'Yes, sort of. She isn't how she was when she came home from Ireland, but this has put her back a bit. She'd just got to feel herself again, going outside and helping, getting involved without looking over her shoulder, and then this happens. It didn't help that Clare witnessed it as well and is still upset. I don't want Beth further upset and I'm not sure she'd be the person to advise Richard. It could re-open all the old wounds. Isn't there anyone else who could help him. A professional?'

'The auctioneer called over to see how he was, you know afterwards, but Richard just sat there, nodding his head, not really listening to him.'

'A psychiatrist?'

'Well, who do you know, Tegwyn? They didn't help Bethan did they? Richard's always been very self-contained. The farm and the family have always been his mainspring. He won't open up to an outsider, I don't care how many letters he's got after his name.'

'In that case, I'm sure there are plenty of famers who'll talk to him.'

'Yes, and several have rung, but he won't take the phone and I have to do the talking for him. No one's getting through.'

'If only his mam were able to, she'd talk him out of himself, show him that not all is lost and that there are things still worth fighting for. She'd know what to do and how to help him.'

'Would it help if I brought him over to see her do you think?' suggested Penny. 'No one better than her in the understanding of the farm. She knows what he's going through and his feelings of loss and his overwhelming sense of failure.'

Elin had been in a similar situation during her tenancy of the farm, and following Ianto's death there was a serious shortage of money that nearly forced them to sell up and lose the farm. If anyone knew what Richard was going through it was his mother, but how could she comfort him without her faculty of speech?

8

Malcolm watched the news with added interest as the map showed the spread of the disease including more places in Wales. He turned the volume up as the camera zoomed in on dead carcasses being moved, switching to the smoke and burning pyres that covered rural Britain in an ugly smog. He hoped it would show Llanfeni and Richard's farm where he could catch a glimpse of Bethan and Clare, imagining the stench of burnt flesh. Never mind, as the newsreader switched to Cumbria, he had other ways in place to keep tabs on them, biding his time like a crow in a branch watching and waiting for a weak lamb, to swoop and extract its tongue, rendering the newborn non-viable. This year with all the shooting, guts, and blood, even the crows were surfeited, luxuriating on the delicacies.

Recently his business interests had made huge gains, not just his horses but speculative land purchases which he sold on with added planning permission for development, making a healthy profit. He continued to reinvest, buying up unused waste land, as Ireland's economy expanded. He'd hit a sweet spot, all the while keeping an eye what was happening in the UK.

Unlike his estranged mother, he had no contact with his ex-wife or daughter. He knew Moira communicated with them, she'd had lessons on how to use email and the internet in the local library and she'd even bought herself a computer which she used in her bungalow. She thought she'd been so clever, the old cow with her silly crossword knowledge. As if a password would keep him from nosing in her business with his wife and daughter. She was also on his surveillance list and they had hardly been on speaking terms since Bethan's departure. All that remained was a mutual wish for the other's demise.

> *It was so nice to get your email and I'm at home now and am slowly getting better at using my own computer but I panic in case I push the wrong button. Silly really – old age and modern technology!*
>
> *I've been so worried about you all and what you must be going through. Horrible pictures on the tv everyday with all the dead animals. What a monumental balls up by your government, but I do hope you'll get proper compensation. If you're hard up Bethan, let me help you, at least finically. It will make me feel better and it's easy enough to get some cash over without you know who needing to know anything. Anyhow as you're not officially divorced,– well that's water under the bridge and it doesn't matter. I hope you're happy at home. Please tell Clare I loved her picture of a cat. I miss you all so much Moiraxxxx*

In exasperation, Penny tried to start an argument, something to ignite him, only Richard wouldn't answer back, wouldn't respond.

'It's not only you, Richard, who've lost your animals. I've lost all my beef and store cattle. Your poor sister's had to witness the slaughter of her ewes and newborn lambs, and there's Mervyn and your Mum – it's not easy for any of us but we have to carry on, Rich, for Sion's sake and the whole family.'

Of course he knew she'd lost her cattle and her organic meat business would suffer heavily as a result, but it wasn't her at the helm, the farm had been his sole responsibility ever since his father's death. And there was the daily routine, as ingrained as breathing, of getting up and working. He couldn't function without such structure. There weren't any animals, so it didn't matter whether he got up or not. He was incapable of making an attempt to move on – to what or where? Empty fields, cordoned off, and still under quarantine.

So it hadn't been the lamb from Martin or anything to do with his fiancée's farm in Yorkshire which remained clear of the dreaded foot-and-mouth. Richard had just been unlucky, picking it up who knows where unsuspectingly. There was gossip about a huge conspiracy theory which said that the disease had been started by people in power who wanted to put the British farmer out of business, thus saving millions on subsidies. Or more improbable still, that the aim was to let the Brits starve, so they'd need help from a big power in the East. It was all wild speculation, spread by panic from a sense of despair.

Anything that made Richard consider a future for them would be a start, but nothing she broached caused a spark, he wouldn't consider summer grazing or a silage crop and Penny worried that he had given up on life, his will shattered. When he did sleep, he didn't wake refreshed but as if sleep had wrapped him in a straitjacket, restricting his body so that he woke all tense and stiff. For the first time in his life Richard felt really old, and with no animals to tend to, he fell into a languid depression which he couldn't shake off. As Penny was considering the Samaritans, spring responded to man's destruction, overwhelming the farm and surrounding countryside with vigorous growth and new life. Perhaps it was this, but for no apparent reason Richard got up from his chair and went outside for the first time in seven weeks.

It was not the cuckoo, nor the bluebells carpeting the floor of the wood under green leaf, nor the rough wetland grasses of the *ffridd* where he'd walked as a boy with his mother, camouflage for snipe and hare and wild orchid among the coarse grasses, but the hill that beckoned. A lone curlew's cry floated in the air as he walked up through heather and gorse in a waft of warming peat that rekindled the open space of his home, following the leylines of his forebears, looking down at the small farms of Rhyd y Meirch and Nant y Gaseg that were part of the old stallion walk of his great grandfather. He walked up to the lake, pooled like a saucer on the top. He stopped in the wide silence and for a long time stood looking eastward to the dried shale rivers of disused lead mines and the rusted lengths of railway that still spilled into the water of a man-made, slate-blue lake, connected to the hilltop by deep shafts that were wide enough for a sheep or a dog to fall into. Then he turned and walked near to the ridge, looking west and out to the sweep of the sea and a distant horizon.

At last here he was free of the smell of burning flesh, and on top of the hill where the absence of stock grazing became less significant, he stood and breathed. Perhaps he stood for a few minutes or hours before he turned, unaware of time, to retrace his footsteps, looking down the familiar hillside to the valley and his neighbours and farmsteads. Llanfeni maimed, but not dead.

Initially, Penny was relieved to see him go, so she could have her kitchen space back to normal and she believed he had turned the corner and was ready to do something, looking around at his farm, fields and land. Every day he set a routine, and without saying where or what he was doing, he walked out of the house and off, without giving his fields a second glance, but making for the hill or cliff path regardless of the weather. He often left in unsuitable clothing, without a hat or coat or boots, and Penny would stand watching at the window, worrying in case he did not come back.

Waking from a fitful sleep, he'd immediately get up and leave and not return until utterly spent, to collapse in his kitchen chair. A lifetime of habits that identified who he was, lost, and leaving him to dangle unhinged, like a broken gate. His folded cap was unused on the kitchen work surface, and his wellington boots, worn at the heel, were clean and unused by the back door mat, under the hook where he hung his overalls. Uninterested in any of his regular habits, he no longer put on the television or Welsh radio station which, until the foot-and-mouth, had been part and parcel of his daily existence, and for all her trying Penny couldn't penetrate the barrier he'd erected around himself. She felt excluded, ghost-like on his periphery.

Until he had been hit by the disease, his whole life had been spent working physically on the farm where there was always more to do, regardless of machinery and modern equipment, and he'd come home satisfied at the end of a long day, knowing his land was producing good wholesome food for the nation: milk, grass, silage and cereals for his cows and sheep in a cycle of reproduction and lactation.

As ever practical, it had been Mervyn who'd seen the risk to what was left of the livestock. With the help of Tegwyn, Beth and Penny, they gathered the cobs and pony who, with no competition for the spring grass, were in danger of getting laminitis if left to graze at will. Putting them in a smaller field, Tegwyn erected an electric fence to ration them. There had already been enough unnecessary deaths.

She had a word with the rest of the family first to make sure they thought it a good idea, without telling Richard. On the Thursday morning she put the tickets and his pristine but still in-date passport on the table.

'We're going away for a few days, Richard. Everything's been sorted and Beth's going to look after Sion. We never had a honeymoon and you promised me one then, and judging from your passport, a holiday is way overdue,' she said, flicking through the unstamped pages, and, seeing him about to protest, added, 'And before you think of a hundred reasons why we can't, we are going even if I have to drag you myself.' There was no point in telling him he needed to get away from the place, but the last two months had also been hard on her. 'I need a break, Richard.' She didn't need to remind him there were no animals, nothing to milk, and the others capable of looking after the empty farm. 'I've already packed for you and we'll only be away for a week.'

He'd never been abroad before, let alone flown, having had to pick up the reins and run the farm in his teenage years, leaving scant time for more than an odd night at an agricultural show. After not more than a two-hour flight later they landed in a different world. Richard found the experience of flying thrilling, especially the power of the take-off and the engine reverse thrust on landing. Following Penny down the plane's steps, he was greeted by a waft of warm, scented air and once on the tarmac proceeded with the other passengers to the terminal, glad of Penny who knew what to do. The airport was not busy but had a strong military presence with armed guards at passport control and check points. It was hot inside the terminal, and the large fan circling from the ceiling did little to lessen the heat. There was a hubbub of people speaking languages new to him. Even the trip to the lavatory, something he hadn't dared do in the airplane, had been a novelty. The farmer in check shirt and jeans, looking every inch a tourist, didn't mind the novelty of standing around to wait for their luggage. Men in white shor-sleeved shirts, short hair, and smelling of eau de cologne, spoke in guttural, quick speech. One grinned at Penny exposing a flash of gold in a white smile, before handing back her passport. He felt a rush of something like pride as his was stamped for the first time and then he was asked to go through to where more soldiers at the main doors watched them, monitoring all departures and arrivals. Then another electronic gate as he was swiped by an armed guard before being ushered on to join Penny in the main lounge. A holiday guide waited to herd the few of them like sheep outside and into the correct coach. And another first, the sound of chirping cicada.

'They're like grasshoppers,' she told him when he asked what the noise was, and in that moment he silently thanked her for taking the initiative that had taken him away from his farm. The bus ride followed the coastline around hairpin bends past sheer grey rock as the coach pulled into various hotels to drop off passengers, and by the time they'd reached their hotel it was virtually empty. Penny had chosen a modest hotel outside the city, a few kilometres along the Lapad peninsula. It was virtually empty apart from a few Germans and Russians. Penny and Richard sat in the evening sun, enjoying a drink with the clear Adriatic and the historic city of Dubrovnik, with its terracotta coloured roof tiles, as their backdrop. Their room had a balcony overlooking the sea below and was functional and cool with marbled floors and the minimum of furniture. A small shower and toilet served as their en suite. It was still early in the season and they were the only Brits. An hour later they were by the hotel's private small rocky beach, a waiter on hand to refill their glasses. For the last eight hours Richard had not thought once of his cows or his farm.

She wouldn't let him say no, bullying him into the water. He tried to step in but the rock forced him to jump straight out into the deep. Never had he swum in such water and the warmth left him feeling refreshed for the first time in months as he let the sea wash out his pent-up angst. For the first time in ages he had a good night's sleep. Swimming in the Adriatic was a tonic to the soul, a completely different experience to a quick dip in the cold surf of Cardigan Bay. Out here he could idle, holding his breath to dive, looking along the volcanic rock at the different species of fish. Even the mundane noises of traffic and building work, of voices in a foreign language, were a new pleasure, and he soon became accustomed to the sound of the planes in their ascent, all becoming reassuringly familiar, yet divorced from him as he lay luxuriating in salt water, dawdling on its surface in cathartic bliss as the heat of the sun spread through the water. It was an indulgence, not needing to do anything other than relax, which allowed him to watch his lovely wife lie on a sun bed, tanning gently, and all against a backdrop so removed from Llanfeni as to be unreal, as the pain of the last months dissipated.

Croatia was breathtaking, the land so unlike anything he knew; strings of uneven lines of low red-tiled village roofs, punctuated by a church, that nestled beside the coves and bays of the dramatic coastline, sheltering beneath imposing bare elephant-grey mountains, pockets of pine forest emphasizing the barren rock towering above. It was easy to relax, to swim and snorkel the days away and with no sand only volcanic rock, the water visibility was superb. They spent hours drifting along the rock, watching the scant bright flash of fish feeding, later to be offered grilled, sardines, mullet, grouper or squid, with a salad and glass of wine.

They took a bus into the ancient city of Dubrovnik to the Catholic cathedral which had begun with funds provided by Richard the Lionheart, who'd found shelter from a storm while returning from the crusades in 1192. It was easy to see why it had been such an important city, its situation pivotal to traders and their ships, traveling from the north-west toward the south-east, a counterpoint to the bigger, busier and vastly more expensive city of Venice. Surrounded by immense walls built from the 11th century on, it had managed to keep modern-day traffic out and Penny took Richard on a tour of the city, walking along the walls, looking out across the rooftop skyline and when that got too hot they dropped down to meander along the tall narrow cobbled streets, where'd he bought her an antique necklace of round silver buttons, apparently typical of the area and a pair of earrings in delicate silver gilt with applied filigree decoration with inlaid stone which set off her fair hair. She hugged him for them, putting the necklace round her neck, and looking in the mirror the shopkeeper held up for her. Then it was out into splendid squares for a Turkish coffee, sweet pastry and people-watching. In a gentle public caress, he put his hand across to touch hers, his eyes thanking her. Penny smiled in return, finally getting the kind gentle-natured man back from the brink.

Before they'd have to pack their bags to leave, she wanted him to experience the local market and made sure they returned to the city on the Wednesday. The weekly market had been set up in one of the city's squares and although they were early it was already busy with local shoppers keen to buy the freshest produce. Penny and Richard enjoyed the bustle, a little like home with the buying and selling of foodstuff from peasant women much as they saw themselves. Here, the food wasn't wrapped in plastic, but there were vine leaves to cover their soft cheese, and the vegetables were loose in boxes or just piled on the tabletop, unwashed, fresh. So much better than the ubiquitous cling film-wrapped, plastic-clad items that filled the supermarket shelves. From a large wooden tub Penny bought some olives which the woman put into a paper box. She also bought some nuts and fresh fruit to eat on the harbour wall. Richard tried to thank them in their language, which got a laugh and nod of appreciation, just as he would feel in Wales if someone made the effort of a *diolch yn fawr*. And yoghurt, he couldn't believe the Knickerbocker Glory-sized glasses of goat yoghurt which the locals ate. Naturally sharp, they savoured them like ice cream. It gave Penny another idea for their home produce. It was something she'd broach with Richard, but not yet.

The woman in Reception had befriended them and on her recommendation they booked a taxi to take them up into the mountains to one of the secluded hilltop villages where she came from. She told them told not to wander off, but to stay within the confines of the village. Beautiful, if remote, it was as if they'd stepped back in time where the pace of life was slower; a donkey or mule as well as car sharing the single-track road. Hidden by trees, they followed the taxi driver-cum-guide up a cobbled path to a Byzantine chapel where inside they were astonished to see beautiful paintings and ceremonial decorations in gold and silver. A rope sectioned off a well-preserved mosaic floor. It was only afterwards as they were walking back toward the small square that the taxi driver grabbed Penny by the arm pointing to a damaged wall of a house. He looked upward making the noise of bombs and waved his finger at them as he pointed to a sign they couldn't read but understood that it was a warning not to go off the track. He spat contemptuously, continuing his rant, pointing to further evidence of shelling and gunfire, the visual signs of the atrocities that had taken place in his country less than three years previously when the British armed forces had played a key role in Nato attacks on the former Yugoslavia during the recent Kosovo crisis.

Richard recalled a discussion with Martin Price who'd served in the Balkans with his unit, helping to defuse mines, restore bridges. It was where he'd witnessed his best friend, Gareth, being blown up in front of him, his-comrade-in-arms whom he'd failed to protect, having failed to spot the buried device.

Standing in this picturesque village, evidence of the war was readily apparent in the form of bombed and shattered buildings that had yet to be repaired, reminding Richard of the soldier who had saved his life and his sister's. Unlike Dubrovnik, up in the hills and away from popular tourist trails, the ravages of war were starkly apparent, where whole village communities had been slaughtered. It was little wonder that the soldier suffered from bouts of depression, and he felt bad about the way he'd pointed the finger of blame at Martin for the foot-and-mouth on his farm. It had had nothing to do with the present of the pet lamb, and Richard made a mental note to apologize to him for his irrational outburst when he got back home. Such visible scars of war, although unsightly, were merely superficial compared to the murder of innocent people, with whole communities fleeing as refugees. That gave a sobering perspective on the loss of animals through disease that he had suffered at home.

Huge efforts had been made to restore Dubrovnik and the surrounding area in order to encourage the tourists back to help Croatia's beleaguered economy, and they travelled back to their hotel in a subdued mood in the late afternoon.

The experience of what they'd seen left them feeling flat and they'd decided on an early night when the receptionist saw them and beckoned them to join her. He looked at Penny ready to decline but she shrugged, 'Come on, we might as well. We needn't stay long.'

She took them to the back of the hotel to a small room that served as a café-bar for the staff to use and relax in after the evening shift had ended. Some local men sat smoking and drinking slivovitz, eyeing the two visitors as they made room for them. They tried to converse, using hand gestures, smiling and nodding and being enthusiastic whether they understood or not, the receptionist coming to their rescue. The plum brandy helped them to lose any inhibitions.

After a few glasses the locals were as merry as any of them. Getting up, one of the old men brought out an accordion from behind a table and started to play. There weren't more than seven or eight of them, but their deep Slavonic voices, emanating from lined, used faces, sang out. Like so many before them who had picked cotton, or mined for coal or salt, there was a communion of suffering in their collective singing that gave a special resonance to the simple folk songs. What is it about men and hard labour that brings out such beauty of voice, wondered Penny, enraptured by their plaintive songs.

In a lull in the singing, she told the receptionist – who insisted on being called Izvorinka now that they were friends – that her husband's brother was the famous opera singer Simon Davies, and that Richard also had a very good voice. Without further ado, Izvorinka clapped her hands telling them that the Welshman would sing for them and although Richard tried to resist, she took him by his sleeve, giving him no choice as the men started to chant, calling him to take his place in the space they'd made for him. If it hadn't been for the Dutch courage he'd drunk, nothing would have induced him to sing so publicly, and he remembered his nerves before going on stage for his childhood performances at *eisteddfodau*. What did he sing then? Hymns, *alaw werin* and *cerdd dant*. He thought what to sing, shrugging at Penny who just beamed back at him before clearing his throat and starting on a light-hearted easy Welsh folk song with the refrain '*Oes gafr eto? Oes, heb ei godro*'. By the time he'd got to the third verse they needed no encouragement having picked up the chorus and with their own words joined in with gusto, singing faster and faster, as the song dictated, building a crescendo that ultimately exploded into laughter.

There was generous applause and more laughter and refilling of glasses, before Richard started on 'Delilah', accompanied by the accordion player, and soon the whole room was singing like Tom Jones. After that, Richard returned to his chair and the men sang another rousing Slavic song. Then, in a lull, Izvorinka changed the mood, joined in a lament by one of the maids and kitchen staff, as the men listened, underpinning the women's voices in low humming.

On their final afternoon a coach load of children turned up at the hotel. They stepped down out of the bus, some excited, others quieter as the women in charge called them on, waiting until all the children had got off the bus. Then they were led over the rocks and down to the sea. The English woman thought they looked an odd assortment. Some had big grins and were exuberant, but there were several quiet children in a mishmash of clothing and footwear. Six or seven had severed limbs, a hand or arm or foot missing. One child looking emaciated, just stood by the bus, his brown eyes overlarge in his young face, unblinking in a kind of vacuous numbness that hid some monstrosity of human torture that he'd been through. It was a look that the foreigners would not forget. One of the older children came back and took his hand and led him to the rest of the group, waiting near the water's edge. A couple of men from the hotel went down, one with a football and whistle to lend a hand. Back in reception Penny asked Izvorinka were they on a school trip.

'They are orphans. You see since the war, we have many children who have lost everything.' She shrugged. What could she say, to start and never stop about the injustices, about what they had been through, to a couple of nice holiday visitors who had no idea of how it is, or was, or ever will be again. All the staff had been told the best healing was to try and move on, and make Croatia good again. So she said little: 'We take in turn to give them a small holiday, so today it is the Hotel Adriatic's turn.'

He would not moan again he promised himself as they flew home, longing now to see his son Sion and the rest of his family and his farm with its green grass. Croatia had been an eye-opener to real suffering as well as being a tonic and a beautiful place where kind, good, simple people – peasants like himself – had been subjected to barbarism and butchery.

Back in Llanfeni while Richard and Penny were abroad, Beth looked after Sion in Tan y Bryn. With Clare's help to keep him entertained the week had proved easy and raced by. He was a contented and happy little boy and on the day before his parents were due to return Beth wanted to give them a treat with a day to remember. Luckily the day looked promising with only a little high cloud which soon evaporated in one of those rare days when the sun's sudden May heat took everyone by surprise. She managed to persuade Tegwyn to take them all out for a picnic.

He drove them along the coast to a cosy village tucked against the side of steep hill, with the sea lapping the harbour at high tide. The slow road meandered parallel with the river revealing the estuary as they came round the final bend and into the village. The fast flowing estuary filled the river mouth and the boats bobbed on their moorings against the pull. Ubiquitous seagulls loitered on the street, insolently waiting for the first careless chip or ice cream cone to snatch in an unguarded moment. The single track railway line ran tightly against the rock, road and sea, barely above the high tide line as it hugged the coast giving it its reputation for being one of the most stunning journeys for views and sunsets along the Welsh coast. Houses perched above the road lining the estuary's front, squeezing up for a window of the unspoiled views across the racing water to another sandy stretch of Cardigan Bay. As the river widened the space afforded a wider pavement to more generous three-storey houses that would soon become cluttered with another season of holiday makers, many of them regulars with wet suits, various boards for surf, wind and sand, as well as the more traditional bucket, spades, fishing lines and nets, all synonymous with a seaside holiday.

Every year, children gathered along the wooden jetty hoicking out the greedy green-backed crabs dangling on their orange lines and lead weights, the crab's claws gripping the bait, unable to resist the limpet or bread. Still clinging there as excited children lifted them high out of the water, swinging them several feet into the air, where some had the sense to let go and plop back into the tidal water, but most held on and were released into buckets to be looked at, and compared by the kids and parents alike. Hidden under bladderwrack growing on the jetty uprights, there were dogfish that were harder to lure. As the sun dropped, the day's catch would be tipped back into the changing tide and the released crabs scuttled under bits of seaweed away from brat and gull.

After watching the crabs being caught on the pier for a while, the Joneses moved on, keen to get out of the town before it became jammed with traffic and people and on up the coast that widened as it broadened into sea with an expansive sandy beach protected from the town by dunes, with the high-peaked mountains of Gwynedd clearly visible to the north. A couple of miles out of town, they parked near a chapel and its sunny, sloping graveyard with polished black granite headstones and flowers that caught the sun where a bench had been erected offering time for reflection. A good place to rest in peace.

Tegwyn carried the basket and took Clare's hand while Beth pushed Sion in the buggy as they went down the rough path, through the circular gates to cross the railway line and over the golf course to the sand dunes where the pushchair sank into the soft sand. Beth lifted Sion out and continued, away from the other few people, walking a few hundred yards to a private spot where they put down their clobber, laid out the rug in a sheltered spot amid swathes of the yellow-green marram grass. The colour had always reminded Beth of sheep's eyes.

Always better with children than adults, Tego lifted Clare into the air laughing and teasing before racing her to the top of a dune and tumbling down, careless of the flat blades of the grass capable of cutting skin-deep if used as a grip to pull up on, as he played like a child, sinking into soft sand slopes with her. It reminded Beth of how he'd been with her all those years ago, his irresistible playfulness forcing her to join in, and so it was again, this time with her daughter and nephew giggling with their uncle playing the clown. It reminded her too of why she'd always loved him, ever since she was a little girl much like Clare. He was a man who made her see fun. And all the unhappy intervening years that she'd wasted. It had been the wrong choice to have ever left, seduced by so called sophistication and the promise of money.

He came flopping down beside her, tickling her toes to make her open her eyes, before kissing her quickly; a happy normal couple with their children on a day out, away from other people and the caravan park, in *her* dunes, as she saw them, home to the bee orchid and the silent lizard and the never-ending motion of the sea. They had a picnic and afternoon paddle in the pools made by the roots of an ancient petrified forest, slippery in its clay grave and only exposed at low tide, before ice cream and home.

9

Caradoc Hughes lived where his family had been for generations, still struggling to make a living on a small, isolated farm on the north side of Llanfeni. Life had always been hard, labouring with wet, acidic clay soil, heavy rainfall adding to the small stream where the damp conditions were prone to give his sheep fluke. Myra his wife was glad to leave for her shift at the local supermarket and their two boys were at school, leaving Caradog to do what he could at Pant y Crwyni to make it pay its way in an increasingly difficult economic climate. As the name suggested, 'the hollow of the skins' was never going to be an illustrious place and, in years past, his family had been the tanners for the area, making use of their isolation, and the water and clay soil.

Although long since gone, evidence of the cottage industry was still there for the discerning eye – the rows of crater-like holes visible under the rough grass where once they'd have been filled with tanning fluid from oak bark, increasing in intensity dyeing process proceeded. It had been labour-intensive, filthy work, the rotten liquor-filled holes mixed regularly using wooden poles, before the sodden heavy hide was moved up into the next hole with a stronger solution. The tanner would have used dogs, for pulling and eating any fat off the hides, and later their excrement would be spread as a paste onto the hide to help soften it as part of the curing process that carried with it an appalling stench – a necessary, dirty business. With knives the tanners would work the skins, using lime to help remove the hairs, their hands hardened by years of chemical misuse. They'd tie the skins down flat to produce a smooth surface. Rubbing and re-rubbing and rolling and polishing them, like kneading dough, until they had worked them into useable leather which was used for making harnesses and other equine tack. Yet some tanners would produce a softer leather for shoes and simple leather garments like waistcoats and workers' slopes.

Through the generations, his family had remained lowly, and grumbling to himself, Caradog shouted at his dogs as he prepared to go and check his sheep on the hill. Closing the door of a shed, he stopped on hearing the sound of a vehicle turning onto his track that served as a drive. It continued to approach and he waited hidden to see a smart four-by-four pull up the untreated road, to turn into his yard.

His dogs gave him away, racing towards the vehicle, not heeding his call, running in front of the tyres trying to bite the mud flaps. '*Shep, Twm, dewch yma,*' he shouted, whistling when they failed to obey.

Two men, both strangers, got out of the car, one with an

Ordnance Survey map in his hand and Caradog immediately became defensive, thinking they were about to cause a problem, accuse him of some misdemeanour, an oversight in his book-keeping that might affect his measly grant in trying to make a living in such a place.

He looked at them, surly, not offering them his hand as they greeted him in a friendly manner.

'Mr Hughes? Pant y Crwyni?' the taller enquired, as the farmer stood mute, not helping him with his pronouncing of the Welsh, hoping to put him on a back foot.

He gave the curtest of nods.

'Ah, good, at least we've got the right place. You're quite difficult to find. There was no sign at the turning.'

'People know where I live without the need of any sign.'

The man smiled, ignoring the farmer's rudeness.

'Quite. Well, have you got a minute as we've got a proposal that we think will interest you.'

'Depends.'

'Before we go any further, can you just confirm that – Mike can you pass me the map?'

The stockier man handed over the map and looking briefly around for a suitable spot, not liking the look of the two dogs who were sniffing around his legs, decided on opening it out on the bonnet of his car.

'There, can you just confirm that this is your hill – here – and that's your boundary, Mr Hughes?'

Caradog studied the map closely where the man's finger was pointing. It was definitely his hill, his land, adjoining the hill of Rhyd y Meirch and further along, Tŷ Coch.

'Yes, that's my land, and has been for generations. Why do you want to know? I haven't done anything wrong.'

'No, no of course not. It's nothing like that, Mr Hughes. In fact it's good news, potentially very good news for you, and could make you a lot of money. Perhaps we could go inside and discuss it all?'

He called on his dogs who were still thinking they might nip the visitors when they weren't looking. '*Gorweddwch lawr, gŵn,*' he clicked his tongue at them and led the way into the back of the small cottage to the clean, tidy kitchen.

'My wife's at work, but I can put the kettle on if you'd like a mug of tea, if you don't mind the style.'

'Tea would be lovely.'

They sat round the table with tea and some Welsh cakes he'd found in the cake tin, and some time later they were still there with files open on the table with various pictures, dimensions and graphs in a very different atmosphere. Now the farmer was all conviviality and humour, on first name terms and in broad agreement.

'There's still a long way to go, Mr Hughes,'

'Caradog,' the farmer reminded him.

'Caradog, and I can't at this stage guarantee we'll be successful and the process can be slow. But, by agreeing with us today, it's the first step forward and we can now discount going to put the offer elsewhere. This way, if we do get planning, you'll be the one to benefit.'

'And, it'll be nothing to do with me afterwards, not my responsibility? I don't have to manage any of it when it's complete?'

'Absolutely not. It will be just as you are now, no different for you or your sheep.'

'And you say it's every year, regardless?'

'Yes, you'll receive a regular income year on year. Like a farm's rent, only this will last twenty-five years and is guaranteed.'

Mike interjected. "If you'd said no we would have made the offer to one of your neighbours, another farmer bordering your land, here on the map, this one on the same ridge of hill and you can bet your bottom dollar they would have jumped at the chance to make some easy money. You'd have had all the hassle, the interruption over your land while they are being erected, the constant noise.'

'Which isn't much and you're far enough away to hardly notice it, once you've got used to them,' Jim reassured him.

'Much better that you get the money rather than one of your neighbours, at your expense,' he added, just to keep the farmer on the right track in case he decided to decline the no-brainer offer on the table.

They shook hands, tidying away the papers into folders. 'We'll get the ball rolling and apply for planning for the monitoring mast.'

'The what?'

'A small mast that measures the wind. We'll have to monitor it for a year to make sure the site is suitable and the project feasible before we go ahead.'

'It's windy enough up there, I can vouch for that!'

'I'm sure, but it is very high-risk with expensive capital outlay and we have to make sure it is right at this early stage, so we erect the mast to be sure that it will yield a good return over the next quarter of a century.'

'See me out,' he thought to himself, eager now.

'How long before they're up and working?' he asked them.

'Hopefully, if it all goes to plan and there are no major problems, five years from now.'

'As long as that?' Caradog's face showed his disappointment, having already accounted for his little pot of gold.

'Yes, I'm afraid it is a long process. But we can move forward immediately and draw up a petition for locals to sign to gather support. We've a local man, Iestyn Williams, who works for the company and he'll co-ordinate this and all the community consultation process.'

'Advertise public meetings in village halls and community centres where he'll explain the project and answer any questions people have,' explained Mike.

'The more support we can create the better our chances for a successful outcome,' said Jim, 'I'm sure you've made the right choice, Mr Hughes, and Mr Williams will be in touch shortly.'

Later that day, Caradog walked up through a patch of scrub oak and onto his hill, looking at the route and the site the men had proposed and then down towards Llanfeni and out to sea, quietly pleased with himself.

'That was easy enough,' Jim said as they drove off. 'Now for the difficult bit.'

10

At the time it happened, Penny was in Scotland, having travelled up overnight, and stood in the middle of a field surrounded by red and white cows.

'You won't see better in the whole of Scotland,' Mr Bruce Flemming was busy telling her as he patted a rump of a nearby flank. 'And look at the quality of their udders. Put your hand there. Dunot mind, she'll no kick you.' Penny put her hand on the cow's udder and nodded in agreement with the farmer.

'I don't know if they'll do so well in Wales, and my husband's family have always kept Friesians.'

'Ae, they'll be fine for you. Good grazers on rough ground and hardy. They're one of most efficient breed for grass converters to milk. You take an average herd, it's as high as seventeen thousand pounds of milk and seven hundred pounds of butterfat.'

Penny wasn't sure how good that was and wished she'd consulted Richard before coming, but she didn't want to be put off, and while they still hadn't received any compensation for the loss of their entire herd, she could, if she had to, foot the bill. She didn't want her husband's innate common sense reining her impulse in. This was her surprise for him and the farm. A fresh start.

'And, with you saying you're into cheese and butter. These cows here have smaller fat particles so it's better distributed throughout the milk and makes for better conversion into your cheese and ice cream.'

'I see,' she said. 'I thought all Ayrshires had long wide horns?'

'We de-horn the calves. They may look good in the show ring with their horns but they're not practical in a modern day dairy parlour.'

'And do they calve easily?' She asked. 'Honestly?'

'Ae. Good vigorous calves, and easy to raise. They're a grand breed though I say it myself. And, another thing, unlike many of the other dairy breeds, this breed of cow does not possess the yellow tallow characteristic that reduces the carcass value of your bull calves. So it's profitable to raise steers with the Ayrshire as they produce good meat for the butcher. You can't go far wrong with them.'

Penny recalled Richard coming home from market having virtually given away his Friesian bull calves just before the foot-and-mouth outbreak.

'Is that so?'

'And, look at their feet. See, good hoof, they have less problem with their feet, they're free of genetic disease.'

'They sound almost too good to be true, Mr Flemming.'

'Ah, I wouldn't sell you anything but the best.'

He stood stick in hand moving a cow into a better position as he walked around the group patiently waiting for Penny to make a decision. She'd come a long way just to look and he felt a deal was there for the prizing; it just needing playing gently, letting the cows sell themselves. Canny lass, she seemed to have plenty about her.

They looked lovely and the farmer had been right, as Penny had already made up her mind to make him an offer. 'I don't know what you want for them?' she started, looking up at him.

'I was hoping fourteen.'

Fourteen? Surely not thousand, unless he meant for them all.

I was hoping nearer eleven – hundred,' she added quickly.

He paused took his time. 'Na, you're too low there. I wouldn't let them go for that.'

'Is there a way between? What if we split the difference?'

'Thirteen.'

'If I buy them all, can you do them for twelve and a half?'

She could see him waiver and added, 'Remember, I'll need something left for the heifers that you're going to show me!'

He shook her hand on the sale and led the way back towards the buildings where he had brought in young females ready for her to see up close. After an inspection, having put her trust in him as being honest, she shook hands on another twelve pedigree Ayrshire heifers, tested in calf to a pure-bred Ayrshire bull. The farmer would make all the transport arrangements needed to move them down to Wales. Potentially, if it all turned out all right there would be thirty-six new head of pedigree livestock for Tŷ Coch before the end of the year.

In the Scottish kitchen, his wife was waiting for them for when they came in. She could tell they had done the deal and had already prepared them a cold lunch of ham, cheese and pickle with a salad and apple tart before Penny was to start back. The television was on in the background with nobody paying much attention, not until the image of a plane flying low into a building.

'Mary, will you turn it up,' Bruce said as they all looked awe struck at what looked like a passenger plane hitting one of the twin towers in the middle of New York.

'Oh my goodness,' Mary exclaimed as the flames spread further into the tower, and people in them could be seen trying to get out. They gasped collectively as they witnessed a figure leaping from a window and falling hundreds of feet to his death. 'Oh those poor people,' Mary murmured as they stood mesmerized. Faces appeared at windows on the different floors, waving their arms and appealing for help. Initially it was being reported as a tragic accident, but that was before another plane flew low and hit the other tower.

Penny sat appalled at what they were witnessing, the rest of her food untouched, knowing that Ralph, who often flew across the Atlantic for his business, was there at the time. More immediately, she needed to make sure her two daughters were not with him but safe in London. She was suddenly desperate to be home sensing a momentous atrocity that would have far reaching consequences.

With her phone back on and within signal range again, it started ringing with messages from her eldest daughter, Charlotte, who sounded distraught.

'At last, Mum, I'm been trying you all afternoon. Dad's in America and I can't contact him.'

'Sorry, darling, I had my phone off. I've only just seen the footage. Are you all right?'

'Yes, but Dad.'

'When did your dad go? I'm sure he'll be OK.'

'Before the bombing, he and Lily flew out and I know he's been caught up in it.' She shouted hysterically down the phone.

'Look, calm down darling, he'll be all right. Are you alone in the flat?'

'Yes, they went over together. He said he'd be away four or five nights.'

'OK.' She was trying to think where he used to stay.

'They went on Sunday. He had meetings all week in New York. I'm sure he said the twin towers and then I saw those awful pictures on the TV and I can't stop thinking Dad's there, under the rubble. He won't answer his phone, Mum.' She burst into tears.

'No, because everything will be down, love. It doesn't mean the worst, it's just that he can't make contact yet.'

'Mum, you have to do something.'

'I will. First things first. Have you rung his office to find out exactly what his movements were? And find out exactly when he was due back?'

'I can't remember which day. But I know he said the working week away, and not to expect them until the weekend. Where are you, Mum? Can't you come down?'

Should they have left her alone for a week, Penny thought, angry that like so many things in her daughters' lives, she wasn't kept in the loop anymore.

'I'm on my way back from a business trip up in Scotland. Look, as soon as I can, I'll ring his office and we'll go from there. Is Sophie all right? Has she contacted you?'

'Yes, she rang when she saw the pictures, she was very upset and wanted to come home.'

'She's better off staying at school until I can get down. Listen. You stay put, make sure you keep the door locked and as soon as I have any news I'll ring you. You have to understand, Lottie, all the lines of communication will have been disrupted and I'm sure Dad is OK.'

'Promise you'll come, Mum.'

'I'll be there, I promise.'

She'd hardly got through the door before she was back out and heading for London leaving Richard to look after Sion and the farm, her surprise of cattle left, no longer important.

He felt an unexpected pang of jealousy, standing on the platform as he put her on the first available train to London, with only the briefest of kisses from her, her mind already miles away. All Richard could do was wait at the farm for her news and watch the events on television.

It was two days before Ralph was able to ring his daughter and let her know he and Lily were all right. They had been in New York at the time, but thankfully not near the twin towers when the bombers struck, sending the city and the whole of America into a state of panic.

'Mum's here, do you want to speak to her?'

'Yes, I'd like to have a word.' If he was surprised that she was at his flat, he didn't say anything.

'Charlotte rang me, worrying about you and asked if I'd come. So naturally I did. I'm glad to hear you're all right. It must have been terrifying, witnessing it.'

'Apoplectic. We were several blocks away, but we all felt the terrible shudder. A numbing delay and then mayhem. Sirens, and everyone running. It was Armageddon here, but at least we're safe and we'll be on the first available plane back. Thank you for coming down to them,' he added.

As if she wouldn't, for her own daughter.

'I'll wait here with them until you get back, and Soph's coming back for the weekend. She needs to be with her family. It's been a nasty fright for them.'

'I'm sure. And the American nation.' (Subtext for sending the money markets reeling, Ralph didn't change.)

It was strange to be back in London, inhabiting his spacious flat in Islington after the rural quietness of Llanfeni, and while Charlotte went for a lecture at her college of art and design, Penny had time on her hands to appraise the lifestyle she'd left behind. They hadn't anticipated a visit from her and so she found the flat as they lived, with nothing put away for her benefit. Minimalist and smart, the two bedroom flat was on the second level away from the street noise. Large Victorian windows overlooked the road, broken by the leaves of the London plane giving the house a sense of shade from the busy traffic. She'd almost forgotten the constant hum of the city; the noise taken for granted, that kept her awake for the first night, lying in their bed looking at a photo of them, Lily and Ralph, on the bedside. They looked relaxed as they smiled for the camera and Penny churlishly put it face down after studying her successor's fine features and her perfect, small frame in a figure-hugging, knee-length silk dress, making her feel suddenly old and dowdy in comparison.

Conspicuous for it's lack of clatter, the flat still oozed money. The few paintings were on the walls for a reason, one in the sitting room opposite the large mirror was a bold original Hockney, its colour filling the room. Other pieces of art – porcelain, oriental in influence, which Penny presumed was Lily's touch – were displayed with unostentatious subtlety to catch the light. It was nothing like Tŷ Coch, a functional farmhouse with nothing of value, and a general clutter reflecting the outdoor life – overalls, coats and wellington boots, the essential waterproofs hanging above rope halters, with buckets, by the door. Everyday-mugs were left on the draining board for tea or coffee, and always a cake in one of the tins; a collection of hair, left by dog, horse or cow, was invariably on the sofa, as the soft smell of animal permeated from the yard into the kitchen.

It was a different world, and she caught herself looking in the mirror, immediately pulling her tummy in, straightening her back, before slumping, kidding no one. Was she envious and regretful of being where she was in life? Superseded and living in the sticks instead of, what? This, she reasoned to herself, as she worked round their nest, looking for any sign of discord or something less than perfect that might make her feel better. It had been a hard year on the farm coping with foot-and-mouth and Richard's depression, and she'd been strong and stoic for them, looking after her son and husband, her boys as she liked to call them. But now, distanced from the day-to-day pace of the farm, she suddenly wondered if it had been worth it. Didn't she miss the buzz of the city, the diversity and stimulus of commerce? Even the cafés offered a sophistication lacking in Llanfeni. Perhaps she was just being a snob; people were just people, the world beneath the veneer.

She pulled herself together, confidence the only way, and decided on a therapeutic shopping trip to make her feel good. She locked the flat door and went down the shared staircase to the front door, eight steps, and out onto the street, looking forward to treating herself and buying a treat for the girls as well. It would be good to see Sophie again, and a little bit of bling would make a nice surprise. Penny got a tube to Regent Street. What she needed, she convinced herself were some smarter clothes, rather than the jeans, shirt and three-year-old jacket she'd travelled up in. Bad enough that she had gone rustic but she didn't want to endorse her children's opinion of her going to seed.

Excited to be back in the melee, enjoying the buzz with no small hand to hold on to, Penny started enthusiastically along the shops, popping into names she used to frequent, where the designers had flattered her. Three shops later, her initial enthusiasm was dented as she failed to find anything that she liked that would fit her.

'A twelve has always fitted before,' she offered lamely to the assistant who was more interested in the length of her nails than in a middle-aged, unremarkable woman, shrugging as she took the garment back.

'I can look in the back to see if we have an extra large?' she offered, making Penny feel vast.

'No, it didn't suit,' aware that her hands were rough and that a nail had broken, no doubt while out on the farm. Sod it, she'd go back to Sloane Square and up the King's Road and if she couldn't find something from one of the boutiques, there was always John Lewis for a quality size twelve, and dependability.

Two hours later she got a cab back to the flat laden with bags, new shoes with a high heel that hurt after flats and wellingtons, but gave her a luxurious lift. She'd also stopped off for a load of fresh groceries. At least she'd do what she'd always excelled at and make them a delicious supper to celebrate being together again. Sophie turned up in a taxi from the station and of course had her own key to the flat and let herself in with a 'Hi, sis. Hi, Mum!' Dropping her rucksack she hugged her mum. 'Gosh Mum you look great, new outfit? And I love the heels!'

Trust Soph to give her a boost.

'It's so good to see you, and Lottie. And Dad's safe and everything's turned out OK and we can spend the weekend together. So let's have a party. I bought you both a little something I found in one of the boutiques. I hope you like them.'

'Cool, thanks Mum.'

Half the pleasure was the unwrapping, to see Lottie open her silver necklace, and Soph her silver bangles which their mother thought would suit.

They wasted no time putting them on, jingling them as they looked in the mirror pleased with their pressies. No reason, just a spontaneous joy, a celebration of being alive.

Later the Islamic terrorist group, al-Qaeda, lead by Osama bin Laden, cited the presence of US troops in Saudi Arabia, together with American sanctions against Iraq, and their support of Israel against Palestine, as reasons for the attack on the twin towers. This was followed by America's declaration of a war on terror, and the invasion of Afghanistan to depose the Taliban. As in the Middle Ages, sanctuary away from an increasingly volatile threat of terror became all the more precious – the centuries' old tradition of milking cow, sheep, or goat, in order to feed one's family, neighbours and village. The aim was the same, whether it was a single cow, or hundreds in a mechanized modern parlour, they all produced nourishment for a world disrupted by war.

11

Political discussion and news updates on the war on terror, that had become part and parcel of daily media coverage since the attack on the twin towers, only slowly subsided leaving an after-effect of a tsunami. Every tremor made people uneasy as they got on with their everyday lives, waiting for another ripple – a suicide bomber using an unmarked car, with a rucksack, or with explosives strapped inside an anorak. Security was heightened in anticipation of another attack which could be anywhere in the world, but was most likely where large numbers of people were gathered so that an atrocity would match public outcry in all the major cities of the western world. Going about their business, people became twitchy in any prolonged queue as they clutched their bags, glancing at the person next to them in a bus, on the tube or in an airplane. Shoppers, diners, pedestrians, all were potential suicide bombers.

Although on the periphery of all this, something of it permeated to the isolated outpost of Llanfeni, and as farmers got on with their lives, they would look up to the sky more often, at the sound of a plane or RAF jet. They'd been through their difficult period from foot-and-mouth and dreaded further calamity in the country, which they could do nothing about. The rural community had begun to get back to normal as it kept an eye on world events, watching the destabilizing of economies as each new terror attack affected the world's stability, and stock markets fell and fuel prices rose, while farmers talked about lamb and beef prices falling and the spiralling costs of fertilizers and animal food stuff.

Buried, but not forgotten, had been their own small parochial disaster which had severely dented the rural economy, leaving it empty of visitors. It was up to the community now to work together and put it behind them, gearing up for another holiday season. With such global uncertainty there could be more holidaymakers deciding to stay in Britain rather than travel overseas, and it was up to the village to make the most of the opportunity. Reopened coastal paths had been freshened up with new wooden signs as efforts were made to encourage footfall and tourism. B&Bs and cafés were all desperate to regain lost trade, waiting anxiously in newly painted premises for a spell of good weather which would encourage holidaymakers back to the seaside, with a flag of approval, good quality water, sand and surf. And the farmers, too, restrictions lifted, had returned to the weekly market as wives' shopped, bringing much needed income to the town. Fields were grazed again by cows and sheep, and tractors and trailers whizzed up and down in the hurry of the first cut of silage.

Tŷ Coch was no exception, but there was a difference as brown and white Ayrshires instead of black and white Friesians now came in for their regular twice daily milking, and there was a new breed of sheep, as well as their Welsh Improved on the hill. There was an influence of Cheviot and Penny had bought a flock of twenty pedigree Lleyn ewes for Bethan.

'Take it as a present for looking after Sion when we went on holiday,' she said to a protesting Beth.

'That was just for a few days last spring, Penny, it was nothing, and I loved having him. These must have cost a fortune,' she added, leaning over the fence, looking at the tight-wool, white clean-faced sheep. 'I can't possibly accept them as a gift. We're talking of thousands of pounds.'

'Yes, but we have been compensated Beth. Look, if you won't take them as a present, pay us back with next season's lambs. How's that? It's what Richard and I want – you to be involved – and there's no one better with the sheep and the dog than you. I know last year was a disaster but not because of anything you did. Look at your lambing percentage, it was brilliant until foot-and-mouth wiped everything out.'

She saw her sister-in-law weakening. 'Good, that's settled then.'

'Perhaps when we've built up the herd we could try and market their wool separately. It's better quality than the hill sheep,' Beth said.

'What a good idea, Beth. Anything that adds to our brand. We've lost a lot of ground, starting again with the organic beef Welsh Black. Well you know, it all takes time. I'm even trying to encourage Richard into looking at ice cream and yoghurts as well as cheese.'

'Rather you than me!' Knowing her brother to be an old stick in the mud.

'It's still early days, but I'm getting there,' she laughed.

When the tall, thin mast went up nobody at first noticed it. Tegwyn had made a detour from collecting the bags of moss on a neighbouring hill to check on Tŷ Coch's hill sheep as Beth was busy collecting her mother-in-law Moira from the train station.

Preoccupied in preparing for Moira's arrival, and wanting her to enjoy her first ever visit to Llanfeni, Beth had decided to redecorate the sitting room, not that Moira would have minded, knowing how when she first went there as a bride, the Connor house was a large, damp mansion, shabby and by degrees crumbling in the salt air and proximity of the sea, but

Beth wanted to let her know how much it meant to them to have Moira come and stay. So Tegwyn had volunteered to go, leaving them to get on with their reunion in private. He didn't need an excuse to go up on the hill, but assured Beth he'd look over the flock to make sure there was nothing that needed attention. No blowfly or maggot attack, nothing with severe foot rot or worm infestation that wouldn't survive until they were brought down at the end of the month for shearing when they would be treated for those common sheep ailments. Unlike their hardier hill counterparts, the Lleyn sheep on the lower slopes had already been shorn leaving only the hill sheep until mid July.

Being observant of the things and places he enjoyed, especially on the open hill, Tegwyn had noticed the rise in heron numbers, often coming across a lone bird fishing silently in hill lakes and streams to the cost of trout, newt and frog. A habitat that had housed grouse in his youth was now void of their quick cackling calls. Conifers and a lack of heather had put paid to their long-term survival. He knew it wasn't all the farmers' fault – the demise of hedgehogs wasn't due just to modern agricultural practices, as was claimed by the new breed of so-called conservation experts. The landscape of his home had changed only minimally when it had already been difficult marginal land, but whereas as a boy he'd regularly find a hedgehog, hear a curlew or grouse, and see snipe lift off from wetland, it was now a rare treat to hear even the cuckoo call in a new spring. The countryside had changed and what had been the common wildlife animals of his youth had become scarce.

For all his education, Dr Trelawny hadn't convinced him he'd got all the right answers. Nor could he explain why bees were disappearing when there were plenty of wasps, and other stinging insects that seemed to thrive. The woodworker had been bitten plenty of times in woodland by biting insects – midges, horseflies and flying ants – and all his hard work replanting a larch woodland for a private owner last spring had been seriously damaged by weevils, and the scientist hadn't an explanation. He continued up beside a small ditch running between the wet sponge of moorland and moss, stopping to bend down and pick up a purple-black beetle which he'd have put in a matchbox years ago. Now he turned it upside down to reveal a large healthy family safely stored on its undercarriage. He set it down carefully and continued onwards lifting a large flat stone in a swampy wet edge of a pool, hopefully to find an eel. They had also become much less common and Tegwyn knew things were changing fundamentally at life's fringe.

Somehow it was right that it was he who spotted the mast on Caradog's hill, climbing over the slate wall that marked the boundary. He walked across to inspect it, not knowing what to make of it. Perhaps it was one of those mobile phone masts being erected everywhere.

'Did I tell you Granny is coming?'

'When, when Mam? Is she going to stay?' asked Clare, excited at the prospect of seeing her Gran again after a long gap.

'Hopefully by the time you come back from school, she'll be here. And, if not then, she'll be definitely on her way.'

'But, you just said today.'

'The trains maybe late, so I don't want you to get too excited and then be disappointed in case we haven't returned by the time you're home from school. Your Uncle Teg will be here in case we're delayed.'

'Granny is coming, Granny is coming today,' she sang, too excited to finish her breakfast.

'Clare, please at least eat your toast before school.' She wondered if her daughter really remembered her grandmother or was it the emails and photos over the internet that kept her a familiar person. It had been more than two years since Clare had last seen her and she'd been very young when they'd left. Then the question she been prepared for.

'Is Daddy coming with her?'

'No, my love, your Daddy can't come, but Uncle Teg will be here.' Clare made a face but before she could complain, Beth distracted her. 'Come on, *cariad*, look at the time, you'll be late. Give your Mam a kiss and see you at teatime with your Granny.'

She thought it would be awkward, but not at all, as Moira O'Connor stepped down from the train looking as she had always looked to Beth, in a tailored suit, a slim and alert woman. Even in her eighties she refused to stoop to age, holding herself erect, and Beth could hear her distinct voice as she thanked a man who she'd obviously got to help with her luggage.

'Bethan,' she called on seeing her daughter-in-law, waiting to be embraced with arms outstretched as the younger woman came to hug her. 'Let me look at you.' She held her from her, standing back to appraise her. 'You look well, radiant.' No longer thin, peaky, or nervous, what stood in front of her was a stronger image of the young woman who'd walked into her life ten years before as her son's wife.

'Come on, the car's waiting. I'm sure you're longing to get in and have a cup of tea after your long journey.'

'A strong gin and tonic and cigarette.' She caught her look and they both laughed as Beth carried her case to the car.

'It's so good to see you.'

Away from her bungalow for a week, her son lost no time in snooping around her sad pathetic home. Not that he needed her gone to do what he was intent on doing – he could have done it anyhow, but this way he had the luxury of taking his time to look through her things and get a sniff of her dealings with his wife and daughter, not ex-wife in his mind, as he slipped in the back door nonchalantly looking through her cupboards to see if any of his mother's habits had changed since living without him.

Still plenty of booze, with little food; she'd always lived light, nicotine and liquor her mainstay. Any food would be bought fresh so there was little evidence of any in her kitchen. He almost made himself a cup of coffee just to use her things so she'd know he'd been there while she was away, but he found the thought of her using the cup a turn off and he couldn't be bothered. Instead he went into her bedroom for a look through her chest of drawers for any correspondence or photos. Apart from an old one of them all together on a beach, there weren't any others he could find.

He pulled back the bed covers and put them back up roughly, his foot touching something that made a slight clink. He bent down and under her bed there was a china chamber pot. He was glad that here at least he'd found something that indicated she was getting more frail, for all her outward bravado, the tight-lipped old bat, behaving as if she hadn't a care.

In the lounge he found what he'd come over for, her computer on a small walnut table. He switched it on, knowing she would have been taught to use a password, but having lived with her for most of his life, he reckoned he knew how her mind worked and with time he'd be able to open it and see her files. As a fall-back he could always call up someone who was a bit of a computer geek who'd soon break any silly crossword puzzle clue that he knew his mother was fond of using.

In the event he failed, hating her all the more for thwarting him, so that he'd need to get someone else to open it, giving them a cock-and-bull story about his mother going senile and forgetting her own password.

'Is there a way to fix it so that I can access it again, because the old dear will be forgetting her password again?'

He made sure he'd have access in the future so he could look at random.

Once alone and with the curtains drawn he took as long as he wanted to savour the images, the emails and photos between grandmother to her granddaughter and daughter-in-law, now living in Wales. He zoomed in to examine the woman more intimately, dragging the mouse across her body and up onto her freckled cheeks, enlarging it again to look into her blue eyes to try and gauge what was behind the smile he wanted to wipe from her face. He clicked back out to see the happy group posing, Bethan next to Clare, grown so much in the short time, with the arm of Tegwyn around them, grinning like a Cheshire cat, pawing over his family. Malcolm still recognized the place where once he'd called to claim her and where he had to pretend he was interested in their cows and Welsh cobs so that he could take her away from them and their way of life. Several photos on and he was able to get an overview of the farm and the yard, and Tan y Bryn where Bethan and Clare were playing happy families. A lick of paint, a new milking parlour, but otherwise it was unchanged. His wife and daughter, in case his bloody mother or anyone else had forgotten, who she'd helped do a bunk.

'Do you remember me, Clare?'

She twisted her shoulders underneath her T-shirt, suddenly shy after all her expectation, nodding as the old woman waited for her to say her name.

'You're Granny.'

'Come and give your Granny a hug,' she said, holding herself ready to embrace her granddaughter, momentarily hiding her emotion in the girl's mousy hair. 'How I've longed to see you again and now it's like a special birthday to have whole week of you.'

She'd never been to the farm before, having only had images of Bethan's home, and she bought little luggage, agonizing beforehand as to what, or what not to bring, apart from clothing and footwear, and whether she should include the more complicated emotional stuff that was part of Clare's first years. In the end she'd decided it was better to leave her favourite, probably forgotten, old toys back in Ireland. The last thing Moira wanted to do was to mar her week with them or upset either Bethan or Clare with memories best left undisturbed.

Instead she'd bought her a colouring book and pencils as she had always loved drawing and painting.

'And, you can do me a picture so I can put it on my mantelpiece when I go back so I have something to remind me of you and this lovely holiday.'

'What shall I draw?'

'Whatever you like. Let it be a surprise.'

'OK, Granny.'

For the next week Moira O'Connor was immersed in the family and the farm. Like everyone she'd seen the awful television images of the foot-and-mouth epidemic that a year before had caused ten million animals to be killed, affecting thousands of farms across the UK, including her daughter-in-law's, and unlike her son who relished their disaster, Moira had felt for them, wishing she'd been closer to hand to offer moral support. Now she was amazed at the power of nature to mend so that the farm was a hive of healthy activity, with no sign of the past, covered over in green. A country woman herself she enjoyed watching the cows file past into the milking parlour, reminding her of her younger days in Ireland – that smell of warm cow and milk, soft doe-eyed calves in straw-filled pens with tails swishing as they drunk the powdered milk from artificial teats.

She stood in the field and watched as Beth worked her sheepdog, Fly, away to the right to gather in her new flock of Llŷn sheep.

'I hope to build up the breed, and Rhian, my niece – she's Richard's daughter from his first marriage – who moved up to London last year and works as a hat designer, says she's in the market for felt.'

It sounded much grander than it was. 'Well, she has part of a stall in Portobello or is it Camden market. Anyhow one of those trendy places, selling hats, and I think it's going OK. And she's got a boyfriend in a band, and seems happy and going places. She says she'd like to source organic wool from Wales, so hopefully she'll be able to use our fleeces from Tŷ Coch.'

'Felt hats, well there's an idea, I don't remember you talking about her much.'

'Rhi's a great kid, well, adult now, but she went through a bad patch when Richard and Nesta were fighting. Like so many other couples they should never have married.'

She shrugged, neither needing to add anything.

'And you were in Ireland with us by then.'

'There wasn't a lot I could have done even if I had been home, and when I heard from Simon that things weren't good, well you know how it was. I couldn't help myself, let alone anyone else.'

'It wasn't ever your fault, Beth.'

'I know that now, and I suppose most teenagers go through a stage where they want to test the system, to rebel, and Rhian chose Goth, and vegetarianism, two issues guaranteed to drive her father mad, especially as it coincided with mad cow disease, and Richard was already under huge pressure. Then Mam had her stroke. Do you remember I came over without Clare? When it all started with me and Malcolm.'

When he'd made his own daughter sick so she couldn't travel with her mother to see her relatives. She remembered accusing him then and if she'd ever thought he was capable of what ensued she'd have got Clare away and over to Wales to be with her mother then, and would never have returned. But there was no point in looking back to the 'if only' in life already past.

'Does she still live in Wales?'

'She and her mother Nesta went to live near Swansea and Rhian did some sort of course in art and design.'

'Hence the hats.'

'Yes. I hope it really flies for her. We all need a lucky break in life.'

'And to make it truly authentic, you could put the sheep fleeces under the saddle like the Mongols use to do and let the sweat from the horses and the rubbing from the saddle do the rest!'

'What?'

'I'm joking, but it was the way felt used to be made and probably still is out there.'

Trust her mother-in-law to know. 'Of course you know where the term mad hatter comes from.'

She didn't wait for an answer, 'Mercury was used in traditional felt hat-making and over time it sent the hatters crazy.'

'You having me on?'

'Where do you think the mad hatters' tea party came from in *Alice in Wonderland*?'

'I'll suggest she call her company Mad Hatters then!'

'Can I be one of her first customers? Could you order a ruby one? Or crimson! Red has always suited me and would look nice, don't you think?'

'I'll tell her, Moira. That'll do, Fly,' Beth called her dog in to allow the sheep to drift back to their grazing and both women wandered toward the house to see the horses. A jet appeared suddenly from the sea, the noise of its engines deafening as it accelerated up into the sky, making Beth jump and for a brief second Moira saw a familiar look of fright cross her face that she'd witnessed while she was Malcolm's wife, and she took her arm in affectionate support, smiling at her.

'He seems very nice, your Tegwyn?'

'We'll never be very rich, but I'm happy with him. I've known him all my life.'

'Money's not always a good thing. Too much can wreck the children's lives.'

They walked back arm-in-arm and although Moira had spoken to him on the phone in the past, she'd never met any of the family other than Simon, until now. It had been her choice not to attend the wedding, prejudiced against Bethan before she'd even met her. That had turned out to be a rash decision which she later bitterly regretted, blaming herself for some of the consequences of her stand-offish behaviour. Richard, Beth's elder brother came across the sea to save his sister, taking them back to Wales over the treacherous water. Her elder brother didn't look like her or Simon whom she had met, but Moira could see the family resemblance, more in the way he did things, shrugging and smiling as Beth did. Relaxed and happy, the epitome of a proud farmer as he showed her round the farm, finishing with a large tea which his lovely Penny had prepared, Richard giving her the credit for turning the place around, financially.

'They seem a good pairing, Richard and Penny.'

'She's been an absolute godsend to him. Without her, the whole place would have gone under. And she genuinely seems to enjoy it all. The animals and muck and hard work. I can't think why!'

'How did they meet? Is she local?'

'No, from London. But, she'd bought a small farm, you know, wanting a bit of the good life for herself and her daughters. Her husband was in banking and never at home and I think Penny got fed up with it all. What she didn't know was he was having an affair at the time with an American business partner. Well, it all blew up in her face when she confronted him and she was left stranded – on her own with an empty farm. And then she met my brother at the local cattle market.'

'As you do! And her children?'

'Two girls, Charlotte and Sophie, both away at school, who didn't take to the idea of their mum living with a Welsh country bumpkin very well.'

'I can imagine.'

'They're a bit spoilt and to be fair were at an impressionable age when it happened. They used them, one against the other, to get whatever they wanted. It bothers Penny, them not wanting much to do with her, or here. They only come down very occasionally and briefly. London has all the caché.'

'It'll change, it's an age thing. Once they're grown up they may look at it all from a different perspective.'

'Perhaps,' said Beth, unconvinced, who had met the two teenagers and had been unimpressed with the way they treated their mother. 'He's very rich and we've benefited from it. I do sound mercenary and I don't mean to, because we'd love Penny even if she didn't have a bean, but her money has been the saving of us. You know how land eats money and it's lucky she's got plenty and is very generous, throwing it at the farm.'

'Perhaps it gives her pleasure, especially knowing it's from her ex.'

It was obvious they both adored their little boy, crooning by him as Richard swung him up onto his shoulders, making him chuckle. The old lady was aware that the baby boy's birth would have brought back painful memories for Beth, having lost her own baby a year earlier. Another cause for regret that she had not acted sooner and seen through her son Malcolm, but at least Bethan looked so much better now than when she'd last seen her, fleeing from the racing yard. She'd put on much-needed weight, filling out her face so she looked younger. The biggest difference was nothing physical, but how she was in herself, and Moira was glad that it had been worth everything, to see Beth well adjusted and happy, vindicating her for her part in the betrayal of her own son. The knowledge still hung between them, unspoken, but needing to be aired with both women waiting but not wanting to sour their reunion.

After a few days, and when they were alone, Moira broached the subject. There was no easy way in, and in any case she'd always been a frank woman.

'I didn't bring anything because I didn't think you'd have wanted any of it and I don't know where he would have put your jewellery.'

'No. I took what I wanted, and I wouldn't want anything else.'

'We don't talk, as you know. But he's there, and watches me.'

'I suppose he knew you were coming over?'

'Not from me, but he'll know. He has his spies.'

'I remember!'

'Sorry, Beth.'

'It's all right, I don't care any more. I'm out of his reach and Tegwyn wouldn't let him get anywhere near me.'

'I can see he's devoted.'

'Yes. I should have married him first time.'

'Instead of my son,' Moira said it to make Bethan smile in apology as she nodded.

'Saved a lot of grief. Tegwyn was always here for me, ever since Dad died, a kind of childhood sweetheart, only, well there were other issues, and I was very young.'

'He seems fond of Clare?' A point close to her heart, her granddaughter's well-being.

'Yes,' she said, knowing Moira was looking for confirmation that Clare was well loved. 'A child at heart is our Teg. You saw the pony he bought her and he enjoys spending time helping her. He's always had a way with kids.'

'I had to come, to see for myself that you're OK, Beth. I felt so responsible for what happened – guilty.'

'Don't reproach yourself, Mam. I'm more than OK, I'm well and happy, so you mustn't worry about me, or Clare.'

'I can see I needn't.' Then changing the subject, 'She took me by surprise, her speaking fluent Welsh.' Moira felt keenly the years missed. 'She'll be seven on her next birthday.'

'Yes and she's been so excited to see you, Moira, and you coming over. You always had a close bond with her and now you've come once, you can make it a regular trip.'

They both knew it would never be vice versa. She'd never go, nor let Clare travel back to Ireland.

'We'll see. It would be lovely to think it isn't a one-off.'

They did the tourist things, driving Moira north up into Snowdonia, to some wonderful beaches along the Cardiganshire coast, past castles built by the English to keep the Welsh at bay, clicking away for something to remember; a brief snapshot, history repeating itself in photos of smiling faces, beaches and ice creams. A memory for when she was alone back in her bungalow.

Time sped by too quickly. Each day the hours raced away and she promise herself she'd come back. She'd left it almost till last, but before leaving Llanfeni, she needed to meet Bethan's mother, Elin. She sat with her, looking at her directly, touching her gently on her arm.

'I needed to say this face-to-face, woman-to-woman, mother-to-mother. To say sorry for what my son did to your lovely, beautiful daughter. I know you can understand me, Elin. It doesn't matter you can't answer,' she added as Elin tried to speak 'But I hope you can find it in your heart to forgive, to believe me when I say I never knew what he was doing to her and to pardon me?'

She glanced out at the farmyard, and the house on the far

side. 'Thank God she's home with her family where they belong, and they are both safe and well.'

She'd carefully placed the picture Clare had done for her at the bottom of her suitcase so it wouldn't get creased. When back home, she would put it up so she could be reminded of her granddaughter and her stay with them.

It arrived with the morning mail, folded in half and stuck with a little adhesive. Pulling it open Penny read a brief outline of the proposed development of a wind farm on the hill above Llanfeni. There was to be a public meeting at Llanfeni Community Centre, where a representative of the company proposing the development would be present, as well as a local, Iestyn Williams, acting as their PR man.

'Rich, have you seen this?' she asked when he came in from the milking. 'A proposal for a wind farm.'

'Where?' he asked, taking the paper from her outstretched hand, glancing through the blurb. '*Duw, Duw* but that's just by us. Who the hell has applied for this?' He read more carefully. 'Pant y Crwyni, I might have guessed. Caradog Hughes. His hill joins ours. It's just above us. We can't have that. When's the meeting?'

'Thursday week. Do you know this Iestyn Williams, who according to this is coordinating it?'

'No, name doesn't ring a bell, but when I see him, I might know him.'

He didn't want the disruption, or the intrusion such a development would bring. No doubt there would be lots of traipsing, busy-bodying over his land and then there was the constant noise and the scarring of the landscape, and inevitably the development would involve more people telling him what he could and could not do on his own land.

'Rich, before you go off at the deep end, keep an open mind? At least wait until you've heard what they've got to say.'

'Oh, I have every intention of hearing their lies. Someone's got to stick up for our rights.'

'But you're not anti-alternative power, Rich, surely? Your family's led the way in green energy.'

'That's not what this is about, Penny. It's not a one-off and I'll fight to keep my land from being industrialized. I don't want it like the slag heaps in the valleys.'

'But that's the point. These would be windmills on top of the hill. Once up that's all there is to it.'

She might see it rose-tinted, but as far as Richard was concerned this was big-time production and not some cottage industry. Nothing like the old turbine his grandfather had, producing electricity for a few farms by the stream, driven by a Pelton. The new proposal would be like the reservoirs where hundreds of acres had been drowned and those farming communities lost, in order to provide drinking water for cities. And this scheme was another for the benefit of the city dwellers living across the border.

Penny had never considered a time without modern conveniences; the touch of a button for instant use, and didn't want a row with Richard about alternative energy.

'Makes you wonder how we ever managed without electricity, doesn't it. If the world runs out.'

'Hopefully I'll be dead by then,' he said unhelpfully.

'Do talk sense, Rich! There has to be an alternative, if not for us then for the sake of our children.'

'They'll have to re-learn how to be frugal, like the old days. Waste nothing. Back to the old ways of doing things. For all this technology, we haven't moved forward have we? Nope, it'll be back to slate tables to keep the milk cool; salted bacon, hanging on hooks, an open fire for cooking and outside boiler for washing.'

'Realistically, can you see the world going back to that? With the population as it is?'

He shook his head knowing it to be impossible.

'Overpopulation. That's the real problem. And I don't see an answer to it.'

Only since the war on terror that threatened regular disruption to the world's diminishing supply of oil, had discussions on alternative green energy became more urgent. Britain's government was no exception, keen to encourage possibilities for renewable energy from wind, solar and hydro. It was a long way from what Richard was describing, and Penny couldn't envisage her daughters settling for such a backward step, dependent on speedy technology, the use of the internet via fibre optics, mobile phones that were all part of the modern life. On the few occasions they visited, they complained bitterly of the farm's poor internet reception. She looked at her husband as he stood there, hands on hips, looking out onto the yard and hill beyond, imagining the worst, and shrugging.

'I wouldn't mind so much if the electric was for us, locally.'

He didn't want her to see him as petty or parochial. She was probably right. He should wait at least until the public meeting before passing judgement.

Later in the day when he had a moment on his own, he rang up Dai, from the farmers' union.

'*Ah, prynhawn da. Oes gen ti eiliad? Rich, Rich Tŷ Coch s'yma.*'

The turnout for the public consultation was expected to be high, with everybody having an opinion on wind turbines in the area.

12

He'd been dreading it, but the country's leader had sealed his fate, failing to conceal the smirk of self-belief, as he gave the camera his sincerity pose and started on his justification for Britain sending British troops to Iraq. The prime minister's announcement came the day after Martin and Katie had booked their wedding day. They had decided on December, to coincide with his leave and a quieter, more predictable period on the farm. He could hardly bear to watch Tony Blair announce his plans to the nation, standing shoulder to shoulder with President Bush, sending Martin and thousands like him back to a war zone in the Middle East.

As he flew out to fight in Iraq, old school mates of his filed into Llanfeni village hall.

It quickly filled up and latecomers had to stand at the back. Not only Llanfeni, but the adjoining parishes had had flyers sent round and turnout was high. Letters had also gone out to local interest groups such as the British Horse Society, the Ramblers, the Open Spaces Society, a nearby trekking centre, and Snowdonia National Park.

On what was the stage, two trestle tables had been erected, with a large logo with the company's name 'Atlantic Energies' on a plastic cloth fastened onto the front of the middle of the table, conspicuous even to those at the back. Four men and a woman sat smiling on the large turnout. A screen had been set up ready for a promotional film and two piles of coloured pamphlets were ready to be handed out. Richard now recognized the face of Iestyn Williams, nudging Tegwyn. It was So-and-so's cousin, related to them at the farm Cwm Pell where they had been encouraged to plant their hill with conifers in the nineteen-sixties. Recently with a change in government policy the whole hill – more than four and a half thousand acres – was being felled and replanted with native hardwood, or in Cwm Pell's case, left for natural regeneration which would mean no future income for the farmer.

Sitting in the front row was Caradog Hughes, wearing his suit, with a white shirt and tie, fit for a funeral. He was accompanied by his wife who, after a double shift at the supermarket, would have preferred to stay at home with the boys, but had obliged her husband in a show of support – anything that would help the family purse, for money always tight. She'd like to think that in future she could say yes to the school skiing trip as a special treat for the children, having never been further than Cardiff. Her husband's comment that there were plenty of hills and snow in Wales and he'd only ever had a bit of roofing zinc as a sledge had been ungenerous. They were good boys.

The farmer smiled, making a point of being seen, feeling that at last he had an advantage over neighbouring farmers like Richard Tŷ Coch. He might only have poor quality rough grazing on an exposed hill, but finally it had the potential to be an unexpected windfall! He didn't want to look too smug, however, not wanting to jeopardize his chance of realizing a regular, decent income, and hoping the local community wouldn't gang up against him and prevent the proposal from going through.

'That's typical. Can't make a go of farming so he's here doing the dirty work for them,' said Tegwyn as he nudged Richard, watching their neighbour meet and greet those around him. 'Shh,' he hissed between his teeth, watching Caradog, the poacher turned keeper, obsequiously rub his hands as he greeted another farmer.

Typically Welsh, the meeting already running fifteen minutes late, the doors were finally closed and Iestyn Williams got to his feet, banging the table for attention, as he started the evening with a few words in Welsh before turning to English to explain the procedure for the evening and introducing the representatives of the company. He also announced that there would be plenty of time for any questions from the floor at the end of the presentation and it would be easier to get through it more coherently if there weren't constant interruptions. So without further ado, the lights were switched off and the film started, and the full room settled down to watch the video.

Slick and glossy, the film zoomed over the coastline and beaches of Cardigan Bay with a voice-over explaining what Atlantic Energies stood for, in a professionally produced, no-expense-spared promotional spiel. It made it all the more personal to the audience as they recognized parcels of land in the area, and there were a few murmurs of approval from farmers and shopkeepers alike as they saw their farms with grazing livestock and Llanfeni high street with its shops and café, and people going about their everyday business. Another long lens shot showed the bustling farmers' market, zooming in to the local auctioneer busy selling store cattle and fat lambs. Quite a few in the audience recognized someone, or shrewd-eyed, an animal being sold and for how much. The camera panned away to the hills, showing them as they were, empty of any man-made structure, until turbines sprouted up benignly, like a circle of mushrooms superimposed on the land, so as to give a true picture of how they would look *in situ*.

Farmers and other interested parties listened to the facts delivered by Iestyn, about the timescale and the number of turbines proposed, and how, if the planning application were successful, the company would bring prosperity to the area with well-paid jobs and training opportunities with the Danish company based in Brande who manufactured the turbines, so that school leavers from the area could learn new engineering skills that would translate into well-paid permanent employment without having to leave their homes as they had in the past.

'We'll need to build an infrastructure for the turbines, and just as an example, roads up onto the hill, and a substation that will feed into the national grid. Skilled labour will be needed for the excavating and concreting of the bases of the turbines, and we envisage using as many local companies as possible. It's part of our company policy.' He felt a subtle shift, hands in pockets becoming still with the possibility of a reliable income. 'We will also set up a process whereby we will put money generated from the turbines back into the local economy, talking with the county council, say, about a community fund for local primary and secondary schools.'

'You sound just like a politician before an election!' shouted a heckler from the side of the room.

'A bribe,' someone added from the back.

Iestyn was not to be put off. 'The way I see it, it's only right and fair. Your area should be the first to benefit from this new initiative of green renewable energy.'

'More bureaucracy.'

'Gravy train for the boys. Snouts in the trough!'

'No, that's where you're wrong. The payments will be put in place annually to help this area specifically and for the duration of the life of the turbines, which before you ask is about twenty-five years.'

A scientist from Adas stood up to discuss the ecological effect of the turbines on the hill. He started with an overview of the world and worrying changes in the global climate.

Climate change was one of the most serious environmental problems facing the world and as a farmer's son himself from Llandeilo, he could appreciate at first hand how even a small change in temperature could cause havoc in farming with erratic weather patterns, drought, and flood that would make the rearing of livestock difficult, and would be catastrophic for crops, with two-thirds of the world going hungry in an ever expanding population. 'Indeed, the world is on the cusp, and some scientists, though not myself,' he assured the audience, 'already argue that we are too late and have irreversibly damaged the world's balance.'

Tegwyn couldn't resist commenting loudly to the farmer the other side of his brother-in-law, 'Look at the telly for the forecast and the weathermen can hardly give an accurate prediction for the next few hours, let alone any long term weather!' The observation caused a chuckle of agreement from the workers of the land.

'That was a bit harsh, Tegwyn,' said Dr Trelawny, smiling at him. 'It's easier to see the bigger picture, than day-to-day fluctuations in the weather. We know from the mosses on the hills and the peat that temperatures are rising. I bet your brother-in-law would agree that weather patterns have become more intense.'

Richard couldn't deny that there was more severe weather with flooding, drought, and periods of bitter cold, as well as the more common gales and short-term snow. But hadn't it always been like that throughout history?

'I remember my dad going on about the snowdrifts in 1947. Went on for months with the country completely frozen. Digging through tunnels of snow to make a path. Dead people as well as livestock.'

'And in '63,' added Ifor who farmed near the top of the opposite cwm on a small farm called Ty'n Brain and was planning to see Iestyn afterwards to see if his bit of hill was suitable for wind turbines. As a boy he remembered the real hardship of that winter when his father had lost most of the hill flock, cut off for weeks and relying on paraffin and firewood to keep the family from freezing, while the sheep starved, frozen under huge drifts. 'That was the first time a machine was used to get through. Do you remember?' he nudged Tegwyn. 'Tommy

123

Llan with his JCB driving through and two workmen with shovels walking behind as slow as you like with their feet at a quarter-to-three. Well, there's no work for a shovel after you've got a machine is there!'

They smiled at the picture, Dr Trelawny nodding politely, Tegwyn grinning, and Richard only half listening. Penny continued to look intently to the front, thinking it rude, and wishing Richard would tell the old codger to shut up so she could hear what the man from Pwllpeiran was saying about the ecology.

'And Sam Davies driving the midwife up to Morris Tŷ Cerrig with his wife in labour. Him in his Austin A55 pickup, with only chains on the back wheels and a shovel, going along the top of the fields' hedges, covered over with packed snow.' He let them imagine the scene before continuing. 'Well, the snow had drifted, ah, you're too young to remember, but it become so hard with the frosts and high drifts, it was way over the hedges. Takes a local man like Sam to know the route and he was able to drive over them. See, he knew the lay of the land, it was bloody dangerous even for him. He could have got stuck, left there for days without anyone knowing.'

'Did she have the baby?' asked Bethan.

'*Beth?* Surely did!' It was not the important part of the story in Ifor's eyes. They had no idea, the younger generation, nesh with creature comforts, just how hard it was back then.

'I remember the drought in '76 and all the leaves coming off the trees early,' said Richard, 'There was virtually no grass for any haymaking that year.'

They were on a roll, remembering the disastrous seasons of the past and not to be outdone Emyr who'd been sitting quietly listening to the anecdotes, piped up.

'And the floods in 1953, with the Royal Welsh Show in Machynlleth in the Llunlloed fields. It's built over now, but I remember sleepers from the railway line floating away down the fields into the Dyfi river.'

'Pah! Weather's always been unpredictable. They don't know what they're on about,' Tegwyn concluded, nodding towards the top table.

Naturally cynical from years of being goaded by the carrot and stick of successive governments, this conservative group was not about to jump on yet another, short-lived bandwagon. They lived and were ruled by the weather and the old rules, watching cloud and wind change, cows lying down before rain, red dawns, and late berries, as accurate as anything from any computerized weather maps.

Fair play to Iestyn, he laughed in agreement but he wasn't to be drawn or distracted. He knew his facts and knew how they thought, playing to their strengths as keepers of the land for the next generation, as their forebears had done for them. He pleaded passionately about love of the land and the need to look after it for their children's children.

'Wales has been depleted of her coal, and the world's gas and oil supplies are being used up. Look at our mining communities, gone from the Valleys. What we have in abundance are wind-facing hills, and wind power is just a way of using this land that needn't upset our way of life, shepherding our hills and farming sheep just as your grandfathers did. Only this will give you a regular yearly income and the country is desperate for sustainable renewable energy which we can provide.'

'You mean you, not us.'

'No, I mean us. This is for all our benefit, not just the farmer on whose land the turbines will be put, but all of you, the whole community.'

'How's that?' asked one of the shopkeepers.

'Let me go through the process, and I'll explain how we plan to contribute to the community and answer all your questions, at the end.'

Like a local eisteddfod, it was going to over-run into a long evening with everybody wanting their pennyworth. Farmers and many of the local community were going to need convincing this was the way forward, being prejudiced and anti any wind-of-change to their way of life.

However, hours later, with the board answering their questions to help dispel some of the doubts about disruption, noise and interference, the audience was beginning to see the proposed wind farm development in a different light, green preferable to nuclear.

'We don't need to be reminded what happened to the flocks of sheep grazing on Snowdonia after Russia's accident,' said one of the consultant's from the table. 'How many years before those sheep were free of radiation and able to go to market?'

'Chernobyl, or Trawsfynydd?' suggested the doctor to Tegwyn. 'We all know it had a leak, and it was on our doorstep. Scottish sheep weren't affected, and they should have been if it was from Russia.'

'It's shut down now. Mind you I wouldn't be seen dead eating any fish from that lake,' laughed Tegwyn. 'Shine in the night!'

Mothers in the audience thought of their children and the clusters of unexplained cancers in remote rural areas which were not natural. At least you could see the wind, and the turbines turning, thought Beth, wanting a healthy future for her daughter, knowing that her mam, Elin, who'd raised them in an organic ethos, would be pro wind farms rather than nuclear. Her love of nature and knowledge of herbs had been part and parcel of her life on the land, and she'd used herbal remedies in treating animal and human alike. Sitting in the hall among the community she'd grown up with, Beth suddenly felt an overwhelming sadness at everything past, with her mam's slipping from them, despite Mervyn's devotion in keeping her with them. The old boy needed her to hold on, desperate not to lose her, knowing he'd have nothing left to live for without her. He'd been a genuine and good stepfather to her children, working to keep the farm together for no reward other than sharing his life with Elin and securing her children's future on the farm. But like his old dog that had had its day, Mervyn spent his time pottering around the yard, getting under Richard's feet.

The pictures of the turbines were impressive, 55.5 metres high on top of a hill, a bit like a colossal lighthouse. There would be three rotating blades and, according to the engineer, they would generate about thirty percent of the theoretical maximum output.

'What happens if there is no wind?' asked a farmer who prided himself on knowing machinery, with a needs-must attitude to mending anything that broke down on the farm. A broken, idle machine cost money and precious time, and he was right.

'If there is no wind then the turbines don't turn and don't produce electricity.'

The farmer looked smug. 'I said they'd be inefficient.'

'However, that's why there is a mast up there which has been monitoring the wind speeds over the last nine months and I can tell you that the readings are very, very positive, which is why Atlantic Energies is going ahead for full planning permission. It's why we've initiated this consultation process, one of many, and why we're all here in Llanfeni this evening and why a representative from Natural Power has come all the way down from Scotland, to answer your questions.'

'We're based in Dumfries and Galloway and like here it's very rural,' he said smiling, at the audience, trying to show them he was one of them.

'As one of the leading experts in the renewable energy industry, Mr Munro will be able to answer any of your concerns.'

So they listened as the workings of the turbine were explained. Blades mounted vertically to a nacelle, mounted on top of the tubular tower housing the generator, gearbox and other operating equipment. A large diagram came up on the white board and the engineer from the company pointed out the finer details of the Siemens turbine.

13

Had Martin Price known, he wouldn't have cared less about any discussion as to whether or not to have wind turbines on the hills and cliffs along the Cardigan coast, or at what cost to the environment, as he sat in sweltering heat waiting for the next wave of insurgents, stuck as he was with his regiment in a foreign country in a modern-day crusade, waging war against terror that could dangerously escalate throughout the world. There seemed in fact to be no end to terror or religious fanaticism, as man was set against man, sect against sect, with indiscriminate bombing, as oil fields blazed uncontrollably, spewing plumes of black smoke into the atmosphere. He wanted to run, shaking and sweating in uncontrollable fear, going AWOL back to the peace and tranquility of the hills. He saw his companions look at him, knowing him to be unsafe, not to be relied on, and he wished it was all over or to be at peace like Garry. The officer knew he was near to breaking point, watching him grip his rifle, his teeth chattering, but there was nothing he could do except order him on.

Martin touched the talisman Beth had given him in his breast pocket. It was suddenly important, would help him, carried like a bible against his chest, even though it was a silly superstition. The whites of his eyes shone in his dust-covered, drawn face. Basra was not the place to be caught with the shakes as they moved out cautiously along the tall grass-lined waterway where Iraqi insurgents watched their every move, silent as snakes. Overhead a helicopter spotted them in the grass, radioing a warning to the troops on the ground to pull back.

They discovered her body amid the mud and slush on the outskirts of Sebastopol and eventually her family back in the Cambrian Mountains would be informed of her death in the New Year in 1855. Nobody was brought home, instead she was hurriedly buried along with others in bloodied fields, a single cross marking her grave – buried in the rags she'd fallen in, muddied and wretched by the side of the road of her final journey. She had been recognized, lying half-frozen and inert, by one of the Turkish Bazouks, whose life she had helped save at the hospital. He would not leave the woman there, picking her up and carrying her as she had carried him, back to a British base.

There a nurse took charge of her body, trying to tidy her to make her look presentable. In vain she scraped at the mud on her tattered skirt, dislodging something in the process. She picked it up and turned it over to reveal a piece of jewelry, a Byzantine talisman that had been hidden within the folds of her skirt. She wondered where she had got the foreign-looking piece from, thinking of the Zouave in his bright uniform, his yataghan slung across his chest, who had delivered her to them, putting her body down gently, his eyes inscrutable as he beat his hand, fist clenched, across his chest in a gesture of respect, before he turned and left without a word. Sure that it was something the warrior had given her for whatever reason, the nurse put the silver piece into her pocket for safe keeping.

It was only after another gruelling shift when she returned to the room she slept in with seven other hospital staff that she found it gone, lost or more likely stolen, while she was on the ward.

There was little for her daughter to remember her by — merely a piece of paper to say she had died. Martha had survived dysentery, serving in the hospital as a nurse under the harsh rule of Florence, but it was her undying search to find her William Morgan somewhere among the hundreds of injured and dying soldiers in the bloodied fields near Sebastopol that killed her a year and a half after she'd run away from her home and family in the Welsh hills, with a romantic notion of saving life with herbs, tincture and moss from a horse doctor.

At Rhyd-y-Meirch, the family grieved, the paper in their hands, which only the minister could read for them, the one tangible evidence of William's passing. In their daily struggle to survive on the cold hills of a New Year which sapped all their energies, there was little time to mourn a lost son and his foolhardy sweetheart.

Only Myfanwy, the eldest, had known of her sister Martha's plan and had been complicit in the romantic scheme that enabled her to leave Nant y Gaseg unnoticed on that fateful dawn. Her parents' concern as to where she'd gone lay heavily on her conscience, a concern that turned to anger when she eventually admitted to knowing where she'd gone. They were vexed at their daughter's folly and cross with their elder daughter for allowing such nonsense to have happened. Their words of accusation played on her mind, until in the end it slowly drove her mad. Her father had no time, and even less understanding, for her erratic behaviour, and insisted she leave the farm.

She didn't seem to mind, or to miss them as she continued looking for Martha, ending up destitute, sleeping rough in the hedgerows until she was stumbled upon by a farm labourer walking home after a day's toil. Mute, with the unblinking eyes of the troubled, she stared at him as he asked her who she was and how had she got there. She did not move as he shuffled the earth under the hedge with his foot, to see if she had anything concealed as she stood there dishevelled with nothing more than what she stood up in. He persisted, but still she was would give no name. Easier to have left her to her fate, yet he could not just abandon her and had no choice but to lead her back to his home. At least with the cows she would stay warm and they could spare a crust and watered milk. The next day he walked her to the village, handing her to his master, who failing to get a response from her, took her to the newly-built lunatic asylum. Myfanwy was admitted as a Welsh pauper.

The Denbigh Asylum was an imposing, almost grand, building built of limestone from the nearby quarry and stood in about twenty acres of land which had been kindly donated by a local philanthropist, Joseph Ablett of Llanber Hall. At least here, the mentally ill had a chance of being understood in their own language. But as she wouldn't speak, they had no idea who she was, where she came from, or how mad she was. Neither a first- nor even a second-class patient, Myfanwy was washed and deloused. She was escorted along a long passage, square blocks leading off, designated for male inpatients only. Each block had an airing court and on first and second floors there were several single rooms, heavily padded for the most violent.

Because of her unpredictability, and as a precaution against further harm, the medical superintendent Dr George Turner Jones had her confined to a single padded cell, until the ugly black and yellow welts that looked like human teeth bites on her arms could be verified as the result of self-harming rather than having been inflicted by someone else. There, wrapped in a coarse strait jacket, Myfanwy would pace her room, banging her head against the wall, suddenly stopping as if she'd seen someone. '*Wyt ti yn nabod fi? Mae'n ymddangos dy fod ti. Wyt ti wedi gweld Martha?*'[1]

It took months to trace her family back to Nant y Gaseg, and eventually to the horse doctor whose herbal medicines had done little to cure her, until she had cut herself loose from them, wandering the hills in her search for her dead sister. There were no cures at the hospital either, with only a meagre budget for wine and spirits that doubled for medicine.

Myfanwy was one of the first patients to experience the newly installed Turkish baths that were used to treat melancholia, and over time she became less chaotic, learning to look forward to the water treatment. The young woman responded to kindness and the attendants, some better than others, would play along with her search, answering her questions, keeping her hopeful that she'd find her sister in one of the rooms, that they had seen her following the lady with the lamp at the end of a long corridor.

Later when she was deemed sound enough, she was allowed outside in an airing court or in the hospital's vegetable garden, and so over time she became a model patient, happy to help, her imaginary lamp in hand, always on the look-out in some dark cranny, searching for Martha as she brushed floors, carried buckets of water, and helped in the kitchen. She became familiar with the hospital, which had become home. The yearly patients' ball and Boxing Day celebrations were the two highlights of her year on the stark bleak Denbigh moors. The patients who were fit enough – some of whom were not insane at all but were there from misfortune, family cruelty or destitution – lined up with the attendants and medical staff in the gallery on the female side of the house, each making an effort to dress up for the occasion.

For days leading up to the ball, Myfanwy had helped with the evergreen decorations, collecting ivy and holly from the hospital's

---

[1] Do you know me? You seem to know me. Have you seen Martha?

garden. Dr Jones had hired a fiddler for five shillings, so that they could dance to music. The patients deemed safe to attend, got up from the chairs arranged around the circumference of the large gallery and danced, the music of the fiddler irresistible, as feet tapped loudly on the wooden floor. It didn't bother them whether they danced on their own, with a female or same-sex partner, despite the staff's attempt to pair them up in orderly lines. Many of the normally troubled patients seemed to be released from their cocooned mental prison, allowing the music to flow over them like a river, sweeping them off their feet in an unexpected outburst of joy. Two or three, Myfanwy being one of them, had a real sense of rhythm and although she did not know the steps, she moved effortlessly in time to the fiddle and the clapping. For several hours they danced and jigged up and down the wooden floor, their demons temporarily danced out, to the marches, polkas and lancers. The ninety-seven females outnumbered the eighty or so males with the attendants making up the numbers while trying to give some semblance of pace and direction of the dance.

For three hours or more, Myfanwy spun and skipped to the strings, laughing and whooping with her fellow inmates. It was like any country hoedown, until exhausted by the exertion, she eventually sat down on the stairs that lined the gallery. Many remained standing as the mood changed with the end of dance, listening to a soloist singing. Any attendant or other member of staff who could sing had been drawn in perform a few verses, and they took it in turns to stand up and walk to the middle of the space, turning during their song to engage with all those present sitting along the wall. Usually it was a few verses of a well-known rousing song – 'John Peel', and 'I would not be an Emperor' were two of the favourites. One of the male nurses, Llewelyn Jones, got up and sang 'Myfanwy', as the patient's namesake blushed in shy pleasure at being so singled out. Afterwards the inmates were treated to a special supper of roast beef and plum pudding, with a half pint of beer for each patient, before they were segregated once more and taken off to their sleeping quarters, Myfanwy leading the way to the top floor where the female paupers slept.

She was used to the place, considered it her home more than anywhere else and the staff relaxed their guard with her, allowing her the freedom of the hospital, where she'd go as she pleased, with the exception of the dangerous patients who were kept locked in their separate rooms, remaining out of bounds to all but a few strong male attendants and the medical superintendent. Myfanwy seemed to positively enjoy the responsibility of helping the auxiliaries with the heavy day-to-day work.

It was never discovered who was responsible, but at some point, Myfanwy had had sexual relations, something which was discovered far too late to do anything about it. The doctor could not decide whether she had deliberately kept her pregnancy a secret, nor could her persuade her to tell him who the man was. The superintendent wasn't even sure if she fully understood she was with child and it was impossible to reprehend her for an action that might have been forced upon her. Perhaps she knew well enough and enjoyed her affair, her little bit of pleasurable attention amidst the buckets and mops, the moans of a different kind to the everyday cries of the hospital, hiding her pregnancy under the folds of her skirt, but she gave Dr Jones no choice other than to let her go the full term and then put the baby, if it lived, out for adoption. He suspected Nurse Jones, who vehemently denied any impropriety with an inmate, but with her freedom to go as she wished, it could equally have been a male patient. He could not apportion any blame, then, but he did punish her by keeping her more confined and under observation, something which she objected to, becoming more surly as her pregnancy reached its final month.

It had been a stifling week of hot, humid weather. As if sensing the coming storm, Myfanwy's waters broke and she cried out in her first grip of pain. Alerted by her calls, the doctor had her removed from the rest of the females, to one of the padded cells. Apart from any possible complication, he did not want news of any pregnancy or birth getting out, and in the event of the labour being difficult, he wanted her away from the rest of the wing. Protracted and difficult it was, but after a day and night the baby finally presented itself in the breech position and before they had to insert a hand, the doctor administered a strong dose of laudanum to her. While she was still under its influence he was surprised to deliver a live baby and had it swiftly removed from her sight. A nurse washed the mother and wrapped her chest tightly in cloth to ease the discomfort of her milky breasts. The birth of any baby was never to be mentioned to her and the staff were to pretend she was recovering from a fever. The healthy seven-pound baby, a boy, was given away to a childless couple, John and Sarah Price who lived on the edge of the moor.

After the loss of her baby, Myfanwy lost much of her energy and although there was no record of her ever having had a baby, a few of the staff thought it wicked at least not to let her know that she'd had a healthy boy who'd gone to a good home. She continued to live at the asylum, but she was more likely now to be found sitting quietly on the sidelines rather than participating with her old gusto in any of the hospital's activities. She never really got her vitality back, dying fifteen years later. She was buried in a pauper's grave in the hospital's cemetery with just her name and date, RIP.

Already past their prime, an adopted son was to prove a blessing and when he was capable, the little boy – who John and Sarah had named George after the kindness shown to them by the medical superintendent who'd given them the baby – was put to use helping them with the heavier tasks on Tyddyn Haf[2], learning to fetch and carry from an early age. Reserved and sombre, they loved him and he them, and as they became more decrepit, George who grew into a strong lad in adolescence, took over more and more of the farm's work, under the frugal hand of the only father he'd known, working all the daylight hours. In return he had a home, and more importantly, no knowledge of being an illegitimate son to an asylum inmate. Instead he had a mother and a father whose love was sparsely given, but given nonetheless.

His father taught him how to make the most of the smallholding. They could not afford a horse or other beast of burden and had to do all the work by hand, making sure nothing was wasted but recycled back onto the land, carrying the dung out to the three acres in a handcart, using a fork to spread the manure. Later in the year, he'd get a hay crop, hoping for dry weather as he cut the grass with a scythe, turning and spreading it regularly But if it looked like rain he'd pile it up in stooks in the field. When the harvest had dried sufficiently, they'd put it onto a blanket and he and his father would carry it back to the loft above the cows. They also dug and turned the peat on the hill so that it would dry ready for another winter's fuel, and gathered dying bracken at the end of the summer be used for animal bedding during the winter. The same with the rushes that grew on wet, undrained patches. He even gathered the gorse that fringed the hill, putting it through the farm's mangle so that it would be more palatable for his two cows and their calves in case of a poor harvest or severe winter.

The farm barely supported its stock of two cows and two pigs, but he was better off than many, and considered himself a lucky man as he collected the day's water in buckets from the farm's

---

[2] Similar to a croft.

well, stopping for a moment to watch the hens scratch around the yard, as the old gander hissed, protective of his goose and goslings, raising and beating his wings in threat. The goslings were a valuable income around Christmas and their down used for pillows. Precious goose fat was carefully stored in stone jars, brought out for a special treat. Before setting off, George would tar their feet to prevent them going lame. Then he walked them the several miles to market.

As part of the farm, old Mr Price had the right to graze fifteen acres on the hill above the bracken line and he kept thirty Welsh mountain sheep that survived all but the worst weather. They were brought nearer the homestead to lamb in April.

Sunday was sacred, with attendance at the Methodist chapel, where the rural community came together in worship. It was a chance to sit quietly and listen to the minister, and to sing hymns, and give what little they could afford to the collection. Afterwards they stood outside the chapel – a chance to catch up with their widely dispersed neighbours, before the three-mile walk back home. Very occasionally the minister would honour them with his presence for dinner and Sarah Price would go to great lengths to give him a good meal even if it meant they ate less well in the days following.

George met and courted one of the girls who attended chapel, and as the old couple grew chair-bound and infirm, he married his sweetheart, Ruth, who came to live with them and help care for his invalid parents.

Always struggling to make ends meet, the mouths of the seven children who turned up year on year, with Ruth only slipping one in their nine-year union, made surviving solely on the farm's produce impossible as they grew up and needed more than breast milk and swaddling clothes. Like others in a similar situation, the eldest son Hugh, though still a child, was sent out to the nearby quarry to work as a *rybelwr* getting work from the gangs of men, odd jobs in clearing up the debris, occasionally given a chance from a gang leader to split a slate from a block. Paid a pittance, he learnt his craft, and it was better than starving. He had a bed in the quarry's barracks, sharing with two other man and another teenage boy. After paying for his bed and food, which consisted of tea, buttermilk, lobscouse and bread, when he could, he put a little aside for his family back at Tyddyn Haf, and although it was only a few pence, he was comforted by the fact that his wage was a little better than his younger brother who had become a farm worker on a bigger farm some twenty miles away. His job was dirty and dangerous and he missed the moor of his childhood and the freedom of working in the fresh air, surrounded by noise, dust and slate waste.

The eldest daughter of Tyddyn Haf went into service as a scullery maid to an English house near Ruthin, leaving the three surviving children to help run the small farm, with wages contributing to the family pot.

Slowly Hugh worked his way up to become a quarryman, with a gang of five men. Perhaps it was because he was the oldest child, and was used to negotiating that he proved better than the others at getting the best from the setting steward. Hugh Price would see him on the first Monday of every month to negotiate the best bargain for his gang over a section of rock. He knew his hands were tied and the price had already been agreed with management, nevertheless he went through the motions, without pushing too far and risking losing the contract to another gang.

Their meagre wages had to fund their equipment and he had to borrow a sub for the ropes, chains and slate tools. Each gang had to cover other tasks as well, including sharpening and repairing, agreeing a loan to be settled up at the end of each week. Twice, work on poor blocks of rock had been so bad that after a week's labour he and his gang had ended up owing the management money, leaving them with barely enough for food. Hugh was used to being exploited, unable to do anything about it in case he lost his place, and another gang filled the breach for less. Slate workers were little better than slaves, like the coal miners. It was the quarry and mine owners who made fortunes at their expense.

Hugh scrimped a living, putting up with the injustice for several years, but he was aware of changes taking place. Like the pit ponies that were giving way to rail and steam, Hugh sensed his own slide, as contractors were brought in to 'arrange' the quarrymen's bargains. He was not prepared to work under them. The cut in holidays without notice or reason was the final straw. Hugh Price packed up his pittance, all he had to show for his twelve years in the quarries, and walked away to the nearest port where he offered himself to the navy. He was the first in the Price family to serve with the British forces.

The talisman was now in the pocket of a Welsh soldier waiting again for the dreaded command, convinced that his luck would run out and that he would die in Iraq, the great-grandson of the quarryman Hugh Price. He feared that he'd perish in the dust and heat with instead of church bells, the sound of the imam calling the faithful to prayer, against a backdrop of war, the smell of burning, explosives, death and fear, fighting with his regiment in answer to the US president's declaration of a campaign of 'shock and awe', dying just like his great-great aunt in a distant land – a part of the glorious ethos of empire.

Sitting behind a partially blown-up wall, he waited with them, his rifle slippery in his clammy hands, a helicopter overhead covering the troops on the ground. Martin cursed his fate through chattering teeth – to be involved in a war that would solve nothing, neither wanting to kill or be killed, just to go home.

'Quick!' He was being commanded, waved on urgently as the six men got up, crouching as they scuttled along the wall like rats, waiting for the single sniper or hidden mine that Price was convinced he'd step on, to be blown apart like Garry and left out to be picked clean in the parched stark landscape without ever having married, fathered children or settled down to till the soil. He'd never known who he really was or where he'd come from, yet his roots were as fixed as any hawthorn in a harsh upland moor where his forebears had toiled as peasants, unbeknown to him.

On a romantic quest, his great-great aunt had gone to the Crimea, searching as a nurse under Nightingale, for her beloved William Morgan, failing to find him among the lost, and dying herself, exposed and exhausted, near Sebastopol. Her death had sent the young soldier's great-great grandmother to Denbigh Asylum and the only thing left of it all, apart from himself, was this Ottoman relic he had in his pocket with no idea of its provenance other than his own superstitious feeling that it was connected directly to his family. He felt it, the soft, smooth silver and rounded lump of stone in his pocket, its touch reassuring. He only had to survive until December when he'd have leave to get married.

'Come on Price.' He stood up cautiously. 'You're next.' Running low, stop and crouch, catch your breath, hold, waiting for the sniper. Move to gain better ground, and close in on the suspected target.

14

Following the meeting, wherever he went Caradog Hughes wasted no time in pushing a petition form in front of the farmer, auctioneer, shopkeeper, or even an unsuspecting holidaymaker in order to get as many signatures as possible to approve the wind farm proposal that would help his case when it went before the planning board of the county council in the next few months. He'd had several copies made and given these out to other farmers so that they could also get their neighbours to sign. Most obliged, to his face at any rate, though some left the petition untouched. Others binned it. His wife had a copy to hand out at the supermarket even though she had been warned not to canvass on the shop's premises. The wind speed where the monitoring mast had been erected had proved strongly positive over the last nine months with better than national average readings. There had been letters in the local press, some for, but many against, and Caradog knew opinion was divided and he would need as many local signatures as possible.

Although naturally taciturn, he knew he had to overcome his usual abruptness and talk to people he wouldn't normally bother with, if he was to get this new income, even if it involved knocking on strangers' doors.

Two such newcomers were the new owners of The Old Rectory. Aptly named, Mr and Mrs Steven Parsons had moved to the countryside, retiring from his place of work in the smoke. They looked forward to days of relaxation, involving themselves with the community, as well as entertaining friends and family from away, with days on the golf course and the obligatory holidays abroad, especially when the British winter took hold. Judging from the renovations they undertook, they seemed to have plenty of money, revamping the house and grounds with lavish landscaping and a pool. Rooted trees wrapped in huge individual bowls had been replanted to give the work an immediate and dramatic effect. Caradog was suitably impressed and intimidated as he lifted the large door knocker, listening for the sound of footsteps in the hallway. He looked out at the manicured lawn and glistening pool while he waited. Nice to have it, even if he thought it a waste of money, disliking water. He would not choose to erect a swimming pool for his neighbours to gawk at. Mrs Parsons opened the door, smiling brightly with an enquiring look.

'Yes'?

'Good afternoon. I'm, eh, Caradog Hughes, and well, we're going round collecting signatures and I wondered if you and your husband would like to sign.'

The woman looked to see the 'we's' as implied, expecting more than the solitary figure.

'Depends, Sign what?'

'It's for the proposal of the new wind farm. On the Llanfeni hill.'

'You do mean the huge turbines?' her question negatively charged.

'Yes.'

Her distinct change in posture emphasized the fact that she didn't approve. The farmer felt clumsy, standing in front of her, but he had a lot at stake and so persisted, without much hope of gaining a convert.

'They do seem big up close, but away over there on the hill, you'll hardly notice them and they don't give out a lot of noise. The energy is clean, using the wind, and it's one thing we have plenty of here!' he said, trying to make a joke.

It fell on deaf ears, nor did Gilly need some glib comment about wind or any other green energy, being content with her oil-fired cooker, electric hobs, and gas central heating. She'd paid for double glazing on her patio doors and didn't need some Welsh yokel giving her a lecture. It was bad enough they wasted taxpayer's money with their pointless bilingual road signs, without getting even more subsidies for wind farms that produced barely enough electricity to make it worth it. Not for a few houses.

'*You* may not notice them,' she replied, emphasizing the 'you' to make her point, 'but I think they're an eyesore, a blot on the landscape, and if you think we've just spent a small fortune doing up our home, to have it wrecked by those hideous monstrosities, you must be joking! And, as for noise, they make a horrible continuous drone. So I hope I've made my point clear; they are unsightly, inefficient and noisy. I'm sorry, but what did you say your name was?'

'Caradog Hughes.'

'Who is it, Gill?' enquired a voice from within.

'Not someone you want to see. Some farmer with a petition for the proposed wind farm.'

'Well, you can tell him where he can stuff it. Tell him to bugger off,' the voice said as a man's step was heard coming toward them on the oak polished floor.

He appeared in the hall, a tall, big-framed, bald man filling the space, his wife sharp and short as he stood next to her.

'I think they're an absolute monstrosity, another waste of taxpayer's money and worse than useless, so you know what you can do with that bit of paper!'

He grabbed the petition from the surprised farmer, ripping it up before he could stop him, the several signatures invalid. 'You've got a nerve cold-calling, and on something I'm adamantly opposed to.' He made a noise from the back of his throat and for a minute Caradog thought he was going to be spat at, but Mr Parsons turned on his heel, dismissing him as he called his fat Labrador and walked back inside, leaving his wife to close the door.

'I think my husband has made his point clear,' she said, leaving Caradog to try to salvage what he could of the petition, as he tried to gather up bits of strewn paper.

Still angered by Caradog's impromptu visit and his petition, Steven looked out of their drawing room window past the pool and sweep of lawn, to the fields rising onto hill and moorland, to where the proposed wind farm would be erected. He sighed irritably, damned if some half-soaked scheme, aided by the Welsh Assembly with the Green Party's blessing, was going to spoil his retirement home. Such a development would seriously devalue the property and their enjoyment of it. He was determined to do what he could to stop the development in its tracks. 'Not in my back yard,' he thought as the sun was blocked out by thickening clouds. He reached for a whisky and soda before supper, reminding himself that he needed to ring a few people to add clout to the opposition. He was not someone to be quiet and would make sure his opinions were known, and would use his influence to prevent the erection of any of the ghastly turbines anywhere near his view.

Only Beth seemed oblivious to the heated debates in village halls and community centres, even to Tegwyn's negative reaction to the turbines, operating in her own rarefied world untouched by any turning blade or regular drone, living by more intimate rhythms as she went about her work at Tan y Bryn, looking after her small patch, and her family. It was an exciting time with the first shear from her flock of Lleyn sheep a success. After it was sorted, cleaned and milled she'd sent it on to Rhian in London, who turned it into felt and was using the product in her burgeoning Mad Hatters business.

It was not just this, or the farm, though, or the fact that Clare was happy in the small Welsh school, but something deep within herself which made Bethan feel she was soaring. She felt a rush, a freedom of the wild, swinging her arms out wide as if to fly, running along the field in a burst of happiness. Everything that had been burdensome vaporized. She had something so precious, and knowing Tegwyn was there for her, liberated her.

On the hill above their home, on a parallel plane, a venerable species felt the same subtle change as she slid gently along the bottom of her pool, gliding over the dark, slippery stones. The sexually maturing eel curled in on herself, the confines of the pool no longer her sanctuary. Both species shared an ancient quickening, rich, ripe in yoke, drawn by the sun's heat, knowing its significance.

This time Bethan would not wait, lingering as she'd done, to make the error that had proved so fatal. She was homed, safe with her childhood sweetheart to look after her. This time there was no right or wrong moment, no need to evaluate a reaction, with each day slipping comfortably one into the next, and she knew he would be overjoyed, just as she was, the knowledge making her shimmer like a new leaf of beech, all soft velvet in spring warmth, as she caught his eye upon her, smiling in the union of their shared secret.

So, too, this primeval creature that had survived man's trapping for centuries, like the tiny thousands of her kind had slipped through history, unnoticed under clouds of darkness. Her inner clock, sensing neap water, she traversed along ditch and over stream, passing the freshly dug up tracks and deep holes that would take such tonnage of metal that would soon be set on the large square concrete bases. She slid alone, progressing steadily downwards, keeping close, following wet courses and only daring to move over open land when she had to, waiting for a starless night; over moss and under browned leaf, passing the cultivated fields, keeping unseen along the borders where long grass hid her progress. She'd waited years, maturing slowly in her lake home and would hole up again for another inky night before she moved on. There was no turning back once she'd embarked on her journey, cautiously, but nevertheless relentlessly on her way back to the sea, back to her birthing place in salt water, undaunted by the dangers ahead of her in her quest for the survival of her species. It was a journey far more torturous than any willow net, during which she would be exposed month on month to a far more lethal toxin.

Years before, curled up like a tiny leaf, she'd floated with the currents for two years, growing in the sea before turning sliver and wriggling her way to the shoreline. Already one of the lucky ones, she'd found a suitable muddy estuary, sliding unhampered upstream to her hill home, maturing for fifteen years in the solitude of freshwater, undisturbed by man. She had grown from that small elver to this beautiful, silver-skinned, mercurial night traveller, as she slid gracefully through the mud and silt in the river's mouth, over discarded plastic bags, bottles, cartons, ropes, and rusting metal, as she sought the taste of fresh and salt intermingling in the tidal water. It was the change that was the beginning of her epic journey, the estuary where boats' hulls bobbed on their ropes in the urgent tug of the tide-race. The pull was too great as she unhesitatingly surged on, her large, open eyes watchful as she swum over bits of debris on the estuary floor, over seaweed-covered stones and blacker rocks that were home to mussel and limpet. She swum out, going deeper along the bottom, rock turning to sand in open water that heralded the real start of a heroic swim across six thousand miles of ocean to get her to her unique breeding place.

Preoccupied with building up his business after the foot-and-mouth debacle, Richard was not in the mood for further bureaucratic interference on or near any of his land. What he needed was to focus his energies on increasing the farm's production to somewhere near what it had been prior the outbreak. The last thing he needed was the time-consuming distraction of a wind farm, albeit on his neighbour's land, that was bound to infringe on his use of his own land. Although he wouldn't admit it if asked, he was also jealous that it was Caradog and not himself who would be the beneficiary of all the inconvenience that was bound to follow, getting compensation as well as income from the electricity the wind turbines produced. Yet it would be him that would have to put up with the toing and froing that such a development would involve. He'd read their literature and the list of bodies consulted, but the most worrying thing was that by avoiding an area marked as 'of special scientific interest', the proposal had pencilled in a route that would go over his land in order to reach his neighbour's part of the hill.

One a market day, he had his first serious row with Penny over the plans. While he was finishing up after the early milking and Sion had gone to the *ysgol feithrin* for the morning, Penny had set up their stall, laying out all the vacuum-packed meat and, on the opposite side, the Tŷ Coch cheeses. Without thinking of consulting him, she'd also put out one of Caradog's petition forms, attached with a bit of string and a biro, ready to catch the customers. Richard noticed it immediately, with a couple of signatures on it already. Instead of selling their food, Penny was discussing the project with a couple of alternative types – what he referred to as hippies. After putting their names down, and sampling some of his cheese, they walked off without a purchase.

'Typical. Fill in the form in the name of some so-called

green protest, but support the local farmer? Na! Not unless he produces mung beans and cannabis.'

'Don't be such an old reactionary! It's a free world, Rich, and most of us have moved on from the Sixties.'

'But they didn't buy anything, did they? No, thought as much. Why have you got that on our stall for? It's not going to help sell our produce.'

'Because I happen to agree with them, about nuclear and fossil fuels, don't you Richard?'

She had a point which he begrudgingly acknowledged.

'They're not right about everything. I don't want to eat their tofu, or soya beans, or biscuits made with palm oil. Look what's happening as a result to the rainforests. The news is always quoting an area the size of Wales, being cut down because of demand for these so-called green crops. You try telling it to the indigenous people or the orangutan! There's never nothing for nothing in this world. Always a payback.'

They shuffled around each other, both grumpy and neither willing to concede, putting off what few customers there were. As if to emphasize the point, two people came to sit on a bench not far from them, the waft of fish and chips reminding them that they hadn't eaten since breakfast, but neither willing to offer to go and buy some. A large gull swooped from the sky and in an act of daylight robbery, grabbed the paper, causing most of the food to spill onto the ground. The man got up angrily, shaking his fist at the unperturbed bird as it pecked some of its stolen meal, squawking in triumph as it finished the scrap and flew up with others who'd flocked in a feeding frenzy to demolish what was left of the dinner, squabbling over the paper scraps. It was funny to watch, and Penny and Richard couldn't help but laugh. He slipped his arm around her waist, kissing her. 'I'll go and get you some, if you watch the stall,' he said, eying the birds. 'Coffee or tea?'

'Coffee, and plenty of vinegar on mine.'

It was only later, when she'd found out that he'd hidden the petition as soon as she'd left to pick up Sion, that he was not prepared to let it drop as a matter of principle. Once Sion had had his bedtime story Penny had it out with him.

'What I don't understand, Richard, is here you are, a really good and conscientious farmer, who like your mam cares passionately about your land and what you put on it, your animals and their welfare, what you feed your family, and yet here is something that has a huge impact for all of us, not just Llanfeni, but for the human race and you don't want to discuss it.'

'Bit melodramatic.'

'No, it isn't. What we're doing to this planet is bordering on the irretrievable.'

'And you think a few windmills are going to stop it? Save the world!'

'Now who's being puerile? We've got to start somewhere. The world's running out of the fossil fuels and I don't want our children to be beholden to the likes of the Arabs, Russia or China, or be dependent on nuclear.' At least he was listening and she went on. 'Wouldn't you prefer it for Sion if he had his own, self-sufficient, clean power source. Wind, sun and hydro, they will all need to be used to replace the gap left by oil. Either that or future generations will be back in the Dark Ages. I thought you of all people would have been the first to support the wind turbines?'

What could he say, admit that he'd have jumped at the chance if they'd approached him instead of his neighbour? A bit of the green-eyed monster, jealous of his neighbour's undeserved good luck? He'd have been only too happy to tolerate the intrusion, the noise and unsightliness, a small price to pay for such a good regular income. Now all they'd be was a reminder that he'd missed out. 'They're not very effective and are very expensive. And yes, OK, Penny, why here?'

'Because it's windy, empty of people. And it'll bring income and jobs to the area, which let's face it, the area could well do with.'

'Then put them up on land already spoiled. Just not here.'

'At the expense of Sion's future, not to mention Bethan's and Clare's? Can't you see, your family is more secure here on the farm because of the wind turbines.'

'How do you come to that conclusion?'

'Perhaps Sion will want to be an engineer?'

'What, and not farm?' He didn't voice the unthinkable thought.

'At least, this way he has more options.'

'Or he could continue to run the farm, as his family have for generations.'

'Quite.' She knew she'd touched a nerve and didn't want his toil devalued. 'Oh, Rich, it's not the turbines, it's everything here that you and your family have safeguarded. I want what you want, to preserve it for Sion and his family. I never used to give all this,' she said, spreading her arms out, 'a second thought, but living here with you has made me realize how fragile the natural balance is. That it's not all about profit, but nurturing as well, looking after the land so it can continue to produce.'

He shrugged his shoulders.

'Would you be so opposed if they were being erected on your hill instead of Caradog's?'

'They're not.'

'What if they did. How would you feel?'

'About what?'

She smiled a wicked seductive smile at him, looping her arm around his back.

'I made some enquiries, that's all.'

'Did you, now?' he asked.

She nodded. 'It took a bit of digging, but the company's based off-shore and if this is successful, they are very likely to consider putting further turbines up and would be interested in including other bits of the hill.'

He was surprised by her quickness.

'Grass doesn't grow under your feet, I'll say that for you. And? Who are they, this Atlantic Energies company?'

'Typical big business – people with money wanting to invest; and this green energy, the current buzzword, has lots of government incentives at the moment.'

'Isn't it a bit odd, choosing somewhere as remote as this?'

'No doubt the incentives are too good to ignore and they need to be early in the field. I read some sort of Tan 8 planning guidance that aims to facilitate the development of wind farms in strategic areas throughout Wales, not just here.'

'How did you find all that out?'

'Oh, I have my ways!" she teased him. 'I rang up Iestyn Williams. He was very helpful and then I went online and looked at the company profile and then I rang round, got someone responsible for renewables in the Welsh Assembly.'

'And?'

'Do you realize, Rich, it'll cost in the region of ten million pounds. That's just for six turbines, not a small-fry investment.'

'That much. Why bother then?'

'If you can afford to wait, it'll pay well in the end. What with grants and tax concessions, it's a good long-term investment.'

'I suppose, and if what you say is right, there are plans for more.'

'Exactly. So it's important to be ahead of the game or we'll lose out to someone else.' She sensed him moving and put in her winning shot. 'I got some useful ballpark figures. If the turbines produce what the blurb says they will, then I reckon Caradog will get a nice earner, an annual income of several thousand pounds. Not bad as an extra, guaranteed. All for having to put up with a few squares of concrete on his hill. Think what we could do with something secure like that every year? It would help the financial security of the farm regardless of the crop, market prices for our meat, or weather conditions. Not to mention the savings to the environment from CO_2 emissions that a coal-fired power station would produce.'

'But they say they're so inefficient. The whole country would have to be plastered with them and I bet they still wouldn't get near producing enough power.'

'No. But combined with other renewables, it's a step in the right direction.'

'And learn to switch off.'

'Yea!' She laughed, both knowing they were guilty of leaving appliances on stand-by mode. 'See, practise what I preach!' She said, switching off her mobile phone.

In the event there was little fuss, and only a few people turned out, milling around outside the council's offices with some banners waving 'no to turbines', the Parsons among them with a large placard. The protesters in fact barely outnumbered the media who'd come to report the event. Inside the chamber, the petition, with many hundreds of names, accounting for a good percent of the surrounding rural population, had served its purpose, showing local support for the development.

The detailed consultation process had thrown up a couple of anomalies, one turbine being refused because of an SSSI survey, which the company had accommodated to the planning committee's satisfaction. Adding this to the Welsh Assembly's pro-renewable energy drive, consent for the turbines was duly given with surveys taken for the protection of flora and fauna all approved. Horse riders, the Ramblers Association, historic sites of Wales, and other such bodies were also accommodated, so that only a couple of disgruntled letters of complaint were to be seen among the positive letters in the local newspaper.

With another three-quarters of a million pounds to be paid by Atlantic Energies to be joined up to the national grid, the cables were to be buried underground to the substation, before going overhead, to limit unsightly cables across the moor. Payments were also paid upfront as a gesture of goodwill to the local communities, a sweetener where everyone felt they were a winner.

Nothing much more was heard of the development, until the actual parts of the turbines started being transported from the ports of entry, craned onto lorries and driven along Wales's roads, highlighting the poor infrastructure of the very rural mountainous countryside. Police convoys were employed, stopping oncoming traffic as the huge lorries pulling trailers a hundred feet in length carried the vast inch-and-a-half thick lengths that made up the steel tower, weighing eighty tons, were slowly transported toward their destination on the hills overlooking Llanfeni. It was just about all right along a motorway or dual carriageway where the lorries took up two lanes, but almost hopeless on the winding narrow roads, and their arrival caused a huge headache for all other road users. With each turbine needing nine such loads to make up a single complete turbine, traffic along any B road became seriously disrupted. And not just roads. Moving such large loads in constricted areas forced whole streets to be closed as well as cautioning off bridges. Double bends and steep inclines all contributed to a virtual standstill of traffic. The tempers of other road users shortened with each week as roads became gridlocked, and local tradesmen and businesses who had been in favour of the scheme became increasingly disgruntled as people tried to avoid driving anywhere along the designated route, staying away from Llanfeni as much as possible, leaving their shops and cafés deserted. Even the local farmers' marts struggled to keep going in the angry snarl-ups as large livestock lorries pulling double trailers, and

Land Rovers, were all forced to give way to the loads carrying the turbines, with their eighty metre blades and motors.

Frustrated by months of delay, with temporary traffic lights causing further headaches, people trying to get through the town rounded on the hapless councillors, giving them an earful as they watched their town and livelihood shrink with a diminishing footfall. Even simple tasks such as the school run and twice daily milk collection from the farms had to run the gauntlet of avoiding the convoy of the slow-moving turbine carriers, and for the best part of four months the area was seriously disrupted.

With such a disturbance, the eel had chosen her time of departure wisely, seeking the sanctuary of estuary, sea and ocean, as the colossal crane lumbered its way along the specially made road up on to the moorland. Its gigantic size was another local talking point in Llanfeni. It had to be huge to have the capacity to lift five hundred tons of metal in order to safely erect and assemble each turbine onto its foundation – a concrete square that was three metres deep and pressure-tested for its twenty-five-year lifespan.

As soon as they were assembled and a final check made by the turbine manufacturers, their blades started to turn in the wind on the three-hundred-acre site and once again Llanfeni, albeit on a very different scale, was producing wind-driven electricity.

Like static giants with flailing white arms swinging round their long bodies, the windmills became quite a tourist attraction, and for a while Tegwyn's hill, as he had always thought of it, become invaded by day trippers. The road that carried the turbines, now an all-too-easy route for onlookers, all rubber-necking in their cars as they sat eating their picnics, bits of plastic left lying in heather, as they stared mesmerized by the turbines, the blades turning in a constant humming. His hill, wild and remote, spoiled by this easy accessibility – the sound of a radio, car doors slamming, dogs being thrown sticks into the lake disturbing more than the surface water, sending him fleeing. There was no longer the plaintive cry of the curlew or the 'jack-jack' of a lone snipe. So much for conservation! Like the shopkeepers, Tegwyn wished he could reverse it all. He'd like to have been able to dismantle them, and the specially-built road and throw them off his hill. He ducked down, hiding from the view of the cars, crouching under the brow in thick heather and gorse, quietly cursing the exposure of his sacred place that had forced the hill to lose her secrets.

Given hindsight, Bethan would never have believed that she could feel the way she did now. Not after what had happened to her when she met Malcolm. Her experience then had been a breathless girly rush that led her headlong, eyes shut with excitement, down a blind alley, believing herself to be swept off her feet in love. Only, she had no excuse to have been so naive. She hadn't been the giggly schoolgirl in the flush of youth, but a woman of thirty, parched from the need to be loved and loving. She was a sensible nurse who should have known better. It had been a silly conceit, or flagrant vanity, to think herself pretty enough to catch him, her handsome rich Irishman. So easy she must have seemed to him, as he kept her hooked, playing her on his line until he had exhausted her mentally, as he held his rod firm, giving her just enough trace before pulling her in, jerking hard. They had been tortuous years and she had almost succeeded in banishing them, only for them to rise to the surface like a trout through brown water, plopping back with a minimal splash, leaving the surface smooth again. Those years when she'd closed her eyes to hide her inner flinching, that made him all the keener. She'd trained herself not to respond to his taunts, his nasty insidious humiliation of her. The face of her baby, the son she'd somehow slipped, never to know, imagined in her mind as she lay on a sheet up against a wall, splayed, bottom up for him to snake around her, his eyes almost yellow in his dislike of her before he took her, his property, in an act of ownership. It was not enough that he caused her to miscarry, he'd broken her mentally, unhinging her, so that she'd struggle to trust, always suspicious, especially of men, doubting their integrity.

When she first arrived back in Llanfeni she'd been unable to sleep in the new double bed Tegwyn had bought for them, leaving the pristine sheets under plumb pillows untouched. Only with time and patience, saying it didn't matter, had she eventually been able to move across the landing and share a bed with him where he held her, leaving his clothes on, as he cuddled her like an upset child. Knowing him from childhood, she'd unfurled to him. Tegwyn who had been there after her father had been killed and always looked after her and loved her; knowing that he would never do anything to harm her, as he'd proved time and time again. Never letting his desire spoil their relationship, he allowed her all the time she needed to feel safe with him before moving across. His love was so solid, undiminished from the time when, years before, had held her in his arms in his clapped-out car when she had been a foolish teenager. Rather than abandoning her when she chose to go with others, he'd always held his candle for her and come to her rescue as she fell drunkenly across his car seat spewing up her evening's alcohol when others would have left her to it.

Now he was just happy to have her with him, his longed-for sweetheart, there as his companion in life and he'd wait, knowing she'd come in her own time, like the eel in her pool, waiting until she was ready. She took his quiet touches, his rough-skinned, honest hands that caressed her, quieting any disquiet, tracing along her arm, her neck line, to her clavicle, a finger touching toward the softening of breast. She learned to look again and not clench her eyes tight or focus on a wall, watching his face as he loved her, his eyes intent, waiting for hers before he leant forward to kiss her. Ripening under the sun, she uncurled, a late flower blossoming in an Indian summer.

When she told him her news, he stood silently, his wide smile speaking his unsaid words of utter delight as he took her in his arms, lifting her up as he hugged her close in unbridled joy. Never had he thought to be a father, content to have Beth and Clare, but now he was going to be a dad, he brimmed with happiness, wanting to jump gates and shout his joy in a wild whoop, to swing his legs in a skittish hop whenever he thought about it.

'When? How?' he asked, laughing at himself. 'You know what I mean,' as she looked at him – really?

'Just a few weeks.' But she put her finger to her mouth as she thought she heard Clare coming in from the yard, lowering her voice. 'I don't want anyone to know. No -one, absolutely no one. Not for now. Promise me Teg?'

He understood, her question loaded with what had gone before.

He nodded. 'I promise.'

Malcolm O'Connor had paid his two million up-front and was pleased when the planning had been approved. Ever since his mother had been over to visit them in Llanfeni, he was able to keep up to speed, with regular updates thanks to her emails and contact through the internet with her daughter-in-law and granddaughter. From a distance he sniffed, nosing through all her stuff, looking at any recent photos Beth had sent, keeping tabs undetected on his stolen family and their lives. Now he had legitimate reason to walk over their bloody hill when he chose, to snoop back into their lives if and when he so pleased. He would wait for now, content to watch, until he saw the right opportunity for a strike that would cause her the most harm.

16

Glad to be away from the house and out of the reach of the lecherous groping of her mother's boyfriend, Les, Rhian walked the sands of Llangennith watching the evening surfers catching the rolling waves on an incoming tide, the off-shore breeze helping to lift the crest of the waves making them an ideal run. She wished she were anywhere but stuck where she was, still reeling from the shock of being betrayed by her own mother who'd sided with her partner. She wished now she could go home, back north to Llanfeni, the farm and family, her dad and aunt, drop out of college and not complete her final year to escape the dirty old git, wanting to bring a crowbar up against his crotch that would kill his urge and if she were lucky, knock him out. She could dream of ways of being the heroine, of sorting him out once and for all, showing her mam what a shit he was. But it was only a pipe dream, knowing that he was much stronger and liked the fear she tried to hide, a come-on for the bastard, her anger and arguments with her mother rolling over in her head like the surf as she walked along the edge of the water, her feet soothed by it in the soft sand. She must have walked for an hour or more and when she turned back, the tide had moved swiftly up the beach. All the day trippers had left and only a group of surfers were still there, two or three sitting by a camp fire as they waited for the others still in the water, enjoying the last of the good conditions as they caught a final wave, coming up to the dunes carrying their boards. One of the boys looked up at her as she passed and smiled.

'Fancy joining us?' he asked, patting a bit of sand as she hesitated. 'I saw you walking along the beach earlier. There's a can of beer if you want.'

She pondered, looking at the other girl in the group, assessing her position and whether they were safe – safer than Les, she could guarantee. The girl didn't seem to mind the intrusion, and Rhian didn't want to go back to her mother – anything to delay the necessity of facing them at home. So she sat down and took the can from the brown curly-haired boy, who introduced himself as Ryan. The fire was cosy, making her feel less of a stranger as she sat down within their group next to the boy who'd made a space for her. By the light of the fire their faces seemed more familiar than the strangers they would have been in daylight. They sat and smoked and drank beer, throwing a bit more driftwood onto the fire as the night grew more chilly, with grey cloud against the darkness and always the sound of the sea in the background as the tide turned again, with white-fringed waves drawn to the waning moon.

One of the group came back from the camper van with a guitar and started plucking it, before strumming a tune the rest of them obviously knew, joining in. Sitting next to her she could hear Ryan's voice that reached above the others, as he took the lead vocal, the guitar keeping the melody. She didn't go home that night, staying out with them in the dunes and from there, without going back to pick up anything or let them know she was leaving, she went down to London. She and Ryan shared one of the rooms and three other members of the band also dossed there. She became used to the transience of youth, with girlfriends and mates drifting in and out of their lives, everything cool, uncomplicated. There was no tight or fixed time, other than gigs in pubs and clubs or wherever else Jim had got a contact, each night hoping someone in the music business would be in the audience and they'd be liked, and get a break to the big time. It was a mixture of indie rock and folk jam-sessions that lasted into the small hours and Rhi loved the excitement of being part of it, sitting or sloughed against a wall, rolling a joint for Ryan as he sang in a light voice, with an edge that made her skin prick.

She learned that the house they virtually squatted in was something to do with Amber's family who, as Tim's girlfriend, had managed to get use of the scantily-furnished house for a few months. Tim played the fiddle, and double bass as well doing vocals. Evenings were spent drinking, smoking and taking the odd high to enhance their creativeness, letting it all hang loose as they jammed into the small hours. It was a place Rhian had escaped to, sleeping and loving Ryan, his foppish hair and his clever way with melancholy lyrics to tunes that turned her on and made her ache for him, blocking out her past. The days became shorter, but London was never really dark, not pitch black like the countryside as autumn slipped into winter and she nestled against him and his smell, with always the noise of life, of coming and going, in the orange glow of an-all night city that was so different from the hills, sheep, and wildlife where nature ruled in darkness. Much later it would be one of those early songs that would help make them, and whenever she heard it, wherever she was, it would always remind her of him, of that first evening on Llangennith beach where they'd met, and he'd invited her to be with him.

Admiring her bangle, Amber introduced her to a friend of a friend who had a stall on Portobello market, selling bespoke jewelry and accessories. For a cut she was willing to have a few pieces that Rhian made, liking her quirky style and design. Amber seemed to have contacts and always some money, and was ready to help Rhian out, calling it a long-term loan until she'd become famous.

It was a good place to learn, selling directly to the public, with the young, bohemian and well- heeled, always willing to try something different and ethnic as part of their creed, their set: jungle, rainforest, Norse or Celt, and for six months she was happy filling in – in between gigs and sleeping with Ryan – learning how to make and use felt, experimenting with shapes and dyes and occasionally remembering to ring home, her proper home, the farm, and let them know how well she was doing and how happy she was. In hindsight, rowing with Les and falling out with her mother had been the best thing for her, as it had set off the events that ended with her making a go of her life. It had been a springboard that had forced her to jump and use her talent as an artist with a new set of friends in London.

The rift with her mother brought Rhian closer to her Dad and Tŷ Coch. Her friends, far from turning their noses up at her being a farmer's daughter, were impressed, especially as it was an organic farm, and they offered to spread the name of the brand by word of mouth, asking for it in trendy restaurants, suggesting she give Penny some contacts for a London delivery which might lead to a regular supply and profitable value-added to their organic cheese, Welsh lamb and beef. It was too late for this Christmas, but it would be a useful foot in the door for next year.

It was just the excuse she needed to go home, at last, to see them, and as she sat down in the train from Euston she was full of optimism that she'd be able to mend the bridges of those awkward adolescent years when she'd stomped and stropped and then left abruptly, with her mother leaving her dad and *nain*[3] and the farm. It was the time to reconnect with them and her home, hoping as she sat on the train, that Penny was nice and would be keen to bring the farm's produce up to London. Even perhaps to bring her dad up to London to listen to the band and meet Ryan and her mates. Though perhaps not, she thought, recalling her boyfriend's reluctance at her suggestion he come down to Wales with her. It was all too early and she didn't want to seem pushy, so she'd backed off and didn't mention a visit again.

She'd started the habit of ringing them, giving her dad news of her success, glossing over any rougher sides to her life. She filled

---

[3] Grandmother.

him in with stories of her attempts at selling her artwork; how it was difficult at first but she was learning and people were coming back and she was beginning to build up a customer base. She had just started on a new development and was into hat making. If the truth be known it hadn't been her idea to use wool felt, but Caro's, another friend of Amber's, who saw the demand for one-off hats – not so much Afghan or Tibetan but a new wave of home grown organic, Mad Hatters. When Caro heard that Rhian had grown up on a hill farm with sheep and cattle, she saw the organic wool as an ideal basis for the felt-making process for the hats they started to make together. With her nous, Amber's contacts, and Rhian's natural eye and artistic flare, she reckoned they could soon have a profitable business, setting up a website, YouTube, Twitter and Facebook accounts to go with the stall. 'Get some footage from home Rhi,' she'd instructed, 'anything off the wall, and the more bizarre the better. Up by those windmills you've been talking about, with sheep and the sea would be great. Can you dye some with the wool still on their backs? And wear one of our brightly dyed fedoras. Orange or blue would stand out.'

Rhian grinned, thinking of the prospect, knowing how conservative her dad was. 'Don't know, I'll see what my dad and Aunt Beth say. See you next week.'

Only in the country did Rhian see the seasonal change from autumn to winter as she travelled home to Tŷ Coch to film and photograph the sheep in their natural surroundings and choose what wool she wanted from her aunt's pedigree Lleyn flock. She'd forgotten how much she missed the place, the light and smell of the farm, as fallen leaves the colour of spices from the orient, littered the lane under a short burst of sun. In the background the sound of the sea in its continuous swell made her smile, remembering the happier times. Waiting for her arrival, as he stood in the farmyard, her dad welcomed her as she got out of the taxi beaming his delight at having her home again and seeing her looking so well, so vital, no longer so pale or thin, and much more self-assured, as she hugged him back.

There was a lot to catch up on and he was eager to hear all her news and to learn about her life in London. He barely touched on Nesta, her reply to his initial question enough to warn him off from asking further. Of course, she'd met Penny briefly as a teenager, but hardly knew her and had never met her half-brother, Sion, who hid shyly behind his mother as Rhi bent down to say hello. She was glad to see the place looking so cared for, with no residual reminder of the ghastly foot-and-mouth catastrophe that had been so graphically depicted on TV, briefly recalling regular phone calls when her dad was near to breakdown. Now he looked so well and happy.

However she was surprised – as children often can be, expecting somehow that their parents never change – to witness his ageing, as if it had come on overnight. What little hair he had, had gone, emphasizing his weathered, lined face, and he stooped slightly and seemed more stiff and less nimble as he proudly showed her some of the farm's improvements. Her grandmother was very frail and Uncle Merv no longer the strong farrier, but an old bent man. Only her Aunt Beth seemed unaltered and happy, broad-faced, smiling to see her again, and grabbing her arm to show off her new flock of pedigree sheep, as Fly, her dog obliged, bringing them down from the far end of the field to be more closely admired. Beth had kept back several of the shorn wool fleeces in large sacks for Rhian to inspect and make her choice for her hat business.

'If it works, Aunt Beth, I'd like to buy the lot off you next year.'

'Fine by me, *cariad*. At the moment it costs more to have the sheep sheared than the price I get for the fleece. But if you wanted to buy a jumper or cardigan, it'll cost forty pounds in the shop.'

'I'll give you a fair price.'

'And a fedora?'

'Any hat you fancy.'

They walked back towards the house.

'I'm so glad things are working out for you, Rhi. I know you went through an awful time when Nain was ill and your parents split up. And I had my own problems and wasn't much help to you when you could have done with someone to offload.'

'Ditto, Aunty Beth. Your plight was much worse than a teenage strop and no one was there for you, not even your own mam, and you had to deal with her, my dad loosening off, and all that stuff over in Ireland.'

'How were any of you to know? And I got through it thanks to your dad, Tego, and Moira.'

'And you are happy now? You seem to be.'

'Blissfully. So always follow your heart, and if this boy, what's he called?'

'Ryan.'

'Ryan does it for you, then don't listen to so-called sensible advice, hold hands and jump off together, which is what I should have done to begin with, instead of listening to Nain for all her good intentions. It would have saved a lot of pain.'

'But you're good now.'

'So good you've no idea. Listen, I haven't told anyone yet, so you must keep it a secret. You promise?'

Rhian nodded her head, keen to have her aunt spill beans.

'I'm pregnant.'

Somehow it hadn't been the news she'd expected, thinking it a bit mundane, but she smiled at her aunt.

'Congratulations, Aunty Beth. Does Tegwyn know? How far gone are you?' she said, looking at her aunt to see any telltale signs.

'Of course he does and he's over the moon. I'm only a few

164

weeks. It's all very early and I want to pick my moment to tell the others.' She paused before explaining. 'Because of what happened, I don't want to announce it too early, just in case I lose it.'

The enormity fell like a stone, Rhian not realizing until then how another pregnancy must be for Beth, considering the tragic outcome of her last one.

'Oh – sorry, I wasn't thinking.'

'That's OK, Rhi. Why should you remember my horrors? Much better that they're forgotten and I've got this little thing to look forward to, to share with Tego and Clare,' she said, gently rubbing her stomach. 'But enough about me, tell me how's your mum these days?'

Rhian shrugged, 'Spose fine, I haven't rung her recently.' Her aunt gave her a questioning look.

'It was because of her, well her foul man, Les, that I left. Filthy bugger came on to me. To begin with I thought I could handle it, keep out of his way. But, you know, he was persistent and contrived to being alone with me in the house. When I told Mum she didn't believe me and when she realized I wasn't joking, she accused me of leading him on! She took his side, Beth! My own mother, with that shit she hadn't known for more than a few months. Well, I did a runner and got the hell out, and got lucky meeting up with Ryan and his mates on Llangennith beach. The rest is, well you know.'

'I'd no idea; your dad didn't say anything. How horrible for you, Rhian.'

'To be fair, Dad didn't know. I didn't tell him.'

'No. I suppose it couldn't have been easy for your mam, either.' Her niece only sort-of saw it. 'The wrong side of fifty, being taken for a ride by a shit only interested in her pretty daughter. Makes her feel suitably dirty and cheap.'

'So why didn't she kick him out?'

'Hurt pride? I bet he isn't there now?'

'No, she's on her own.'

'I know she deserves your absence, but don't leave her out in the cold for too long, Rhi. She is your mum and has no one else. Forgive her, you'll feel better if you do. Anyhow changing the subject, what are you doing for Christmas?'

'I would have come home, but The Lites have got some gigs lined up and so I'll be staying in London.'

'Perhaps bring him up in the New Year?'

'Perhaps,' she replied non-committally.

'I suppose you'll be staying here?'

'Yes, over Christmas, but it's very busy what with Clare in the school concert and, guess what, we've been asked to a wedding.' She nudged her.

'Oh? Whose? When?'

'Between Christmas and the New Year. You remember the soldier, Martin Price, who came to our rescue on the beach? He's getting married up in Yorkshire and has asked Clare to be a bridesmaid.'

'So you're all going up?'

'No, just the three of us. Your dad, Penny and Sion are staying home, what with the farm and relief milking at that time of year when everybody wants to be home with their family. It's too difficult to find a relief milker, and expensive, and Mervyn is too frail to cope on his own. They'd only fret and anyhow on top of the day-to-day jobs, we've got all the Christmas orders to get out as well as everything else. Actually, I feel a bit guilty going up, but your dad and Penny insist we do.'

'You could make it a secret celebration as well.'

'Yes, it'll be nice to have a night away and, well, if everything goes right, there won't be so much opportunity when a little one arrives.'

'And Dad'll cope.'

'Yes, and your stepmother's a very efficient lady. She turned it around for him in the foot-and-mouth crisis. That holiday abroad she took him on, saved him, and then she bought the new stock and kept him going. She's quite a woman.'

'I take my hat off to her! I know she's been great.'

'And she's a really nice person and your dad's happier than I can ever remember. They both dote on Sion.'

'Yeah, it's cool.'

17

'I hope you've passed the cost on to the consumer. Have you seen our fuel bill this month?' asked Richard, the bill in his hand. 'I mean, is it worth going all the way up to London when it costs so much just to drive there? Two fill-ups, we're talking two hundred quid, and the time it takes.'

Orders for their organic range of meats and cheese had increased steadily with the build-up to Christmas, with popular restaurants and delicatessen shops placing orders, ready for the festive rush. Husband and wife were fully stretched to get the orders vacuum-packed and delivered in a three-times fortnightly run up the motorway in a refrigerated van. On top of the extra work, they still had the daily running of the farm, their weekly local farmers' markets and their regular shops to supply. They worked long hours and even Penny struggled to keep the operations flowing smoothly, twice having to phone Tegwyn at short notice, needing a driver.

'We have to Richard or we'll lose our place in the market. I'm not prepared to throw it all away, not after the work we've done to rebuild our brand since the foot-and-mouth. Let me look at the bill, it can't be that bad.'

'See for yourself. They've hiked the price again.'

'It's the war in Iraq, that's the trouble,' she said, studying the invoice. 'It's making everything so uncertain, the whole world seems to be on a knife edge, and we're top-heavy and very vulnerable in the West, being so dependent on oil.'

Which reminded Richard that he would need to order some more tractor fuel before prices rose again.

'At least we've got no one in the army. I'd hate to be a mother or wife of one of our troops deployed out there. Beth told me Martin Price has had his leave shortened and he can only have a week's compassionate leave before he has to go back out – enough for his wedding and a few nights off, but no time for a proper honeymoon. His fiancée must worry sick about him. I hope he'll be all right, he's longing to quit the army altogether and settle down.'

'He can thank our prime minister for it.'

'Watching the news fills me with horror, seeing those images on the telly.'

'The country's in a bloody mess, and I don't know how they expect us to survive the way petrol prices are rising. I mean I can't just pop on a bus or tube, can I? Or walk ten miles with the milk and cheese on my back like the old drovers, driving my cattle to market! Ah, so much for progress!'

'Which makes green energy all the more viable, and something we should consider on our hill. That Caradog bloke is no doubt pleased with the turbines. They seem to be rotating almost constantly and you have to agree they're not so much of an eyesore now we've getting used to them, are they?'

'S'pose not,' he grudgingly agreed, 'but for the moment, I'm up to my eyes in it and can't think about bloody windmills.'

'Of course not now. Perhaps, though, after the New Year we could make some serious enquiries?'

'I'm not promising, but in the meantime how do we pay these extortionate fuel bills?'

She hugged him, kissing him for his generosity in moving his ground to accommodate hers, believing renewable energy to be the only way forward if the world hadn't been blown to bits by then.

She'd left the wet side of a ditch a month before, her pool olive-green and brown, and slithered silently, invisibly under the night, towards salt water and open sea, leaving no trace that she'd ever been there. Critically endangered, this ancient breed, a maturing female eel knew her time was approaching, instinctively heading south along the coast that was the expanse of Cardigan Bay, away from the hills of Llanfeni and the land that had nurtured her. Travelling past Trwyn y Bwa and Strumble Head, she turned west away from the islands and sounds, to the open sea, diving at dawn a thousand metres down to avoid predators, keeping away from nets and propellers as she swam without feeding on into the Celtic deep, along ancient sightless lays, feeling along the bottom, weaving her way to Cork and Ireland's southern tip. Only at night, safe from pointed wing and hawking bill, did she venture up to shallow water to warm her body on the sea's surface, continuing her swim, only to dive again to avoid discovery as grey light broke upon the ocean, hiding in the depth of the sea's mystery, suppressing any further development of her eggs, the eel kept them stable until that optimum place was reached. Only then, in a sea defined purely by current, would she feel safe from man and his meddling.

As if by sudden pull, she swung southward towards the Azores, searching for that body of water that would help propel her ebbing strength towards her ultimate goal. It was an incredible journey which, if she managed to stay healthy and alive and negotiate her way to her destination, would take half a year to achieve. In their different ways, she and Beth were each on a unique journey, carrying their precious cargo for safe delivery. To return to this special place, home to shrimp and white marlin, and young loggerhead turtles, seeking sanctuary among the mass of floating sargassum – oh clever eel, that we should learn so much!

They hadn't been away at all since Beth's return to Wales, and she was looking forward to a trip up to Yorkshire as a family, just the three of them. Clare was very excited, having never been a bridesmaid before, and couldn't wait to get there as she sat in the back. Recommended by Katie, they'd booked into a pub near the venue, and Beth wanted to get there in good time for the rehearsal so they could relax before the wedding the following day and make it more of a break.

She didn't like the look of the weather as they pulled out of the yard.

'I hope it won't snow, Tego?'

They'd already had a brief cold snap in late November and although the skies looked leaden, Tegwyn shook his head. 'It's too cold for snow and I saw the gritters when I helped Rich with the cows first thing, so we should be all right. The main roads will have been treated and I won't drive fast.'

She put her hand to her tummy.

'And, if it snows I've put the chains in and we've got lots of time, so there's no hurry.'

He reassured her knowing what she'd meant and had no intention of any silly driving up the M6.

She could imagine it would be attractive in the summer months, with stone walls and burbling brooks and steep-sided, wider-topped hills than those of home; a place more popular with ramblers and walkers. But in midwinter the scenery was cold, grey and bleak, with no sense of sea or warmer Atlantic air but a northerly blast from the Arctic as they got out of the car after a long journey and rushed quickly into the solidly square, stone pub, leaving the cases until they'd had a pee and warming cup of tea by a welcoming fire in the lounge.

Lights on the Christmas tree glowed in the hallway although Christmas seemed long past in the no-man's land of the official holiday between the end of one year and beginning of the next. Beth thought it a funny time to choose for a wedding. It wouldn't have been her choice, what with everybody else in party mode, which somehow detracted from their own special day, but she knew why Martin and Katie had chosen the time, and she thought how brave the young farmer's daughter was, to commit herself to a soldier about to go back out to the war in the Middle East. A happy, sad time with it's a mixture of remembrance of the past, and hope and optimism for what was to come.

After a hot supper, a few beers and a good night's sleep, the Jones family woke to a whitened landscape in a heavy hoar frost that softened in the early morning sunlight, the frost melting from the branches as they dripped in the sun. Too bright a start was not auspicious for a sunny afternoon, and all too quickly the winter sunshine was replaced by the blanket of silent grey cloud of another dead December day.

With the wedding at twelve, Beth decided to risk leaving her umbrella in the pub as she and Clare set off to the church just along the road to meet up with the other bridesmaids. Tegwyn had left earlier to keep Martin company and as they hurried towards the church, Clare looked very sweet in a soft pink dress pulled in at her waist with a raspberry pink satin bow.

Inside, the church was not fully filled, and the wedding guests had been ushered to the front. A large display of white lilies mixed with seasonal holly on a stand, with trailing ivy, gave a focal point in front of the lit altar candles, as the guests chatted quietly in expectation of the bride's imminent arrival, with the groom and best man suitably nervous in the front pew.

Uncharacteristically, there was no sign of any military presence, no polished brass buttons and shining black boots, no arch of honour from flashing swords no sign of a uniform. Martin himself was dressed in a plain dark suit with a white carnation in his buttonhole, his shaking hand gripping the order of service as he kept his gaze firmly to the front, like many a groom suffering wedding-day nerves. Along the leaded windows, variegated ivy interspersed with sprigs of mistletoe surrounded a night-light candle on each sill, that flickered in the draft from the church's open door.

Then the music got them to their feet, as a proud dad led his daughter down the aisle, followed by the two bridesmaids and a page boy. It was a solid, down-to-earth place and the people sang out heartily, their breath rising as one in the December air. The couple walked down the aisle together, arms linked, with Katie smiling broadly, while Martin was more shy and tentative, with only a smattering of Prices in the pews, not knowing many of the faces offering congratulations.

Three days of bliss away from it all, with Hogmanay in Scotland, staying in secluded comfort before he had to return to his regiment, flying back out to Iraq, promising a proper honeymoon in some exotic island in the sun on his return.

'It was good that we went, there were hardly any of his family or friends as far as I could see,' Beth commented on their drive back across the moors in a cold thick fog-filled day, thankful that she had Tegwyn with her, trusting him to drive them safely home.

Now she was pregnant, because of the potential risk of toxoplasmosis, she couldn't afford to take the risk of doing the lambing in April, and although she was delighted to be in her condition, the two months lambing and calving, not to mention the milking and other jobs she mucked in helping out, would be out of bounds, and she was not looking forward to being cooped up and unable to help when the farm would be fully stretched at its most productive period.

'You know, we're going to have to spill the beans, and tell them before lambing,' she said, looking at his eyes in the car mirror, her hand on her tummy as she put her finger to her mouth not wanting Clare to understand.

'Tell them what, Mam?'

'Nothing, just about the wedding and how absolutely pretty you looked and so grown up and well behaved. Did you enjoy it?'

'Yeah, it was OK. Bit boring and Uncle Martin wasn't very jolly.'

'He had lots on his mind, what with the wedding and everything.'

'Lambing?' Tegwyn seemed puzzled by her remark. 'Why?'

'Toxoplasmosis, not safe for me, or you know.'

The penny dropped. 'No, of course not. I didn't think. You're not to go near them, or the cows or any of the milking.'

'Why not, Uncle Teg?' asked Clare. 'Mam always does the sheep. They're hers.'

'You're right Clare, they are her sheep and she's the best shepherd.'

'So why say she can't go near them? I don't understand.'

'I just meant when we get home, she'll be tired and I'll do them for her.'

It was impossible to talk in the car, but when they were alone he needed to have explained all the possibilities that might infect their unborn child.

Martin had prayed that the capture of Saddam Hussein would bring about a swift end to the war in Iraq, but far from quelling the turmoil it had resulted in an upsurge in violence, not just among the warring factions, but also directed at the Coalition soldiers. The thought of another tour of duty in the country petrified the engineer, so much so that it affected his performance in bed, and in the short time they had together before he had to leave her, his erection failed him, leaving him embarrassed at having to apologize to his new wife for his lacklustre performance. When he eventually managed, instead of being elated, he felt somehow unmanned and vulnerable, something which was made worse by her sympathetic understanding. Fuck him and the world for making him so reduced, so impotent, as he sobbed quietly into her neck. And for the loss of his best friend, Garry, that still haunted him in nightmares, for the loss of his nerve, for everything that had rendered him so useless. Welcome to 2005!

His uniform gave him a veneer of strength, belted and braced, ready for the shit as he rejoined his comrades with their innuendoes about his recent marriage – time off for a bit of nooky, leg over, lucky bugger. Then it was helmets on, guns cocked, to face a bitter and hostile populace, a sitting target in the middle of Iraq. There was no sign of any goodwill, with electricity and clean water in sparse supply, and little evidence of any sign of reconstruction in the country that had been promised after the war by the politicians. Half the employable population was without work, as the unstable country tried to hang on to its tenuous hold on peace where cities, towns and villages were still in a shambolic state. Civilians faced an even worse infrastructure than before the war, hampered by a clumsy bureaucracy, and ever-present security worries made it a hell hole, ripe for suicide bombings, kidnappings and beheadings among civilians, foreign workers, Iraqi security forces and Coalition soldiers alike. It was a foretaste of ISIS and their jihadists which Martin Price returned to in January, just as the country was going to vote in the first national election, when Iyad Allawi, a Shiite Iraqi Council member, became prime minister, and Ghazi-al-Yawar, a Sunni, the president.

18

The freezing cold weather that brought Britain to a virtual standstill in the last days of January played into the hands of Rhian and her fledging company, Mad Hatters, as a photo of a mini-celeb in one of the tabloid glossies wearing one of her brightly-coloured felt fedoras had caused a sudden demand. With the cold snap persisting, the young were flocking to buy the new trendy warm headwear – not just the more usual black, olive green and dark brown, for Rhian was using damson purple, crimson red and blood orange, all adorned with different silk bands in leopard print, paisley or wild flowers. She knew she was onto a winner when the singer Cerys Matthews was seen wearing one of her hats on television, talking about her music, her love of folk, and her Welsh roots, as she walked along a Pembrokeshire footpath, waxing lyrical about the unspoiled beauty of the place and joking that she was on the lookout for a Welsh farmer!

It couldn't have happened at a better moment for Rhian, whose relationship with Ryan had cooled, for somehow the famous singer's endorsement of her product re-addressed the balance of her relationship with him. There had always been an unspoken understanding that it had been a loose hook-up, Rhian knowing he'd offered her a bolt-hole, but not much else, as his gaze drifted across a venue, eyeing young girls as he sang and played. Suddenly the hat, or the person wearing it, rekindled his interest in his own Welsh girl and Ryan was not quite so blatant when he looked at the females in the audience as the band performed, his arm latching into Rhian's when she was there. She had been transformed from hanger-on to flavour of the month, a cool chick who was suddenly able to contribute to the success of the band with her own brand of trendy hats, as well as being in possession of a much-needed cash injection towards their costs, including the more prosaic needs such as bog paper and groceries. Talk about good product placement, as orders poured in causing the Mad Hatters website to crash with Rhian frantically ringing round for help to restore it, recruiting friends to help pack and send out the huge increase in orders, in an attempt to catch up. Weeks later, when she had a minute, she emailed Beth to let her know she'd be wanting all the Lleyn wool after the sheep had been shorn, and if she knew of any other organic wool producer in Wales, seeing as there was such demand for her woollen felt hats.

It was a very different picture in the country, away from the perpetual movement that generated its own warmth in a twenty-four-hour city. The countryside was bleak in comparison, where days of hard frost burnt off what little winter vegetation there was, and an east wind made life on the hillsides a hard place. Not here, the warmth of a conurbation, cocooned against the icy wind, and with the exception of the wind turbines that continued to turn regardless, the Llanfeni populace stayed indoors, venturing out only when they had to. Red-faced, with runny noses, pinched in cold, farmers and outdoor workers wrapped up like onions to face the biting wind, with Richard no exception.

Milking at Tŷ Coch became an arduous fight with pipes and water freezing. Only in the parlour when the cows were in, was it a degree or so warmer, but with the changing over of cows any heat was soon lost as they stood miserably in the collecting yard, slipping on any ice.

It went on for weeks, Britain gripped in an iron fist that made winter feel interminable. There was a general longing for longer days and spring. Richard came in, cold, shutting the door to keep in the kitchen's heat, thanking his luck he'd ordered oil before the Christmas shut down, which would be enough to keep the machinery running and the house operative for another couple of months. More out of habit than any hope of change, he tapped the glass of the barometer, the needle staying stubbornly fixed, knowing he'd have to help Beth and Tegwyn gather the hill sheep, or at least get fodder up to them on their scorched hillside if the freezing weather persisted much longer. At least his sister's Lleyn flock was already down and being fed whole sugar beet to boost their energy levels so near to lambing.

As if farming wasn't difficult enough, without the added complication of increasingly unpredictable and severe weather patterns. It was no longer just rain, but weeks of persistent downpours that caused huge swathes of the country to flood. Then a hot dry spring with no rain at a time when it was most needed for spring growth in grass and newly planted crops. Now they had a freezing Arctic spell that brought the whole country to a shuddering halt. Penny was convinced that the imbalance resulting in global warming was man-made, and as if to emphasize the point, Clare had come home from Llanfeni school with a painting competition on the subject for all the local children to try. The competition was open to all children living in the area using any medium, crayons, paints, collage, or clay, under the title of 'Your Environment,' and the classes were to be divided and judged by age groups. There would be prizes for all the winners and an overall winner would receive an extra special prize. It came as no surprise to see that it had been sponsored by Atlantic Energies and it reminded Richard to ask Penny if she'd had any response from the company regarding his own bit of hill. If this weather didn't relent soon, the only thing left up there that would bring in some money would be wind-generated electricity.

It was a near miracle she was still alive three months after she left her Welsh shore, swimming through unknown waters to her goal in the northern Atlantic subtropical gyre. She had not been eaten, caught, or attacked, although her journey had been treacherous for all her guile, and she only narrowly missed being killed by the ruthless sweep of a vast dragnet along the bottom that scooped up everything in its path. The wily eel just managed to slip through the tightening net. Now she sensed another danger, not this time the distant vibration of a trawler's engine, or swirl of the current in an ever-changing ocean, but something she smelled in the sea's swell.

Above her, the water was still whipped up by the tail end of a seasonal hurricane, yet it was not the churning water but something altogether unfamiliar, a physical heaviness above her that made her hesitate, keeping her low near the seabed. When the sea calmed, she ventured upwards, still sensing that something was wrong with the water. Nearer the surface there were no light rays breaking through, only a strong, heavy smell. It was not floating seaweed but something like a vast black blanket, with globules inches thick stuck to the water's surface. From beneath she could see the pathetic paddles of birds' feet, covered in the sticky black stuff that seemed to entrap them in a treacly glue, unable to take flight, their wings and body covered in stinking crude oil. A turtle, eyes and shell thick with tar, dived to try and rid itself of the substance that stuck to its body. Overhead a plane monitored the oil slick drifting in the current, killing any sea creature unlucky to get caught in it. Worse was to come as smaller planes flew over dropping powerful chemical solutions into the water in an attempt to break up the mass of crude oil before it got close to a shoreline.

What a change in the sea during her years holed up in a deep peat pool. Now the oceans were almost bare of fish but littered with debris – all sorts of plastic, oil derivatives and other human waste, only sometimes crudely disguised with chemicals which poisoned in another way, equally destructive. While she struggled in her primeval urge to negotiate her safe passage, the whole world seemed hell-bent on destruction.

Bombed oil plants burned uncontrollably in Iraq, adding to the soaring price of the black gold as oil-dependent nations were panicked into stockpiling in a vicious spiral. Although far removed from such hot spots, Llanfeni was not immune to the knock-on effects, for even the most humble home relied on fuel and electricity that had no connection with the wind turbines on the hill above the coastal town. The last three months of fuel increases had seriously eaten into Tŷ Coch's profits and the business could not go on as it had if oil prices continued to rise.

The cold weather only exacerbated the problem, with everything needing fuel to run efficiently. It was not just the farm machinery, the milking parlour and the diesel to get around and make deliveries. They also ran their Aga and central heating on oil. Animal food stuffs and artificial fertilizer had become increasingly expensive, especially in relation to meat sales and although Richard and Penny were paid a premium for being organic, it was hardly worth their while economically.

'I don't see the point of it,' he said one night after supper as they sat down to watch the news. 'Here we are scrimping and saving trying to economize on our fuel consumption, but let's face it, whenever we need to go anywhere we have to use a vehicle, and then all they do is blow the bloody stuff up. The rate they're going global warming won't be an issue. There'll be nothing left to blow up,' he said, pointing at the pictures on the screen that showed another plume of burning oil somewhere in the Middle East.

The world news was grim, and as Beth watched the footage she thought of Martin, worrying for his safety as she saw the pictures of Coalition troops – British boys running in the dust under gunfire, with oil fires in the background. She felt grateful and at the same time guilty at being safe, remembering that wretched bleak early morning on the beach when Martin had come running down to help her, picking Clare up from the water's edge and dragging Tegwyn up the beach, taking it in turns to give him mouth-to-mouth resuscitation, not giving up, telling her to hold on and everything would be OK. He had waited with her until help arrived in the form of a helicopter and ambulance back-up that saved their lives. She owed him everything, warm and snuggled up by an open wood fire, her baby fluttering within her womb, Tegwyn's arm protectively over her shoulder, shut in against the winter cold.

'I hate seeing it, it makes me think of Martin out there instead of being with his Katie in Yorkshire. I hope he'll be all right, Tego? I wish our troops could come home and let someone else fight. It's not our war.'

'He'll be all right. He's made of hard stuff. You mustn't worry. It's not good for you to get yourself upset. Why don't you switch it off, or over to the other side? Martin's survived worse and he's due home in not much more than a month. You'll see, and he'll be really pleased with our news.'

Only, Beth knew – she'd seen Martin's look, and for all the outward bonhomie, it didn't conceal what was going on behind the soldier's smile. She knew those signs. She had been a victim to them herself, and when he'd last called, and again at his wedding, she'd noticed the clamminess of a fear that had nothing to do with wedding-day nerves. She shuddered, blocking out the unwelcome memory of her past with Malcolm that proved stubbornly persistent and would haunt her dreams.

Tegwyn squeezed her gently.

'You all right, sweetheart?'

'Yes, fine. And, you're right I'll have to tell them soon,' she said, raising her eyes toward the farm. 'I'm going to tell Clare first and then we can let Richard and Mam know.'

'And Moira?'

She paused before answering. 'Yes, I can't not tell her. She should be the first, but I'll wait to give us more time. I don't want to put the jinx on anything.'

'You won't, my darling. It's all right to be careful but you mustn't let superstition get the better of you. Nothing bad is going to happen. I'll be here for you and won't let it. I can't wait to see the look on their faces. I don't think they'll be expecting it, will they!'

'No. I wasn't.'

'And you feel OK? Don't you, *cariad*? Not so sick now?'

'It's getting better. You'll come with me for my next scan, won't you. Twelve weeks?'

'Try and keep me away from seeing my own baby.'

'I wish this weather would break. I can't wait for spring to come.'

'But, no lambing for you.'

'No, but I can still help with other things, feeding and stuff. I'm not going to sit like an invalid but I promise I won't be silly. It's not just for you. I want this baby more than anything.'

Perhaps the bad weather reminded both siblings, Rich and Beth, of the terrible first winter without their father, Ianto. His unexpected death on a tractor that turned over on a hillside left them to manage a farm while they were still children, and as if out of spite, nature had thrown her worst at them. It had been a winter of freezing weather, followed by snowfall, with no prospect of a thaw. Elin and her children couldn't manage, and as the eldest, it had been Richard who was the most acutely aware of his failings, as they lost the daily struggle to run the farm in such conditions. Somehow this was etched in his mind whenever a period of snow and cold persisted, and unlike his wife and son, he hated the white stuff and could not be cajoled into sledging with them. Nearly fifty years on and for all the technology, Britain still seemed to grind to a halt at the first flutter of snow. Salt gritters were out in force as were JCBs and other powerful machines, scraping away the snow to keep runways, motorways and train tracks clear, only for them to be covered over once more, the new snow freezing before dawn.

In the countryside it took longer to clear, with the small rural roads remaining impassable, and farmers well used to depending on their own resources, helped open up their community, clearing roads to the elderly, the doctor's surgery, the hospital, schools and shops a priority, using their tractors to force through a path. Although it wasn't as bad, or as long, it still made Richard anxious and uneasy – give him wind and rain any day to ice and snow.

Penny's brief joy at such a winter wonderland, taking Sion out on a sledge, soon soured as the cold persisted day after day, making even simple farm tasks difficult and dangerous. Everything slid – tractors, machinery, cattle and people. The council was unable to keep up with the need for constant gritting as salt stocks became dangerously low and the snow continued to fall, drifting as the wind picked up.

Richard and Tegwyn attempted a trek up onto the hill to see if they could free any of the sheep caught sheltering by the slate wall, the snow making it a tomb as it piled up against the wall. They took the tractor as far as it was safe to go and then proceeded slowly on foot, using their shovels to test the depth of snow. Both men knew the lie of the land but their progress was laborious and for the first time Richard was thankful for the improved road made for the turbines that undoubtedly saved some of his sheep from dying. He and Tegwyn dug and dragged several sheep out from under the drifts that had built up along the walls. The animals staggered at first and then miraculously found their little feet and stumbled away from their white prison. Heavy in lamb, they were weak, and once back onto the frozen road the men were able to put down some high-energy cake. There was no way they could get them off the mountain until there was less snow and the road became safer for vehicles. As it was the tractor slid on ice and with a trailer full of sheep behind it, would have been a lethal weight. There were bound to be some losses, weak sheep giving up in late pregnancy or stress – they were exceptionally hardy, but susceptible to stress of a kind that could bring on a heart attack.

With heavy snowfall after a period of freezing, just before the lambing season, it was surprising that more ewes didn't succumb, giving up their struggle and becoming food for carrion once the snow melted, left there regardless of the rules for the removal of carcasses that caused as many problems as they solved and deprived wildlife of a little bit of protein in bleak months. No minister in a grey suit was going to trek up the side of an uninviting mountain in the middle of a winter freeze to check, and if they did, by the time they got there, buzzard, fox, badger and crow would have demolished the evidence, leaving only a remnant of wool and scattered bone.

When they came home they glossed over the severity of the problem, but Beth, unlike Penny who hadn't been brought up in the hills and had never witnessed what could happen to sheep stuck in snow for any period, was not fooled, knowing they would have lost a fair number of the flock.

When the weather did break, it didn't come with a more normal shift to warmer wetter snow that would wipe away the colder stuff underneath, but with an icy rain that froze the top of the fallen snow, entombing any trapped animal even further. Only by degrees did the cold eventually ease, lifting enough to start a thaw, revealing the grey deadened grass underneath.

'At least the pedigree sheep are down and Beth can look after them, but I don't hold much hope for the hill sheep. They'll be lucky to bring with a single, let alone any twins.'

It was no one's fault but his own, trying to do too many jobs. By taking his eye off the sheep to get the Christmas orders out and watching for the early calvers, he had left the sheep to their own devices on the hill. He should have got them down before the bad weather set in, but at the time, as the farm was always squeezed, with virtually no grass growing, and fields often wet, Richard had been thankful to have them away, grazing up on the hill, secure in the knowledge that they were tough and used to fending for themselves. Even in snow they were better than other softer breeds and were more likely to survive a short cold snap. Only he'd miscalculated, and when prolonged snow fell on already frozen ground, it proved fatal, burying his sheep alive. Although a great insulator, their wool also a trap, becoming too heavy for them in their weakened state to enable them to clamber out of the snow.

With the thaw came the carcasses, at least forty, several together as they'd sought shelter, lying under a wall or tucked under a stunted hawthorn that had taken the brunt of the snow storm. It was a depressing job, loading what hadn't been picked by scavengers, onto the cart to be carried back down to the farm and into the special container ready for disposal, which Richard would have to pay for, making it a double blow.

Perhaps Penny was right after all and the best thing was to have windmills and not livestock to help bring in an income from their part of the hill. At his age he didn't need many more hard winters and livestock loss to lose heart in a marginalized, remote industry, distanced from a public who no longer seemed to care where their food came from as long as it was cheap. Looking at Sion asleep with his toy tractor and farm machinery on the floor, Richard silently thought his son would be better off not following him into the farm business, but training to do something else, instead of slogging his life away for very little, no matter how beautiful the view.

Thinking in this way, he was aware of history repeating itself, as he recalled his own mother begging him, after his father's death, to stay on at school and not commit to a lifetime of toil on the debt-ridden land. At least Rhian, who'd never been given an option, had done well for herself in the fashion industry and as her dad, he was hugely proud of her, with her hats in magazines. And she had not forgotten her roots, fair play – she was doing better than the British Wool Board in promoting wool by using it in a way that caught the public's imagination. Who'd have thought that Rhi, his awkward, argumentative girl, who'd professed her hatred of the farm and disliked living in a rural backwater, now waxed lyrical about everything green and natural. And of course she was hugely pro the giant turbines, seeing them as part of everything she considered 'organic and renewable', not so unlike her grandmother, whose philosophy had been similar, working with nature, destroying as little as possible, using natural products rather than artificial, manure rather than 20:10:10, and herbs instead of antibiotics.

Sitting on his son's bed watching him sleep, Richard felt he'd come full circle, having spent all his energies trying to improve and better his farm to produce more. Now circumstances were shunting him back to where his family had been generations before, for modern practices were not the answer, even if they led in the short-term to greater productivity. Perhaps his great-grandfather, the village horse-doctor, had understood the rhythms of nature better and had got the best from the land – better in fact than he had himself. For all his efforts to improve his farm, instead of progressing it seemed to him they'd gone backwards – TB, foot-and-mouth, blue tongue, MV, scrapie, lice, antibiotic resistance and worm infestation. There was an endless list of what animals could become infected with for all the modern hygiene practices, including antibiotics, washing down, rubber gloves, antiseptic spraying. Boundaries provided no immunity against contagious diseases when the waste drained into water courses.

He'd lie awake in the small hours, Penny sleeping peacefully by his side, her rhythmic breathing accentuating his lack of peace. Once started, he couldn't stop fretting about the jobs needing to be done, the cost of it all, the sums not adding up, as he worried about the future of the farm. Perhaps his forebears' way had been the only sustainable way – a couple of cows to milk by hand with a pail in the field, giving enough milk for the family with a little over for bartering. Milk, occasional cream, but usually buttermilk sufficient for a healthy if spartan existence, with a few chickens and a pig, wool from sheep and wood from coppicing for fuel. Perhaps micro was all along more sustainable than macro, obviating the need for big machinery running on oil, milk churned out in a factory line, sold too cheaply to the giant supermarkets.

Where was the sense in working all hours ploughing, fertilizing the land, putting down seed to harvest it in order to feed the animals over the winter – silage, maize, stubble turnip all needing hours of tractor work and the right weather, for what? Milk, meat and cheese which, without the EU subsidy, was produced at a loss on a small family hill farm that nobody but it's inhabitants gave a jot about. The world had moved on like a giant spider, whose websites dominated and controlled peoples' spending, Amazon and eBay the new highway. Deep down, he knew the answer to his questioning, that regardless of any effect he might have on the global economy, his farm still mattered to him. It was why he got up every morning, the animals demanding his attention, his cows waiting by the gate, their warm breath rising in the early dawn, eager to get into the parlour for their breakfast as they were milked. There were small things that surprised him, giving him an unexpected uplift – a new life, a March hare or flock of starlings, existing under his stewardship in his fields. His care of a small patch of marginal rough land was infinitely more meaningful to him than any paper exchange.

He'd seen bad springs before and although there was no longer snow it remained bitingly cold keeping any new grass or leaf bud at bay. More than once he looked enviously up and across to his neighbour's hill, watching the long arms of the rotating turbines earning Caradog Hughes money, while he struggled. The cold snap could not persist, with the lengthening days and strengthening sun, even though the sheep huddled together in the bottom fields waiting for another bale of silage and some sugar beet nuts after their ordeal on the hill. The winter was enough to make the farmer look forward to having turbines and fewer sheep for his survival. Better to be at the source, than have a line of the 'A' framed pylons all along his land that would eventually be needed to connect wind power from the uplands to the national grid. He was glad that Atlantic Energies had agreed to phase two of the Llanfeni wind farm development.

With moss frozen to rock there was no gathering, and it was lucky that Tegwyn had more time to help on the farm. What with Beth's condition and the freezing temperatures, there was a need for manual labour where machinery couldn't yet be used. Leaving the tractor in the lane, Tegwyn could walk over the frozen snow drifts to get to the young stock and check they were all right, throwing them a bale of hay where they couldn't forage. With a hammer he was able to break through the ice on the water troughs, keeping water supplies flowing. The demand for winter fuel, especially wood, with the escalation in oil, gas and electricity prices, had trebled. Seasoned hardwoods were particularly sought after with wood burners and new huge biomass production being increasingly used in businesseses and homes as an alternative to oil-dependent appliances.

Spring would come, but in the meanwhile the cold weather produced a huge rise in demand for Tegwyn's business and he had plenty of seasoned and stacked firewood. Demand came not just from his regular customers with open fires. There were enquiries for wood in a large quantities, tons to be used in boiler systems to heat buildings, as well as to provide underfloor heating, hot water and other domestic uses. Wood and biomass were the new flavour of the month, becoming big business, and although Tegwyn wouldn't thank you, and remained adamantly anti the turbines, his wood business complemented energy from the wind as yet another sustainable resource. Tegwyn himself was more interested in the welcome boost to his cash flow in an otherwise slack time of the year, so both he and Beth had an extra reason for their grins, and something to celebrate at their small holding of Ty'n y Bryn.

Whether it was because of her condition, or just her state of mind, Beth seemed oblivious to the cold, running on a different fuel to the rest of them, wrapped up in her own protective shield that was more than mere clothes. She carried with her an aura of happiness, and seemed to be always jolly whether out and about or at home. She walked with a jaunt as she picked her way over the frozen ruts in the lane between the two houses, carrying a quantity of cake over her shoulder to her sheep. Her dog Fly sat waiting on the back of the quad bike, ready to jump down and help if asked. From across the yard her brother watched her, she waved at him, lifting her hand to her mouth, indicating a cup of coffee, enough to make him smile.

'I knew there was something up,' he said when she'd told them her news. 'I've never seen you looking so radiant. Everybody else is cold and glum but you've been going around as if you've won the lottery!'

'Better than the lottery, Rich!'

'Many congrats Beth,' Penny added, giving her a kiss as she handed her a steaming cup of coffee. 'How far gone are you? You don't show.'

'We've been for two scans.' She hesitated, seeing their faces.

'No, everything's fine. But they didn't want to take anything for granted, knowing my history, so the doctor wants to monitor the baby every few weeks.'

'And, how does the father feel? Tegwyn going to be a father for the first time!'

'Thrilled. He can hardly believe it. He and Clare are already planning for its arrival. She can't wait, she's always wanted a brother or sister and has often asked not to be an only child. Look how she adores Sion.'

'I hope that doesn't mean I'll lose my best babysitter! He dotes on her and trots round after her like a dog.'

'Have you told Mam and Uncle Merv?'

'No. I'll go over this morning and give them the news, but I wanted to tell you first.'

'That'll brighten up the day and give them something to be cheerful about. Congratulations, my little sis. Here, come and give your brother a hug.'

'There is one fly in the ointment though.'

'Oh?'

'I won't be able to help with the lambing.'

'You're not that big?'

'No, but it's not safe. Toxoplasmosis.'

'Of course, I didn't think. Well, you've chosen the right year, there'll hardly be any lambs after this winter!'

'I'm sorry, Rich, leaving you all the work and my load as well.'

'Don't you worry, sis, I'll charge you for every lamb I have to pull on your Lleyns and I'll make sure you have double the work as soon as your babe's born!'

'Listen to him. You can see he's as pleased as punch.'

With good news to brighten a leafless dank day, she left them to discuss her and her condition in private and went down the yard to Y Bwthyn to tell her mother and uncle.

She knew Uncle Merv would be pleased for them but wasn't

sure if her mam would understand and if she did whether she would be able to communicate her joy. It wasn't quite the same sharing her news with her invalid mother and as she leant down to give her a kiss, the smell of incontinence wasn't masked completely by the liberal sprinkling of lavender water. Beth felt mean, unkind for even thinking her mam not fit – too old and infirm for something so pristine and young. For a split second she thought about not telling her about her baby, not wishing to sully it by sharing her news with the wrinkled shell that had become her mother.

'I'm pregnant, Uncle Merv,' she said quietly to him by the sink, with her back to Elin. Like an old person his response was exaggerated surprise and pleasure as he threw out his arm to hug her. 'You clever girl! Have you told your mother? Elin, have you heard Beth's good news? There, go over so she can see you close to. Beth's got something to tell you, Elin.'

'I'm expecting a baby, Mam,' she said almost shyly, looking at her for her response. She couldn't speak to form her words, instead her head nodded as it always did so Beth couldn't tell if she'd understood.

'Isn't that good news, *cariad*, our Beth having a baby. Tegwyn must be pleased, he'll make a brilliant father, there'll be no stopping him now!'

He thought, but didn't say, how the news of fatherhood in his middle years had bowled him over, when Elin had told him she was expecting Simon all those years ago. It was very different then, all hushed up in case it upset Richard and Bethan, so soon after losing their own father. Nothing said, allowing the youngest to be brought up thinking he was Ianto's final leaving present and not the result of an illicit affair, kept quiet because of the fatal accident and subsequent inquest into the farmer's death. Only Elin and Mervyn knew the truth, leaving the gossips unchallenged, speculating about the possibilities behind hands that covered their mouths as they filed on a Sunday morning into chapel. Nothing and no one could have daunted his overriding joy and pride as she carried his seed, his baby, and when it was duly born, the same fingers that covered the sanctimonious mouths, counted off the months, disappointed in the realization that it could possibly have been Ianto's child, leaving only a whiff of scandal in another 'open verdict' against the farrier.

Only Mervyn saw himself in the baby's skin and almond eyes, and he'd had a lifetime to get used to living with gossip, being illegitimate himself, and caring now only for his new family. That he was known as Uncle Merv didn't matter if it made life easier for the baby, Simon, and he hadn't disappointed them, becoming a famous opera singer travelling the world. It was, in fact, his visit to Ireland that was instrumental in finding out about Beth and her unhappy state, and his intervention that started the process that brought her and her daughter home to the safety of the family home in Wales.

So history was repeating itself and like an iceberg that showed only a little of what made Mervyn the man he was, the people of Llanfeni, the farmers and their sons who remained on the same land, knew the history and what lay beneath, as part and parcel of their own community. Marriage was no longer so socially significant, as couples happily co-habited, needing no church ceremony, law or bit of paper to raise children, though a sense of where you'd come from and who you were was as pertinent as ever it had been. Even if married status had become less relevant, finding the right partner was still crucial where land and ownership were concerned. There was nothing more devastating for a family farm than divorce. There would always be room for stirring things, for gossip, but a family needed to stick together.

In Mervyn's eyes, Tegwyn was a bit like him, a misfit and underdog in the community where everybody knew everybody else's business and could also recount a family's past, being the first to remind them of any misdemeanour. At least Tegwyn had been born in wedlock, unlike himself, the horse-doctor's grandson being treated with contempt by the community, especially by Richard's father, Ianto, who'd been loud in his dislike of Mervyn, knowing they shared the same father. Being an outcast and aware of the ignominy it caused, Mervyn had always sided with the wild, free-reined Tegwyn, who'd been left to find his own way in life. So when he came to help the Davies family after Ianto's sudden death, it was Mervyn who fought his corner, reminding the family that without his help in those ugly frozen months, the farm would not have carried on; that Tego was not bad – unfettered perhaps – who'd made the mistake of showing his hand, his interest in Bethan, Elin's little girl. When Mervyn had finally moved in with them after the inquest, and took over the running of the farm, they'd had no need of Tegwyn's help. Nonetheless, he'd had felt bad about sending him off to search for other employment, knowing there was little for him at Tan y Bryn, and from the sidelines he'd watched him make bad choices that led him to drink and poverty. He felt a twinge of guilt each time he heard of Tegwyn's downward path. The accident that proved almost fatal was the saving of him, bringing him back from a drunken abyss. This and his belief in Bethan, his lifelong dream, just as Elin had been a rock to him.

Mervyn was glad it was Tegwyn's time at last, and he'd make sure he'd do what he could for them, to right what he saw as his wrongs. Tegwyn had finally got his girl, just like he'd got his Elin and he deserved good fortune, as he'd risked his life for her. She may have come to him late, carrying baggage, but her news of a baby would be the icing on the cake for Tegwyn. Old and one armed, Mervyn vowed to help them, to do what he could as a stop-gap. A knowledgeable pair of eyes in the lambing shed were better than nothing, even if it was just for a few hours at a time, to relieve them, and he'd done his fair share of pulling lambs on the open hill in all weathers, reviving others after a difficult birth. He'd had a lifetime to get to know the tricks that made the difference between life and death – a bit of straw down a newborn's ear, to tickle the senses and make it sneeze and start breathing, clearing its lungs of mucus; a heavy slap across the ribs, seemingly callous, to induce a first gasp, or a swing in the air, holding the slimy back legs, to clear the airways of a breech, put back down forcibly onto the straw – anything that would stimulate life. Only then could he stand back and afford to croon. All these things were second nature to a man whose life's work had been tending to animals.

Elin couldn't speak or show any of the emotion Beth's news had brought about. Raw with the frustration of being trapped in her useless body, she allowed herself to cry, tears escaping down her cheeks unchecked, to mingle with loose-lipped saliva from her mouth. How she longed to stand up so that she could hold her only daughter and hug her fiercely to her old body and tell her how much she loved her. How much she had been vexed with herself for not being there for her in Ireland when she had Clare, who would never really know her *nain*. There was so much she'd wanted to share but it had all been too late, her stroke putting paid to her plans for the future. Imprisoned by her condition she had to accept things as they were. At least they had come home for good and it was enough to know that they were around and everything was sound until, that is, Bethan's morning visit which had been like a stick that stirred up an ant's nest in her head. How to tell her it wasn't safe for her to have a baby? That she would have to have an abortion? Not just how, who would tell her such a thing, even suggest it, knowing it could easily send her over the edge. Not for the first time, Elin seethed with inner anger at the typical selfishness of Tegwyn, allowing her daughter to get into such a predicament with precautions so easily available, and just like him not to have considered the consequences for Beth of getting pregnant. He'd always been a careless, feckless fool.

With Mervyn spending more time in the lambing shed, he didn't devote quite so much time to Elin and failed to notice her agitation which only someone close who knew her from day-to-day would pick up on. He didn't wait, spoon to lip, to help her finish off the last of her porridge, or hold her cup for the last of her tea. Instead he threw it half drunk down the sink, promising to be back to make dinner, leaving it to Beth as they swopped roles.

The harsh winter had left the ewes weakened and many needed help lambing. Somehow they hadn't the energy or urgency that labour demanded, lying down and pushing half heartedly, knowing they hadn't the reserves left. It didn't matter that belatedly they had plenty of haylage and cereal, it was too late to alter what would turn out to be a disastrous lambing season for the upland farmers of Wales, and Tŷ Coch was no different with half the ewes giving birth needing assistance and then rejecting their lamb. The sheep hardly had the will to live and many had no milk for any newborn, walking away and abandoning them.

Richard and Tegwyn helped put up a special pet lamb crèche in the corner of one of the sheds, and feeling that it was he who should be doing Beth's work, Tegwyn felt obliged to help out. He wasn't a natural shepherd, and didn't like lambing; it made him feel squeamish, putting his hand into a ewe's back-end in order to find a hoof or nose. Nor was it safe for Beth, as his clothing could be contaminated with lambing fluid and he had to be extra careful hosing down his waterproofs in the yard and making sure he took off his coat, wellingtons and any other item of clothing that had come into direct contact with the ewes. Any trace of amniotic fluid on a sleeve or trouser leg was a potential risk, so to be doubly sure, he put everything in a bucket of disinfectant outside the back door. All the extra bio-security might have been worth the effort if he'd been proficient at the job but as it was he wasn't much good with a permanently bent finger, making the whole lambing procedure all the more clumsy, and Tegwyn was only too glad when Mervyn returned to take over, waving his finger as the excuse for his lack of competence.

'Remember to keep those clothes out of the house.' As if he needed reminding, the knowledge that he was going to be a father was a happy constant in his mind. No, he was happier helping with the milking – wash down and wipe, claws on, automatic feed in their manger and a steady pish-pish as the cows were relieved of their milk. Give him them, or better still, leave him to the wood, to his timber, moss and open hill, and let the old boy tend Beth's flock of awkward sheep.

Seeing the number of lambs without mothers, Mervyn was forced to buy in bags of expensive powdered milk with a feeding system of buckets with several teats that he refilled three times a day and once in the night. All newborns had to be taught to suckle from rubber that didn't bleat or smell like a mother. Newly orphaned lambs were even more difficult, refusing the taste of rubber and needing a lot of persistence to get them suckling efficiently enough to live. Once they got the hang of it, they demanded an on-tap supply, their constant bleating an added irritant when he was overworked and tired from lack of sleep. Cade lamb-raising was time-consuming, expensive and loss-making, but the old shepherd couldn't leave them to die even though he knew they'd never grow properly or be as robust as naturally reared lambs. Their potbellied appearance was a giveaway of how they'd been reared that would put off any potential pedigree producer from buying them. Nor would they be ready for the fat market at the end of the summer, so he was damned if he did and damned if he didn't, trying to keep as many of them alive as possible, often thinking it would be more economically sensible just to knock them on the head at birth and write the season off.

Out of the lambing shed he painted a brighter picture to Beth than the reality justified. At least the wool wouldn't be affected and Rhian had already ordered the entire production, wanting the sheep sheared as early as was possible for an awaiting market. The way it was going with such a late spring and the sheep in poor condition, their fleeces would reflect this and would not have 'lifted' from their skin, making it impossible to shear until the sheep's condition had improved sufficiently. Just as human hair is a reflection of a person's inner health, sheep's wool was the same. The way the year was going, he couldn't see them shearing until mid-July at the earliest.

It didn't help that the months of freezing weather caused the spring to be late, and being organic, Richard couldn't throw as much fertilizer down as he would have liked to make the most of the warm wet weather in late May and give his worn-out fields a quick boost of growth. With better light he worked all hours to get some slower-releasing farmyard muck onto his land to help the grass and encourage the purple-and-white flowered clover. The price of organic fertilizer was prohibitive and he could only afford enough rock phosphate on his best fields to help push the belated growth.

All too quickly the small window of opportunity closed as the weather turned unseasonably hot and dry. This was good for the lowland farmers whose depth of soil retained the short plentiful recent rainfall, but on the thin, acidic shaley soil of the Welsh uplands where rainwater ran off the hills into the streams and lakes, it left the soil dry and his grass exposed to drought. Without enough ground cover, or depth, the new growth soon died back, the weather conspiring to thwart their efforts. Mervyn could not remember such a difficult year, season following season full of problems that put the whole farming cycle out, so that despite Richard's slog, the farm looked scorched and bare and would yield less than needed to keep the livestock fed in the following winter.

'Os cân y gog a'r llwyn yn llwm, gwerth dy geffyl a phrynu dy bwn,' he remembered his mother Mair singing to him as a little boy, hearing the cuckoo's call in the bad spring, the old saying proving right.

19

Exhausted by her six thousand mile journey that took her back to the home of her birth, the eel lay spent resting on the bottom, the gentle swell of vast water swaying her tired body, helping her relax. High above, swaths of floating seaweed, the sargassum grass, offered her shelter from the filthy accumulation of all the non-biodegradable plastic waste of man that she'd been affronted with throughout her arduous journey. It had mixed with organic matter, becoming another trap for some of her newly spawned, critically endangered brood, the ancient *Anguilla anguilla*, curled up like small leaves drifting with plankton under the flotsam carried by the Gulf Stream on a new journey that would take them back in a reversal of their mother's migration, toward the coasts of Europe.

Beth returned from her anti-natal clinic, held in the newly renovated community centre close to the primary school. With half an hour to kill, she stayed on to help tidy away before collecting Clare from school on her way home. She didn't know the community nurse but knew of the family she'd married into, the farm Maes Llymystun, where they bred prize-winning continental cattle on fertile flat parkland several miles east and inland from Llanfeni.

'Amazing what they've done to this place, isn't it?' the midwife said as they put the last of the cups and saucers back into the new cupboards.

'It was very different in my day. I remember coming here as a little girl with Mam, very basic. Now they've got everything in the new block – the internet and computers that drop down into the surface when they're not being used.'

'It's very up to date, isn't it! Nothing like when I was at school which just goes to show my age. My daughter knows so much more than I do about the computer, the mobile phone, and what's more she's no hang-ups about using them.'

The nurse agreed, adding, 'They've grown up with them, as if they've always existed. They haven't thought of it as learning like us, just like we used to switch on electricity or the TV without thinking.'

'All this, and the sports hall, all from the wind turbines? Amazing.'

'Yes, all part of the promise, funded by the company.'

'A sort of payback. Well, all I can say is lucky us and lucky Llanfeni. A good wind!'

Back at the house Clare wanted to show her how her painting was coming on for the competition, pulling it carefully from the special folder that kept it protected. Beth was impressed by her daughter's talent and obvious good eye for nature.

'Did you do this all by, *cariad*?'

'Of course I did, Mam. But Miss Elfed helped me to begin with. To get it started.'

'It's amazing Clare, it's really very good. You must show it to Tegwyn and Uncle Rich. It's brilliant,' she said, trying to lean down to kiss her, her big tummy getting into the way, at which they both laughed.

Even if she had been able to, Elin would not have laughed or celebrated the news of a baby. Plagued by a capricious memory, she fought to catch the threads to confirm her fear. The more she struggled to recollect, the less she could, angry at her lack of recall. If only she could get up and walk to the places of her past that would reconnect her to it. Instead, she only had fragments of memory to draw on that were unclear in the blur of her brain. Mervyn would know, or would at least understand enough to second guess if only she could bring it to his attention. Yet how was she to do this, immobile and chair-bound as she was, and him distracted in the lambing shed.

Having Beth with her instead only adding to her angst as she watched her, growing, preoccupied and happy, tidying up and cooking for them both. Smiling indulgently, as if looking after another child, she bent over her to feed her mother, her hand across her tummy, failing to pick up her mother's worry, as she looked into her cataract-clouded eyes, patting her frail heavily-veined hand gently as she pulled the blanket around her shoulders, feeling that her mam was cold.

'Oh, Mam, brrr, here let me pull this over, there that's better. You're cold,' she said, tucking her mother in the woollen blanket.

She tried to point, her voice an unintelligible garble. She wouldn't eat until Mervyn fed her and when he did, she tried to take his sleeve, to make him see where she was looking at.

'You're trying to tell me something. I've got that much, pet. But I don't know what it is you want?'

She raised her voice as if to agree as she attempted to nod encouragement. He could tell something was amiss, knowing her so well, and looked around to follow her gaze. Slowly he pulled himself out of the chair.

'I'll go round the room. Let me know if I get warmer.' In a child's game of hide and seek, the tone of her voice let him know when he got warmer, a grunt when colder. He touched objects, a plate, cup, kettle, picture, went to the fridge, cooker and larder, his coat and wellingtons by the back door, the dog basket that now housed the cat, the telephone, radio, television, knick-knacks, dried flowers, her herbs. Photos on the dresser brought her strongest response. He touched each one, like a doctor feeling a patient waiting for the pinpoint 'ouch'. Partially hidden, there was an old photo of her and her family, the four of them together. She'd only kept it because it had been a particular good picture of the children; Richard standing next to his mam, sitting stiffly for the pose while Beth perched on her father, Ianto's, knee.

'Is this what you want?' Mervyn asked, fetching it from the dresser, and wiping away the dust with his fingers, as he took a closer look to see if there was something he hadn't noticed before. It had never been a photo he'd liked, seeing their father, his half-brother smiling, full of himself, at the lens. 'Always been a show-off of a man, full of cock,' he thought to himself, bringing it back to her and sitting down beside her as he held the photo for her to study.

'This what you wanted, Elin? This photo? Why?'

She tried to point, to touch the portrait of Ianto, to make Mervyn understand what she was trying to tell him.

'Yes. He would be proud of her, if he was here. Is that what you're trying to say? But no more than I am, *cariad*. You know I look upon her as a daughter, and I'm very happy and proud for her, and it's lovely and right that she's come home for good and to raise her family. Tegwyn will be a good father. You mark my words. They'll do all right together. She is happy, Elin, really happy.'

Elin tried to remonstrate, and Mervyn could see his

sentiments had upset her, but he didn't understand why, as her tears flowed. Was it the memory of her past, her marriage with Ianto, and that her failing health had made her regret something? Or that she might not be there to see the birth of her grandchild? Was that the thought that so bothered her. Her own mortality?

No, he put the photo back on the dresser. Elin had never been a conceited woman and would never worry about getting old. Her feet had always been firmly on the ground, a down-to-earth sort of person. She was not, and never had been, sentimental, but was practical and kind. So what else could it be, he wondered, pausing to take another look at the family group, Ianto's hands were gripped around his daughter's middle, probably trying to tickle her, knowing him, to make her giggle in front of the camera. What was in this group photo that Elin was trying to tell him as opposed any of the others he brought down for her to inspect?

It didn't resolve itself and Elin continued to fret, refusing most of what was put in front of her.

'Mam, come on, Penny's made this specially for you. To please me. You used to love fish pie, it's one of your favourites.' Beth coaxed her with a spoonful of freshly made pie with coley and smoked haddock, a boiled egg in the creamy sauce and topped with mashed potatoes and some steamed broccoli to tempt her.

She took only a morsel before refusing more, wanting no yoghurt or cup of tea. Beth took her pulse, her blood pressure, looked at her long shaped, hard-worked feet in their slippers for any sign of circulation problems. Perhaps she had a urine infection, yet there was no temperature. Her mother carried no excess weight, diminished now in age with her back hunched, like an old mare who'd done her days in the field. Her daughter asked her if she had a tummy upset, and if her water was OK. Was she sore below, knowing that her bowels were functioning all right considering the little amount she was eating. She inspected

201

her mother's commode as she emptied it down the toilet. Elin was deteriorating and Beth considered ringing the doctor for advice.

As is often the case, overtired from too much work, Mervyn couldn't sleep, so he went down to make himself a cup of tea and to check on Elin who was worrying him. He listened to her breathing, quietly pulling the door to. Back in the kitchen he got down the photo that had seemed to bother her so and in private, studied it at length thinking back on those days, when he'd been only a part of her life. How he'd wait and watch from Yr Efail, ready in case she had need of him. Even after all this time, he'd never once regretted Ianto's death. The man had carried the arrogant stamp of his father, making light of people less advantaged, as if by doing so it promoted their own self-importance. His own mother, Mair, had been used – getting her pregnant, denying it had anything to do with him, and abandoning her to her fate in the days when a pregnancy outside of marriage was a disgrace.

Mervyn had plenty of reasons to hate the Davies family, his own father no better than the son. So what was in this photo, telling him that he didn't know and Elin did? Something that made it significant to their lives now? He sat with the clock ticking as company, letting his mind slip back, to hear the voices of his younger days again, airborne across summer fields of cows grazing overlooking the sea. He turned the photo over, looking closely at Beth as a little girl, noticing her father's hands wrapped around her and his crooked middle finger.

Was this what it was all about? The whispering of tittle-tattle? He put the frame down on the table. Shhh. Nothing said, just a look, a wink of complicity, remembering. Paternity, it was always about paternity. Was that wound to be re-opened to spread its poison again? He hoped not, as the likelihood dawned on him of the implications of what might be the cause of Elin's stress. Now he understood, he would ask her quietly if this was at the root of the problem and what, if anything, she wanted him to do about it. Was it not already all too late, and did it really matter in the modern world?

'Dear Elin, I got up in the night and came downstairs and as you slept I thought about the photo you wanted me to see. I think I've finally understood what's been bothering you and why you wanted me to look at this picture in particular,' he said to her 'It's about Ianto, isn't it?'

He knew her attempt at a nod was a 'yes' and continued. 'I know this is painful for you. Look, take my hand and if you want me to stop just squeeze it and I will. You think that because there was some history between Elizabeth and Ianto before he met you' – he didn't add and afterwards, as well as several other women – 'Ianto could possibly be Tegwyn's father because of his crooked finger in the picture, and Tegwyn has a bent finger? Is that it?'

She looked at him, tears forming.

'Oh, *cariad*, please don't cry. I don't think you're right, but even if you were, what can we do about it, now? They don't know – nobody does. They haven't a clue they could be related. Much better to let sleeping dogs lie.'

She screwed up her eyes, trying to impart her wish.

'You're worried about the baby? How do we tell them? Beth cannot go through another pregnancy to lose it, or worse, to have to have a termination. It will send her insane, Elin. So what do we do?

He sat holding her hand, considering what was the best course to take in such a delicate situation.

'Does Richard know?'

She squeezed his hand.

'He's no idea?'

She shrugged.

'Do you want me to ask him, to see what he has to say about how we should tackle the problem? Isn't it all too late? I don't know how many weeks Beth is, but if she has to have a termination the sooner the better for everyone.'

How was he to broach the delicate subject with Richard, knowing the implications of such a disclosure, especially if it turned out to be wrong? It was a task he did not relish but nevertheless knew he had to, and promptly, if they were to avoid a complete catastrophe. Better for him to have Penny present, a witness as well as good influence in preventing flared tempers in case things got out of hand, which knowing Richard, they might easily do.

Untypically, he used the phone first, ringing them to forewarn them of his coming over, choosing the evening when he'd normally be with Elin. When asked, he wouldn't say why, other than that it was something personal that involved them all; something that had recently come to light and needed addressing.

'That's strange. I've never known Mervyn to ring first. Usually he just pops over unannounced. Sounds rather ominous,' Penny commented to Richard as she vaguely picked up some farm papers, plumping up the cushions on the easy chair, before putting the kettle on. Luckily she still had some coffee and walnut cake in the tin. Better than cheese, she thought, that might keep the old boy up in the night.

'I wonder what's bothering him?'

'Hmm,' replied Richard with his own thoughts firmly on his mother and the need for more care and whether Mervyn was coming over to say he could no longer cope with looking after her and she needed to go to a home – something he had been dreading, knowing how badly it would affect her. He shouldn't have agreed to the extra work in the lambing shed as it had obviously been too much for Mervyn.

'It's your mam.' Just what Richard had predicted, as Mervyn started to relate his concerns, cup of tea in hand and slice of cake ready on a side plate for him. 'She's very concerned about Beth.'

'Beth? Oh?' He was surprised and relieved at the unexpected announcement. 'She's all right isn't she? The baby's growing and her last scan was fine, wasn't it?'

'Yes. No, it's not that.'

'If not that, what then,' thought Richard. Surely there can't be anything else important. Beth seemed so well and normal. It couldn't be that she was going mental again.

'I'm sorry to bring you in on this, Penny, but Elin and I felt you had to know, because of the implications.'

'Sounds sinister, Mervyn.'

'If you'd prefer, I can leave you and Rich in peace, and he can tell me later if it's easier?'

'No, there is no easy way to say this.'

'Then do you have to say anything at all? suggested Richard, fearing more bad news on what had been a difficult year.

'Now you are worrying me, Mervyn.'

'You know your mother's been poorly recently. Off her food and the like.'

'Yes.'

'Well, I knew it was something other than being under the weather. When you live with someone as long as I have, you intuitively know when something's not right. With her not being able to speak very well, I had to second-guess what's been troubling her. It must be very frustrating for her. That was until yesterday, when I spent some time with her. I've been that busy with the sheep, I've neglected her recently.'

'No one can ever accuse you of that, Mervyn. Don't beat yourself about that.' Penny got up to take his cup from him.

'Anyhow, we sat down together yesterday afternoon and I tried to go through all the topics I could think of that might be of a concern to her. I wasn't having any success until I brought down the photos from the dresser.'

'I know, the ones of us. They're just pictures of the family.'

'Yes, it wasn't the recent ones, but one at the back, half-hidden by the big platter on the top shelf. That was the one she wanted me to bring over to her. So I got it down and held it for her. Then she started crying. Great sobs of grief. I couldn't understand why.'

'Who was it of, Mervyn?'

'You and Beth with your mam and dad. Beth sitting on your father's knee.'

'I think I know the one. It was one of the last photos we had of him, before he died. The four of us. Good one of him and Beth. Me next to Mam and she frowning at the camera.'

'That's the one.'

'Why should that bother her, now?'

'It was Ianto, the way he held his hands around Beth's waist. His fingers.'

'His fingers? What about them? I don't follow.'

'Your mam thinks your father is also Tegwyn's father.'

'What?' blurted out Penny before she could stop, putting a hand over her mouth and apologizing.

'Dad can't be. Mam's got it wrong,' Richard said.

'Think back, Richard. Do you remember how she used to hate Liz Tan y Bryn coming over? How she used to flirt with your father. Do you remember the killing of the pig? It wasn't just the animal's squealing that upset your mother. You must remember Sam, Tegwyn's father, coming over with his wife Elizabeth to help with the killing of the pig.'

'No, I don't. Only stories from Mam and how she hated the day.'

'How silly of me. Of course you wouldn't remember, you hadn't been born then! Before your time, they used to kill a pig every year at Tŷ Coch, and it was the custom for neighbours to come round and help, and as a thanks for their labours they would share supper and go home with a bit of the pig, and the next time some other farm would kill a pig or sheep and share the meat and so it would go on – meat, milk, wool, horse shoeing, and tanning. It was all part and parcel of how we shared. I remember Sam Tan y Bryn had the best technique. His knife was the sharpest and fair play to him, he was quick and accurate, slitting the sow's throat.'

Penny grimaced at the thought of an animal, especially a pig with its intelligent, knowing eyes, held down by men as it bled to death.

'There was talk, no more than gossip, that Liz and your father had a bit of a thing.'

'You mean an affair?'

'If you like. I don't think it was serious on your father's side and then he met your mam, married her and you know the rest.'

Oh, he knew the rest all right! This man sitting in front of him, telling them a story that mirrored his own past shoddy behaviour. Didn't he sneak round to see Elin when Ianto was away? The open verdict following his accidental death never completely exonerated Mervyn, the farrier, in Richard's eyes. Had he forgotten Simon and his untimely birth? Only just able to come under the radar as his own father's, even though Richard had always known his so-called brother was only a half-brother for all their papering over cracks. No one there to witness the blazing rows he'd had with his mother about having Mervyn on the farm, usurping his dad's place, a petty thief stealing in the night. And now, all these years later, Mervyn had the cheek to bring up such a story. He'd wanted to hit him when he'd been a teenager and tell him to piss off and leave them alone, and now, well, he clenched his fists in agitation, going red in the face just like his father did when he lost his temper, looking as if he could kill the old man.

'And now you're suggesting Tegwyn is my father's child! That would make him my half-brother. Another one, Mervyn?'

Mervyn understood his accusation, choosing to ignore it as Penny sat stunned by all the revelations.

'I'm not saying that definitely, Richard. I don't know, but he may be. And I understand your anger and I'm sorry I've had to bring it up. But just say for a minute he is, for argument's sake. That makes them related, like a brother and sister. And, then the baby, you see?' He shrugged, raising his hand. 'That's why your mam is so upset. Apart from anything else, it's the baby. Beth cannot go ahead and have the baby if Tegwyn is also Ianto's son.'

'Incest.'

'Without knowledge, but still incest. What a bloody mess.'

'Yes, and me and your mam, well, we don't know what to do, which is why I'm here. It cannot be left.'

'Oh, I don't know. I'd have preferred never to have known. Why did you have to tell me? You of all people.' Once said impossible to become unsaid as the three of them struggled with the implications. 'I've no idea what to do or how to go about telling them. My own sister for heaven's sake!'

'Rich, I think Mervyn's right, and they have to know, so they are in a position to make their own choices, given the facts. Then at least you've done everything you could for them,' said Penny, trying to defuse the tension.

'And, what if we're wrong? What if it's just malicious gossip. What damage do we cause by interfering? How will Beth react to knowing she is living and sleeping with her brother and carrying his child? It would kill her if she has to get rid of another baby. I suppose you've thought of that Mervyn?'

'Why the need to tell her? Penny asked. 'Surely, since we know Beth's parentage, hers isn't the issue. It's Tegwyn who must be told.'

'And do what? Nullify their union and abort the baby?'

'No, don't you see, nothing so drastic as that. Start by him having a DNA test and go from there.'

'So Beth need never know, unless it proves they are related?'

'Exactly.'

'Is it possible to do a test, with Dad dead?'

'I'm sure it can. If they can catch a murderer or a rapist years after the crime with a tiny bit of DNA on a bit of clothing, they can surely trace Tegwyn and your DNA to prove if you are related or not, and that would solve that particular dilemma without it ever having to divulge it to Beth.'

After Mervyn had left, Richard went out into the yard to check on his stock before bed, avoiding the lambing shed knowing Tegwyn would be switching over with Mervyn before midnight and not wishing to face either of them. Not yet. He needed time to consider Mervyn's bombshell before he was ready to share the information with Tegwyn. He may have helped save all their lives, but if it hadn't been for him in the first place, Beth may never have gone away. Elin had only encouraged her in order to remove her from Tegwyn's influence and attention. So, no, Richard wasn't ready to look upon him as a half-brother or to have that discussion, or ever accept it, and would do nothing, at least until he'd slept on it. When he came back in, Penny had already gone up, leaving the kitchen lamp on. Instead of joining her, he knew he wouldn't be able to sleep, so he poured himself a small tot of whisky, sitting down in the armchair, his mind full of the things that had been said and all the memories it evoked.

Here he was more than fifty years later and he was still tangled up in the net of his family's history. Sitting in the small hours, mellowed by alcohol, he recalled the threads that had frightened him at the time, leaving a lasting impression. The rows between his mother and father. The slamming of the kitchen door and sound of hobnailed boots retreating across the concrete yard.

His fear of his father's cob stallions, who belittled him at the local show for being so timid, while praising Tegwyn who went on to come first in the pony races on Ianto's horse. No consideration had been made for the fact that Tegwyn was several years older, and had the strength and confidence to hold an excited pony. Richard had felt keenly exposed by his father. No wonder his mother would cry, having learnt to keep her thoughts to herself, letting the bully have his way. In hindsight who could blame her for taking comfort elsewhere, in the arms of Mervyn, the gentle giant. The irony of it, that they were all tied by blood to the Davies family who had been as good as the stallions they took round in mating, spreading their seed. Two generations on and Richard felt no less encumbered with the thoughtless, careless sex of his father and grandfather, and Mervyn. Only in Mervyn's case, he could never accuse him of being casual or careless about it. Nothing had been more calculated than getting Elin, and having achieved his goal he had lived his life devoted to her, to Simon, and the farm.

So where did that leave the eldest son? Had the rogue gene jumped a generation and might re-appear in his own son, Sion. It was typical of a farmer to look at his family as if they were livestock, knowing that traits re-occur, and that it was difficult to breed a colour or horn out of a beast without drastic culling. Mervyn's news couldn't have come at a worse time with everyone over-stretched on the back of a hard lambing season and a lousy spring.

Richard waited until Beth had taken Clare to school, knowing she would call on in their mother on her way home. Tegwyn, who'd been up much in the night in the lambing shed, was in the yard chain-sawing oak and ash branches to log size. He didn't hear Richard with his ear muffs on and only when his blade got stuck, causing him to stop, did he notice him watching.

He wiped his face, pushing his ear muffs to rest around his

neck. 'Why didn't you tap me on the shoulder? I didn't see you there. Something wrong? Do you need help with a calf?'

'No, she calved down on her own.'

'More than I can say about those sheep. I lost another couple of lambs in the night. Then the ewe wouldn't take a twin as hers, kept pushing it away and knocking it so I had to take it out, give it a bottle and put it with the other orphans. The mothers just don't want to know. I'll be glad when it's over and Beth can do it next year!'

'The sheep are weak. They can't cope with the stress, after all the snow.' He didn't say that if Tegwyn had bothered to take more time, taking the lamb to the ewe so that she had no option other than to lick the less favoured twin, before reintroducing the other lamb back, they might have bonded as a threesome. It was too late now, for nothing would make her accept it as her own. If it lived it would be another poor specimen raised on an expensive bottle.

'Have you got a minute, Tegwyn, there's something important I've got to talk to you about. Can we go inside?'

'Sure, I could do with a coffee.'

Inside, Beth had transformed what had been a plain house – previously a council-owned small-holding – and her touches reminded Richard of their mother's influence. There were dried flowers and driftwood, amid amid greens and blues, giving a sense of the sea. He didn't want to be the bearer of such bad news that would destroy her.

'What are you staring at?' Tegwyn bent down, thinking his flies had opened, following Richard's intense gaze.

'Nothing.' He couldn't help noticing Tegwyn's bent middle finger, just like his father's – proof, if more proof were needed.

'Spill the beans, Richard. Something's obviously got your goat and if I don't get a couple of hours kip before dinner, I'll be no damn good in the lambing shed tonight!'

211

'Mervyn called last night, because Elin knows the truth about you.'

'Oh she does, does she. And what's that then?'

'There's no easy way to say this.'

Tegwyn's smile left his face, as he realized that what Richard was about to say was serious, something that could change his life.

'Just tell me then. What the hell's wrong all of a sudden?'

'You're not who you think you are. You're not Sam's son.'

'Oh? And how the hell do you know that?'

'Because you're Ianto's.'

'Ha ha, sick joke, Richard! Ianto's?'

'I'm serious. He's your biological father. You're not Sam's son,' he repeated.

'You stop right there if you've any sense. Hey! Where's this all come from all of a sudden? Do you know what you're saying? If you weren't my brother-in-law, I'd bloody hit you! I've never heard such a load of shit.'

'I wish it was, Tego.'

'You really are serious?' he asked, realizing that Richard wasn't playing a badly chosen April Fool joke. 'You think that I'm Ianto's bastard? Never. Sam was my dad and I should know, I lived with them all my life. This was their home and you've no right to throw up these accusations. You remember that.' He banged his coffee mug down, spilling some of the contents.

Overtired and rattled, Tegwyn always had a quick temper that never came to very much. Richard knew that what he said had upset him and made him rightly furious. Who wouldn't react the same in his position.

'I've been up all night worrying about it and if I thought there was any doubt, I wouldn't have come here with it, Tegwyn. Do you think I want to give you this news?'

The last thing he wanted to admit was that they were half

brothers. 'Can you think what it will do to Beth, my sister? And the implications. Do you think I'd wish them on her, or you, after all we've been through together? No, you're right, it's the last thing I want to burden you with.'

'So why come out with it now, after all these years. I mean, how old am I, Richard? It's a bit late in the day to tell me I've got a new father, isn't it, even if it is true, which it isn't.'

'Because of the situation. Because of Bethan.'

Tegwyn knew what he was insinuating.

'The baby. What makes you so sure all of a sudden? And why now?'

'Mam – and –'

'Trust her! It would be. Even half-gaga she's still got it in for me. Never bloody good enough for the likes of her! But I thought better of you, Richard. I thought we were friends. You want to take her word against mine? Dribbling out gibberish, and you believe her?'

'I don't want to believe her, Tegwyn, but because of, you know, I have to take what she says seriously.'

'No, I don't know. I don't believe you, or her. It's just a ploy because in your eyes I'm still not good enough for your sister. And now because she's having my baby, your mother wants to put a stop to it.'

'If that was the simple case, Tegwyn, you could tell her to mind her own business and get on with it. But, you know it isn't. How much evidence do you need? Apart from Mam never liking you, everyone knew your about your mother and dad.'

'She's got a lot to answer for, and she's not so lilly-white as to be able to afford mud-slinging. She needs to look closer to home before pointing the finger. We all know who Simon's father is, and she didn't even wait until he'd got rid of your father. So I suggest she keep her smutty lies to herself.'

They both knew that what Tegwyn said was the truth, that Richard's youngest brother, Simon, was Mervyn's son.

'So before you go spreading nasty rumours – all my mam and your dad had was a bit of fun flirting, and so what if they had a fling? They were teenagers, before she met my dad.'

'If you need more proof, look at your finger.'

'What?' He looked at Richard, not understanding. 'What's wrong with them?' he said, holding his hands up.

'Ianto had a bent finger exactly like yours. It's a hereditary problem.'

'Pah! Rubbish! I wasn't born like this. It was an accident. A winch nearly took it off. And if it's so hereditary, why haven't you got one? It's bollocks, Richard, and you know it. Your mother's jealous, that's all this is about. She can't stand that I've won. I've got her daughter, and Beth chose to come to me against everything Elin tried to do to prevent it. She can't stand to see us together and happy.'

'I know it's not that, Tegwyn. Mam knew she was wrong, what she did sending Beth away. And she's paid dearly for her mistake.'

'Meddling.'

'OK, she interfered when she shouldn't have. But it's not about that, it's about now. I – don't you see, the baby won't be right. It'll come out deformed or mental or something.'

'Don't you fucking start that with me, or I'll hit the head off you. You've said enough. And you can get out of my house, now.'

He moved towards the door, stopping by it.

'What about Bethan? Think about her Tegwyn. It's not fair.'

Tegwyn jumped up and across to Richard grabbing him. 'Don't you dare. Fair, with me! What's not fair? Me, her, you, your father, your grandfather. Your brother, Mervyn. Where to start on fair. Now get one thing straight. I won't have her involved, understand, or I'll wish I'd thrown you overboard with Pete. I should have let you join your father in the bottom of the sodding sea.'

'You've every right to be angry, Tegwyn and I wish it was different. And it could be, if you wait to hear what I've got to say.

'I've heard enough.'

'Listen, we needn't get Beth involved in any of this.'

Tegwyn was about to ask why, then, bring any of it up, but Richard pushed on. 'You've only got to agree to have a DNA test. Then she need never know about it. It's not her fault,' he added, 'or yours, Tegwyn. I know that and I'm not blaming you.'

'Blaming me! Why don't you just piss off out of my house. And, you tell your bloody mother I hope she drops dead.'

Forget it ever happened! Just stuff it back in its box and pretend your ears weren't burning at the nudges and innuendoes when he was a boy. Two fingers to all those the prissy, small-mouthed village gossips. What did he care, back then, what they thought or said. And if his father didn't bother, why should he? Now it had re-emerged like a viper from the long grass, vicious-tongued and with a deadly venom. It was impossible to push away or ignore – the rogue gene in a wild game of poker.

20

For three days and nights Martin had been stuck in a hell hole, unable to break out and make a run for it. Here was gunfire, then nothing, though he knew the snipers were there, taking aim behind a wall of a house, resting the barrel on a windowless frame until someone moved. It was May, the prettiest month, with white- and black-thorn in creamy blossom, and crab apple and wild cherry, and the cuckoo's calls echoing through the lettuce-leaf foliage of beech and birch, with, up on the hill, wild space and heather. He'd give anything to be back there, to go home to the hills and sheep and wild weather. The soldier had a longing for rain, sitting crouched, clammy with cold in an arid country whose boundaries had been ripped up and so misaligned that nothing was left. Nothing that Martin Price could interpret, sent out to try to help dismantle the vehicles of a war that he didn't understand, that maimed indiscriminately.

He'd been waiting a long time, ever since Gareth had been killed, and when it finally happened, at the split second of impact, he remembered thinking before he was catapulted into the air, how it came as a relief, releasing him at last, and how he'd no longer have to think, anxious in the expectation of being hit. He would no longer fear the unknown.

In the event, he couldn't hear himself screaming. There was a loud deafening roar around him and within him, like the roar of water crushing him under its weight and magnitude. The soldier was unaware of any pain or injury, but somehow he couldn't or didn't try to move, his face to one side in loose dirt, suspended in time. A second, minute or quarter hour – he'd no idea, blacking out, embracing the loss of feeling and control. It was as if nothing had anything to do with him anymore. He no longer needed to worry about bombs, land mines, or children being blown to bits on his watch, as he let go in bizarre sense of joy.

In rheumy light, on a mattress of something wide and soft, he saw outstretched pink arms with yellow fingers come to caress him, to make him better. His harsh burning throat meant that he could only croak, his mouth split open by the heat of the blast. Was that his old friend and comrade Gareth come to him? There was a searing hot pain from his leg to his groin as he felt himself being lifted. Then he mercifully passed out. When he came to, he had no idea where he was. The room was dark. There was no sound, no voice, nothing. There was a stir in the air as a figure bent over him to check that he was still breathing. There were no words of comfort as hands felt over his clothing and through his pockets for an identification, not caring when he called out in pain as his open wounds were prodded and his burnt flesh seared. He knew he was very weak and could feel blood seeping through a crudely tied cloth. A hand hesitated, fingers feeling inside his breast pocket, not for any heartbeat or sign of fever but latching onto something solid. Pulling it roughly out, the figure took it over to a covered hole, pulling back the makeshift blackout to let in a shaft of light so that the object could be examined more closely, rubbing it gently with a finger. Furtively it was slipped away in a concealed pocket, and as silently as the figure came, he or she left, leaving the soldier alone.

Had he been captured? Was he a prisoner of one of the insurgent groups? Or had he dragged himself to this blown-up hut, picked clean by a scavenger of war and left to die? He had no idea of how he came to where he was, no recollection after the explosion. He drifted in and out of consciousness, the pain always unbearable when he was awake. Yet he listened through his laboured breathing for any sound that might connect him to the outside that would acknowledge him as existing, as being alive still. He forced his eyes open and stared at the ceiling, the simple structure that hid the night sky and stars. He had no concept of time, or of place, other than a room he was in. Lying on what was left of his clothes, with no blanket or pillow, he shivered in the cold. It wouldn't be long, he thought, before his body would be drained of its blood and he'd be allowed to die.

The pain brought him back, searing and penetrating as any dagger, making him gasp as a man wrapped cloth on his throbbing leg. Another rubbed his burns with some strong sweet smelling ointment, and a woman – he could tell it was a woman from her touch, her hands smaller and deft – poured a little water between his parched lips. Without a word he was lifted and carried out. He could not remember any details of the journey, blissfully unaware of the jolting trek over the rough terrain, carried like baggage over a shoulder, or was it a donkey, with its strong smell?

That he survived the blast was a miracle, but more so that he'd been taken, but not tortured, kidnapped or killed, and treated, then left in a place where he'd be found by Coalition soldiers. He had been stretchered off to a waiting vehicle and taken back to camp to the field hospital where the medics worked on saving his life.

They heard it on the news, as Huw Edwards, one of their own, reported the death of two soldiers in combat, Paul Jenkins, aged twenty-seven and Darren Rogers, thirty-three, from Cardiff and Pembroke Dock. Their next of kin had been informed. Martin Price, an engineer with the regiment, had been badly injured. His condition was critical.

They flew him home, when he was fit to travel, to the specialist burns unit for the beginning of what would be a long process, He would need many operations to reconstruct his body and face, using the latest plastic surgery procedures to rebuild the blown-off side of his face that had taken the brunt of the blast. The loss of a limb was less problematic as he could hop to get around and learn to use a prosthetic foot. His face was an altogether more complicated proposition, apart from his obvious disfigurement, the practicality of using it to function was almost impossible.

Left with only half a jaw, Martin couldn't eat or speak properly. His hearing had been seriously impaired and his eyes would need several operations. Although his wife Katie had been forewarned that his face had been badly disfigured, and that he would be heavily bandaged and sedated as he had lost losing thirty percent of his skin on his face and arms, she was unable to disguise her shock on seeing him lying there up on the hospital bed. His eyes were open but askew in a face mostly hidden by bandages which nonetheless failed to conceal its contorted nature. He couldn't smile to show any pleasure on seeing her, or grimace as he watched her trying to hide her shock. He felt sorry for her, having being lumbered with him. It was not what she had said 'yes' to, a few months previously. He was too sedated to be able to express his mental anguish, and because of the nature of his injuries he had no functional eyelids, so he could not shut out the world. It left him with a perpetual unblinking stare as he watched her and her dawning of horror at the thought of having to look after him.

He did not wish to hold her to her promise, even though she continued to come dutifully to see him, trying to sound encouraged by his small progression which the nurses breezily informed her about. She couldn't see any big improvement herself. Their meetings were awkward and restrained as Katie went through the motions of saying how he looked better and was told he was coming along. She tried to block the awful details of how she'd have to cope to help him with his eating, going to the toilet, not being able to do anything for himself, a knack the specialist nurses encouraged, which once learnt made handling him easier for them both.

There were endless surgical procedures that would eventually help him regain some use of his face. His life was an endless round of operations, grafts, and physiotherapy, with the nurses cajoling, teasing and praising him for any seemingly insignificant improvement, not allowing him to become morbid, wheeling him into a roomful of other injured soldiers, lifting his spirits by sharing experiences. From the outside, Katie tried to join in with the ward's sick humour, to laugh rather than wince, to sound positive at any improvement, the plates in his jaw to join it back, and false teeth after everything had been pinned together; a perfect plastic smile to go with the plastic-looking skin of his unnaturally stretched face that made him look like a fish with bulbous unblinking eyes. The hair on his scalp grew back in tufts that made him appear mad. Later, when he'd been discharged, she'd wheel him about, away from the safe seclusion of the hospital, his appearance to the outside world being a truer indication of how he really looked. People didn't hide their shock on seeing him, they would move out of his way, disguising their abhorrence with a sympathetic smile. Their children were more honest. 'Ugh! Did you see that! What's wrong with him?' they'd asked, pointing and looking back as Katie hurriedly pushed pass to escape their gawping.

For all their skill, no surgeon or psychiatrist could repair the damage inside his head, as he sat looking out of a bedside window onto a British summer, blue sky above green grass, the sound of birds, of playground games at a nearby primary school, wishing he'd been killed alongside Gareth rather than sent home, mauled like a dog's dinner. Nightmares would cause him to wake up screaming, hands over head, curled up in an act of cowardice while his wife tried to soothe him, at the same time hating to touch him as he shivered in his misery. Better by far the solemn dignity of a box draped with the Union Jack and a military funeral, hailed as a fallen hero, as a crowd clapped sincerely, throwing down a flower in front of the cortege as it passed at a sedate pace, his regiment sombre, yet relieved that he'd gone, one liability less, dispatched honourably. But, no, as fate would have it, he had been saved by a precious Turkish relic, knowing nothing of the family history behind it, of the life that had been laid down for love, as Martha searched for her William so many years ago.

'Poor bugger,' he thought, seeing a clip on television of badly injured men, smiling through horrific injuries at a rehabilitation centre, as they learned to walk, to climb a stair, or play a sport from a wheelchair in a PR exercise to boost morale and raise money. Only Martin knew what they'd have to go through to get where he was, better men than he, having to come to terms with their injury and to make a new life with plastic limbs.

From the comfort of his kitchen, Richard watched the report, vaguely wondering if he would see Martin, knowing he'd lost a foot and had had intensive reconstructive surgery. Seeing them struggle with grim determination to do a task he took for granted, he thanked his stars he had never been in the army, or been called up to any war. By comparison, he had little to grumble about. So what, that the harvest had been of poor quality and late; they still had plenty and would manage. They had their health, a beautiful place to live, no real threat of massacre or bombing to mess up their backwater, their safe lives. After seeing what the soldiers had to put up with, Richard left the house, crossing the yard with a spring in his step, thinking how lucky he was, the only immediate blight being the dilemma with his sister and how to persuade Tegwyn to take the test. Beth was beginning to show signs of a tummy, and the time for any termination, was becoming critical.

'Why are you looking at me like that?' she asked, catching Tegwyn studying her as she bent down to get a casserole from the warming hob.

'Can't a man admire his woman for no reason? I was looking forward to my tea, if you really want to know. Nothing to do with you as it happens!'

She served up, calling Clare from the sitting room where she was playing on the computer.

Again she caught his sideways glance, but let it rest, not questioning him as he wiped up the last of his the gravy with a slice of bread.

'I'll clear up. Why don't you put your feet up and I'll bring you a cup of tea. You look tired, Beth.'

'Thanks, Tego, you are an angel. Where would I be without you?'

Later when they were alone, the telly on in the background, Tegwyn sat down beside her, putting a hand gently on her stomach. 'You're OK, aren't you Beth? I mean feeling everything is all right, you know as normal as pregnant women are?' He sat patting her tummy gently.

'Yes, of course I am. Why, do I look that washed out? You'll get me worried, Teg. Do I look so terrible?'

'No, of course not, *cariad*. It's just I've never been in this situation before and I don't want you under any extra strain, that's all. I want to take care of you.'

'Sweet man,' she thought, his concern etched across his brow. 'Having a baby's a natural process, Teg. It's what millions of us women do every day so why should I be any different from all the other women going through the same process. Look,' she continued, rubbing his arm in reassurance, touched by his apprehensiveness, 'I know you're concerned about me after what happened before. But you needn't be. This time it is totally different. You can see for yourself, I mean, look at me, I'm positively blooming,' she said, showing off her bump as she pulled her T-shirt tight to accentuate it. 'And I'm well, safe, at home with you, and the rest of my family on hand. I've been given another chance, Teg, to be happy and I am here with you, and although it's late to have another baby, I'm not really too old, I mean look at my brother and Penny, they had no problems, so you mustn't worry. My check-ups have all been fine and I'm being monitored for any complications. So there's nothing to worry about.'

'I know, it's just me wanting it all to be all right.'

'We're both very lucky and come the autumn you'll have your work cut out, so I'd make the most of the peace while you can.'

Boosted by Beth's assurances, he sought out his brother-in-law to explain he'd got things wrong.

'She says she feels fine, Richard. There's nothing wrong with her, or the baby.'

'It needn't show up on a scan, but it doesn't mean there won't be. What if it's mental in some way? Or, because of its genetics it dies very soon after birth? Can you afford to put Beth through that risk? You, above all people, know how she was, and that she must not go back to that time, not at any cost, not if you love my sister as you say you do. That's why you know you have to have this test, Tegwyn, if only to safeguard her.'

They went together, concealing their true intent, pretending they were looking into a potential purchase of a bit of farm machinery Richard had spotted advertised in the *Farmers Guardian*, and that he needed Tegwyn to accompany him to the sale. With his superior mechanical knowledge, Richard would be less likely to bid for a dud with Tegwyn to guide him.

It was a cover that allowed them to sit in a hospital corridor, waiting for a quick needle and sample of their blood, uncomfortable with the collusion and the thought that they could be so closely related. Had Tegwyn's initial attraction to Bethan been because of their shared genes? No, he would not believe that, although he'd become self-conscious of his crooked finger, crossing his hands when he sat, hiding his left under the opposite arm as if anyone would notice other than himself, exposed thanks to Richard.

Afterwards he nearly came undone, pulling off his shirt and vest to get into bed when Bethan noticed the small round plaster in the fold of his arm.

'You all right Tegwyn?'

'Yes, why?'

She pointed to his arm which he tried to cover, laughing it off as he pulled the plaster away.

'Oh, that. It's nothing.'

'You've been for a blood test? Why? You never said you needed one.'

'Because it wasn't important.'

'So why didn't you tell me?'

'Because it was so unnecessary, I forgot, that's all. They said I needed a check-up after that cut with the chainsaw. Something about checking my anti-tetanus. It took all of two seconds and everything's fine."

Not quite the medical procedure, if she remembered correctly, but he obviously didn't want to make a fuss or talk about it and she let it be. He was a law unto himself, but who was she to question him when he'd never deceived her, never let her down. She would not let herself start to doubt him, he was nothing like Malcolm and would not suddenly change. He had always been hopelessly honest, wearing his heart on his sleeve. He had never hidden anything from her in the past, so why would he start now?

How to explain that he'd loved her all her life, not because of an attraction he couldn't justify, but because of something much deeper and closer that he'd kept earthed, undisturbed and left to decompose with time. It had not been easy to have it dug up, when the exposure would force him to consider it, with the imminent arrival of their offspring and the consequences it would bring.

Tegwyn was nervous, eager to be out in the morning and in the yard ready to take the post whenever it arrived. The time was less predictable than in the old days when one could count on the post being delivered to the nearest five minutes. Nowadays, anything between ten and noon was normal, making waiting for the mail a nail-biting and time-consuming activity. He was lucky, he had things to do about the place, as he watched for the red van swinging down the lane, anticipating that all-important buff envelope that contained the vital confirmation.

Bethan had two weeks or more of him being edgy, not irritable exactly, but not the easy, affable Tegwyn either, and she wondered if it was the unseasonable hot dry spell, or more probably the likelihood of more wind turbines on their hill that made him so unlike his usual self. Bethan knew he'd had a recent run-in with Richard over the windmills, but it wasn't his land, it was her brother's, and in the end what he said, went. Tegwyn knew that both she and Penny were in favour and he was seriously outnumbered in the family now that his former ally, Richard, had changed sides and come out in favour of the turbines. He'd been bought, of course. Persuaded by the promise of a regular income to help with the farm's viability, so the outcome shouldn't have come as a great surprise, not when you added it to the general situation of the farm – the general phasing out of Tir Mynydd subsidy, for less-favoured uplands, not to mention the general cut-backs in agricultural grants that made a big difference to the farm's income. Organic prices were holding out better than commercial farming, but the cost of organic inputs all but negated any gain. The hill farmers were back to where they started, struggling to make a precarious living, off sloped fields and sharp hillsides looking out over Cardigan Bay. Was this what made him so uncharacteristically on edge? Or, was he ill, there being more to his blood test than he was letting on?

She hadn't seen him searching for old family photos, any snapshot that might reveal the relationship, waiting for a time when the house was empty so he could rifle through her possessions for old pictures of Ianto and them as children; that he looked at her, not as she supposed to see if she was well, but to spot any shared resemblance in feature or habit. Was it that he tortured himself over the fundamental reason for his attraction to her all those years ago? An unknown bond, conjugated by the same root? It was not only affecting his bond with Beth, but with the rest of her family. He didn't want to come into contact with Richard, not until it had been resolved, and he resented the fact that Elin and Mervyn had ever brought the possibility up. It would have been so much better to have let sleeping dogs lie. Now the balance between the three units had been fouled, causing it to alter irretrievably. Bugger them all for interfering.

Beth had no inkling of what was really bothering Tegwyn, puzzled as to why he'd got up suddenly, leaving half his dinner, in a rush to go out. Perhaps he had money worries, or he really was concealing something about the doctor? Only, Tegwyn had never really bothered himself with either his health or his finances, having the philosophical attitude that tomorrow would look after itself. Perhaps it because he was about to become a father for the first time. Perhaps he felt too old, too set in his ways?

'I know what's wrong with you, Teg,' she said, when he returned with the day's post which he plonked down on the table.

'Oh?' Taken off guard. 'There's nothing wrong with me.'

'You're worried about the baby. That's it, isn't it?'

Concerned at once that someone had said something or that she'd found some proof, his reaction made a poor show of hiding his startled feelings, as he almost jumped away from her. 'What do you mean? Why, has something happened? Of course I'm not. Why, who have you been talking to?' Trying to cover his anxiety, waiting for her reply.

'No, nothing, Tegwyn. But we will manage, you know. The noise and sleepless nights won't last forever. The first three months are the worst, and it's not going to cost a fortune, you know, it'll be on the breast.' She smiled at him and he relaxed letting go of his held breath. She didn't know.

'If it cost the world, Beth, somehow I'd find a way.'

'Dear sweet Teg, I know you would, and in case you've forgotten, we've got the wool money accounted for. Rhian's bought it at a much better price than we would have had from the Wool Board. So you needn't go fretting your little head over our finances, and I'm sure Mam or Richard would help if we got really short. We'll be fine. We're one big happy family who look after each other.' He was so good with children, happy looking after Malcolm's daughter as if Clare was his own, but perhaps a new baby would be more of a challenge for him and the thought of crying, nappies, teething and infant ailments were too daunting for him.

For a horrible minute Tegwyn had thought someone had spilled the beans, but Beth was still thankfully in the dark.

'I know we will be, sweetheart.'

'So, promise me you'll stop worrying. I prefer the old Teg, the one who laughs, who hasn't a care,' she said, giving him a playful kiss, her hand on her tummy. 'Only a few more months.'

There was nothing loud, or profound in her ending. No last gasp, as Elin let go, her breathing less regular and shallower during the hour before her lungs stopped. There was no bedside vigil to witness her dying, in her own bed at three in the morning. Later he would wake, looking across at his bedside clock. Quarter-past-four and as he'd done for the last couple of years, Mervyn got up for a pee and went down to make himself a cup of tea and check on his wife. He could tell before putting on the light that she'd gone, and he sat down heavily next to her, picking up a frail hand and putting it to his lips. '*Cysga mewn heddwch, fy nghariad annwyl.*'

His life's reason for getting up each morning had now gone. There was no glorious fanfare to acknowledge the passing of a quietly prestigious life, holding her family and farm together in a community she'd lived in since the war. She'd witnessed changes, had worked tirelessly to keep the farm afloat as it adapted to fluctuations in market forces. It was always a time of uncertainty, and she'd held her ground, kept them going forward to where they were today, finally letting go like an old dog on its mat, in sleep. He sat with her there, having no wish to go across and announce her death, which would make it more real, preferring to recall the bygone age that had been his and hers. He didn't want to have to listen to their sympathy, their embraces and handshakes, or to witness any release of grateful tears, secretly relieved that the matriarch had finally let go, obviating any need of future homecare and cost. Their kind words would be platitudes, about a long, a blessed life, about a loving mother and grandmother who would be missed, and about how he couldn't have done more for her, or been a more devoted partner, etc.

'Oh my sweet Elin', he said, stroking her arm, 'where to go without you by my side.' He sat quietly beside her as another morning broke into the room, with a lifetime of memories that bound them together on a path that had been far removed from the modern world. They had lived at a different pace from this new world, and although from the outside, it would have been looked on as a simple life, it was no less profound. Eventually stiffness forced him up and he went out to their small garden. He left the roses, but bent down to cut off a few sprigs of lavender, her beloved herbs, thyme, rosemary, mint and sweet marjoram. She would have liked the scent of them in her room as he put a few sprigs in a small vase and placed them on the windowsill next to her bed, the smell evoking memories that were so her that it made him cry in pitiful slow sobs for all their time now gone.

'I wish she could have waited until the baby,' Beth commented as they sat round the kitchen table discussing the funeral arrangements. 'I know she couldn't have done anything, but I would have loved her to know she had another grandchild and whether it was a boy or girl.'

Richard deliberately looked away from Tegwyn and Mervyn not wanting to catch their eye, instead changing the subject abruptly. 'Simon rang to say he was sorry but by the time he could get a flight from Sydney the funeral will have been.' Simon rarely came home these days, busy with his career that involved a lot of travel. After the Sydney Opera House, the WNO was on tour, travelling to Melbourne, then Adelaide and on to Perth. Another flight home was not what he needed and her death had not been unexpected.

'At least Rhian's coming up from London. She was always very close to her Nain,' Richard said.

'Richard wasn't very sympathetic, was he?' Beth said to Tegwyn back at Tan y Bryn. 'It's almost as if he's glad Mam's gone and won't see our baby. As if she was in the way.'

What could he say – that he was also relived that she'd died and so wouldn't witness any similarity? Let her take it to the grave, because Tegwyn had made the decision that, whatever the result, there was no way he'd tell Beth.

'I don't think that's the case, *cariad*. It's just he's got a lot to organize. You know, Richard was never one for sentimentality.'

'Unless it's about Sion. Then it's a different story.'

Considering her age and health, which had kept her out of general circulation for several years, Elin Davies's funeral was still well attended. Most of the older Llanfeni residents, Elin's contemporaries, came as a mark of respect. It helped she'd died in summer when the weather was hot and the chapel cool, rather than that chilly damp of winter, and the event, because it was seen as an event, offered a good chance for a bit of a social get-together, with the comfort of community singing of well-known Welsh hymns. Although chapel attendance had fallen away drastically in the last twenty years, for the older generation chapel still held an importance in their lives, especially at Christmas,

Plygain, Easter, and Thanksgiving, as well as weddings funerals, and many came to see Elin off, knowing there would be a good tea afterwards and a chinwag. When all the hand-shaking and pleasantries had been done and said, the tea eaten, and people sated with talk, they departed in dribs and drabs until it was only the family left.

'You sure you don't want to come back with us, Uncle Merv?' Richard asked, not wishing to leave him on his own in the graveyard.

'No, you go on, I just want a little time on my own. I'll walk down after.'

'If you're sure.'

He sat to the sound of the sea and the call of gulls, and the salt smell of the sea, in a place she had so loved, her beloved farm fringing cliff and mountain. He walked a little way along the cliff path to capture an essence of her there with him, like a soothing unction. The odd walker nodded as they passed, looking back at the old man, incongruous in his black suit on a sunny day, standing so near the cliff's edge, wondering if they should stay in case of an incident. Tufts of pink thrift trilled in the breeze upon perilous rock, where nestled the fleshy creep of flowering sea sandwort. A gull glided down onto a nearby outcrop of granite, giving Mervyn the once-over, superior on its domain with its sharp yellow bill and imperious eye. It was a bird Elin had always admired and Mervyn felt heartened by its call of defiance, two fingers of indifference to him as he had no food to pinch. It took off again, crying as it flew over the sea, leaving Mervyn to his thoughts. Only after the sun dropped did Mervyn retreat back along the path to his cottage, less sad than if he had not sat on the cliffs. He would go there often in the following weeks, making the most of the dry summer, evening or early morning, in the times he missed her most, so that he could sit by the cliff to be near to her, hearing her voice as she spoke to him through the beauty of nature. He was lonely, for all that the family rallied round keeping an eye on him in his solitude. He was patient in the time left to him, as all he wanted was to join her when his old body would allow.

21

At least her Irish granny was still alive, and unlike her Welsh *nain* who she never really knew, Clare could remember talking and being read to by her, and although she had only seen her once since they'd moved back to Wales, the family had stayed in touch, Clare emailing her often with photos of what she was doing. She explained to Moira that her *nain* had died, but she had been old and she hadn't left her bed for ages and couldn't speak and although Mam was sad, she said it was a blessing that she'd gone. Moira emailed back to say she was sorry and to give her mum a special hug from her. In a following email, Clare attached a picture of herself on her pony Merlin. She was proudly wearing a pretty felt cloche hat, with embroidered foxgloves circling up from the rim and Beth was standing by her daughter, holding onto the pony's head collar as she smiled at the camera.

Dear Granny,
This is me with my pony Merlin, who is a Welsh mountain section A. He is very sweet but sometimes quite naughty and sometimes puts in a buck when he's feeling frisky. Uncle Tegwyn says I can take him to the Llanfeni show this year without being on the lead rein if we practice enough around the farm a lot first.
I'm busy doing a painting for the school competition and when I finish it I will send you a picture.

Mam has a big tummy and says the weather is too hot,
but i like it as i can play outside until late. I cannot wait to
have a little brother or sister to play with.

My hat is from Auntie Rhi, who made it just for me. I love
it and wear it all the time and everyone at school wants one.
Would you like one as well?

lots of love
Clarexxxx

He sat staring at the image, his expression unreadable except for his eyes. Unblinking like a snake's, they held her gaze as he looked at her smiling face on the screen, his pupils concentrated to small black pricks in his silent rage. So, his wife was happily pregnant, it would seem, with another man's seed. Well, he'd see about that and this time he'd do it properly without any interference from his old mother. At least Beth's mother had had the decency to die and clear out of the way. He'd monitored them long enough and now she was pregnant, it was time. He savoured the thought of her, incapacitated, swollen in late pregnancy, or better still going into labour, leaving him a clear field. There would be dates available, falling conveniently for him to execute what he'd been planning ever since she'd left him and done a runner. She'd be shown graphically that she had lost, and that he was more than a match for the likes of her. She'd not behave like she had and get away with it, not if his name was Malcolm O'Connor.

At the sound of a tread on the pebbled path, he clicked the computer window closed and started the shut-down before she had put her key in the lock to open the door. He moved lightly and swiftly to the kitchen door, half opening it for her, the unexpected sight of him in her locked house made her half cry out as she started in alarm. A sly smile stretched across his insolent lips as he looked at her with hate.

'Ah, did I startle you. You jumped like a ferret, mother,' he paused, emphasizing the word, 'mother' for effect.

She chose to ignore this, accusing him instead. 'What are you doing in my house? How did you get in? I don't remember inviting you.'

'Does an only son need an invitation from his own mother?' Never missing an opportunity to twist the knife. 'I came to call on you, but you weren't here, so I let myself in. I wanted to see how you were keeping.'

She knew it was a lie as he made a show of stepping aside to let her pass with an obsequious bow.

Sarcastic little shit that she'd ever given birth to, and he was not her only son, Kieran was a better boy dead than he was alive.

'The only time you'll want to know how I am is when I'm stiff as a board.'

'It can be arranged.' He gave her one of his lop-sided smiles. 'Anyhow, shouldn't you be at your old cronies' playing bridge?'

'Since when were you my keeper? What business is it of yours what I do and where I go? And, what have you been up to in here? I don't like you in my house, you bring a bad smell. You came deliberately, knowing I wouldn't be in. What have I caught you up to? No good, you can be sure.'

'Don't you trust me? Your own flesh and blood. How your words can hurt.'

'Now there's a word you've never understood. Trust.' She wouldn't trust him as far as she could throw him.

'You, of all people, mother, should know more than most how much I did trust. Only to be undone bit by bit, and I'm sure you don't need any help in remembering the day when you finally shattered any self-belief I might have had.'

'Pah! If it's sympathy you want you've come to the wrong place. I won't lower myself to your level and I'm not in the mood for your games. What are you really here for?'

'Nothing, as I said. I just came to call as a dutiful son. But I can see I'm not welcome.'

'Knowing I'd be out! Well, whatever it is, you'll get no help from me. No alibi, nothing.'

'Charming. As if you could ever help me.'

'Now I want you out, before –'

'Before you'll what? You stupid old crone. How could you ever think, even in your wildest dreams, that you could possibly have anything I'd ever want! Do you think I'd come here for anything from you. Love or affection for your little baby boy! Hah! As if!'

Did he give the last word a slight inflection, or was she imagining it? Hold your ground, don't let him read any flicker that might give anything away. Worse than a raptor, he'd sense it. Was that what he was in her house for? Snooping for morsels?

He looked at her, holding her in contempt. To think she had so much to answer for. His milky angst that had soured into hatred for her. He put his foot in the door as she tried to force him out.

'You were never born innocent. Not like –' He cut her off in mid sentence, finishing it for her

'Like my little, perfect brother, Kieran. You and my fecking father never stopped telling me. He was a saint and should be canonized, I know. But he's dead and there's only me left. Oh, and then there's my sister, but of course she doesn't count.'

'You're pathetic!'

'I'm truly touched.' He put his hand to his mouth, quickly making the sign of the cross and bringing his hands together in mock deference. 'But enough, I cannot banter here with you all day, much as I'd like to. I have other fish to fry, dear mother, and I'll wish you a good day.' He smiled again, his eyes like nails. 'Don't worry, I'll see myself out,' as she made to push him, his body stiff in resistance as he stared with a look that could kill.

After he left, she slammed the door, shaking in shock.

It was time for a reconnaissance, as he hadn't been there since their wedding day, and he wanted to examine the exact lay of the land for himself and check his assets for the windfall he anticipated. 'Uh!' He thought, excited at the prospect of getting so close, up onto their hill, totally legit, to observe them, unseen until he chose to expose himself. The shock it would give them to see him there and to learn that they had unwittingly sold the right to him, as a director of Atlantic Energies, to inspect the turbines whenever he chose, walking over their land willy-nilly and paying him indirectly for the privilege to boot! To see him once would be enough for the Davies's, but with the freedom to come and go as he pleased and never knowing when that might be, would prey on Bethan's mind, just as he intended it to do. It was a costly revenge, worth paying if it achieved what he wanted. He wanted to watch her from the initial shock until he'd worn her down and broken her. He wanted to see her squirm, quickly losing her new-found lustre. He wanted to witness at first hand her disintegration, so that she would come to him and beg him to leave her alone in her precious Welsh home. There would be nothing her family could do about it – brothers or boyfriend.

He flew into Cardiff, hired a car, and drove up over the Brecon Beacons, going north-west to Llanfeni. Approaching the hill from the east, he followed the specially-built mountain road to the substation, stopping briefly. Then he drove on past the grazing sheep that were unperturbed by the hum or the rotation of blades. The turbines were impressive close up. He got out of the car, enthralled by the size, with each turbine turning their three huge blades in the steady wind. This is what he'd invested in, each one fifty metres high on a concrete base that supported the eighty ton steel pillar. He sensed the enormity of them, filling the landscape, and for a while he stood entranced. They gave him a sense of power over the people below. He sniffed, pulling his overcoat closer, firming down his hat before slinking off along the road to the newer development over on the Davies's hill.

It felt good standing on their land, on top of the brow looking down at the town barnacled against the sea, with dwarfed farmsteads divided by hedge and field boundaries with small lanes like blood vessels linking them together. He felt like a bird of prey, preparing its pounce. He produced his racing binoculars from his pocket. Well used to bringing a distant object into focus, he easily found the pinpoint of his interest, zooming in on Tŷ Coch, then following the hedgerow down to the roof of the old blacksmith's. He scanned across the patchwork of fields, looking at their stock – Ayrshire cattle and Lleyn sheep – hoping to catch someone outside, uninterested in the expanse of the pewter dull sea. He noted the crop of oats greening on long stalks and the fields empty of animals, left for the first late cut of silage. Like a connoisseur, he savoured the intimacy of being there, walking where their feet tread, prying into their personal things. Malcolm swung his binoculars over the two fields, keeping the best to last, to what he knew was Tan y Bryn with it's neat little yard, the stacks of timber, round saw and mobile saw confirming that it was the right place. He felt an evil satisfaction as he zoomed in on a garment of hers drying on a clothes-line next to his daughter's frock, T-shirt, pants and bras, ignoring the male underwear of the usurper Tegwyn.

He lingered before finally moving away to a pony, his daughter's, in the paddock by the house, with a plastic, brightly-coloured feeding bucket by the gate. He mustn't lose sight of his purpose which was to make a careful mental map for future reference. It was fortunate that he himself was a man of the soil, able to read the signs. Wild life was an excellent warning system in case someone should catch him unawares – the sudden alarm call of a small bird, or the shriek of a jay, even something less obvious like a sheep lifting its head. He watched as the cows grazed their quota of fresh grass, their noses all but touching the electric fence as with dexterity, their tongues curled round the tempting grass just under the fence line, avoiding any shock.

The young cattle looked well, growing fat on the land, and as he studied the layout it gave him an added thrill to see them looking so comfortable in it all. It was so much better this way than if they had been slummy and impoverished by the foot-and-mouth epidemic, which would have lessened his satisfaction at their imminent demise. It was something to look forward to. He would enjoy the hunt, the coming and going in order to familiarize himself with their farm, hidden by the turbines like an elaborate hide. He would be ready when the time was ripe, slipping between high hedges and banks that would shield him so that he could show himself to maximum effect and scare Beth out of her wits. There was no hurry, as it was he who was in control. He would choose the time and place, checking Google Maps and and the Ordnance Survey map in the back in his car, until he knew every blade of grass, every gate, and all their comings and goings. For now, though, as it was the first of many visits he planned, he was content to stand on the hill, anticipating her shock with a quiet malice.

The family were quite unaware that they were being spied upon, as work on the farm continued at a frenetic pace, as they tried to catch up on the months lost to bad weather. Everything was late and the first crop of silage was well down on the previous year due to the late, hot and unusually dry spring. The lack of water did not suit the thin porous land, more suited to Welsh downpours blown in from the Atlantic.

Although there was less of it, the grass was nonetheless high in sugar and very nutritious, and hopefully as Richard spread the cleared fields with slurry, the second crop would be denser, with a wet July forecast.

Penny's high-end meat products were selling well, but they were still working on the catch-up from the lost market following the foot-and-mouth. By the time Richard accounted for the cost of producing the bullocks ready for slaughter, and the expense of packaging and delivery, together with work on their revamped website, which Penny spent hours each night replying to, it was still a business that only just made a profit, and that was without adding any proper wage to the equation. Like so many other small rural businesses, the farm was only just staying afloat. It was all well and good to say it was a way of life, Richard thought to himself, driving his tractor over the fields with muck spewing out of the spreader, but with all the hard work and long hours, the truth was that without the EU farm subsidy and Penny's much-needed cash input during and after the foot-and-mouth, the farm would have gone under, and the only way that farmers were going to survive the promised cut-backs was to diversify into renewables, borrowing more and amalgamating small family hill farms into big single units that would be able to produce the cheap food the consumer demanded. Although he was well aware that his farm came under this heading of being small and unprofitable, Richard continued to work his land the only way he knew, content to work from day to day, his family by his side, in the hope that, it would still be there for his son to follow in his footsteps.

When she arrived, Rhian was in great form and delighted to be home. She hit them like a blast of warm air, rushing up from the city full of its vibrance. She was doing very well with her millinery business. The hats she created had been flying off the shelves and she had great plans for the future. Her dad had never seen her look so stunning, with a new-found confidence that gave her a light quality that was infectious, taking him out of himself, so that for a few days he stopped worrying about the farm's finances. Her being there with a completely different take on the world helped lift the family's spirits and she was a brick at her *nain*'s funeral, taking round tea and scones, listening to the chat about the old days and taking the time to talk to the pensioners about a period she didn't remember. She had another day before she was due back in London and, giving up on the poor mobile phone signal to get her emails, she popped across to catch up with her aunt. If no one else in the family seemed pleased for Teg and Beth, Rhian made up for it with her spontaneous enthusiasm, commenting on how well Bethan looked and how pregnancy suited her.

'Honestly, you look years younger, Beth. If this is what it does to you, perhaps I might be persuaded one day!'

'You thinking of settling down with Ryan?'

'No, but, we're still together, and with the band, it's pretty cool. I don't want to just yet. I'm enjoying my new-found success and am far too busy running my business for now.' The baby moved, Beth's shirt rising and falling as it changed position. 'Look at it kicking. Can I put my hand there?'

'Sure. It's very fidgety, never stops moving. The only time I get any peace is in the swimming pool. As soon as I get in it suddenly stops moving, and seems to relax in the water. Perhaps I've got an Olympic swimmer in the making!'

'Well, you know what you must do, make sure you book yourself in for a water birth.'

Beth's tum had become quite extended, the skin wriggling under her lycra top, and to Rhian she looked fantastic, her face aglow and happier than Rhian could ever remember her. If anyone deserved having a bit of good luck in her life, it was her kind and generous aunt.

'I can't understand why your dad doesn't seem very pleased that I'm pregnant. He didn't say anything to you?'

'Dad? No. Why shouldn't he be? You'd think he'd be the first to be absolutely delighted for you. You probably got him on a bad day, he's always been prone to be a bit grumpy when he's faffing about the farm. I wouldn't worry, it's just Dad being Dad. I'm sure once it's arrived he'll be a very proud uncle. And, I know Penny's really looking forward to you having a baby, she said so just this morning at breakfast how it'll make a world of difference to have another young person around and a playmate, a cousin, for Sion, otherwise he'd become impossibly spoilt!'

'It's a real tonic having you home, Rhi. I wish you could stay longer.'

'I can't, but as soon as you get your first twinge, promise to let me know and I'll do my best to get here, to be with you during your labour. How's that?'

'Would you, Rhi? I'd love it if you could. A bit of moral support.'

'Just book the birthing pool.'

He ran, covered in sweat, as quickly as he could, breaking cover toward a helicopter, as a volley of gunfire ricocheted over his head and he fell to the ground, covering his head from the falling debris. Pain, searing pain, rotor blades throbbing in the background, as a hand grabbed him. No Garry or friendly face, but wrapped up in black, slits for eyes as he jabbed him with a knife, slipping away before he could scream.

'Martin, Martin it's all right. You're safe. You're here, home. Shhh.' Katie put an arm on his clammy, shaking body as he became aware of his surroundings. The wallpaper and curtains, the armchair that he spent most of his time in with its added arm, that helped him manoeuvre in and out of it, needing a little less help from her. She was careful not to sit near the stub of

240

his lost limb which still caused so much pain. And the burns, the scars, that had changed his features out of all recognition, so that he was no longer the good-looking man he had been, the expression in his eyes permanently changed, open-eyed and blind.

'And, sex, I hear you ask? My wife can hardly stand to be in the same room as me, and my injuries are an excuse to keep out of our bed in an act of compassion. As if I could even contemplate sex! Ha, would any living thing lie next to me.'

Martin Price could not even tolerate a sheet on him and when she lay on top of the blanket to try to appease him, to let him fondle her breasts, it was a thrill-less torture. A sick man with his false limb resting by the chair, his charred body being stretched back together with skin graft by slow skin graft, and the human mind thinks of sex. As Price does, unbalanced when sober, with nothing in his flaccid penis, drooping bal- less between his thighs. There was no honour for this soldier, no looking at such damaged goods, and no such military covenant that had promised to care for the injured veterans, at least not long term. Just a quick fix to sew him back together as best they could, then out, with not even a placebo to mend his broken head, leaving him to his family with nightmares for company. Rhubarb extended its fingers under yellow light searching for him, his fear always giving him away as he whimpered like a puppy, waiting for the slick beating, or steel knife that left him screaming.

'I've nowhere else to go. I've tried everything. I had to ring somebody.'

'No, Katie, of course you were right to ring. I'm sorry it's been so difficult for you. And for Martin.'

'He's been through hell and it's not his fault. He's still there if you see what I mean, living the war, fighting.'

'Poor sod. You know, you see them coming home on the news and you think what they've sacrificed, and then you get on with your life and tend to forget. Not like you having to live with it, seeing your husband suffering twenty-four hours of every day. It must be physically, let alone emotionally, exhausting.'

'It is, and if he was getting better there'd be some hope.'

'Beth told me he was improving with each operation?'

'Oh, they're patching him up slowly, and he can just about walk now he's got his new limb, but there's only so much the rehabilitation therapy can do. Whenever he goes out people stop and stare. It was easier for him in his uniform, at least they could see then that he'd been fighting for his country, but now he's in civvy street, he's shut himself out. I can't get close and nothing I try to do for him helps him.'

'I'm sure it does, Katie, even if you don't feel it is.'

'He shuts me out, Richard.'

'He needs specialist help. Isn't the Ministry providing support? They must have special teams trained in this sort of long-term trauma.'

'They were very good to begin with, you know, helping him, skin grafts for his burns and fitting him with a new limb, and the rehabilitation centre helped at first, but now he's on his own and there's no funding, what with so many injured soldiers coming back suffering from post traumatic stress and I don't think they know what to do. They're only scratching the surface, leaving our lads to cope on their own.'

'It's a disgrace, if that's how it is.' He stopped himself from ranting on about the gung-ho policies of the politicians, quick-fixing nothing and causing a whole lot more instability.

'I'm frightened for him, of what he might do.'

'Do you think he's suicidal?'

'He doesn't want to live.'

'Of course he must be depressed, anyone would be after what

he's gone through. He's lucky to have you and your family to support him.'

'But, that's the problem, you see. He doesn't know anybody else up here, except us. I mean we got married and then he had to go straight back out to Iraq, and he's come home blown to bits and with nowhere to go. And he's very self-conscious about how he looks, especially to strangers. People who don't know him stare at him as if he were some sort of monstrosity. So he won't go out anymore.'

'I can appreciate that. So how can I help you? What can we do?'

'He's put me in a very difficult position but he's asked me to ask you if he could come to stay for a bit. I know it's a huge imposition and I wouldn't ask if I wasn't desperate.'

'No, of course you wouldn't, and I'm sure we can do something. Tell him, will you. But first I will need to talk it over with Pen, and she's out at the moment. Let me ring you back this evening.'

'I would have rung Bethan and Tegwyn but I know her baby's not far off and, well, I hope you don't mind.'

'Of course not, and you were right to ring me. It's the least we can do. We owe it to Martin. I'll speak to you later, and chin up, Katie, it'll all come good, you'll see.'

Coming through the door carrying her shopping bags in one hand and Sion in the other, Penny was in need of a coffee, and was surprised to see Richard in the house.

'Something wrong? Has something broken down?' They didn't need another hefty bill, hoping it wasn't one of his tractors out of action.

'The power drive's gone on the Massey, I came in to ring the engineer and they're sending someone out. I can't afford to have the tractors idle. Did you have a good morning? *A ti Sion? Ysgol feithrin yn hwyl?*'

243

'I need a caffeine fix, town was heaving with holidaymakers – you couldn't move.'

'Kettle's just boiled.'

He waited until she'd unpacked the shopping and taken her first sip of coffee before he brought up the phone call.

'While I was in, Katie, Katie Price, you know, Martin's wife, rang from Yorkshire.'

'Sorry? I was miles away. Oh, so how was she? And Martin's recuperation.' She caught his expression. 'He's all right, isn't he?'

'Katie's fine. No, actually she's not. In fact, Penny, she sounded a bit desperate on the phone. At her wit's end.'

'Poor thing. It must be hell for her. Everybody praising Martin, coming home a hero, leaving her to pick up the pieces once the news interest has passed. They hadn't been married very long had they?'

'A few months.'

'And here he is, shot to hell and a complete invalid needing constant care. She's had a raw deal. Do you remember the last time he was here? Before he was posted back to Iraq, he had those terrible shakes, panic attacks, and didn't Beth find him sobbing in the lane?'

'They should never have made him go back out, anyone could see he wasn't in a fit state.'

'So what's happened? Has he had a nervous breakdown or something?'

'Pretty close.'

'It's the army's fault, sending them out unfit for duty. He'd already done his duty in Bosnia.'

'She's asked if we would help?'

'Us? But how? Do they need money?'

'He wants to come and stay here. She thinks he'll be better among people he knows, by the sea, in a place he knows well, where he used to run with his old mate Gareth.'

'Wasn't he killed?'

He nodded.

'You're not serious, Richard. Him staying here with us?'

Richard didn't answer, waiting, knowing her to be a compassionate woman.

'For how long? Do you know what it means, to have a real invalid to look after with mental problems? And where would we put him? I mean, can he even get up the stairs? And there's Sion to think about. It'll upset him, to see someone like that. Couldn't you house him out with Mervyn?'

'He's just lost his wife and he is in his late eighties, Penny.'

'I know,' she sighed, 'It was really awful of me to suggest it – it's just that there is a bedroom made-up downstairs with a window overlooking the yard, so he'd feel included and he might be company for Mervyn. Don't look at me like that, I was only thinking aloud – it could be a short-term solution. Look around, Richard. It will be really difficult here, there are steps coming in and out, steps down to the buttery, the stairs from the hall are narrow and there's only a small bathroom which is full of Sion's stuff, unless he uses ours, en suite, and I don't fancy him hobbling through our bedroom every time he wants a piss. It's very impractical for an invalid.'

What did he expect, that Penny would jump at the idea of having a virtual stranger, mentally unstable, sharing their house, however good he'd been to the family in the past? Bethan was the nurse, not Penny, and it should be she who should have Martin if anyone. 'After all,' he thought to himself, it was his sister who'd got them into that frightful situation in the first place. He knew he was being unfair but he was cross with her for the mess of it all, Tegwyn, the baby, and now Martin Price.

'Do you think I want him any more than you? But what was I to say, I mean, he saved all of our lives didn't he.'

'That was a bit different, you were on the beach, nearly

245

drowned, and he happened to be there and helped pull Tegwyn from the water.'

He looked at her, knowing what she said wasn't quite fair.

'Don't look at me like that, Rich. You're right. I'm sorry, and what he did was heroic and we all owe him. It's just that if I'm being totally truthful, I'm not good with deformity or other peoples' illnesses. I know I shouldn't think like that, let alone admit it, but it's the way I feel.'

'You're not the only one, Penny. I don't know how I'll react on seeing him disfigured, as Katie says he is, but I owe it to him, and it's too much of an ask to dump him on Beth and Tegwyn, just before the baby. It needn't be for long, just to give Katie a bit of breathing space.'

He didn't tell her that Katie had said she thought the marriage was over. Martin no longer wanted to live with her. It was better for them both to get a divorce. Take it one step at a time.

'So what shall we do? I promised to ring her back tonight after talking it over with you.'

'No option, is there. You'll have to say yes, but it can only be for a very short period and if we can't cope with him, Katie will just have to take him back, she'll have to understand that.'

He came over and kissed her.

'It's very generous of you, and I'm sorry to have lumbered you with it. Most people wouldn't have agreed, so thank you.'

'No more than a week, as a respite for Katie, that's all we can do for him.'

When he told Bethan of Katie's plea for help, she was indignant that he hadn't agreed for Martin to stay with them instead of at the farm.

'He should stay here with us, Rich. I'm the most qualified to look after him and I'm home the most. Clare's at school all day and Penny's got the business to run and Sion to look after. It would be much better if he stayed here with us. Poor man. He should never have gone back out. He wasn't himself was he? Hadn't been for months. He was shaking at his wedding, dreading leaving. Even during the foot-and-mouth, he showed classic signs, jumping at loud noises and trying to hide his shakes. They don't care about them, they're just a rank and a number.'

'You're hardly in a fit condition to lump a fifteen-stone man up and down the stairs.'

'Then he can sleep downstairs. Tego'll help me make a bed up in the living room.'

'You're cramped enough.'

'That's as maybe, Richard. She should have rung me, poor girl, it must be awful for her, on her own with him and so early in their life together. These politicians have got a lot to answer for. I'll ring Katie, and tell her he must come here.'

'Let's play it by ear. Wait and see until he arrives and what he's like. I haven't told Penny but when you ring Katie, well, she told me on the phone she and Martin, well, it isn't working out and he says he wants a divorce. I thought I'd better let you know before you make the call. Don't over-commit.'

'Is it that bad?'

'Sounds like it, Beth.'

'Where will he go?'

'Exactly. Even if he comes, and it's OK, and he and we manage, he still can't stay here forever. What do we do then? If he won't return and it's all through for him here, I don't want him cutting his ties with Katie, otherwise where will he go, and what will we do with him? I mean he can't work and there's nothing round here. You know when Mam was poorly, how little there was in social services, and they're fully stretched, and virtually non-existent for his type of injuries, and who's going to drive him the hundred-mile round trip every time he needs to go to a hospital?'

'To begin with, perhaps we can share him and lessen the

strain on you both. And if Katie has a break, some space, it'll help them and may bring them closer together.'

'Or drive them further apart,' he thought.

'And your baby's due in the autumn. What then?'

That's if she managed to have it at all, the baby being another potential unresolved nightmare ahead of them. He wished the DNA results would hurry up. He thought he'd made it easier for the scientists, producing his late father's flat cap, the one that he always wore, which he had found tucked away with his mother's things. He couldn't believe it was so slow, unless Tegwyn had had the results and was keeping the news from him, which could only mean one thing.

22

It was going to be an exciting day and Rhian had woken early, helped herself to a pomegranate fruit juice from the fridge, a quick cup of coffee and an apple to eat on the tube. She checked that she had everything in her portfolio, before she bent down to kiss a sleepy Ryan who'd hadn't come in until the small hours after a gig.

He muttered, half asleep, raising a thumb at her for good luck before he pulled up the duvet and turned over. She pushed her hair that lay across one side of her forehead, so that it looked more like she wanted it, made a face at herself in the mirror, wishing her image luck, and left the house, pulling the front door shut behind her. She checked her mobile for any text messages as she walked to the nearest tube station. It was still rush hour and she knew the tubes would be heaving, but before she got to go down the escalator she saw that there was a problem with people pouring out from the underground, and police ushering crowds away from the entrance.

'What's happened?' she asked a bystander.

'A fire or something,' he shrugged, turning away from the rush.

'Damn,' she said aloud, looking at her mobile to check the time, thinking it was lucky that she'd allowed herself plenty of time. Clutching her portfolio closely, its size inconvenient in the crush of people which was made worse by the added inconvenience of a station out of order, with police forcing everyone out of the area and along unfamiliar routes to work. Rhian considered hailing a taxi as she couldn't afford to be late for her meeting, looking for a black cab in the gridlock.

It was busy on the farm, the second cut of silage needing to be collected before the Royal Welsh Show, where Penny had a stall in the food hall for their organic mountain range of meat and cheeses, and where, if she could get it ready in time, she planned to launch of their new soft, creamy brie-like cheese which had a blue vein for an extra kick, 'The Llanfeni Blue'.

The cows out and grazing until three, and the milk away, Tegwyn was ready to help make a start on the first of the silage fields, while Richard started on the top field furthest from the barn.

It always gave him a thrill as he put the mower down, driving along the outside to make the first rip, keeping a close eye at the side as the swathes of grass fell tidily under the blades, all the hard work of spring behind him, rewarded now by the smell of sweet, thick meadow grass with red and white clover that added valuable nitrogen to the soil, making it more productive. Before he'd gone round twice, a red kite had appeared, hovering above for the easy meal of an unlucky mouse scampering from the tractor's wheels and machine's blades, or crushed, to be taken later as the wilting grass was scavenged at dusk by owls.

Seeing the post van from the field, Tegwyn stopped the

tractor and walked the two fields and lane home. He knew its route and judged the time that he'd meet it before it pulled into Tan y Bryn.

'*Dyma dy bost i ti, Tego. Dirwnod da am y cynhaeaf.*'

'*Ydy. Gobeithio bydd e'n para hyd ddiwedd yr wythnos.*'

The van turned round, saving time and diesel by not having to deliver right down the lane and into the yard. At last, the brown envelope he'd been waiting for. He ripped it open using the high hedge as a screen from anyone looking. He read it and then re-read it, focusing on each word, to be sure he hadn't misunderstood. Then he whooped for joy, putting the letter back into its envelope and into the back pocket of his jeans, bundling up the other bits of post and junk mail as he raced down the lane like a boy on holiday.

Coming into the kitchen from the bright sunlight momentarily blinded him and he had to blink, to catch his excited breath, seeing Martin start.

'Sorry, Martin, I didn't mean to startle you. It seems so dark in here after the sun. I should wear sunglasses. It's very strong. Is Beth about?' His suddenly bursting in like that was tactless, but he was so over the moon at the news he'd received that nothing else seemed to matter. For weeks he'd been living in a secret dread that his whole life had been built on a falsehood and now, whatever they had said, it hadn't. He was who he always assumed he was.

'There's been some bad news.'

'Sorry, what did you say, Martin? What bad news? Is Beth all right? Where is she?'

She's gone over to the farm, to find Richard. There's been a bomb in London.'

So what, was his immediate reaction, thinking only of himself and Beth and his good news. Perhaps it had something to do with Penny and her family who lived there.

'Are you all right on your own, Martin, if I go over and see what's bothering them? I won't be long.'

'You've only just missed her.'

He'd come across the fields to meet the post just as she'd walked away down the lane to the farm. Tegwyn didn't wait to see if Martin needed him to stay but, eager to show Richard and Mervyn the letter that held the proof, he left and walked quickly down the lane to Tŷ Coch in bright sunlight that dappled the hedge's thick covering of leaves, his heart glad and full of life for his baby, *his* now, with every chance of being born normal and healthy. If he'd been alive, he would have hugged his father and mother for being his parents.

The mood in the farmhouse was sombre, Richard still sweating from his work, his unwashed hands not touching the full mug of coffee. The was a strong smell of tractor oil and grass as he stood next to his sister, both studying her mobile intently as she scrolled down the messages.

'She sent me this text, the first, look, it was before eighty-thirty, asking me to wish her luck for her meeting.'

'Then what? How do you move this?' her brother asked, handing the mobile to Beth to scroll on down.

'I texted her back saying good luck, see, only she didn't need it, I knew she'd be fine. Then about half an hour later she sent this saying there'd been a bomb scare and she had to change her route as her tube station was affected, and it was heaving with people trying to get to places via different routes. I texted her back asking to keep me posted. I heard nothing from her after that. And I put the television on for Martin while I took Clare to school, and when I came back I saw there'd been another explosion, this time on a bus. I think it's the route she said she was being made to go. I can't raise her. There's no answer to her phone. I've tried and tried.'

The atmosphere along the Euston Road was very different to a normal working day, heaving with more people along both pavements. Many were commuters who'd been ordered off the underground by the police, who were trying to find an alternative way to their places of work. Rhian tried to walk back down toward King's Cross but was prevented from doing so by the police who sent her back to Euston. She, and many like her, only added to the crowds already on the Euston Road, all searching for a way through the city's gridlock and she felt suddenly vulnerable, trapped in the city's network.

Being relatively new and unfamiliar with London, she didn't know any short cuts, or trust herself to try and walk another way, so she could not hope to pick up a bus, even if she managed to manoeuvre round the blockages. She no longer knew in which direction she should go and tried to ask a man in a suit, but he just said something very quickly, heading off in another direction, leaving her with many others who confused, not knowing what to do or where to turn.

Her mobile wouldn't work to ring Ryan for directions, and anyhow he wouldn't pick up, probably still asleep. Equally frustrating, she couldn't contact the department store to let them know that she was caught up in the snarl up after the scare. Moving with the crowd, she found herself by the bus station and got on a bus. It was already full downstairs, so she made her way to the top of the double-decker, having been forced to leave her portfolio in the luggage space on the lower deck since she couldn't get it up the stairs. It made her even more anxious, not having it to hand, and although the back seats had already been filled, she tried to position herself near the mirror as that way she could see down the stairwell to her folder. At least then she'd have a chance of calling out if anyone tried to nick it. She wasn't even sure where the bus was going, or if it was even remotely on her route, but at least it was moving away from Euston. Once clear, she'd find another tube station, where it would be easier with its maps to work out where to go, and in which direction. Perhaps by then, too, the traffic would have cleared and with time so short, she'd be able to hop into a black cab.

She tried her phone again but there was still no signal, so she tried to relax and not think of the pressure of time, or what she had rehearsed to say, keeping an eye on her large folder, thinking of its contents, its inspiration coming from her childhood – the Welsh uplands and woolly sheep, gales from the sea; the natural environment transformed into the pictures, photos, and prints of her hat designs for the following autumn/winter collection. She wished now she had an old Walkman or something so she could listen to music to distract her. In the house, Radio 6 would be playing, as she liked working to music, hoping the DJ would choose to play something from The Lites and then she'd be able to tell him later that she'd heard them on the radio. She looked across at her fellow passengers and then out of the window at lines of cars parked up, as they moved at a snail's pace toward Tavistock Square. The way the traffic was going, she'd be lucky to make the meeting.

From her vantage point she saw a policeman walking to the front of the bus, beckoned over by the bus driver. Diverted from his usual route, he also needed directions. She remembered looking at her watch, it was past nine-thirty and she had forty-five minutes until her appointment. She could just about make it in time barring further traffic disruptions.

Then it hit. A huge roar, as the roof of the bus tore off, taking with it bits of red metal, with glass flying everywhere. Like a sheet ripped from a washing-line, the top of the bus flew off down the road behind them. She remembered standing up, of feeling strangely exposed, her ears numb, not hearing the screams, seeing the carnage at the back of the bus and below her, as she and those around her stood, bleeding and shocked by the explosion. People stood watching in horror as, in slow motion, they witnessed the blowing up of the No. 30 double-decker bus.

People on the pavement were stunned by the sight of so much carnage in what had been transformed in seconds into an open-topped bus. On the lower deck, too, many passengers had been killed, with several severely wounded. Luckily, the parked vans and cars had served as a shield from the flying shrapnel of metal and glass. Soon, only shreds of paper still floated like confetti in the air.

Rhian couldn't recall how long she stood there, how she was helped off the bus, or how she got down from the top deck, her head and face bloodied by bits of flying glass. She remembered seeing police, hearing sirens and watching doctors, all running to the scene. She saw the bus driver, being led away by a policeman and two ladies standing on the pavement, blood on their faces and clothes and someone by them treating them as if she were not there but watching it all unfold like bystanders. Then someone took her hand and asked if she was all right and she nodded, still too stunned to form words. Only much later, after she'd been taken to hospital and her cuts and bruised lesions had been dressed, did she shake in delayed shock, aware now of how close she had been to losing her life, images of the dead and mangled bodies jumbled in her head. She recalled the goodness of others who came to help with no guarantee that there wasn't another bomb onboard, the efficiency of the professionals who treated them, moving the worst of the injured first, and the police cordoning off the area for the public's safety. She thought of Martin, his war more real now, brought violently into the heart of London. The terrorists, who killed thirteen people on the bus, had been indiscriminate in their destruction.

Penny had phoned Ralph in London to make sure their two girls were not involved and after he'd confirmed that they were fine, she concentrated on finding out where Rhian was, ringing the central emergency number given out on the news bulletins. Richard paced around the kitchen, unable to settle, and at her suggestion, eventually went back outside to his fields of hay.

'I promise as soon as I hear anything I'll come and get you. There's no point in both of us watching the phone. You're better off occupying yourself. Keep busy, Rich. Remember, no news is good news.'

Reluctantly, he left her by the phone to return to the harvest. The grass, having wilted, needed to be chopped and put in the pit before it dried too much. At the top of the yard Tegwyn was waiting for him with a tractor and forage trailer attached.

'Heard anything?' he asked, as Richard approached.

'No, nothing. It's all chaotic with the tube bombs and the bus, the police can't confirm how many people have been killed or injured. They haven't been able to get to everybody yet. It's terrible, Tegwyn. The pictures coming out of London – I dread looking at them. What if I see Rhi there?'

'But you don't know she was anywhere near the explosions. London's a huge place. And even if she was around there, they say thousands of people had been diverted by the police, so more than likely she's been re-directed by the police and is stuck somewhere.'

'I hope you're right, Tegwyn. I can't sit in there and watch, and I can't think about the bloody harvest. I need to know my daughter's safe.'

'Of course you do. If you like, I can get on with the silage on my own.'

'No, Tego, it takes two and I can't stay indoors, waiting for the worst. Penny's promised to come over straight away. She's much better than me at getting information. She knows the area, the places Rhian said she was going to, so she has a better understanding of where the explosions are and how that might have affected Rhian's journey. I've no idea of how London works and where's where.'

'She'll be all right Richard, you'll see. And I know now is not a good time, but at least I've a bit of good news that will lessen one of your worries.'

'Oh,' he didn't seem very interested.

'I've had the letter and it proves I'm not related to Beth or you. I'm not Ianto's son. Here, look for yourself,' he said, taking the envelope from his back pocket and handing it over to Richard. Squinting against the sun, he read the short paragraph with some analytical data that showed that there was no match between the two DNA samples, confirming that Tegwyn Jones was not related by blood to Bethan O'Connor née Davies.

He proffered his hand, and Richard, his mind elsewhere, seemed slow to take it.

'Good. Sorry, Teg,' briefly shaking the offered hand, 'I can't think straight, not until I hear she's OK. But it's good news for you and Beth,' he added, handing him back the letter. He said no more but got up into his tractor, driving off toward the cut fields. Tegwyn followed with the trailer, miffed at his brother-in-law's response.

He understood he was anxious about his daughter, but the chances of her being caught up in the bombing seemed remote, taking into account the millions of people in London going to work on any given morning. It was Richard who'd made the stink about his relationship with Beth. Richard who pointed the finger, throwing out the accusations that had caused Tegwyn such doubt, and for what – nothing that he didn't know already, even if he couldn't prove it, until now. His word had not been enough for the doubting Thomas. And now he had his proof, Richard had waved it aside, barely taking the trouble to read the letter – six weeks of worrying unnecessarily, tossed aside as if it hadn't even mattered. Not that he would ever have told Beth.

And in any case, it would have been too late if the results had been the other way. He'd have taken the risk, never mentioning their connection, hoping the baby would be all right. He was innocent. There never had been a wrong to put right or anything to own up to. Thinking about it, he didn't feel inclined to help his brother-in-law with the silage.

He got back into the tractor, sitting stubbornly in the seat without turning on the ignition. He sat there brooding, putting the letter back in its envelope and, lifting his bum off the seat, slipped it into the back pocket of his jeans for safe-keeping. Then he started up the tractor, following Richard along the field of mown grass. Later he'd make sure that Mervyn and Penny saw it before he destroyed it. Bethan was never to know that there had ever been even the slightest suspicion of a taint on their relationship.

It wasn't until mid-afternoon that Penny had confirmed that Rhian was alive and all right. She had been involved in the carnage, a passenger on the No. 30 bus that morning, trying to get across central London, and had been one of the passengers caught graphically on someone's mobile phone, dazed and in a state of disarray on the top of the bus. She wasn't recognizable as herself, standing amid the debris. Rhian Davies was one of the lucky ones.

23

After she'd been treated and discharged, Ryan came to collect her from the hospital, taking her back to the house in a taxi. For a few days he stayed with her, making sure she was all right before he went back to his music and the band. Rhian didn't want to be left sitting in London on her own, feeling the need to distance herself from the bombing, to be away from the constant noise of the city's traffic, so she went home to Wales, back to the bosom of her family, to recuperate. Now she understood, more than most, what Martin had been through, and was still going through. Her experience on the London bus had left indelible internal scars, as well as marks on her face and neck, but unlike the soldier, her bomb blast had been a one-off, happening in her own, normally peaceful, country. She'd had all the support the rich capital could offer where the medical teams had been excellent, proficiently stitching her up so there'd be no long-term ugly scars, and she had her boyfriend there for her.

She'd not been bombarded day after day, anticipating treading on an IED, or being captured and tortured in a hostile land, fighting against her will. Nor had she had to witness the murder of her best friend, failing, when it had been the soldier's job, to spot the buried mine that his comrade had trodden on. And she had youth's resilience on her side, knowing that, with time, she would get over it and get on with her life. Her Mad Hatters business was a saving grace, making her fight against her new fear of claustrophobia, of being stuck in a metal casing; needing a window seat in a train, plane or car, fighting the nausea of paranoia and determined not give in to it. She had been so close to death that she could say to hell with it, and live her life, determined to recreate her portfolio and take it back to the buyers, with the farm and the natural world her inspiration.

When her cousin showed her the painting she'd done for the school competition, Rhian was genuinely impressed, and quietly pleased to see Clare showing signs of following in her footsteps with an eye for art. She studied the composition in front of her, the skill belying the child's years. She'd painted a rock pool, full of sea creatures with, centre stage, an enlarged hermit crab, its claws and legs sticking out of its periwinkle shell. The pool also had some green-grey rock shrimps and a starfish at the bottom on the sand. On the sides, dark red anemones clung to the black rock, their sticky tentacles outstretched, waiting for a meal. At the other end, Clare had painted a dogfish hiding beneath seaweed, while a gull perched on a nearby rock. For the background, she'd put in their farm, with the sheep and cows and her pony, as she proudly pointed out. On the skyline there were wind turbines on the hill. It wasn't just the imagination that impressed Rhian, but the way she'd put it all on paper, aware of each space without swamping the scene. And she'd painted it all in bright colours that gave it a contemporary feel. It didn't matter that the perspective was wrong – the pool too prominent and the crab too big, with some of the farm animals larger than life as well, and the fields and mountain too steep. It was the colours she'd used which held it all together, whether by chance or instinct, Rhian wasn't sure.

'Did you do this all by yourself, Clare?' she asked her.

Clare nodded. 'I asked Mam what I should paint and she said anything but it ought to be something special to me.'

'And you chose this.'

'I can't paint people, so I didn't do Mam or Uncle Tegwyn and I tried doing Merlin but he didn't look very good, so I sent that one to Granny in Ireland and Mam said why not draw the beach and seaside as I love it so much.'

'And you came up with this. Well, I must say, Clare, I think it's good, it's very good indeed. You are really talented, you know. You've got a natural eye and should take up art seriously when you go to the high school. Have you shown it to your mam or Aunty Penny?'

'Not yet. I wanted you to be the first to see it finished.'

'Well, I'm honoured. Thank you, *cariad*.'

'Have you seen Clare's picture?' she asked Richard and Penny at supper. 'It's really good.'

'I heard she was doing one for the competition. It's sponsored by the turbine company as part of their community benefit promise, a goodwill gesture to get the local kids involved and interested in their environment.'

'I wish I'd had something like that when I was at school. I think it's a really great idea.'

'So do I, Rhi, and they are giving generous prizes to the winners in the different age groups, as well as some art materials for the schools. I think they're planning to turn the best artwork into posters and Arriva Trains have agreed to hang them in their stations along the Cambrian coast.'

'Very enterprising. Well done them!'

'How did you find Martin?' asked Richard. 'I feel bad that we haven't had him staying here.'

'He seems OK, Dad, considering.'

'Is Beth managing with him? It isn't a big house and he must need a lot of room, you know with all his needs.'

'Remarkably well, considering.'

'She is a nurse. I suppose she's used to all this.'

'Hardly, Dad! That's not fair. I don't think she ever had to work as a nurse in a war zone, did she? It's very different looking after someone like Martin than a person having an appendix out. I mean he's been through so much.'

'Yes, but he's getting better and there're others, you know, badly wounded. I see them on the telly, smiling, who seem to be coping and make something of their lives.'

'For the camera, Dad. And, Martin is coping, as you put it. Better than I would.'

'I think he's very brave,' said Penny.

'After what happened to me, I know I wouldn't manage in his situation. I had one lunatic that I had no idea about when I got on that bus, but Martin has had to face hundreds of them, all wanting to blow him apart every hour of the day and night.'

'It's his job, what he's being paid to do.'

'OK, Dad, it might have been. But he's done his job, and been put through hell, and I know I wouldn't have coped, that's all.'

'He was never the same after he lost his school friend, Gareth.'

'Would you be? If you saw one of us blown to bits. And he blames himself. Look at you over your cows. You nearly went to pieces then.'

'They were my life's work, Rhian. And the sight of all that death.'

'Exactly, Dad. Think if they had been humans. People you knew and worked beside. I think it's terrible that they treat Martin like they do. He's an absolute hero and ought to be recognized as such by the government. Do you know how much it has taken me to try and get my life back together these last six weeks? I wasn't even really injured, Dad, nothing like Martin. He's had to live with bombs going off all around him every time he's been out there. Bosnia and Afghanistan and now Iraq. I had one small device at the back of a bus and I've been an emotional wreck. Came running straight home to a loving family who've wrapped me up in cotton wool, protecting me.'

'I think you're being a bit hard on yourself, Rhian. You were incredibly brave.'

'No, I wasn't, Dad. I didn't make a choice. It was just random, and I had to be on that bloody bus at the time. If I'd thought there might have been a chance that this would have happened, even a million to one, do you think I would have gone near it? Never. Martin knew. He was scared stiff but still went. That's real bravery.'

That was telling them, sitting in their comfy safe kitchen with no more to worry about than the weather, milk prices and a few turbines.

261

'You're right, Rhian. We've been the lucky ones in life.'

'All I know, Dad, is it's taken me – What I'm trying to say, to explain is, I've found it so difficult to pick up where I left off. To contact the buyers and re-arrange another meeting.'

'But it wasn't your fault what happened, they must understand.'

'But you don't understand, Dad. John Lewis have been really nice to me, they couldn't have been kinder or more understanding and patient. It's not them. It's me. I have to fight, physically fight with myself, to pluck up enough courage to go back to London. To get on another tube or bus, or whatever, and take myself into the middle of the city, full of people jostling, the noise, and fighting the fear that there may another explosion. I know this is highly unlikely, but I've got to travel, get there with another portfolio, and sit down with them and try and sell my designs again, when all I want to do is hide down here, with the land and sea, and be with you lot.'

'You can, if that's what you want, *cariad*. You don't have to go back.'

'But I do, Dad. If I'm ever to make a go of my life, it's exactly what I have to do – face my inner demons, put them behind me and move on. So I begin to understand just how much Martin is going through to arrive at where he is now. And I think he's truly heroic, just incredible, and deserves all the support we can give him. You, me, Beth, Uncle Merv, the whole family.'

'If he wants, and Beth needs some space, he can come down here for a bit. Mervyn's too old to look after him.'

'I'm sure he's knows he's welcome, Dad, and I'll tell him tomorrow, before I go.'

'You're not going, not after what you've just told us?'

'Yes, I am.'

'Not yet, stay a little longer, Rhi.'

'No, I've made my mind up, and Ryan'll meet me at Euston.

It's Martin I've got to thank. And you, of course, that goes without saying, but he's given me the courage. Do you know, I saw him in the lane yesterday. He was on his own, no sticks, with his new foot. He was using the high bank to support himself as he walked. I don't think he saw me, but it took a lot of effort to take each step, to keep himself stable on the pebbles and uneven ground, and he didn't give up when he nearly fell, pulling himself up against the wall. Got his breath back, and carried on. So I think I can get on a train to London.'

The smell and the sea cliffs brought it back to him, imagining he could hear his voice, his teasing behind him as they pushed on in some youthful fitness test, Gareth always the one to win, the first up the summit, fit as a flea. How they'd shared everything, lying back in the bracken, exhausted and happy, with the rush of the waves and the call of gulls, the smell of his body intimate and familiar. He caught his look, his shrewd sideways glance, before he teased him in playful dismissal as if he were still there beside him, two young country lads with the world at their feet. Gareth, the leader, where Martin followed, always looking out for one another, closer than brothers.

He could almost smell the exhalation of his breath, as he envisaged him lying in the grass, knees up looking at the sky under racing cloud, waiting for the 'old plodder' as he affectionately called him, several minutes behind, to draw level.

'What took you?' he'd tease as Martin, breathless, couldn't speak. 'Come on, we can run down this side, meet you at The Sailors' Safety. Last one's down pays, and mine's a pint.' Knowing Martin would be coughing up. But Martin didn't mind, couldn't care less if it was he who picked up the tab. He'd happily share his last sip of water with him. When he had got concussed on the pitch and thought he'd broken his neck, Gareth had been the first on the scene, the game stopped, his face in anguish as he bent down to him. 'You OK, Martin?'

Winded that's all, and later laughter in the bar after the game when they'd drink away their inhibitions, teasing him about his lack of success with the girls, arm over shoulder in support as they swayed back to a bed, farting from excess beer in an aching easy sleep, with their own dreams of red shirts and glory. Gareth who'd continued to support him as they trained, and then the real thing, in the army, Gareth a shield from any bullying or loneliness, covering him in battle, totally dependable.

He would could catch him looking to make sure he was still there with them, accounted for. Gareth was the first to lead, never thinking of his own safety. He wasn't foolhardy, just brave and honest, doing his work to the best of his ability. He just happened to be much better than his Welsh mate, who was a good engineer but not a natural soldier.

It had been one of many bloody days when they'd been in a hidden place full of unseen danger – buried land mines being a constant hazard, needing sharp eyes and the sense of a dog to detect them. The one time Gareth had needed to rely on him and he had failed, seeing his friend blown to bits, his call just before he realized, too late, haunting his sleep. Life would never be complete without him and he knew he had to live in the place where they'd been such friends. Gareth didn't banter in front of the men, but when he sought Martin in privacy, his dark eyes looked upon him, lighting his soul. Martin preferred to remember him best as they were before any wars, there by the sea's edge among the wheeling gulls.

He drew on his dead friend's strength, to make himself fight to live, not just perfunctorily but to have some purpose when he saw none. Gareth would never have thrown in the towel, not while he had breath and he'd expect no less from Martin, even if he wasn't there to chivvy him on. He could hear him, see him, standing nearby, encouraging him with each step, calling him a Dobbin, urging him to get up and walk again. Giving in to grief and despair would only serve as a final betrayal of his memory. Gareth would never have given in to self-pity, or been pitiful. It was not in him to gripe about his lot, he was always there to do his utmost, however the dice had fallen, and Martin knew, felt his driving force at his back in the whisper of the hedge above the bank he rested against. 'Come on Martin, you can do it,' laughing as he urged him on, while he wanted to break down and cry, needing Gareth to be there, still alive.

He didn't know how long she'd been there or if she'd heard him thinking aloud to a dead friend. Slowly he twisted his upper body and turned to see who it was. Rhian, Richard's daughter, whom he hardly knew but with whom he shared a bond, both casualties of terrorist explosives. She came along the farm track toward him, and when she drew level she didn't look at him with concern or pity, instead sniffing some honeysuckle.

'It's a smell that always reminds me of home, of here, and growing up. Here,' she said, breaking off a stem full of flowers, 'Smell that,' and he bent his face to the flower, the sweet fragrance so much a part of late summer. 'That and drying cow pats baked in the sun, all part of my growing up. Only you don't appreciate it then, do you. Not until it's past and perhaps they're dead, the people who were important to you then, my *nain*, even Mum here among the cows and farmyard that she used to complain about. And now I'm all grown up and they're only there as part of a childhood memory. Placed and yet displaced. I love it here, but when I was young, all I wanted to do was get away. Odd isn't it? And without you, I wouldn't have had this,' she said, raising her hands to embrace the countryside, 'to come back to.'

'They've been very kind to me, your dad and aunt. I know I've been an imposition.'

'Martin, without you, there would have been none of this. I love you for what you did. You saved my dad and aunt and Tegwyn. If you hadn't been there that day, and risked your life to save them from drowning in that storm with those wild seas –' She paused touching his arm. 'Don't you see, I would have lost everything. So, this is your home as well as mine, for whenever and however long you want it to be, and you must never feel you're imposing upon us, Dad or Beth. If anything it's the other way round and we owe you, so you stay as long as you like, and come and go as you please. I know I speak for all the family.'

Her words warmed him and he looked at her, the scars on her forehead still prominent, even under her make-up.

'Thank you. It's the hurt, the loss of everything. It no longer exists, but I feel it as if he's still here.'

'I'm sorry Martin. I wish I could do more for you,' she said, misunderstanding his meaning, looking at his prosthetic limb, knowing he had the pills, the medication, to help him with the pain. Beth had told her that amputees suffered from the injury to the nerves, a chronic pain following amputation that could take several years to lessen. This branch of medicine had not advanced greatly. The injured may have better prosthetics, but doctors were no further advanced in understanding the pain they got from their phantom limbs than when the soldiers returned home with lost limbs from the First World War.

'It's all right. Me and my ghost foot,' he tried to make light of it.

'I came to say goodbye because I'm going back to London tomorrow, and much of it is thanks to you. I mean if you can get up and go, after all you've gone through, I should be able to cope with what has happened to me and get over it. You've been an inspiration to me, Martin, and it's only a train journey after all. So thank you for everything you've done for us and me.' She bent forward her kiss, taking him unawares, without cringing or shutting her eyes to close off his image, her young, full mouth soft on his sore, sensitive skin, in an impetuous gesture, and he felt a huge sense of gratitude, holding this young woman in his crummy arms.

A month later, they shook hands with her, her original drawings, photos and pictures in a new portfolio on their desks. Material switches passed between the two of them as they listened to her talk of her journey, of studying art and design in South Wales before moving to London. They looked carefully at her pictures as she explained her ideas and inspirations, curious but trying not to look at her face too intently, to see the telltale scars left from her recent injuries. Both buyers had already had a meeting to discuss her beforehand, agreeing to buy something from her, as she'd shown a tenacity to succeed following such a severe setback. It would make good publicity, something the British public would want to support, a young, bomb-blast victim succeeding.

However when she turned up in person, they were genuinely keen on what they saw, as she spread her portfolio across the table, showing them her designs. Her hats, not just her trademark woollen felt fedoras, but her berets with a twist, a black cherry, damson, or raspberry at the centre of the top as the tab; traditional flat caps for men redesigned for women in a modern take. Their favourite had to be the hats for young wearers – Rhian's selection of children's hats, especially her cloche hats, depicting beetles, ladybirds, caterpillars and grasshoppers, had immediate appeal and they had no hesitation in buying up her entire stock ready for the following autumn/winter season and they wanted to arrange a photo shoot with her with the children wearing their colourful bug hats.

24

There was a heatwave in August and the beaches heaved with holidaymakers and day trippers making the most of the last bank holiday before autumn. Family groups spread across the sand, covering the whole of Llanfeni beach with towels and beach paraphernalia as the sun rose in strength in a lucky cloudless sky. Children shrimped excitedly and, too hurriedly, in the little rock pools, failing to lift a prawn or cautious crab from under the camouflage of bladderwrack, and too slow for the shrimps jumping along the sandy bottom in front of any bright net. In the distance there was the sound of bat on ball, cheers, and 'run', as desk-stiff fathers chased an easy dropped catch, much to the delight of the young, running between make-do stump and crease to add to their score. Mums, watching vaguely, lay back, enjoying the sun's caress and peace from the 'I Wants', reading a paperback or just dreaming – the picnics, cool bags, crisps and canned drinks, enough and more for the few hours on the beach, with an ice-cream van in the car park waiting to catch them, a last treat before heading homeward.

Striped candy-coloured windbreaks served as a shield as the Brits caught the sun, taking small heed of sunburn or the threat of skin cancer. Girls in skimpy beachwear sat behind their sunglasses, people-watching. For the more sporty, there were surf boards waxed up, the surfers in their wet suits as if tackling a huge Atlantic surge, with would-be surfers standing knee-deep in the water, waiting for the next wave that bubbled them along on polystyrene boards, before fizzling out in a gentle ripple up the beach. Copied from Australia, beach guards now patrolled the stretch between the markers for swimmers and surfers alike, but today their only call was for a child lost in the colour of people, a cut finger or painful prick in a heel that had been put down on the back of a weaver fish hidden in the wet sand of the incoming tide. Further out, black-suited long-board riders bobbed astride their fibreglass boards, turning in to the land when they saw the chance of a roller, paddling fiercely to catch it, strong enough to stand, then letting it carry them briefly, before it petered out, as they swerved their boards into the failing crest to come off the dying wave, then paddle out again and wait for another. From the land the wind turbines like sentinels stood idly, watching from the hill.

Not her family, but others of her species, were near their goal, sliding silently toward the shore through their chosen estuaries, looking for fresh water in their migratory journeys. From larvae-leaf in the Sargasso Sea, they'd drifted in their thousands on plankton-carrying currents, curled up like snails, many never completing the journey from sea to river. These young glass eels wiggled in their silvery, semi-transparent bodies in the Gulf Stream for three years, until they searched out their shoreline, turning darker as they came on up into the brown rivers as elvers. Here they gathered in large numbers waiting for the right moment to slide their way upstream in the rivers of their mothers. Only this month, the moon and water had chosen this ill-fated date to coincide with a public bank holiday. The very traps which had been put in place by the electricity company in a concessionary gesture to the eels, wishing to felicitate their migration upstream, were unmanned and acted as their chamber of death. Falling on a holiday, the hydroelectric power station was left without supervision and the traps were unchecked. As instinct lead them on, along their mother's trail back to the quiet rivers and streams to undisturbed dark pools, they came across a hindrance to their journey. As more and more piled into the cramped space, the elvers squirmed and wriggled pushing their snouts and bodies at the solid wall, searching for a way through and out as they fought to breathe, drowning in the brown sea of suffocating writhing bodies, as humans lolled in the sun's heat on near-by beaches, unaware of the young eels' quiet catastrophe. All of a hundred and twelve kilos of juveniles – more than three and a half thousand of the critically endangered species, were unnecessarily suffocated to death through human error. Already persecuted by humans, their numbers were ninety percent down and had been in serious decline since the 1970s. Now the eels suffered the ignominy of being starved of oxygen in a place built specifically to aid them.

Later, on a regional news programme, a spokesman was quoted as saying, 'I know mistakes have been made. People have been caught off-guard both in terms of elver trapping, and the assisted migration programme, as well as the monitoring of elver numbers. It is quite clear that this has not been done properly.'

The fields lay quiet, reaped and the harvest gathered in, in early September, as if late summer drew a long breath before the dying of the leaves that turned from green to yellow and brown. Now wind and rain signalled the arrival of autumn. A hard spring had been followed by a dry hot summer that allowed the farmers to harvest their crops, putting them safe under roof or wrap for use in the winter months. It had been a difficult year for Richard, working against nature to force the best from his land, and he was not the only one battling the odds.

The wildlife had felt the same squeeze, hunger making them more daring, coming into conflict with the farmer who wished to keep them from eating the fodder he'd grown for his farm animals. It was not just the farm rats who were a persistent problem, or the rush of starlings who'd swoop down on the corn he'd feed to the cows until he covered the whole central alley with netting, but new laws which caused other wildlife to suffer. With the obligatory removal of any fallen or dead stock, it denied wildlife the chance of scavenging a meal, depriving them of a rich source of protein just at the time when they had their own young to feed, forcing them to become emboldened in their fight for survival.

During the lambing season, Tegwyn had come running down the yard to tell Richard he'd had to chase a red kite trying to carry off a live lamb from the field. Never before had Tegwyn witnessed any bird of prey pluck a live lamb from its mother's side, and only after a frantic chase on the quad bike, hollering and shouting after it, did it let go of its prey. And that had nothing to do with its pursuer, as the kites had got used to being hand-fed by humans, but the fact that the lamb was too heavy to lift high enough before it could clear the hedge, forcing it to drop the lamb as it lifted over, failing to bring a meal home to its starving chicks. It was a year when pairs of ravens worked to harry a ewe giving birth, distracting her as one ripped out a live lamb's tongue or eye, maiming it so that it was unable to suckle, a knock on the head being the only humane solution. It was a season when the ever-growing badger population sought fresh food supplies, with young lambs bitten and left for dead, or dragged bodily into their set. And with ever more farmers opting to lamb inside, there was a scarcity of any afterbirth or stillborns on open fields and hills, forcing the hungry wildlife population to become more daring, invading food sources close to people, risking being poisoned or a shot.

Even herons had to make do with frog spawn drying by the edge of a shrinking pond in their need for food, as the small fry and elver numbers had crashed to the extent that they were in danger of becoming extinct. Wild animals that had been common in his childhood had changed places with the ones he now saw daily – badgers and foxes were a common sight, but hares, hedgehogs, pine martens and weasels were a rare treat. At least the dry spring had brought an abundance of rabbits that helped redress the imbalance, but Richard thought it a pity that those who were responsible for making laws were not there to witness the consequences of their legislation. It was doing more harm than good in his mind, leaving the countryside a poorer place. It was the result of a knee-jerk response – poorly thought-through regulations made by people who understood nothing about the land.

The animals lower down the food chain were being decimated by the protected dominant predators that killed off the smaller species – mice, voles and shrews, ground-nesting birds whose eggs were being eaten. The same was happening to fish and eels, to frogs and toads and newts, with fewer worms or beetles left to help the soil replenish itself, that had long since been dug up and eaten.

He didn't like the way modern trends were going, the economics that would make only big factory farms survive in the future, where there would be even fewer scraps for the surrounding wildlife. It was unhealthy, he thought to himself, a feast-or-famine attitude, that housed animals, milk and meat under one roof, with zero grazing. Vast lakes of slurry were poured onto large hedgeless fields. There was no room for weed or copse or bumble bee, no tree or margin for vole or barn owl and bat, and the only poppies to be found were on the graves of soldiers. For the first time, as he stood by the barn door looking at his store of crimped oats, he was glad to see the end of the summer. Normally as he felt the change in the wind, he'd wish for a prolongation of the warm, light evenings, but not this year. Perhaps it was because he was getting older that he was pleased to see the summer fade, so he could put his feet up by the fireside, as the wind changed, heralding a wet autumn.

Beth was also eager to see the season change and the cooling of the days for a different reason. Since early August she'd found the heat, with her heavy stomach, a real burden. It hadn't helped that her legs and especially her ankles had swelled with her extra weight, forcing her to sit down more than she wanted, staying in the house and shade, making the hot summer days drag. As if feeling her frustration, her baby would not lie still, wriggling around like a dog in a basket trying to get comfortable, forcing Beth's tightened skin out as a tiny elbow or ankle poked in its sac. She'd had enough of Tegwyn's jokes that it was going to be a footballer or play for Wales in the lineout, as all Beth wanted it to do was settle, engage into the pelvis to start her labour.

With Martin still in the house, they hadn't been able to prepare the small bedroom as they'd planned, but as soon as she went into hospital he was ready to move over to Richard and Penny. Only for a short period, as he'd decided to settle back in Wales and was looking for a place of his own. He wasn't going back to Yorkshire, and although he was sad at what had happened, he knew that Katie was relieved to be set free and not have to shoulder the responsibility of looking after an invalided soldier with few prospects. At least here he could be of use in the house when Beth was out, so there was someone there for Clare when she came home from school, not that she needed babysitting at eight and a half.

On the Friday she got off the school bus and came skipping down the lane, a huge grin on her face as she was greeted by her mother, preparing the dinner and making a few Welsh cakes at the same time.

'You'll never guess, Mam, what I've done,' she said proudly, unable to contain her excitement. 'Mam, look!'

'What is it?' asked Bethan, wiping the flour from her hands as she turned round to give her daughter a proper scrutiny.

'I got First.'

'First, well done, Clare, First in what?'

'I got First Prize for my painting. The best in the whole school!' She was holding out the acknowledgement. 'Look. And I'm going to Cardiff for the presentation.'

'Good heavens! Congratulations, Clare! Let me look at what it says.'

'I'm not the only one who won. Rebecca John won the collage, and Josh's dog got highly commending or something in reception class.

'Highly commended.'

'And Iwan and Glyn's picture got the prize for Year Six.'

'Well done Clare,' she said, reading the bit of paper, '"The overall winner of the school for the most imaginative piece of artwork".'

'Look, Mam, I'm going to be given a special prize and we're all going down to Cardiff to the Millennium to receive our prizes from the judges. And there's going to be a special trip after the ceremony to Techniquest. Ooh, I can't wait, Mam.'

Not just the primary school but the local secondary school pupils from Ysgol Uwchradd y Dyffryn had also competed and their winning entries would also be included in the prizegiving trip to Cardiff, the best option being to share a bus with pupils, teachers and parents all traveling together. Parents not wishing to go on the trip to Techniquest, preferring to shop instead, could arrange a pick-up point later in the day.

'When is it?' Beth asked, wondering if it would clash with her dates.

'Here, Thursday, the twenty-seventh of September.'

The week she was due to give birth.

'I'd like to, but the doctor says I shouldn't go. I mean would it matter if I went into labour? I could nip into the Heath.'

'No, Beth, you'd better not. You're nearly there. Don't take the risk just at the last minute. Does Clare mind you not being there?'

'No, not really. She's got her classmates, and three teachers are going with them, so she'll be looked after. It's not as if they're unsupervised.'

'It wasn't about that. It's if she minded me not seeing her go up and get her award. I don't want her to begrudge the baby, if it comes then, that's all.'

'As if she would. She's not like that – she's been longing for it, and can't wait to have a little brother or sister to spoil. She'll be fine and much happier to know you're safe at home than if you go into labour on the coach.'

'You wouldn't want to go?'

'Me? She's nearly nine, Beth, and she's with the school. I don't think she wants me traipsing around after her, spoiling her day. She'll be much happier with her friends. She won't want her old uncle hanging around, and the teachers will watch her. They'll understand why you can't go.'

'I suppose you're right. Leave it till nearer the time, I might have had the baby early.'

'Even if you do, the last thing you'll need is a school trip down to Cardiff and back.'

'But you could go. Give me peace of mind.'

He could see she wasn't going to let it drop and that appeasement the only answer.

'If on the day you insist, then I will, but I'd find it awkward, with all those mothers, and it's so unnecessary. It's not fair on Clare, treating her like a baby, it's as if you don't trust her. And I know you do, she's a very responsible girl. Look how good she's been with Martin. Much better than I would have been as a

275

kid, she's so sensible and reliable. I understand that you worry whenever she's away from here, but you mustn't displace your fear onto her. She's so excited and to get top prize for her picture in the whole school. Wow! Let her enjoy it, Beth. She's got her mobile so she can ring you and stay in contact. It's not as if she's leaving the country!'

Two early frosts brought the yellowing leaves, the colour of over-ripe lime, tumbling from their ash, a welcome bonus for sheep and cattle alike who seemed to relish them, congregating under their grey trunks to lick up the fallen leaves, the land giving way to brown and red as cows were less keen to graze, loitering by the gate, waiting to come in to the milking parlour for their cake boost.

For Beth, the sudden change in the weather came as a relief and her baby obligingly dropped down finally, becoming less fidgety as it prepared for its birth.

> *Hiya Granny*
> *Guess what – my picture got 1st prize for the whole of my school and i'm going down to the Millennium to collect it from the energy company. A bus is going from the school with the high school as well, and some of my teachers. And after we've going to techniquest. Isn't it great, i'm really excited.*
> *lotsof love Clarexxxxxxx joio mas draw! (that means have fun!)*

25

With so much going on on the farm nobody noticed him like an old cat, spending his days mooching around the farmyard doing very little and resting by a sunny spot near the back door. Mervyn drifted in and out of the yard where someone in the family might notice him, to raise a hand. Usually it was Penny who kept an eye out, as she took Sion off to playschool, knocking on his window in case he wanted to call in for a cuppa later.

He nearly always refused, shuffling away out of the yard in a regular routine, along the lane to the spot where he'd buried his old dog, turning to face the sea and the cliff for a short while before coming home down one of the fields adjoining the coastal path, always stopping to spend some time in what had once been Elin's herb patch. It had gone to seed with many of the herbs overtaken and strangled by couch grass, only the hardy species surviving – a straggle of mint dying back into the grass, marjoram, but no thyme. Part of a rosemary bush protected by the hedge remained where the more delicate lavender had been lost to frost. He bent down, slowly going onto his knees so he could pull back some of the weed and grass with his hands, taking in the waft of herbs that had been part of her. He picked what was left of the year's rosemary to hang back in the cottage. Taking his pocket knife from his pocket he carefully cut some, leaving the stem intact. Using the hedge for support he pulled his old body upright, his joints unwilling, as he proceeded to walk back to the cottage.

They didn't need him on the farm, he was no longer helpful, but a liability with animals and machinery, not that they said as much, but he knew himself he could never run out of the way in time if a cow kicked out or sheep panicked, barging into him. The new machinery with all its high tech, gears, and instruments was anathema to him, and even the old tractor cab was too high for him to clamber into, yet he counted himself lucky, keeping his marbles and his eyesight and hearing, able to be independent and get about, and still in the home that he'd shared with Elin, with the family around. He hadn't been shunted off into one of those homes for the elderly. He hoped to remain capable enough to continue to look after himself.

They didn't look right in a vase, sitting uneasily, knowing Elin would have hung them suspended from a hook on one of the ceiling's beams. She'd insisted that her herbs infused the room better hung from above, their properties releasing their cleansing and calming aura to the whole house. In silent agreement, Mervyn got up and tied the bunch up with a piece of string. Then he pulled a chair to stand directly under the beam, and struggled trying to pull himself up onto the seat. Cursing quietly as he was unable to get the leverage he needed, he moved the chair next to the sideboard so that he could use the solid top to aid him. It wasn't quite where she'd have wanted them, but better than on a table. The large ceiling hook that once would have hung curing joints of pig would have to do.

This time he managed, using the sideboard to push himself up, so that he stood on the seat of the chair, and stretched up to latch the bit of string holding the herbs together, onto the black hook. He was pleased with his effort, looking at the bunch, knowing she'd approve, and without thinking he let go of his support, to step down just as he would have as a younger man. His old leg reached for the drop, higher than he'd remembered, to touch base with the floor, and not finding it as he'd gauged, he lost his balance to come crashing down against the oak sideboard, as the chair skidded from under him on the stone floor.

Fortunately it was Tegwyn, and not Penny, who found him there the following day, cold and still on the stone. Blood had congealed around his pallid face. He didn't touch anything, but noted there had been no sign of a break in or burglary, with nothing taken or disturbed, and with the chair still on its side, it was obvious that the old man had fallen, very likely hitting his head on the corner of the dresser before banging down onto the hard floor.

After the police had satisfied themselves that the cause of death was accidental, the body was removed for burial. The family gathered in the kitchen, brother and sister searching the rooms, in case he had made a will. Bethan was surprised to find one in the top drawer of the chest of drawers where he and Elin kept what little relevant paperwork, they had.

Not until now had they ever known his exact age, since, as he had been born illegitimate, his date of birth and early upbringing had been kept private, with only Mair's father standing by her and his only grandson.

'Can you believe it, Rich,' said Bethan, trawling through the meagre possessions from his spartan bedroom. 'He was in his nineties and we all thought he was eighty-six.'

'I don't think even Mam knew his real age. He kept that very much to himself.'

'And, look at his beautiful writing,' she said, pulling out a couplet, a simple thought beautifully crafted, a love poem to Elin. Beth sat on the bed reading the words that Mervyn had written for her mother, bringing her to sudden tears, remembering her childhood with a rush of nostalgia.

'Who would have thought such a big man like Uncle Mervyn was capable of writing so precisely, and of being so eloquent.' She sniffed, wiping the tears away. 'It's beautiful – really old-fashioned, like he was.'

'Yes he was a good sort. Come on, sis, you mustn't upset yourself. Merv wouldn't want you to. It's not good for you or the baby and Uncle Merv had a good innings.'

She sniffed, pulling herself together.

'I know. I'm just being sentimental. Thinking of Mam and when we were young and the farm and how it was, after Dad had gone,' she sighed. 'And reading this, and his will, it's just brought it all flooding back. Makes me realise how much has passed.'

'Yeh, I know. And we're all getting older, Beth, together, if it's any consolation! I'm surprised though that he wants to be cremated and have his ashes scattered along the cliff.'

'Oh why? Where do you think he should be buried then?'

'He was such a man of the soil you'd think he'd have chosen to be buried next to Mam.'

'I'm not. He was never one for convention and I think it's his way of being tactful for our sakes. Not wanting to upset anybody.'

'After all this time? Do you think anyone cares about that any more, Beth?'

'Perhaps not, but he did it then, for the sake of our children.'

Richard felt a bit hypocritical, as it was only a few weeks ago his prejudices had caused him to prejudge his own brother-in-law and his sister's unborn baby. 'That was different,' he reasoned to himself, it would have been genetically unsound and had nothing to do with anything else, remembering how he'd hated the thought of Mervyn moving in; how he'd resented the farrier replacing his father, even though his dad had bullied him and Mervyn had been a fair and altogether kinder man. All the angst had worked itself out, turned like a fallow field, to grow again with new seed as the last of the old generation was laid to rest. Soon it would be the likes of Sion, Clare, and the new baby, to take over the reins, as they relinquish their hold on the land into the hands of their children, to run things as they may.

'Come on, Rich, let's go, it's morbid sitting here and I'm longing for a cup of tea and a sit down to take the weight off these feet of mine.'

They left the cottage, brother and sister, his arm on her

shoulder, walking back across the yard to the farmhouse, with a view of the sea through the hedge. 'I can see why he's chosen it, Mam always loved the sea and the cliffs, and it's his way of being close to her, his spirit free to join hers.' she said, instinctively sure that that was what had been in Mervyn's mind when he made his will.

The old boy had very few personal possessions, and he had left everything to them – his share of the cottage, his farrier's tools, his old anvil and mobile forge – the only things he'd ever owned, given back to the family he'd adopted as his own. There was a gold ring for his son, Simon, and an engraved silver coin from the British Horse Society depicting a shire on the front, dated 1922 for Beth's unborn child. It had been his final way of showing them his unstinting support.

26

Beth took Clare down to meet the bus, which was already parked waiting by the primary school gates, as all the winning entrants and their respective parents were loading up, overseen by teachers. It was cold in the early morning with a sea mist hanging over Llanfeni, but with the prospect of a sunny day once the sun rose. Clare waved as she saw one of her chums already in a seat by the window, pointing to the saved seat. She ran toward the bus, almost forgetting the picnic her mother had prepared for her, then hastily came back for it, kissing her mam quickly, before dashing off to join her classmate, her mother's 'Have a good time and be careful', unheard, as Clare raced off and onto the bus.

Bethan stood waiting by the side of the road, saying hello to the only teacher she knew, while Miss Lewis, the other new appointment, was preoccupied making sure everyone had arrived, looking over her list as she got on the bus to take the roll call, ticking off each child's name as they answered against the excited chatter. The driver started up, closing the doors, and the bus drew away, leaving Beth and a couple of other parents waving the jolly party off as it drove into the mist down into the town to pick up the secondary school children at Ysgol Uwchradd y Dyffryn.

The ceremony was at eleven o'clock in the Weston Studio at the Millennium Centre, chosen because of its more intimate atmosphere so that the younger children would not feel daunted as they went up to receive their prizes. Afterwards there'd be photos with the local press and in the afternoon the visit the Techiquest Centre in the Bay, where a special show had been arranged for the younger children.

The journey was interrupted by the inevitable stops for a toilet break, and Clare, who didn't travel well, had to move up and sit by one of the teachers at the front, having to stop twice when she and another older child threatened to be sick. Since it left so early, the bus nevertheless still made good time, with little traffic on the A470, and only minor road works on the approach to the capital. With time in hand, the teachers allowed the children to stretch their legs in the piazza, walking around the outside of the building, the fresh sea air blowing away any residue queasiness. Then Miss Lewis called the children back to her, keeping them close, as she heralded them, with parents in attendance, through the wide glass doors, where a member of staff waited to greet them. After another visit to the toilets, with hand-washing and hair-brushing, the schools reassembled with their teachers to be escorted up the stairway to the Weston Studio on the first level.

He hadn't needed to look at his mother's computer before he left. It was pathetic that she'd changed her password, as if that had made any difference to his prying. He knew exactly what was happening in Llanfeni, but all the same looked over Clare's email to her granny, a smile forming as he read how excited she was to win and to be going down to Cardiff to receive her prize. He already knew Bethan wouldn't be going, because of the baby's imminent birth.

It had been agreed that Malcolm, as a shareholder and director, would represent the company, awarding the prizes, and he'd arranged to meet Iestyn Williams, the local co-ordinator for the Welsh area, in the Bay the day before to run through the following morning's schedule. He wanted to make sure that there would be no hiccups or loose ends. He needed a translation of Iestyn's Welsh-language speech so that he could mark it up, ready to smile, clap, or look serious at the appropriate place. He knew how important it was to have part of the ceremony in Welsh, it would give the company some brownie points and perhaps help toward another grant from the Welsh Assembly government – that, and the promise of more turbines and more work in an area of high unemployment and low wages – important points to make when he stood up to speak, knowing it would get the right media coverage in front of the Assembly Members attending.

Afterwards, the children's artworks were to be framed and hung in one of the galleries as part of an exhibition on renewables at the Centre, before being taken back to Llanfeni, where it had been agreed with Arriva Trains Wales that the paintings would be turned into posters and displayed on station platforms. The prizes were wrapped up ready and looked suitably large and exciting for the children, each one being different for the various categories. Malcolm had made sure Atlantic Energies hadn't stinted on them, wanting to make a favourable impact as well as a good photo opportunity. There would also, of course, be the presentation of enlarged cheques to the teachers of the schools involved, enabling them to buy valuable equipment –

all connected with sustainability, green energy, and the future prosperity of the area. Naturally with such a big investment the company expected good returns, but he wasn't about to broadcast the killing the directors expected to make over the ensuing years.

Everything was in place, and as he went back to his hotel for the night he felt excited at the prospect of the following day, thinking of the years he'd waited patiently, planning for his day of retribution. He strode about his room, unable to settle, the television offering no distraction as the newsreader droned on. His thoughts centered on matters closer to hand.

Pob lwc, cariad – meddwl amdanat ti
Mamxxxxx

She read her mother's text before they filed into the studio, where they were guided to their seats by a member of the Millennium staff, Miss Lewis reminded them all to switch off their mobile phones. Exactly on time, directors of the company entered with the Welsh co-ordinator Iestyn Williams. One of the men then smiled broadly at the group of assembled children and teachers, before giving a short speech.

'All the judges, whom I represent today, were unanimous in their praise of the high standard of work that was submitted by the two Llanfeni schools, and you gave us a very difficult task to choose the winners, but we're here today to celebrate those who, in the judges opinion, were the best. But before I announce the winners, I'd just like to say how impressed I was with how you all handled the subject matter. "Your Environment" was not an easy subject. The way we live our lives and treat our planet is hugely important and affects us all, not just now, but crucially in the future, and it took a lot of foresight on your part to envisage this, and I commend you all for having a better understanding of your surroundings and the natural world than some of our politicians. However I'm not here to bore you with a lecture but to congratulate you all and celebrate such excellent achievement! Thank you all very much.'

Iestyn Williams lead the clapping as Mr O'Connor sat down, opening a bottle of Welsh mineral water and, pouring himself half a glass, took a sip. Iestyn stood up, waiting for the clapping to die down. It had been agreed beforehand by Malcolm that Iestyn was to read out the names of the runners-up, and then the winners in each category, in case of a difficult-to-pronounce Welsh name, to save Malcolm from any potential embarrassment as each pupil came up to receive his or her prize.

After the fifteen children had received their prizes but had yet to opened them, the two overall winners were announced. Malcolm had scanned the room from his vantage point, picking her out where she sat with her friends. He felt a sudden surge of excitement, his hands increasingly clammy as the moment drew near. First there was a Paul Simpson who was called forward to receive the overall prize for the high school entries, and then Clare. She trembled as Iestyn called her name, 'Clare Davies', and she stood up to the clapping around her, walking toward him. Malcolm stood smiling at her, as she came up to greet him, her face happy but shy. His hand was ready, outstretched to take hers, as he offered her his hearty congratulations. He touched her skin, holding her small hand in his a moment too long so she looked up at him, before he released it.

'Well, we have a real budding artist here, Clare. What an excellent composition you've produced, your mother must be very proud of you.'

Clare nodded, blushing under his scrutiny. 'Tell me, Clare, you must like the sea. Do you remember the beach, the one in Ireland?'

She shook her head. 'This is the beach and that's my farm, see above it, and the windmills on the mountain,' she said to clarify.

'Yes, I see. It's very good and I love your rock pool with all the sea life. Well done, Clare. Here's your prize for being the overall winner in your whole school.' He turned round to take the prize from Iestyn – an artist's easel, as well as an array of paints, oil, acrylic and watercolour, as well as a selection of brushes and several different sized canvasses.

'Wow! What a lot to carry. Enough to keep you busy for a bit. Many congratulations.'

She stepped back, turning away from him, laden with parcels, as Miss Lewis came to her rescue, helping her to carry them off the stage and back to her seat.

Teachers from both schools came up to the stage to collect their cheques from Malcolm and afterwards all the prizewinners were gathered together, holding aloft some of their prizes for the camera, with several Assembly Members wanting to muscle in on the action. A further ten minutes were taken up with press photos and interviews.

Malcolm allowed the time they needed to get to the Techniquest Centre and eat their picnic lunches before he joined them. The high school pupils had two hours to do what they liked and there was a special show for the younger children – 'The Electricity Show' – which linked in nicely with Key Stage 2 of the school curriculum about The Sustainable Earth.

Malcolm went across nonchalantly, pretending he was easy and relaxed and that what he was about to do was a normal occurrence. First, he found Clare, calling her over to him.

'Clare, do you remember me? Do know who I am?' he asked.

'The man from the Millennium Centre,' she answered.

'Yes, but more than that. I'm your father, Clare. You don't remember me do you? From Ireland.'

She shook her head. 'But, you remember your granny, don't you? You know Moira O'Connor?'

'Oh yes, I know Granny.'

'I've got some photos of her I want to show you. And as I'm over here, I thought I could take you to this big toy shop and buy you a special present to remind you of your day in Cardiff. You'd like that wouldn't you?'

She nodded, not so sure, but not wanting to say.

'You needn't worry, everything's all right and I've had a word with your mother. And I'll get you back here in time for the bus. Now I need a word with your teacher. Do you have a mobile phone?'

She produced her phone for him. 'Ah, good. Let's go and see, now, what's her name?'

'Miss Lewis.'

Taking his daughter's hand, he beckoned to the teacher, who came over to join them as she ushered the children toward the area where the show was to be shown.

'Miss Lewis, I'm Clare's father and I've arranged to take her out for a treat just for a couple of hours while you're at the show and bring her back ready for the bus.'

'Is this right, Clare?" Miss Lewis looked enquiringly at the child who sort of shrugged but didn't confirm the arrangement.

'I don't remember your mother saying anything this morning?'

'She probably forgot. Didn't Mam tell you, Clare?'

'No,' she said.

'I tell you what, why don't you ring her up? Here I'm sure Clare won't mind if you use her phone,' he said, handing the teacher the child's mobile. 'Always best to double-check.'

He stood smiling, his hand in Clare's, waiting as the teacher dialed her home number, but because of all the interference and background noise in the Centre, the teacher was unable to make a connection.

'Perhaps it would be better if you go out and find a quieter spot,' he suggested helpfully. 'We'll wait here for you. Everything's fine and I'll make sure she's back in good time,' he added to her retreating back.

Quickly, without waiting, he hurried Clare in the opposite direction and out through another pair of doors, using the exhibits and the mass of children as a decoy as he escorted her outside and away from the Centre. He didn't want to appear anything other than calm and casual in order to reassure her, as he felt her hand reluctant in his, her steps faltering as he led her to the car. He didn't want to do anything that would attract attention, or make her call out.

'Well, this is going to be fun isn't it?' he assured her, as he put her beside him in the front seat, making sure that she wore her safety belt and locking the door from the inside as he got in beside her and gave her one of his brightest smiles. 'What do you think you would like as a present from your Dad, Clare? Hmm? Any ideas?' – trying to distract her from feeling insecure and not wanting a busybody traffic warden or policeman stopping them, he drove more slowly than he would have liked. 'When we get to the hotel I'll show you all the photos I've brought; ones of your granny and of you and your mam with me, when you were a little girl. Would you like to see them?'

She nodded, hesitant. 'I thought you said I was going shopping for a toy?'

'We'll do that as well, Clare. I promise. You can have anything you like in the store. How's that?'

That seemed to cheer her as she sat mute, slightly frightened, with this stranger in his car, gloves on his hands even though it wasn't cold, not like winter cold.

By the time Miss Lewis returned, she was surprised not to find them still waiting, but seeing none of the children, or Diane Davies the new temp, she assumed she'd already taken them through ready for the show. She had failed to get hold of Clare's mother, Bethan, at Tan y Bryn, but had left a message to explain the arrangement.

The show was very good, starting with a black-out before light, generated by electricity, was switched on, a little at a time, to show the everyday use of electricity and how we all take it for granted. How it was not just a question of lights but everything from kettles to computers to charging mobile phones, to ovens and heating, and how it was all possible thanks to fossil fuels. Then they were shown how a power station worked and the problems created by our dependence on fossil fuels and what types of renewable energy could be used instead. It was only toward the end of the show that Miss Lewis was able to catch the young teacher's eye. Moving to the side but still keeping an eye on the children, she was surprised by Miss Lewis's question, knowing nothing about Clare or her father. No one had come up to her and asked her anything and she had seen nothing. They scanned their group for Clare and Mr O'Connor, but there was no sign of Clare among them. There was no need to panic Miss Lewis reassured herself, knowing who he was, having just spent the morning at the Millennium Centre watching the director of the company giving out the prizes. There had to be a simple explanation and she must have misunderstood him. As soon as she could get outside, she'd check the child's mobile.

27

When Beth returned to the house, she noticed the flash of red to indicate there was a message on the answering machine, picking it up to replay the message. As she listened to the teacher's query, her throat contracted and her heart started to pound, not quite understanding, but nevertheless fearing the mention of her ex-husband in any connection with herself or Clare. She immediately returned the call to tell Clare not to go anywhere with anyone other than school party. She didn't want to frighten her but she needed to make sure she stayed close to one of the teachers. What was Malcolm doing in Cardiff, if not to cause some sort of mischief.

'Hello? Mrs Jones?' as the teacher saw 'Mam' in the caller ID of Clare's phone.

'Who's this? What are you doing with my daughter's phone?'

'Sorry Mrs Jones. It's Miss Lewis from the school. I tried to ring you earlier, but you were out and so I left a message, and I borrowed Clare's phone.'

'You've got Clare with you?' – relieved that her daughter was with the teacher. 'She's all right isn't she? I want to speak to her.'

'I'm sure she's fine. But, well you see, as I said in the message, her father came and said he'd arranged it all with you and it was fine for him to pick her up, while he was in Cardiff and take out shopping, and –'

'What?' Beth shrieked down the phone. 'You let her go off with him? A complete stranger?'

'He wasn't a stranger, Mrs Jones. He'd been with us this morning in the Millennium Centre giving out the prizes, and I assumed it had all been agreed between you both.' She refrained from adding that he'd seemed perfectly nice, very convincing in his tailored dark blue suit, with a warm, easy smile. 'I'm very sorry if this wasn't the case, but I'm sure there's no need get alarmed, Mr O' Connor has arranged to bring her back here, to the bus for six. He was very specific that he wouldn't be late.'

Bethan sank down on the chair, still not fully understanding Malcolm's involvement with the school trip. She felt faint, light-headed and sick, trying to keep her composure and not to rush off at the deep-end, fearing the worse. Only she knew her husband better than anyone. Where was Tegwyn, or Richard, to think clearly for her, to put it in perspective and prevent her racing off in a mindless panic?

'Mrs Jones are you still there?'

'Yes, I'm here. I don't understand why he was there? What was he doing at the Millennium Centre in the first place?'

If the teacher was surprised by her lack of knowledge about her ex-husband's involvement with the energy company, she tried to hide it in her answer, even though alarm bells were beginning to ring. If Mrs Jones knew nothing, then she surely hadn't agreed to the father taking Clare off, and with an increasing sense of dread, she tried to sound convincing to the near-hysterical mother.

'Mr O'Connor is a director of the company, Atlantic Energies, the company who own the turbines in Llanfeni. They have sponsored today's event and organised it with the local schools.'

'Yes,' she suddenly saw, it would be just like him to concoct such a plan out of revenge.

'Are you sure it was a Malcolm O'Connor?' she asked the teacher, clutching at straws. Perhaps they had it wrong, and felt momentarily relieved that it couldn't be him. Her husband was a racing trainer from Ireland. He had nothing to do with any energy company, it was something completely out of his field.

'Let me find his card. Yes, here it is,' the teacher said, pulling it out from the folder she had with all the other paperwork of the day. She read it out to Bethan.

Based in Ireland, the head office in Dublin, with the company logo and website address.

What to do? Where to go from here? Alert the police, report a missing child feared abducted.

She couldn't even ring her, to tell her to go to someone, wherever he might have her, in a hotel room or on a boat or plane, convinced he was planning to take her out of the country. The stupid teacher still had her phone – the safety net that had persuaded Beth to let go in the first place, rendered useless.

'You need to ring the police and report her missing.'

'Don't you think you're over-reacting Mrs Jones? Shouldn't we at least wait and see. I'm sure he'll bring her back for the bus as he said he would.'

'No, you must ring them now.'

After she put the phone down, she screamed, rushing out of the house calling for Tegwyn and Richard, a severe chronic cramp catching her in the base of her stomach, her legs wet as she bent down groaning. No, please God not now, not until she had Clare safe.

In a central car park he stopped, and opening the glove department pulled out a plastic folder, which he opened for her. 'Look, Clare, here are some of the pictures I promised to show you. Do you recognize anyone in them? Here, take it and look for yourself.' He handed her the compact album and she started to look at the figures and faces in the photos.

'That's Granny,' she said, relieved at the recognition, 'And, that's Mam, isn't it?' He leaned across, stroking her hair.

'Yes, my darling, that's your precious mam. And, do you know who those two people are?' he asked, pointing at a man and a small child standing next to each other on a beach. 'That's you as a little girl and me standing beside you back in Conor, in Ireland, where you used to live. Don't you remember?'

She shrugged, not sure, but not wanting him to know that she couldn't remember other than what she saw in the photo in front of her.

'Don't worry, it doesn't matter and you were only a little girl then. Look there's another of your granny outside her bungalow, and one with Bethan, and then me and my dog, Big.'

She did have a vague recollection of a large smelly dog who had a rough coat, the photo helping to nudge the recall. 'See, we were once a happy family altogether, you and Mam and me and Granny, and Big, all living by the sea.'

'Were there horses?'

'Yes, there were lots and lots of horses, Clare!' he replied, delighted that she remembered, as he hugged her to him, her soft hair against his chin.

'Come on, we can look at these again. Now didn't I promise you a shopping trip to remember? I'm a man of my word, so off we go!'

He took her to the new, smart department store that had recently opened in the capital, up the stairs to the third floor where there was an extensive array of toys for all ages. Mechanical, electrical, sporty, arts, soft, puzzles, board games, all and anything one could think of, and wrapping his arm around her, he encouraged her to go and choose anything she wanted, always careful to keep her in his sight, in case she decided to run off or speak to somebody. But Clare's thoughts were on more immediate pleasures, her attention on all the toys, the must-haves. My Little Pony and then a Barbie doll with her pink carriage, caught her eye, on top of a display, as she picked it up, waving it to him while he hovered, smiling indulgently at her. He put it in the basket, encouraging her to look for more.

He found her bent double, holding onto the wall for support in the farm lane, as he was bringing the cows down from their pasture, ready for their afternoon milking. He realized immediately what was wrong – the baby was already a few days overdue. He rushed past the cows, to get to her before they did.

'You all right, Beth?' he asked unnecessarily, knowing she wasn't. 'You started?'

'It's Clare. You've got to ring the police, Richard.'

'First things first, sis. You need to get to hospital. Someone else can pick Clare up from school. How long have you been like this? Why on earth didn't you ring, instead of trying to walk across. Have your water's broken yet?'

She nodded, grabbing him by his sleeve. 'Malcolm's taken Clare. He's stolen her.'

'What? Beth, you're not making any sense.'

She groaned as another contraction took hold of her, leaning on her brother for support as the cows mooed, wanting to pass and carry on to the milking parlour, not liking any disruption to their routine. Once her contraction had eased, he helped her down the lane toward the farm, ringing on his mobile for Penny to come and help them, and to try and contact Tegwyn who shouldn't be far away.

As it was, Tegwyn was already in the yard in the middle of replacing the universal joint on the power take-off-shaft of the muck spreader, when he saw Richard escorting Beth. He dropped his tools, wiping his hands on his jeans, as he came running over to help her.

'Beth, why didn't you ring? I had my mobile switched on. I told you I was here. Let me take you. We need to get you to hospital. It's the baby isn't it?' he asked as an afterthought.

'No, yes, but it's Malcolm. He's stolen Clare. You must go down to Cardiff and find them. Now!' she screamed at them, staring stupidly at her, not understanding. 'He's taken her. Don't you see, abducted her.'

She wasn't making any sense. 'But how? How did he know where she was Beth?'

'It was all part of his scheme, the school trip and everything, just so he could get close to steal her. I need to go to her.'

'You're in no fit state to go anywhere other than hospital to have your baby, Beth. We're here to help and sort all this out. I can't think for a minute that the school would let a total stranger just take Clare off. And she'd have something to say about it, knowing our Clare. You must have got your wires crossed.'

She started remonstrating with him, hitting him to make him understand.

'OK Beth. Let's get you sorted and then we'll see what's happening. I will ring the school while Tegwyn drives you to hospital. We'll soon see what's going on. Tegwyn, you need to get Beth to hospital now,' as his sister started another contraction. 'We've no time, I'll run you back in the car.'

They met Penny ready in the yard and quickly half-explained the situation. 'Can you ring them and let them know she's on her way and I'll try to get hold of one of the teachers. Has anyone tried ringing Clare on her mobile? Or the school?'

Ten minutes later, with Beth on her way to the hospital, still protesting she needed to be going down to Cardiff to search for Clare, Richard had managed to make contact with Miss Lewis via Clare's mobile. The teacher sounded very concerned as she explained what had happened and that Clare was now overdue and there was no sign of her, or her father, and that she had a busload of tired fractious children needing to travel back to Llanfeni, with an increasingly irritable bus driver who only knew that the little girl was late returning to the bus. She hadn't mentioned anything about a disappearance.

As always, it was the woman who'd been left holding the fort, as the men jumped into action. Penny left to look after Sion and man the phone. Minutes earlier, Richard had driven off to the police station, a wedding photo of Beth and Malcolm on the seat beside him, so that the police would have some ID in case they needed to advertise the abduction on the news. Penny hoped it wouldn't come to that, and that it was still a misunderstanding. In the meantime she rang to get a relief milker to milk the poor cows who still waiting in the collection yard. She stayed in the house within earshot of the phone, in case of any developments, trying to keep Sion amused as she researched Atlantic Energies online to find out more about the company and to what extent, if any, Malcolm O'Connor was involved with it.

'Did you know he was involved with this company?' she asked his mother, Moira.

'No, we don't share confidences any more, I have very little to do with him. I may live near him but we don't talk, not more than I have to. I can't forgive him for what he did, and now you tell me he's kidnapped Clare? His own daughter.'

'That's what it increasingly looks like, I'm afraid. If we knew he had any connection with the wind turbines, Richard would never have agreed to having them on his land. He was reluctant enough as it was and I feel I pushed him into it.'

'Can I speak to Beth?'

'She's been rushed to hospital, her waters have broken. I'm sure the shock started her off.'

'The poor love. You weren't to know my son was behind any of this. None of us was, but it's just the sort of way his scheming mind would work.'

'But why? Clare's his own daughter? What's he got to gain? He doesn't want her to live with him, does he? He hasn't done anything or made any attempt to see her for years.'

'He doesn't care about the child. It's to get back at Bethan. It's got nothing to do with my granddaughter, he's just using her as a pawn in his foul game. It's the most powerful weapon he can have to hurt Bethan with. And, he's waited, the bastard that he is, planned it no doubt, until she's about to have a baby. If I can do anything from here –'

'Yes, yes, I'll let you know, Moira, and if he does get in touch with you, or if Clare suddenly appears back in Ireland, you'll ring.'

'Immediately, and let me know when you have news, and give my love to Beth and tell her not to worry. It'll be all right. Malcolm may be a bastard but I don't think even he would sink so low as to hurt his only child. It's Beth he's out to damage and as long as she is safe. Well … she must concentrate on delivering her baby into this world and leave us to sort out Malcolm and retrieve Clare. You tell her from me – and nobody knows him like I do – he won't harm her. It's Bethan he wants to damage in revenge for leaving him.'

'I'll tell her, and thanks, Moira, it'll reassure her.'

What a sick game to play, and how awful for a mother to witness a son's ruthless jealousy, no doubt because of Clare being pregnant and having another man's baby, Penny reflected, making her feel thankful that her own marriage break-up had been less malicious. Ralph might have cheated on her, but he'd never been dangerous, never threatened her or their daughters, and he'd made a generous financial settlement, with no ill feeling, but rather relief that she'd found someone else and was happy. She even liked to think that, perhaps, for all his high-flying and wealth, he was a little envious of her contentment with her little boy and stick-in-the-mud farmer.

In the hospital, Bethan had been very difficult with the nurses, trying to get up to leave, so that she had to be restrained by Tegwyn, as she screamed at him that she'd never forgive him if anything happened to Clare, her contractions becoming progressively stronger, the pain forcing her to give in to them as nature took over. Every minute seemed like an hour to Tegwyn who had never witnessed a woman giving birth. He felt helpless, standing near her, as she gave in to her contractions, lying on the bed, her knees up, moaning, not quite fully dilated or ready to push.

28

She had a collective responsibility and couldn't leave them sitting in the bus indefinitely. There were other parents to consider as well as Clare and her mother, and although the other teachers from the secondary school had been patient and supportive, they also had a duty to get their pupils back home. Most of the parents had been contacted by the schools to explain that there had been an unforeseen delay and that the bus would be returning later than the time stated. They hadn't given out further details, but the children had, texting home to say there'd been a kidnapping and that a girl from the primary school was missing. The chief suspect was one of the company directors who'd been at the award ceremony and the place was crawling with cops. This was a slight exaggeration as there had been only a minimal police presence, and now there were only two liaison officers by the bus, in the unlikely event Malcolm returned with the girl, who was by all accounts his estranged daughter.

The local police station was not manned round the clock, and Richard hadn't realized that it was bound to be closed at this time of day, so he arrived only to find a small light on in the porch and everything else locked up, with a notice in the window giving contact details. Cursing the decline of yet another service, he hurriedly dialled the number given, only to be told to go to headquarters. It would take him hours to get there, with valuable time lost, but there was no alternative, and so he got back angrily into his car, stopping at the garage to refuel. He rang Penny to find out if anyone had rung home and to let her know what he was doing.

'When you need one they're not there. No wonder Joe Public takes the law into his own hands, and I've got to drive all the way to Carmarthen, must be more than a two-hour journey, so I'll be on my mobile if there's anything new to report.'

'Don't you worry about us, Rich, the cows have all been done, and Phil very kindly helped finish up and he said he'd be able to come over in the morning if need be. Sion and I are fine, and we won't expect you home until late.'

'Let's hope he turns up with her and this is just a wild goose chase.'

'And I'll let you know as soon as I hear from the hospital. It couldn't be worse timing for your sister. Poor Beth, going into labour and unable to do anything, worried sick about Clare.'

'Yes, it's terrible for her, but at least she's got something to focus on whether she wants to or not, and in some ways I'd prefer her laid up in hospital than screaming frantically and doing herself an injury trying to find them. You saw how she was carrying on. She's just hysterical.'

'As I would be, Rich, if I thought someone had taken Sion or one of the girls.'

'It's what he wants, to hurt Beth. This way he can get to her and she can't do anything about it. Beth has to stay put and let her family and the police find them. And we will.'

Neither voiced any doubt that she wouldn't be found, or that Malcolm wouldn't harm her, or take her back to Ireland, although they both thought of the possibility.

'Mr Davies, I understand that this is very stressful for you, but we're doing all we can to find your niece.' It sounded very much like a domestic matter, which the police would not get involved in. 'However Mr O'Connor is her father?'

Richard nodded. 'They're separated.'

'Nevertheless, he is her father, and there has never been any court order preventing him from seeing his daughter?' Again Richard agreed.

'So, in the eyes of the law, Mr Davies, however unpalatable to you and your sister, Mr O'Connor has done nothing illegal and we can't go broadcasting an abduction that isn't in the legal sense of the term. As her father, he has every right to see her.'

Richard was about to protest, but the policeman continued. 'Now, I understand, and of course it must be very distressing for you and for the girl's mother, but we have to be very sure of our facts before we send these photos out to the media. More than likely they're having fun and he's forgotten the time and by the time you get back home she'll have turned up. We're liaising with our colleagues in Cardiff, and we'll keep you informed of any progress. Leave these photos with me and the best thing you can do is go home and leave us to investigate her whereabouts. We'll be in touch, Mr Davies, as soon as we have any news.'

What to tell Beth, that the police thought it a domestic and were doing nothing about finding her? They had all the details and were doing everything they could behind the scenes. South Wales, Dyfed-Powys and North Wales police forces had been notified, and a photo of Malcolm and another of Clare, circulated to them from the Carmarthen headquarters. Cardiff airport had been alerted to look out for a middle-aged man and young girl, as were the ferry ports, but for anyone wishing to slip away undetected, Wales's ports were an easy option, except that the police didn't know how much Malcolm hated the sea and would never willingly choose to take a ferry. As the child hadn't been officially missing for more than a few hours, at this stage the police decided not to release any information or photos to the wider media, still hopeful that they would both turn up, and as the girl was with her natural father, who wasn't an immigrant about to flee the country, but a respected, wealthy businessman from the Republic of Ireland, who as far as they could deduce, had committed no crime, there was little else they could do other than discreetly continue their search for her.

Eventually much to the relief of the kids and teachers alike, the bus was finally allowed to leave, escorted out of Cardiff and north toward home several hours later than scheduled.

It wasn't quick, as she'd thought it would be, and now she needed Tegwyn by her, having spent the last few hours telling him to go and look for Clare. The pain was unbearable as each contraction intensified, with nothing to show for it in a slow protracted labour that needed all her strength and mental reserve to see it through. The baby wasn't coming as it should, presenting itself at an angle so it wasn't moving through her pelvis. Beth pushed and fought for it to straighten as each contraction made her push deep into her backside, the nurse encouraging her to keep trying, saying that it was moving and that everything was all right and she was doing very well. In fact, the mother's condition was more worrying than that of the baby as its monitor and heart rate were all normal. But the mother had become increasingly fragile and was physically exhausted. She still fought them, however, to watch the door between contractions, telling Tegwyn to move so she could see in case anyone came in with news of her daughter, waiting all the while for the police.

Tegwyn had already explained to the nursing staff what had happened, but he hadn't revealed her previous history, not the full extent of how and why she'd lost her last baby, nor did he say that she'd suffered a mental breakdown following the miscarriage. He didn't want to alarm the fully-stretched medical staff, especially as her labour was becoming more complicated, feeling it would be an act of betrayal on his part if he let them know of a time she'd wished to forget.

In his room at the hotel, Malcolm let Clare open the presents she'd chosen so she could play with them while he attended to some business on his laptop and phone. He looked through his emails, and texts. There was one voicemail. 'They rang me to tell me. If you have a modicum of decency in you, you'll return her to them forthwith without so much as hurting a hair on her body. She's your flesh and blood, your daughter, for God's sake Malcolm.'

'Yes, she is my daughter, mother,' he thought, looking at her playing on the floor with her Princess Barbie and pink coach and white horses, 'my daughter who should be living with me, not them.'

She'd grown a lot since he'd last seen her. Was it five years, so long ago? Far too long to be estranged, father and daughter. And it pleased him to see her look so like him still – her small bone structure and light frame, with freckled face and distinctly Irish colouring that was unmistakably his – an O'Connor. As he watched her he thought perhaps it would be good, after all, to have her with him in Ireland, back to where she rightly belonged.

'So when is your mam's baby due, Clare?'

'Now, any day, that's why Mam couldn't come down to Cardiff with me.'

'Oh? So the baby stopped her from seeing you receive your award. That is a pity isn't it?'

Clare nodded.

'Are you looking forward to having a new brother or sister Clare?'

'Yes. It can be a bit lonely on your own.'

'I always wanted another child after we had you, my lovely. I wanted you to have a little brother, but sadly your mother lost our little baby. Did you know that?'

Clare shook her head, surprised at the news.

'How did she lose it?' Beth's miscarriage and the circumstances that had brought it about, and her subsequent trauma, had never been discussed in front of her.

'She didn't take enough care of herself when she was carrying it, and, well, she had a miscarriage and the little boy, it was a brother for you, Clare, couldn't survive, being born too early.'

'That's sad,' she said, thinking about it, adding innocently, 'Like a lamb we had at home that came too early and couldn't take the bottle and died in the night.'

'Yes, a bit like a lamb. Do you know if it's going to be girl or a boy?'

'No, because Uncle Teg didn't know what colour to paint the bedroom and so I chose a bright yellow.'

'That's nice. Is the new baby going to share a room with you?'

He remembered his own brother, Kieran, coming into his life, ousting him from first place in his parents' affection, outshining him in sports and geniality and becoming everyone's favourite. Then he died, and they blamed him for it, his parents left with the dregs, the older, disappointing wayward brother.

'No, I've got to move out, and it's going to have my room. But not to begin with. Mam says at first it'll have to sleep with them.'

'How very cosy. And aren't you good, giving up your room. I hope it doesn't keep you awake. Babies do a lot of crying and will demand all your mother's attention.'

'I'm going to help. Mam says I'll be very useful.'

'And I'm sure you will be. But, if it takes all your things and makes a mess, you'll always have a special room of your own with me and your granny in Ireland and you can come and stay whenever you like and for as long as you like. And I'll get you a pony, just for you to ride along the beaches. How would you like that Clare?'

'Very much,' she said enthusiastically, 'but I've got one at home.'

'Well that's fine, one for Wales and one for Ireland. Aren't you a lucky girl!'

Time ticked and he sat with his own thoughts, wanting to meddle, to upset any apple cart. He knew their house was small and money tight, and perhaps they weren't as happy as the photos he'd seen. Anyhow a picture could lie. They wouldn't be pleased to discover he was behind the wind turbines and there was sod all they could do about it. He could be in and out of their lives on a regular basis causing her some mischief. But first he had to wait for her to turn up, the bloated swollen cow, and beg to him to give Clare back. In the meanwhile, he wouldn't divulge her whereabouts, wouldn't let her know what he'd done with her, or if she was safe. He woulde play his ex-wife like a hooked fish – anything to prolong her agony.

It had been a long day and Clare was becoming increasingly overtired. The novelty of the new toys had worn off, and she was bored of playing in the hotel bedroom, not liking his intent stare as he lay with his feet up, head on the bed board looking at her.

'Please. When can I go home?' she asked again, having sat and waited as he'd asked her to.

'Why, don't you like it, being with your dad? You always used to be such a daddy's girl, waiting up so you could run to greet me when I came home.'

He watched the line of her leg, curled up, flexible and gangly, like a young racehorse, as she sat aware, under his gaze, that her skirt had ridden up her leg, so she wriggled, pulling her hem down, uncomfortable. She wanted to leave, to go home to her mam and the man she considered her dad. This man, for all his kindness, gave her the creeps with his crooked smile and hard eyes, making her pull her cardigan tight across her blouse to blanket out his looking.

'Can I go home now? I want to go to bed.'

'Are you cold, Clare? Come up here on the bed, sit with me and we can watch a film? Would you like that? And I can order you some supper. You must be hungry?'

She nodded, though she wasn't really cold as she reluctantly got up onto the bed to sit in the place he was patting with his hand.

'There that's better, isn't it?' he said, smiling as he put an arm around her shoulders. 'You snuggle up to your daddy, now what shall we see?' As he flicked through the Sky options, his hand stroking her silky hair, feeling her body next to his, her thin legs outstretched to reach his knee, and he squeezed her close. 'There, this is fun, just you and me together.'

'Why didn't you come, when Granny came?'

'Because your mother wouldn't let me, Clare. I wanted to come, every week I wished to see you, but she stopped me from seeing you. And I didn't want to upset you. One day you'll understand. But I'm here now, that's the main thing, and I'll never leave your life again, Clare, I give you my word.'

After the food had been delivered, Malcolm getting up to take the tray without letting room service see into the room, he put her plate of chicken and chips with salad garnish onto her lap, pushing up to her as he ate his sandwich. Clare tried to watch the film as she toyed with her plate, not feeling like food. She tried not to cry, but her eyes filled and tears spilled down her cheek as she sniffed, lowering her head so he wouldn't see, knowing he'd be cross.

'Hey, hey, little one? What's all this? You're not crying, are you?'

She tried to shake her head, her tears running as she sobbed and the floodgates opened.

'Come on, come to Daddy,' he crooned, removing the plate from her knees and taking her in his arms. He cuddled her, but she was still upset, wanting to go home.

'I want my mam. I want to go home.'

'Say Dad,' he thought, as her crying got louder the more he tried to soothe her.

Suddenly she looked like her mother, sniffling and crying, all puff-cheeked and red-eyed. It was not going as he'd planned it – Clare all loving and glad to see him, the photos he'd brought to remind her how it had been, remembering him as it was back then, her daddy, her special person who she had adored, sitting up late waiting for him to come from the races, calling out 'Daddy, Daddy' as she race into his arms to be swung high in the air by him, laughing.

Who was he kidding! Liar, as if he'd ever thought of her feelings, intent only on causing as much trauma to Bethan as he could. Life had moved on and his daughter had a new life, remembering little of her infancy, leaving him in a void of hatred. It's why he'd planned all this, buying into the energy company, meticulously calculating his disclosure to cause Bethan optimum damage, to derange her, without a thought to how it would affect his daughter. Now that she was sitting there with him, her distress obvious, he felt unsure as to what to do. He didn't know how to stop a bawling child, never having been a hands-on father, always busy away at the races, doing deals and making money.

'Shh, Clare, there's a good girl,' but she couldn't stop her sobbing as he held her and his grip instead of reassuring, became tighter, frightening her further and making her cry the more.

'Shut up, can't you, for Pete's sake!' He held her more intently, looking at her sobbing face, as she recoiled from him, frightened now, trying not to cry.

Seeing what he was doing to her, he let go of his grip, and she jumped off the bed and ran into bathroom, sobbing miserably, calling for her mother.

His clumsy handling was not the way to win her over – treat like a young filly, quietly, gently, with a low voice, nothing to startle her as he stretched out a hand to let her smell it, to touch a silky neck and stroke it to allow the frightened horse time to gain some confidence in him.

Time for him to think, the other side of the door, to plead with her to undo the lock.

'I'm sorry, my little princess, it wasn't meant to be like this. All I wanted is for us to be one big happy family. I never meant to frighten you. Will you forgive me? All your presents are here for you. Please open the door.'

Her tears behind the door lessened, an uh, uh, replacing the heart-wrenching sobs.

'I promise I'll never hurt you, Clare, my little girl. Please come out and forgive me. Come out and give your old daddy a kiss and say you forgive him. And then we'll talk about what you want me to do. How's that? You can decide, if you open the door and let me in.'

He waited hearing her move to the door and the lock turning before she opened it, standing in front of him, her hair falling over her face as she held her head down. He took her hand, gently in his, leading her back into the room. 'I'm so sorry, my pet, for scaring you. I never meant to. This was meant to be our special day together, a good day that you'd want to remember. Here you are, as pretty as a picture, my little girl Clare, the best in the school. And you painted a magnificent piece of artwork, good enough for any gallery and so I thought you'd enjoy a treat with your dad. I'm sorry if I threw it on you. I should have come over to the farm first, I see that now. It's been a bit too much for you to take in all at once, hasn't it? Say you've forgiven me?'

307

He put his hand under her chin, lifting it, and as her hair fell away from her face, he smiled his lopsided smile that had once entranced her mother. 'Please, say you're all right now, my sweetie. Can we forget this ever happened. Start again. The last thing I wanted to do was upset you, poppet.'

He put his arm around her, loosely this time, so she could pull away if she wanted, pointing to her presents on the floor, offering her a drink, a hot chocolate to cheer her up.

At last the baby started to make some progress, moving toward the world, and its first breath. All Beth could do was concentrate and push when the nurse asked her, knowing that the birth was imminent. Tegwyn hovered excitedly, trying to encourage her, longing to see the birth of his baby, all thought of Clare's whereabouts momentarily forgotten. Then it came with a burst, as Beth was told to stop pushing and pant, as the nurse held the little head in her hands, ready to catch the rest of its lithe body as it slipped out from its mother. She didn't need any encouragement, quick to open her eyes and cry her first breaths in her brand new world, as her umbilical cord was cut.

'You've had a beautiful baby girl,' said the nurse, beaming as she handed the wet bundle up to Beth who snuggled her in her arms, mother and daughter looking at each other for the first time.

'She's beautiful, Beth.'

'Is there any news?'

'Not yet, but the police are searching for her and you mustn't worry. Richard and I will make sure we find where Clare is and bring her home. You wait till she sees her. She'll be over the moon. And she *will* see her. I know she'll come home safe.'

For a minute she didn't connect the two, not recognizing the voice on the other end of the phone, expecting either Richard or Tegwyn to ring.

'She's with me. I want to speak with Richard Davies.'

It must be him, Malcolm, though she'd never met or spoken with the man before. She had to be very careful, say nothing to alarm him that would make him put the phone down. What was the priority? That Clare was alive and unharmed. Then where was she? What was he planning to do and what did he want, if as she thought it had to be some sort of sick game of ransom he was playing.

'Is Clare all right. Can I speak to her?'

'No.'

No what? She isn't all right or I can't talk to her? Penny thought frantically trying to stay calm and think clearly, wishing Richard was back from the police. Could they get a lead on the phone, if she stayed on it all enough? She knew she had to keep talking to him, coaxing him into saying more than he wished, that might give away their whereabouts.

'It's Malcolm, isn't it? Is your daughter all right? That's all I want to know.'

'Why wouldn't she be, with her own father.' It wasn't a question, more a statement of intent. He was taking her back to Ireland, if they weren't already there.

'I want to speak to Richard or my wife, Bethan.'

Did he know she was having a baby? It was not the news he'd want to hear and Penny avoided answering him directly.

'They're not in at the moment, but I can try and get a message –'

He cut her off. 'I have something to tell her, but if she can't be bothered to come to the phone –'

'It's not that. I'm sure she would if she could, but she's tied up at the moment.'

'Having another man's baby when I've got her daughter? You tell her from me.'

'Please Malcolm, if Clare is with you, can I at least speak to her, just a few words?'

'Why? Don't you trust me? What were you expecting I'd do to her? She's done nothing wrong, an innocent. It's her whoring mother who caused all this.'

He was deluded. Penny knew what he'd done to Bethan, but she didn't want to argue or dispute any of his wild accusations, not until she could somehow secure Clare's safe release. She wanted to ask him where he was without raising his hackles and as if he sensed her hesitation, he answered her unasked question.

'I've got her, she's safe with me, and I know you want to know where we are. But don't you go getting the police involved. This is between family.'

She prayed that the police hadn't spread Clare's picture across the media. That would only enflame Malcolm, making him more unpredictable, and putting Clare's life in danger. She knew what he'd done in the past, the lengths he was prepared to go to get what he wanted, that she was dealing with a maniac prepared to kill. She needed to tread like a cat, softly without alerting attention.

'Where are you?' She felt him hesitate and not wanting him to hang up, she tried to sound as gentle as she could. Was he still in the country? She had no way of telling, the phone giving no indication of long distance or overseas.

'Clare and I were having such a wonderful time we completely forgot about the bus. This hasn't anything to do with you or any of them, so don't think there is anything you can say to persuade or influence me. This is all about me and my daughter. Do you understand? I want to make this absolutely clear, it has nothing to do with you and nothing you can to or say will have any impact on me.'

'Yes, I understand. I'm not trying to push you or tell you what to do.'

'No, you're bloody well not! I know what's best for my daughter and you can tell her mother that.'

He was getting angry and agitated. She needed to calm him down.

'Of course you do. I'm not suggesting otherwise. I'm only concerned, as you are, I know, for Clare's welfare.'

'So now we've got that straight. I make the decisions and know what's best for Clare and the rest of you can go to hell.'

It had nothing to do with any of them, his mother, his ex-wife, or Richard, and certainly nothing at all to do with Tegwyn. It was only his daughter that swayed him from his intention. The look of fear in her eyes, eyes that reflected his own when his father had beaten him with a leather strap, unhindered by his mother as he crouched down under his father's vile temper, shielding his face from the blows that rained down on him. It was that same look which halted him absolutely, wrapping his arms around her and telling her it was all right and nobody was ever going to hurt her.

It was an unforgivable sin to let a child know it is not loved, and he did love her, more than his father had ever loved him, and he would be there for her, whenever she needed him. Penny tried Richard's mobile which was out of signal range, so she left a message, telling him that Malcolm had made contact and that Clare was with him and unharmed. 'Please ring me as soon as you get this message, Rich. I don't know what to do, but I think he may ring again.' Tegwyn's phone was also switched off and she left a similar message for him but remembered to tell him to tell Beth that Clare was OK, and hoped it was all going all right in the labour ward.

It came from a mobile on the move, the signal intermittent so she wasn't sure she caught everything he said, not wanting to ask him to repeat himself. She tried to repeat what she'd heard, enough to be sure she had understood him.

'You want me to meet you?'

'Only because I say so. It's my decision and mine alone. No funny business, if you know what's good for you. Come alone.'

'Of course, I'll start now. Where did you say?'

'I love you, my little sweetheart, and although you're going home now, I'll be close from now on. You've only got to look up at the windmills above your farm, and I won't be far away.'

He put her on the back seat of the car, her toys and prize beside her on the floor, and drove out of the Welsh capital, on up through the Valleys and onto the coastal road going north.

She couldn't leave him on his own in the house and Penny was forced to disturb Sion's sleep, lifting him in his blanket, and carrying him to the car, fixing him into his car seat, hoping he wouldn't wake fully and start crying. She had no way of contacting Richard or Tegwyn as she started out, headlights on, towards an unlit empty lay-by to meet him.

Epilogue

It had taken a considerable amount of courage and perseverance, but Martin had mastered his own technique for climbing the metal rungs of the ladder, pulling himself up with his arms and good leg as he hopped, his prosthetic foot useful as a wedge to help balance him. Once up, he could look out across the hill and enjoy the uninterrupted view, the sweep of Cardigan Bay, from his vantage point. He'd counted himself one of the lucky ones. He'd got himself a new qualification and long-term employment as a maintenance engineer for the Siemens group, keeping the several wind turbine farms in his area operational and properly maintained along his stretch of Welsh coast and hills. It was good pay, at least double that of any farmer in the area, and he had more than enough for holidays or treats, if he wanted. He rented Y Bwthyn from them, the cottage that had been Elin and Mervyn's.

When he wasn't working he had plenty to occupy his days in a place where he and Gareth had grown up. Recently he'd taken up swimming, liking to keep himself fit. He had a new purpose now, training for a reason, doing lengths in the local pool as a paraplegic swimmer, proud to represent Wales in the forthcoming London Olympics, in honour of his lost friend.

His adopted family muddled on, with farming always hard and tight, and now it wasn't the turbines that brought the rural community together in opposition, but an uglier threat that would be a permanent blight on their landscape – the proposed route for the huge permanent pylons. In the event, no amount of campaigning would have any effect on a decision already made.

Clare still loved her ponies, but now in secondary school other interests had taken precedence. From time to time she did see her father, Malcolm, and her granny, occasionally flying out to Ireland, or when he came over. She preferred the former as whenever he was in Llanfeni, her mother became very jumpy. It was a big gap, too big now, but she loved her little sister and let Buddug sit on her pony, holding onto her chubby leg so she wouldn't slide off as she laughed, bouncing to the pony's trot, their mam watching anxiously, over-fussy as usual. In the summer her Aunt Rhian had promised her a trip to Italy to take in some of the world's greatest artwork.

For all their talk, the politicians had failed to solve any of the problems that beset the Middle East, as war and human suffering escalated.

Unnoticed, a tiny victory slipped its glassy, earth-brown way up the tributary from the river. The young eel had come a long way, drifting with the current to find her mother's home, high up in the hills above Llanfeni, sliding silently into a pool below Bugailyn, beneath the rhythmic sound of the windmills, a small triumph in a chaotic world.